PASSION UNLEASHED

Samantha sagged against him, her tears dampening his shirt. Jake's arm tightened around her. She trembled and Jake felt his body stir with something more than the promise of comfort. She looked up at him, her eyes large and crystal blue from tears.

Jake leaned down to kiss her. Gently at first, for there were still thoughts of comforting mingled with his desire. But then he felt her responding and his passion exploded, blocking out all else.

He overwhelmed her. His arm locked her body to his and his hand cupped her head, dislodging the pins holding her braid. His scent surrounded her, his taste filled her, and she could scarcely breathe. Yet all she could think about was getting closer . . .

* * * *

"KANSAS KISS is a tender, moving novel that touches the heart. Ms. Dorsey's star shines brighter than ever."

— *Romantic Times*

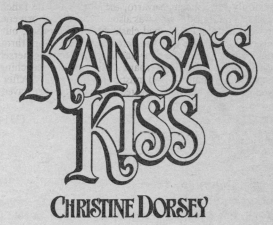

KANSAS KISS

CHRISTINE DORSEY

ZEBRA BOOKS
KENSINGTON PUBLISHING CORP.

To romantics everywhere . . .
believers in the power of love.
And as always to Chip.

ZEBRA BOOKS

are published by

Kensington Publishing Corp.
475 Park Avenue South
New York, NY 10016

First printing: March, 1992

Printed in the United States of America

Is anything worth it? This fearful sacrifice —
this awful penalty we pay for war?
> — Mary Chesnut, *A Wartime Journal,*
> July 26, 1864

Prologue

Appomattox Court House
April 9, 1865

Nothing.

He felt nothing.

No regret that defeat was at hand. No righteous anger aimed at the enemy. Not even a modicum of relief that the long four years of suffering were nearly over.

Nothing.

And the worst part — the part that made him want to bury his face deep in his hands — was, he knew he should feel . . . something.

A pained groan sounded, seemed to echo through the hollow shell of a man he once was, and Jacob Morgan turned. Scanning the sea of men stretched out on makeshift pallets around the hospital tent, he searched for the one who had made the noise. From habit he moved through the cool, gray dawn toward the man who had called out. Habit, not compassion, Jake noted without emotion.

Mechanically he dropped to his knees in the moist Virginia soil to offer the dying man a drink of water.

The war's end came too late for the nameless soldier staring up at Jake with pain-glazed eyes. He'd been gut-shot, no chance of recovery. Jake had seen him earlier—was it yesterday or last week? He couldn't remember. But he did recall he'd been able to do nothing for the man except wrap him up. No treatment. No cure. The wound was mortal. God knows he'd seen enough of them to recognize it. This man wouldn't be marching home. No warm welcome from loved ones for him.

The riotous chatter of morning birds caught Jake's attention and he looked over the dawn-tinged landscape. Gently rolling hills, hazy from April mist and smoldering campfires. And men, many of them rolling out of their bedrolls, wondering what this day would bring.

Jake glanced again at the soldier beside him, then started to rise. It was so unfair, and Jake tried to grieve for the injustice fate had dealt this man.

But God help him, he couldn't. It simply wasn't there.

The hand weakly grabbing his arm stopped Jake, and he sank back down on his heels. "Doc, is it true what I'm hearing?" The voice was feeble and rusty from disuse, or maybe from crying out in pain. "Bobby Lee really givin' up?"

Jake tried to look somewhere other than the man's face but couldn't. He swallowed, hunching over. "Looks that way."

"Shit."

Jake thought of all manner of replies he might make, but none of them made any sense—nothing made any sense. He shook his head, his hands dan-

6

gling between his legs. "I guess that pretty near sums it up."

The man's eyelids fluttered shut, and Jake thought him drifting to sleep. Standing, Jake stretched his stiff, aching muscles. He was thirty-three years old and he felt like an old man — an old man ready to die.

"Hey, Doc."

Apparently the soldier was fighting sleep for now his eyes were open, and he appeared almost lucid in the gray dawn.

"What you think them Yankees is gonna do with us?"

Didn't the man realize he was going to die? A day, two at the most and all his earthly concerns would be over. But Jake didn't tell him — he didn't have it in him to tell this soldier the truth. So he squatted again, hands on knees.

"Word is we're to be paroled, sent home."

This news seemed to please the wounded soldier. The brackets of pain around his mouth relaxed. "Home," he whispered, then turned his head away. But Jake had seen the shimmer of tears in his eyes and shifted uncomfortably on his heels, ready to leave.

"Where you from, Doc?"

Oh God, he didn't want to talk about this, but the soldier was staring at him, and he had no choice but to answer. "Richmond."

"Richmond," the man repeated, then added, "I'm from Georgia myself, Jasper County. Getting well nigh planting time." Again the man's parchment-thin lids lowered. Again Jake started to rise. Again the hand stopped him. "You going home, Doc? You going back to Richmond?"

It happened before Jake could stop it — the sudden flash of his wife's face, his son's. Empty, ashen . . . lifeless. Jake started to answer but his voice was thick. He cleared his throat. "No. No, I'm not going home."

"Neither am I."

The words were spoken softly and Jake was so intent on fighting back his own memories he almost didn't hear them. It was light enough to see clearly now, and Jake watched the soldier's face, waiting. His eyes were closed, but surely he'd open them, ask another annoying question.

Jake waited, his legs stiffening up. More men were waking. Jake heard orders yelled, answers grumbled, and still he waited. His eyes strayed down to the man's chest, and abruptly he yanked the cover away, flattening his hand over the soldier's heart.

Tears burned Jake's eyes, and he let out a shattered breath before pulling the blanket up, covering the soldier's face.

One more dead soldier. What was one more dead soldier? He'd seen hundreds of them, maybe thousands. He'd tried to help and he'd watched them die. What was one more?

But the tightness in his throat wouldn't go away, and blinking only made his eyes smart.

There were worse things than feeling nothing.

Chapter One

Southeastern Kansas
September 1865

"They're coming back, Sam!"

Samantha Lowery lifted her cheek from the cold, metal gun barrel that rested on the windowsill and peered through the broken pane. She'd smashed the glass herself, but now she felt a rudiment of regret thinking how much it would cost to replace. Yet in the scheme of things one damaged window was nothing.

The echo of gunfire still rang in her ears and she didn't know if she could stand any more. But Will was right. They were back. Except this time they'd only sent one man. A solitary rider galloped toward the house.

Toward Willy and her.

Samantha's back stiffened and she gripped the musket's stock, her fingers white against the well-worn wood. The gun was still loaded. She hadn't fired when the others came. She'd watched them shoot holes in the barn, knock down the fence, and trample her garden. And she'd ached to do something — anything — to stop them. But she hadn't.

It wasn't cowardice, Samantha had told herself as she watched the dozen or so men attack her clothesline and mangle the clean sheets in the dirt. If she'd been alone, the gun barrel would have scorched her hands from firing. She'd have shot, praying that her unpracticed aim was true. Anxious to taste revenge.

But there was Willy. And he was her responsibility. All that was left — all that the war had left. If she shot at the gang of bushwhackers, they'd fire back. It was as simple as that. And they wouldn't be wild shots into the barn or air. They'd be carefully aimed into the house. And then there'd be more than just property to mourn.

So Samantha had dragged her father's old hunting piece down from above the mantle and she'd watched all her hard work pummeled beneath the horses' hooves.

Then she'd collapsed over the gun when the men rode off toward the Missouri border. But they hadn't all gone. And now the one they left behind rode straight for the house, his sidearm in hand.

"What are we going to do, Sam? . . . Sam?"

Samantha spared a glance toward her younger brother. He was scared. And who could blame him? Thirteen was too young to have to deal with all this violence, this hatred. But he *had* dealt with it, and this wasn't the first time.

Focusing back through the shattered glass, Samantha watched the man gallop closer. He wore gray — she could make that out. That and the gun. His hat shadowed his face, though she doubted she'd recognize him anyway.

Landis Moore added more border ruffians to his gang every day — men who straggled home from fighting the war. But then no one could prove that, any more than they could prove Moore was the one behind terrorizing Unionist families in the area.

"He's going to shoot us, Sam!"

"Get down, Will." Samantha didn't dare take her eyes off the man racing toward them now. Her hands started sweating and she gripped the stock, her finger bent around the trigger.

She wanted to fire a warning shot. But then she'd have to reload, and by that time the stranger would be in the house, emptying his pistol into Will and her.

"He ain't stopping, Sam!"

She could see that! He was almost upon them, his powerful horse lathered and snorting, the sun gleaming off the pistol wavering in the air.

She'd have to shoot him. The realization came to her the same moment she heard Will yell for her to do it. Samantha thought of Pa and of Luke. They'd shot men, surely. They'd . . .

"The barrel throws to the left," Samantha mumbled to herself as she took aim. She'd never hit him. She never hit anything. Her older brother Luke used to take her behind the corn crib and try to teach her to shoot. But she never got the hang of it. And now Luke was dead. Killed the second time the armies clashed at Bull Run, fighting men dressed in gray . . . like the stranger riding toward her.

The deafening explosion from the gun startled Samantha. The stock slammed into her shoulder, and the smoke stung her eyes. From somewhere in the back of

11

her mind came the warning to reload, but she couldn't make her fingers move.

"You got him. You got him, Sam!" Will jumped up beside her. He sounded as surprised as she felt. He lurched toward the door, but not fast enough to escape his sister's grasp. "Let me go, Sam." Will wriggled, but Samantha only clung more tightly to his cotton shirt.

"Maybe he's not alone." Samantha let loose of her brother when her words sank in. Jumping to her feet, she reached for the ramrod, pulling it clear of the musket with trembling fingers. Luke had taught her to load the musket, and the process was almost second nature. But not today. Not with a man lying out under the hot Kansas sun. A man she'd shot.

When Will reached for the musket, Samantha gave it up readily. Let him do the loading . . . she'd do the killing. Working quickly and efficiently, Will poured gunpowder and shot into the ancient gun—the gun her great-grandfather had used at Breed's Hill. Will handed it back, acknowledging her nod of thanks, and looked toward the door.

Will's excitement had drained when she'd pointed out the possibility of more men coming after their fallen comrade. But as minutes passed, and no horse's hooves thundered into the yard, he seemed anxious to check outside.

And Samantha couldn't let the man lie there forever.

She glanced through the window and saw him . . . face up in the dust. He'd lost his hat, probably when he fell from the horse. His hair was brown, light, streaked from the sun, ruffling every now and again as the wind sifted through it.

But that was the only thing about him that moved.

Oh God, she had killed a man!

Samantha tried not to think of that as she opened the door. It was cooler outside than in the house. Cool, and pleasant, with birds singing, and puffy white clouds billowing across the sky. Cradling the heavy musket on one arm, and using the other to shade her eyes, Samantha scanned the horizon. No spirals of dust thrown up by galloping horses marred the landscape. Whatever prompted Moore to send this man back, Moore obviously thought he could handle it alone.

What would Landis Moore do to them when he discovered what had happened?

A shiver of fear ran through Samantha as she moved toward the stranger. Cautiously. The gun aimed at his prostrate body, her finger on the trigger.

"I ain't never seen this one before."

Will's words made Samantha study the stranger. She'd never seen him before either. His face was lean, she could tell that even through the layer of dust and the whiskers shadowing his jaw. Lean and deathly still.

She moved closer, kicking his pistol out of reach and nudging his arm with her musket.

"You think he's dead?"

"I don't know." Samantha swallowed, forcing herself to look at his blood-covered chest. Scarlet soaked into the butternut gray of his jacket. "Here." She shoved the musket toward Will. "I'm going to see for sure. You watch him." Samantha wiped her hands down the sides of her drab brown skirt, and knelt on one knee.

A few yards away the stranger's horse whinnied, and Samantha's reaction made her realize how nervous she was. She took a deep breath, and reached out to touch the man's cheek.

It happened so quickly Samantha had no time to fight. She was grabbed and flopped over onto the packed ground. Her head hit the dirt, painfully, bringing tears to her eyes. Air whooshed from her lungs. And something hard, and heavy, loomed over her, pressing against her.

The stranger.

She could smell him, his sweat and his blood . . . and his fear. His breath rasped harshly in her ears, almost blocking out Will's frantic cries.

"Should I shoot him? Should I shoot him?"

Samantha tried to answer, but couldn't form the words.

Then she opened her eyes and looked straight into the stranger's. They were green, pale green like the spring leaves on a cottonwood tree, and they were the saddest eyes she'd ever seen. Deep and clear, they held her mesmerized. The sounds of the day, Will's near-hysterical voice, the birds, the horse calmly munching grass, blurred, and became hazy. Samantha tried to hold on to reality, but she couldn't.

Then his eyelids fluttered shut, hiding from her those sad, sad eyes, and the momentary glimpse of his unhappy soul. His weight crushed down on her, ending her fanciful thoughts. She yelled for Will to help roll him off her.

"Did he hurt you? Jeez, Sam, I didn't know what to do."

"You did right." Samantha brushed dirt off her skirt and looked down at the stranger. He was unconscious now, flopped over on his side, and Samantha could almost believe she'd imagined that moment when their eyes met.

"I didn't know if I should shoot him or what." Will still held the musket, and Sam could sense the effort it took for him not to shake. Stepping away from the man, Samantha draped her arm around Will.

"There was nothing you could do, Will. He didn't hurt me." All this had been so hard on Will. He'd been too young to be without a mother when Ma died, too young to understand when Pa was killed . . . and then Luke.

"What are we going to do with him?" Will's question reminded Samantha that the bushwhacker couldn't be ignored. He was unconscious, but not dead. She could see the telltale rise and fall of his chest as he breathed.

And honest to God, she didn't know whether to be sad or glad about it. If he were dead, they could just bury him, and hope no one linked his disappearance to them. Of course there was little hope of that since Moore had sent him.

"We could take him into town," Will offered, looking down at the man, then back to Sam.

"How?" Samantha sighed. "You know the wagon has a broken wheel, and besides . . ." Sam paused to wipe her face and realized her hands were covered . . . with the stranger's blood. She rubbed her palms down her skirt. "And besides, Sheriff Hughes isn't going to like us bringing a wounded Rebel soldier into town."

There was no need to elaborate. It was common knowledge that Hager's Flats' sheriff had Southern leanings. His ability to look the other way when Moore's gang terrorized pro-Union families made Samantha detest the man.

"We could take him into the house."

"No!" Samantha softened her voice. "No, I don't want him in the house." Sad eyes or no, she couldn't forget that Moore's men had killed her father, or that men wearing gray had killed her brother. "We'll pull him into the barn . . . and keep him tied, too!"

"Tied? But he's wounded and—"

"And we'd most likely be dead if he weren't. You remember that, Will." Samantha grabbed hold of the stranger's arms. "You take his legs."

Together they dragged and pulled him into the sod barn. Once as they crossed the yard, the stranger opened his eyes. But they were dull from pain, and he only groaned before drifting back into unconsciousness.

"Where?" Will was out of breath from carrying his share of the load, and so was Samantha. The man was heavy even though he seemed too thin. But then she guessed war had a way of doing that to people. Goodness knows, she and Will had gone hungry a time or two. And now with the garden ruined . . . Sam tried not to worry about that as she motioned toward an empty stall.

When they first moved to Kansas, there were horses and mules to fill every space in the barn. Now there were just Pru and Hope, the mules; Lovey, the mare; and Faith, a moon-eyed cow. And now the stranger's horse.

Samantha dropped his arms. "I'll muck out the stall and throw in some clean straw," she said, wiping the dampness from her forehead with her sleeve. But Will had already started, and with a word of thanks, Sam collapsed back against the rough wall.

The Rebel was bleeding again, and she felt a twinge of guilt. Unwarranted, Sam reminded herself. She should be thanking God things weren't the other way around. She imagined the stranger would most likely have left her and Will bleeding in the dust. But that conclusion didn't stop her from going back to the house for some clean linens.

Thanks to the bushwhacker's friends and their penchant for trampling clean wash, Samantha had to strip sheets off her bed to use for bandages.

"Serve you right if I just let you bleed to death," she mumbled, heading back to the barn. Will had put clean straw in the stall and together they spread out a blanket she brought. Then they maneuvered the wounded man onto it.

"We're going to have to get his jacket and shirt off so I can tend to his wound." Easier said than done, Samantha thought a quarter hour later as she and Will struggled with the sleeves. She finally sent Will to fetch the shears.

Cutting the hated gray uniform gave Samantha more satisfaction than she cared to admit. But slicing away the uniform didn't change anything—there was still the raised CSA on his belt buckle.

Besides, Samantha was too busy staring at the gaping hole in his upper left chest. She pressed a wad of linen against it and pushed. Blood seeped through the cloth and onto her fingers. But she kept up the pressure and in a few minutes it slowed. Motioning for Will to take her place, Sam wrapped a torn strip of sheeting around his arm and body, then stood.

"Is that it?" Will looked up at her, his eyes questioning.

"I don't know what else to do."

"But he doesn't look good."

"Well, he's been shot, Will." Samantha softened her tone when she saw her brother's expression. She'd become hard, and it wasn't good for that to rub off on Will. Besides he was right, the Rebel didn't look good at all. He'd gone pale beneath his sun-bronzed skin. "Why don't you check his saddle for a blanket?" She'd already sacrificed enough of their bedding for this man. "I'll try to get him to drink a little water."

But he couldn't drink.

As much as Samantha tried, the water simply rolled from his mouth, and she finally gave up. Perhaps letting him sleep was best. Will came back, leaving the door open enough for Samantha to see the dust motes dancing in the slice of sunshine. He carried a rolled blanket in one hand, and had saddlebags thrown over his shoulder.

Samantha covered the stranger, and tossed the saddlebags in the corner. "Come on," she urged when Will stood staring down at the man. "We've got lots to do." Too much to worry about one Confederate soldier, she thought, even if he hadn't been bent on hurting them.

When she stepped into the brightness and saw again the destruction done to their small farm, she pushed any thought of compassion for the man in the barn from her mind. Or she would have if Will had let her.

But he was full of questions, and her inability to answer a one of them didn't stop him from asking. While they hauled water from the stream behind the house, he wondered aloud where the stranger came from.

"I don't know," Samantha answered. "Probably someone from Missouri back from the war and too

18

wild to pass up mischief. Hand me that bucket, Will."

Will watched his sister bend, scooping the water into the wooden-slatted pail. "He doesn't look like them other ones."

"Those other ones," Samantha corrected automatically, then wondered why she bothered. It wasn't as if her schoolteacher mother, or minister father, would know how Will talked. Or anyone else for that matter. Too many things had changed for her to worry about Will's speech, but she continued to correct — out of habit? "What are you talking about, Will?" Samantha asked when she realized what her brother had said rather than how he'd said it.

"The stranger." They trod the path to the house, stepping on some wild mint and releasing the pungent scent into the air. "He seems different from the others."

"Well, he's not." Maybe she'd thought the same thing when she'd looked into his eyes, but Will hadn't seen that. Besides, Samantha wasn't certain now it wasn't a trick of the light. And she didn't want Will making this man into some kind of hero or something. "He's like all the others . . . mean and spiteful. And don't you forget it!"

"I'm sorry, Sam. I didn't mean nothing."

"Anything. It's all right. Oh, would you look at this mess." They emptied the water into the wash pail and Samantha trudged through the downed sheets, picking them up, shaking off what muck she could, then sloshing them into the water. "We're going to have to let them soak," she sighed, shaving off slivers of lye soap. They were not just soiled, but torn, and Samantha mentally tallied how many evenings' work it would

19

take to stitch them back to the way they were two hours ago. That time would cost her money. Money she could have made sewing for one of the ladies in town.

The garden wasn't a complete loss, though it took the rest of the afternoon to restore it as best they could. By the time the sun dipped in the western sky amid a blaze of orange and red, Samantha's back felt ready to break. She stood between the rows of pumpkins and leaned back, fighting tears that stung her eyes.

"That's about all we can do for today," she said, nudging Will as he patted dirt around some squash roots. "Let's get washed up and eat supper."

She wanted a bath more than anything, but thoughts of her aching muscles hauling more water, and work yet to do tonight, made Samantha settle for the wash bowl in her room.

Uncovering cornbread and cold stewed apples, Samantha hoped Will wouldn't complain about their simple meal. But she was just too tired, and too emotionally drained, to cook a meal.

They ate by the light of a single lamp set on the hand-hewn table. Shadows danced across the uneven surface. Pa had fashioned the table from split logs when they first moved to Kansas. Samantha smiled, remembering how proud he'd been of it, not even noticing how it leaned to one side. But Pa was a dreamer, not a carpenter, or so Ma said as she managed to sneak the wedge of wood under the short table leg. And now they could stop eating off the wagon tail and move inside.

They'd been so excited Samantha didn't tell either of her parents how much she enjoyed taking meals in the fresh air. She even liked it after the long grueling trip from Massachusetts. Eating outside seemed like a picnic to a girl of twelve.

Samantha sighed. How could she think anything about Kansas was a picnic?

"Willy," Samantha said. Her brother hadn't complained about the cold meal, but he'd barely eaten a bite. Now she shook his shoulder, nudging him awake. He'd fallen asleep at the table. "Will, why don't you go to bed."

"What? Oh, no, I'm awake."

Samantha suppressed a smile as her brother jumped to his feet, obviously embarrassed at being asleep during supper. He grabbed a hunk of cornbread, stuffing it into his mouth. "I'm not even tired," Will assured her as he headed for the door.

"Where are you going?" Samantha brushed crumbs from the table into her hand.

"Thought I'd go check on the stranger. See how he's doing."

"Wait!" Samantha shook her head when she saw the expression on Will's face. "I don't want you going out there. I'll do it." How could she have forgotten about the man she shot? But Samantha knew she'd almost done just that. Without Will's reminder, she'd probably have gone to bed without giving the stranger another thought.

"Shucks, Sam, I go out to the barn all the time."

True enough. "But not when we have a dangerous man out there."

"Well, if he's dangerous, I should—"

"Stay here and clean up the dishes." Samantha shoved a tin plate in her brother's hands.

"Hell's bells, Sam, washing dishes is woman's

21

work." The look his sister shot him made color rise in Will's face, almost obscuring his freckles. He knew better than to curse in front of her, but shucks . . .

Samantha handed Will a dish towel, deciding to say nothing of his slip into profanity. He already knew how she felt about it. "It's true enough that most would think of cleaning as woman's work. But then plowing is usually done by a man, and I've done my share of that. So maybe we shouldn't be so concerned with which of us should do what and go with what's expedient at the time." She took a deep breath. "And right now, I think I'm the one to be checking on our visitor." Samantha reached for the musket she'd left propped in the corner. "After all, I'm the one who shot him."

Will didn't like it, but reluctantly he sloshed the plate into cold dishwater before she closed the door behind her.

The lantern she carried spilled a puddle of light on the packed earth in front of her, but it didn't do much to dispel the blackness of the night. No moon, she thought, glancing up into the darkness. But lots and lots of stars. Tiny pinpricks of silver patterned the sky.

Her mother had known their names. She'd told Samantha some of them, but those lessons were long since forgotten. At the time it didn't seem a necessity to remember. Asking Ma was much easier.

"But now she's gone and I can't remember the names of any of them," Samantha mumbled, then hurried off toward the barn.

One good thing. Landis Moore and his men hadn't returned to search for the stranger. All day Samantha had expected to look up and see them riding toward her, demanding to know what happened to him. They wouldn't take kindly to her shooting him. They'd probably . . .

The noise from inside the barn startled Samantha. My God, she'd forgotten to tie him up, and now he was yelling and scolding, and Lord knew what else. Taking a deep breath Samantha raised the musket and used the barrel to prod open the door. The creaking noise didn't interrupt the tirade from within.

Samantha shifted, holding up the lantern and allowing her eyes to adjust to the darkness inside the barn. She wasn't certain what she expected to see—a raving bushwhacker coming at her with the pitchfork maybe—but it wasn't what was there.

Not that the stranger wasn't raving. But he was doing it from the stall where she'd put him, and he was writhing around in the straw. He'd tossed his blanket aside, and somehow managed to push the one she'd used to make his bed to the back of the stall.

Delirious.

The word popped into her head, and she knew that's what he was. He kept yelling, calling out for a Private Jones, or James, Samantha couldn't tell for sure. She edged toward the stall, keeping the gun ready even though its weight tugged at her arm. Tomorrow she'd bring the Rebel's pistol instead.

Now that the light from the lantern splashed over him, Samantha could see how awful the stranger looked. His skin was pasty white, and she knew it would be hot even before she touched him. Leaning the musket well out of his reach and hanging the lantern on the hook overhead, she bent over to confirm his fever.

But just as her fingers grazed his cheek, he reached up and grabbed her wrist, pulling her to her knees in the straw beside him. Samantha screamed, trying to twist away, but his hand clamped tight, and his grip was like steel.

"Let me go." Samantha pried at his long fingers but he held her firm.

"Stop it!" His words rang loud in her ears as he dragged her closer. "I don't *want* to hurt you. God knows I don't want to saw off your leg. God knows I don't want to. God knows . . ."

Saw off her leg? Samantha scurried to get as far from him as she could, but he still held her wrist fast and he didn't seem inclined to let her move even an arm's length from him. What kind of man was he to talk of cutting off her leg? Bile rose in her throat and she opened her mouth to scream again. Maybe Will would hear.

Before she could make a sound, he yanked her across his body. His eyes were open, but Samantha didn't think he saw her. But then she was so scared, how could she be certain of anything? All she knew was a primal need to escape him. But now he clutched her shoulder with his other hand, and pulled her even closer.

"I don't want to hurt you," he repeated, and Samantha began to tremble. Was he going to talk about cutting off her leg again? How could he be wounded and still be so strong? "I never wanted to hurt any of you," he continued. "I only wanted to help. Oh, God."

Samantha kicked and squirmed, pushing against his chest, but stopped suddenly when she heard the sob. It seemed to come from his soul, but it reached out and touched her heart. Samantha's breathing came in harsh rasps, but she stopped struggling and looked at him. He turned his face to the side, but she could see the sheen of tears in his eyes. His sad, sad eyes.

Then before she realized what she was doing, her hand splayed across his cheek. He was ranting about hurting people again, beseeching God to understand he only tried to help. Then he rolled his face into her palm. She could feel his hot breath on her skin, and her fingers curled.

"Hush now. It's all right. Everything is all right." Her softly spoken words accomplished what all her struggles had failed. His face relaxed and he dropped her wrist. The hand on her shoulder seemed more caress than hold. She could move away from him with no trouble at all. Maybe that's why she stayed pressed against him.

"Lydia? Is that you, Lydia?" His voice now was low and sensual, and before Samantha could answer him, he continued, "I knew you wouldn't leave me, Lydia."

Samantha jerked her hand away, scrambling back against the rough wood of the stall. He thought she was somebody else, and suddenly it seemed wrong for her to be snuggled against this wounded stranger. Who was Lydia anyway? Whoever it was, this man wanted her. The moment Samantha pulled away, his voice became more frantic.

"Lydia! Lydia!" He struggled to sit, falling back against the straw-covered planks with a thud that made Samantha suck in her breath. She wasn't surprised to see fresh blood soak through the bandage. "Don't leave me, Lydia. God, don't leave me all alone."

"I won't."

Samantha closed her eyes on the look of relief filling the stranger's face. He quieted instantly, allowing her to pull the blanket over his bare chest. His skin scorched the back of her knuckles. He was so hot with fever.

He was going to die if she didn't do something.

Samantha leaned back on her heels, studying him. She wasn't sure why she pretended to be Lydia, but maybe it would help. Maybe he'd drink for Lydia.

Standing, Samantha brushed straw from her skirt, only to have the deep timbre of his voice pull her back to his side. "Don't leave me," he whispered, and she bent closer.

"I'll be right back. You need to drink some water. I'm going to get it."

"Thirsty," he mumbled, licking his dry lips.

Grabbing up the lantern, Samantha ran for the house. She didn't want Will worrying that she'd been so long. But he wasn't in the parlor and no sound came from the loft where he slept. After climbing the ladder, Samantha saw him sprawled on his mattress, sound asleep.

She plunked the ladle into the drinking bucket, grabbed it up, and hurried out the door. It wasn't until she crossed half the yard that she realized she'd left the musket in the stall with the stranger. Grabbing up her skirt she ran, water sloshing onto her legs. But when she burst through the stable door, all was as she'd left it.

Samantha pressed her hand to her rapidly beating heart, and sank down beside the stranger. He seemed asleep, but within moments he began ranting again

26

about only wanting to help people. A touch of her hand quieted him. Hearing her say she was Lydia made him choke down water.

She almost left him then. Lord knows she was tired enough to long for her bed, even if there were no sheets covering the sweet-grass mattress. But she couldn't leave him. Every time she tried, Samantha decided to wipe his face with a damp rag just one more time.

She wasn't certain, but maybe his skin felt cooler though he still babbled on about sawing legs and arms, and for once Samantha was too tired to calm him. She sat back, hugging her knees, wondering what kind of man would have nightmares about such things, even when feverish.

Arms and legs and blood . . . and sickness. Samantha leaned forward, listening intently to the words he mumbled. If she sieved through the gruesome details of his dream, one thought rang clear. He had tried to help.

Samantha wasn't sure when the thought occurred to her, but she dipped the linen in the pail and laid it on his forehead. "Are you a doctor?" she asked, leaning close to his ear.

"Lydia?"

"Yes, I'm here."

A smile softened the pain-etched planes of his face as he drifted off to sleep.

"*Now* you're quiet," Samantha complained. She sat back on her heels, wondering. It didn't make sense for him to be a doctor, but she couldn't shake the feeling that his ranting had meant just that. But then why would he join Moore's gang? "Doctor's aren't saints, for heavens sake," Samantha mumbled to herself. But it still didn't fit.

"Who are you?" she whispered, but for now the stranger's sleep seemed peaceful. And sleeping is what you should be doing, Samantha told herself as she leaned against the stall. But before she closed her eyes, her gaze snagged on the saddlebags she'd tossed in the corner of the stall.

Casting only a cursory glance at the sleeping man, Samantha shifted to drag them toward her. After unbuckling one side, she flipped open the bag. Samantha didn't know what she expected to find — what did doctors carry around with them? But there wasn't anything in his pack but clothes, fairly clean and rolled up, trail equipment, and a leather sack.

Samantha guessed what was inside before she opened it. The sight of the gold coins made her palms itch — there appeared to be enough money to keep Will and her for several years — but she gave the drawstring a yank and stuffed the sack back into the saddlebag.

The second pistol was another story. That she quickly stuck in her apron pocket. She sorted through the iron skillet and coffee pot, the pack of Lucifers. She did find a harmonica, and her eyes strayed to the stranger. Did he play?

Shaking her head at her foolishness, Samantha began repacking the saddlebags. She wasn't going to learn anything about him, and she should get back to the house and sleep while she had the chance.

And then she felt something in a jacket pocket. Reaching inside, Samantha discovered a folded paper. Opening it, she found a parole awarded to one Jacob Morgan, Captain, late of the Confederate Army.

Well, that was no surprise. She knew he was a Rebel.

28

Shaking her head, Samantha stuffed the paper back into the pocket. That's when her fingers encountered something cold and smooth. She pulled out the frame, turning it over carefully in her hands. Scrolling gold flowers framed maroon etched velvet. And in the center was an oval daguerreotype. Of a man, a woman, and a young boy. They all looked so beautiful and so happy.

Lydia. Somehow Samantha knew the woman had to be Lydia. She had dark hair and eyes, and a face that shone with love for the man beside her. But that meant the man was . . . Samantha swallowed. The man in the daguerreotype was well dressed and clean, and handsome, nothing like the —

"What in the hell are you doing with that?"

Samantha squealed and her gaze flew to the stranger, who now leaned on one elbow, looking very much awake and very fierce.

Chapter Two

She couldn't answer, only stared at the stranger—
no, Jacob Morgan, she knew his name now—and
clutched the daguerreotype tighter. He gazed at her
through narrowed eyes, and Samantha wondered
how she could ever have thought them sad. *Angry*
was the only word that came to mind.

He shifted, the brackets around his mouth deepening in pain, and Samantha flattened herself against
the stall. Her eyes strayed to the musket still leaning
in the corner and her heart sank as she realized it
was out of reach. Carelessly she'd placed the gun on
the other side of him. He could seize it easily.

Samantha's gaze flew back to his face to see if he
was aware of it, but he wasn't looking at the musket.
Though somewhat relieved, Samantha now realized
he probably wouldn't need it to hurt her. Even
wounded, he possessed a strength she couldn't
match. His shoulders were broad, and though he was
lean, the stark white sheeting wrapped around his
torso emphasized his muscular build.

But at the moment he didn't seem bent on hurting

30

her. He looked at her now, a frown furrowing the brow she'd soothed with cooling cloths. "Who are you?" he demanded in a voice with just a hint of a drawl.

"S—Samantha Lowery."

He seemed not to understand her, his head cocking slightly to the side. A lock of hair, shining gold in the lantern light, fell over his forehead. Samantha leaned forward to brush it back, jerking away when she realized what she'd almost done. This man wasn't Will, for heaven's sake.

He didn't seem to notice her actions as he continued to study her, an expression on his face as if he didn't comprehend what was going on.

He was getting weaker.

His wound had opened again, and his eyelids were drooping. He took a deep breath, keeping his focus on Samantha with difficulty. "What happened to me?"

"You were shot."

"Yeah, that's what I thought," he said before falling back onto the straw-covered floor.

Samantha scurried to her feet, staying as far from him as she could. He swallowed, and Samantha watched the muscles in his neck as she inched back toward the gun. She reached behind her with the hand not clutching his daguerreotype. Her fingers just grazed the muzzle when he spoke again. Samantha jumped and knocked the gun over.

"May I have my picture?"

Samantha looked down at the frame she'd forgotten she held. Her heart beat faster than a midsum-

31

mer rainstorm as she moved toward him. Quickly, hoping he wouldn't grab her, she leaned over, dropping the picture on his lower chest. His hand came up and covered it, nearly hiding it from view.

"Thank you." The words were barely a whisper, and Samantha ignored them as she dove for the musket. She shouldered it and turned, aiming toward the man lying in the straw but he didn't notice. He was asleep or unconscious, Samantha couldn't tell for sure.

Taking a deep breath, Samantha lowered the gun and leaned against the rough wood. She tried calming herself. "It's over. He didn't hurt you," she mumbled, reassured. She'd felt vulnerable, hardly a new feeling, but with him it was more intense. And she didn't like it.

Looking down at him now, he didn't seem frightening. Samantha studied his face closely as a vision of the man in the daguerreotype flashed into her mind. Was he the same person? His hair was lighter, his face darker, and leaner. But she imagined those changes could come from the war. And of course he looked older and sadder. No question *that* could be the result of war.

But now that she studied what she could see of his features beneath the beard, she thought maybe they were the same. Same eyes, framed by long dark lashes that now rested in crescents above his cheeks, same straight nose, same mouth. His lips were firm and nicely shaped, and she imagined he'd look good smiling — as in the daguerreotype.

Pushing that foolish thought aside, Samantha

32

started toward the barn door. She'd done enough to help him. His wound had stopped bleeding, and he seemed to be resting as well as could be expected. Glancing over her shoulder, she noticed his bare chest. Why did she have to see that? Grimacing, she moved back to cover him.

When she did, his hand slid from the golden frame to rest on her arm. It wasn't an aggressive move, but still it frightened her. Steeling her heart, she did one more thing — what she'd threatened to do this afternoon — before leaving the stable.

Something wasn't right.

Samantha knew it the instant her eyes opened. Sunlight streamed through the window, superimposing squares of brightness on the patchwork quilt. Pretty, Samantha thought vaguely, wondering why she'd never noticed it before. She sat up, brushing corn-colored curls out of her face. Why wasn't her hair braided, and why was it so light outside?

The answer hit her like the recoil of a gun and she jumped off her bed, stubbing her toe on the leather shoe carelessly left out on the floor.

The stranger . . . Jacob Morgan. He was the cause of all this. Sleeping late — she always rose before dawn; going to bed in her clothes, without even taking the time to brush and braid her hair. She glanced down at her pillow and began gathering the pins that had escaped her hair during the night.

She felt wrinkled and scruffy, and one glance in the mirror her parents had brought painstakingly

33

from Massachusetts told her she looked that way too. And regardless of her "stay abed" problem this morning, mauve crescents shadowed her blue eyes.

Samantha bent back, hands on hips, trying to rid her body of its aches. She had stayed up way too late last night. And it was all the fault of Captain Jacob Morgan, late of the Confederate Army. Well, today would be different, she decided, taking a brush to her hair with a vengeance. She didn't have time to fool with an ex-Confederate soldier and a member of Landis Moore's gang to boot. He'd make it or not without her assistance. Will could check on him now and again. No need to worry since she'd tied the Rebel up before she went to bed. She wasn't taking any more chances.

"The one smart thing you did," Samantha assured herself. All that worrying about his identity, and Lydia's, was a waste of time. Samantha leaned forward, grabbing her hair in one fist and circling it around her head. She jammed one pin through the wrapped curls, then another, but the third, along with the others she held in her mouth, went flying to the floor when she heard Will yelling and the dog barking.

Tearing out of her bedroom, she ran into her brother as he and Charity, the dog, burst through the front door. Samantha grabbed his shoulders. "My heavens, Will, what is it? Moore's men?"

Samantha glanced toward the window expecting to see hordes of ruffians headed their way, but she couldn't see out. They'd draped a blanket over the broken window yesterday in a futile attempt to keep

34

out the flies and mosquitoes.

"It's not Moore," Will said. "It's the stranger."

Samantha searched around the room for the musket. Where'd she put it last night? With a sigh of relief, she turned and reached for it over the mantle. Some habits die hard. "What about him?" she asked Will as she headed through the door. Had she failed to tie him tightly enough? Had he gotten loose and—

"I think he's dying, Sam. He keeps calling out, and he's hotter than blazes."

Samantha stopped and swirled on her brother, Kansas dirt drifting up around her skirt hem. "You mean you scared ten years off my life because that bushwhacker has a fever?"

Will swallowed. "But Sam, you don't understand. He's mighty sick."

"I understand perfectly." Now that the imagined crisis was over, Samantha's knees felt weak. She took a deep breath and started back toward the house.

"You mean you ain't going to do nothing?"

"Anything." Samantha glanced over her shoulder. Her brother, his too-short trousers showing pale skin above his shoes, just looked at her, his face incredulous. It struck her how much he reminded her of Pa. She sighed again. "I'll see to him. But first I'm going to get dressed." She shouldered the musket. "Fetch me some fresh water. I'll brew some ginger tea for Captain Morgan."

Will was back from the stream before she'd finished fixing her hair. Samantha could hear him banging around in the other room looking for the

35

tea leaves. Stepping out of her bloodstained skirt, she pulled on a clean one—same color, same style—and went to help him.

Walking to the barn, Will carried the tea and a pail of water while she carried Captain Morgan's sidearm.

"How do you know his name?" His hands full, Will blew at a fly buzzing around his head. "Did he tell you last night?"

"No." Samantha could hear her patient raving again through the open door of the barn.

"So how did you find out?"

"I looked through his saddlebag," Samantha confessed, hoping he didn't fault her for invading the man's privacy. But he only shrugged, spilling some water in the process. "You hear him?"

"Yes, I hear him." It was like last night, only his voice sounded more hoarse . . . and weaker. Was he dying?

"I done fed the animals," Will told her. Though a part of her registered the need to correct his speech, Samantha was too engrossed in looking at the captain to do it.

"Thanks, Will. Set the bucket down. I'll call if I need you." She worked on the knot she'd tied around his wrists, finally getting them loosened.

"I think I should stay here."

Will's tone made Samantha look up from where she'd knelt in the straw. The Rebel's skin scalded her hand and she dipped a cloth into the bucket, wiping it over his face, before she answered her brother. "There's too much to do for both of us to take time away from the chores—not to mention the work made yesterday by this man's friends. Now if you want to nurse him, it's fine with me. I'll work on re-staking the fence."

"Naw." Will kicked at the floor. "I'll see to the chores. I don't know what to do for him."

I don't either, Samantha thought, though she noticed he'd quieted down with her ministrations. "Will."

Her brother jammed his hat over his nearly white hair and glanced around.

"Don't stray far from the house, and let me know if you see any sign of visitors."

"You think Landis Moore will be back today?"

"I don't know." She dragged the cloth back through the water and wrung it out. "Just let me know if you see anything."

By the time Samantha finished sponging off his face, neck, and chest, he was calm. She figured it was as good a time as any to fill him with tea. He fought her at first, spitting out more than he drank; making her inexplicably angry. She wanted him well, well and gone, and he was doing nothing to speed the process.

Was she losing her mind? No one wanted to feel the way he obviously did. She couldn't blame him for that. Samantha brushed at hair curling over her forehead and tried again. Lifting his head, she guided the tin cup to his mouth.

"Drink for me, Jacob," she said, her voice soft and coaxing. His lips opened. She poured a little tea into his mouth then, with the fingers of her other hand, massaged his neck. He swallowed, and she smiled, repeating the process until he'd drunk most of the liquid in the cup.

Then she lay him back down. But she couldn't help noticing how uncomfortable he looked lying in the straw. The blanket he'd writhed off of was bundled in the corner of the stall. Samantha grabbed it and, moving away from Captain Morgan, gave it a good shake. Laying it out flat beside him, she slowly inched his body onto it. She didn't want his wound to start bleeding again, and it only took a moment to remind her just how heavy he was. But she finally had him on the blanket.

The day was hot, no breeze as yet to soften the sun's heat. Samantha leaned against the stall side, wiping perspiration from her brow. But she had no time to rest.

Carefully, Samantha unwrapped the bandage and covered the wound with a fresh pad of linen. The heavy bleeding had stopped, but the wound still seeped. She couldn't tell if infection had set in, and didn't know what to do if it had. All she could do was make him comfortable and hope for the best.

His skin needed bathing again, and so she started. Down from his forehead, across his cheeks, under the chin she could barely see beneath the growth of whiskers. Then she rinsed the cloth and skimmed down his neck and over his shoulders, careful not to disturb the bandage. His chest was broad, with a wedge of curly hair that narrowed into a line which arrowed down into the waistband of his uniform pants.

She washed his arms, wondering if maybe his skin felt a little cooler. His hands were large with long tapered fingers. And clean nails. Samantha sat up, his right hand resting in her lap. Turning his hand over, she studied it, noting the calluses on his palms and the pads of his fingers . . . and the lack of dirt. His fingernails were trimmed short with no crescents of grime.

It suddenly hit her that he was clean all over. Oh, not spotless to be sure, but not filthy. He'd been covered with dust and sweat and blood yesterday, but even then there hadn't been the foul stench of uncleanliness she'd expected . . . expected from one of Landis Moore's men.

She had to squeeze by several of them in town when they taunted her on the sidewalk. And she always wished she were upwind of their foul odor.

What had Will said? This man seemed different? Samantha sat thinking about that until his moan stirred her from her musings. "Silly, Samantha. You're being silly," she chided herself. But she did it in a soft tone that quieted the Rebel.

By the time she'd sponged him down again and taken care of his personal needs, Samantha's back was stiff and sore. She stood, hanging his butternut trousers over the stall divider and stretching. It made more sense to keep his clothes off, she told herself, trying to ignore the blush she felt creeping up her neck. What with all she had to do, it was stupid to repeatedly pull his pants on and off.

Knowing the truth of something and being able to deal with it were two different things. She knew that yesterday when she lowered his pants for the first time. And today, she realized, the chore was not getting any easier, or any more routine, as she'd assured herself it would.

If anything, she noticed more about him each time she undressed him. Like his legs were long and sturdy and covered by thick, curly, brown hair. And his hips were narrow, with protruding hip bones that emphasized his thinness. And other parts of him were . . . Samantha squeezed her eyes shut, trying not to think of the other parts of him she'd seen. It was disturbing. It was unsettling. And it made her skin burn as if she were the one with a fever.

But he was covered now, and resting quietly, and she could use a rest herself. Samantha moved, kicking something with her shoe as she did. Bending over, she saw the gold frame sticking out from the straw. He must have dropped it. And she'd come near to forgetting about it. But now that she held it, nothing, not even the threat of Captain Morgan waking and finding her with it, could keep her from studying the daguerreotype.

In the light of day, even the filtered light inside the barn, the woman—Lydia—looked beautiful. Delicate and fragile. In contrast, the man—she was certain now it was Jacob Morgan—seemed strong and protective toward her and the little boy. And sinfully handsome.

Annoyed with herself, Samantha crossed to the saddlebags and stuffed the picture back in, then hurried outside. When she stepped from the shaded stable into the bright sunlight, Samantha saw that Will had been busy. Her clothesline was intact, and the sheets they let to soak yesterday were billowing in the breeze that had whipped up from the south.

She walked over to the fence and gave her brother's shoulders a squeeze before lifting the other end of the split log rail he was trying to refit.

"Thanks." Will removed his hat and wiped a sleeve across his heat-flushed face.

"You've done a lot of work. I could use something to eat. How about you?"

"Cold cornbread?" Will asked, and Samantha laughed.

"No." She grabbed him around the neck. "I was thinking of something a little more substantial. Stew and hominy, maybe," Samantha said, then laughed again at Will's expression. He loved stew. But that wasn't the only reason she decided on cooking it. Captain Morgan needed nourishment, and beef broth seemed as good as anything.

"How's he doing?" Will motioned toward the barn as they passed.

"Maybe a little better. He's sleeping now. I'm going to brew some more tea. Hopefully he'll be better in a day or two." And then I don't know what we'll do, Samantha finished silently.

But he was still feverish two days later. And Samantha was exhausted from taking care of him. But every time she thought to pass the chore over to Will, something inside her balked. She couldn't put her finger on the reason, and truthfully didn't want to think too much about it. She finally decided she'd put so much darn work into saving him she couldn't let go now.

But he wasn't saved. If anything, he seemed worse. His rantings were quieter, but she blamed that on the weakness that seemed to settle over him like a shroud. Samantha quickly pushed aside that thought. She didn't want to think of him dying.

She was afraid that might happen if she didn't do something. But what?

Slowly, careful not to hurt him more than necessary, Samantha uncovered his wound. It looked worse each time she changed the dressing. Today it was all puffy and red. And the smell! Samantha forced herself not to shrink away. It wasn't healing right. It didn't matter that she had no experience with such things, she knew.

But again came the question, what should she do? A sudden memory of Jacob Morgan's earlier ravings swept over her. In his mind he'd been cutting off limbs and she'd decided he was a doctor. Samantha wiped sweat from her forehead with the back of her hand. She could use a doctor now. But she couldn't risk leaving her patient to go into town. And even if she did manage to drag old Doc Shelton out here, he'd probably be too far gone in his daily consumption of liquor even to tell her what to do.

That's what she needed, someone to tell her what to do. Samantha's eyes widened, and she sucked in her breath as the idea formed. It probably wouldn't work, but leaning toward the Rebel's ear, she decided it was worth a try.

"Jacob," she whispered, her nose brushing the soft wavy hair along the side of his head. "Jacob,

I need your help."

"Lydia?" He drew the word out lovingly, and Samantha swallowed, wondering why she felt this odd sense of jealousy. She wanted him to think she was Lydia. It made things much easier.

"Yes, Jacob." She started to tell him she was Lydia, but didn't. The expression on his face made it clear he already knew. Taking a deep breath, Samantha continued. "Help me, Jacob. Help me make you better." She paused. "I want you to be well again."

"Lydia."

His voice was weak and Samantha sighed in frustration. "Jacob!" Samantha slapped her hand against the straw-covered floor. "For heaven's sake, you're going to die."

"Good." The word was barely more than a whisper but Samantha heard it, and her breath left her with a whoosh. *Good?* He'd said good. He wanted to die?

"Jacob. Jacob." Samantha tried to push aside the panic in her voice. "I don't want you to die. Please live . . . for me."

"Want to die."

"No!" Samantha ignored the tears streaming down her face. "No! I don't want you to," she repeated. "Now tell me what to do. You were shot." Samantha pushed ahead before he could say any more about dying. "You have a fever and your wound looks awful. And smells. It smells bad, Jacob, and I'm afraid."

"Get the bullet out."

Samantha sat back on her heels. She heard him

43

clearly, but it wasn't only the volume of his voice. He sounded different. She didn't know how, maybe more authoritative. Then she thought about what he'd said, and she glanced at the wound. "I don't know how."

"Cut it out, damnit."

As if that order drained his remaining strength, the Rebel settled back into the unconscious state he'd drifted in and out of for days. Samantha just stared at him for a moment then she gathered up her skirts and ran from the barn.

Charity lifted her head sleepily when Samantha burst through the cabin door. But by the time she'd gathered up the few things she needed, the dog was snoring softly, her nose cradled on her furry paws.

Samantha didn't bother to light the extra candles till she was again inside the stall. She could easily find her way from the cabin to the barn in the dark. But she couldn't find a musketball without plenty of light . . . if she could find it at all.

Staring down at the knife she'd taken from the hook beside the stove, Samantha felt a shiver of dread flow through her. What if she killed him? She'd never done anything like this before. Oh, she'd nursed the sick. Her mother had lived a few pain-riddled weeks after coming down with the fever and Samantha had taken care of her. But that was nothing like cutting into someone's flesh.

Samantha sank to her knees, watching the play of light and shadows on Jacob Morgan's skin. Tentatively she touched the area around his wound. He was hard and firm until her fingers wandered too

44

close to opening. The contact made Samantha wince, but the Rebel didn't move a muscle. She supposed he would be thankful for his unconscious state, as she replaced her hand with the tip of the blade.

Her probing didn't seem to affect him, but Samantha had a difficult time keeping her hand steady. She forced herself to ignore the fresh blood and continued to carefully explore the wound with the blade tip. And then she felt something hard.

Samantha used her fingers to remove the ball. It looked so small and innocuous cradled in her palm. She dropped it in the tin pan and went about cleaning his wound. Then she pulled out the needle and thread she'd attached to her bodice. It occurred to her to wake Jacob up if she could and ask about sewing him up. She wasn't sure if it would help or hurt him. But waking him would allow him to feel the pain and she didn't want that.

Quickly and efficiently she stitched, pretending her needle flew through one of Peggy Keane's vulgar gowns. After she tied off the thread, Samantha cleaned herself and the knife, covered her patient, and leaned back against the stall divider.

When she woke, it was still dark outside, the little oasis of light coming from the lantern and flickering candles. Samantha thought Jacob Morgan might look a little better. But it might be her imagination tempered with hope. He was still hot to the touch, but he slept more peacefully.

Samantha thought back over his nightmares — tormented dreams — as she watched the slow rise and fall of his chest. In his ramblings men screamed in pain and died. And were sometimes saved. By Jacob Morgan? Samantha was fairly certain the answer to that was yes.

She sighed. As difficult as it was for her to care for one man, what must it have been like to minister to scores . . . during wartime.

Samantha looked down at the Rebel. "What kind of man are you, Jacob Morgan?" she asked, then shook her head. He was in no condition to answer for now.

She was so tired. Last night, after Will had climbed into his loft, she'd brought her pillow out to the barn, planning to sit on it awhile and sponge Captain Morgan down. But she hadn't used it, and now the grass-filled ticking lay beneath the captain's head.

Samantha sighed again, her chin on the bend of her raised knees. His skin seemed a little cooler. And she was so weary. She should go back to the house and sleep. But she couldn't make her tired limbs respond. Her lids felt heavy, and thinking only to give herself a brief rest, Samantha slid down into the straw.

Jake came awake by slow, painful degrees. His eyes slitted open, then slammed shut. Something—the sun?—shone brightly overhead. Where was he? And what happened to him?

Smells surrounded him, ripe and musty, reminding him of the stable behind his house in Richmond. But he couldn't be there. The stable was gone, like the house on Franklin Street. Burned. He'd seen the charred remains for himself when he'd returned to Richmond after the war.

So where was he? And why did his chest hurt like hell? More to the point, why did he hurt like hell all over?

His right side was nestled against something warm and soft, and though it had been a long time since he'd experienced the feeling, he knew it was a woman. He could hear her breathing, and smell her, a faint clean scent vying with the stronger odor of straw and animals.

It wasn't Lydia. He was sure of that. Though it vaguely seemed as if he'd been with her recently, he knew Lydia was dead.

Jake swallowed, then slowly opened his eyes, squinting toward the source of light. A lantern of pierced tin, not the sun, illuminated what appeared to be a horse stall. It hung from a low, roughly hewn rafter. He probably was in a barn or stable of some kind, he thought. Twisting his head to the side, Jake decided to see if the assumption he'd made lying there was right.

The pain that shot out from his chest made him suck in his breath, but didn't stop him from shifting to see what was cuddled against him.

Blond hair, thick and mussed, lay on his shoulder, and beneath it a face that seemed oddly familiar. Yet he didn't remember knowing this woman. She was young, with fair skin tinted slightly by the sun, a short straight nose, and full lips that curved slightly in her sleep. Her lashes lay thick against the few freckles that spattered her nose and cheeks.

And her eyes were blue. Jake paused in his study of the woman. How in the hell did he know what color her eyes were?

But Jake could swear if she opened them, he'd see they were blue, soft and gentle, and turned up slightly at the corners. He didn't know her, he was certain of that, but there she was, strong in his memory.

She stirred, the hand resting on his chest coming up to brush at her nose, and Jake watched as her lashes lifted. Then he was staring into those deep blue eyes he knew she'd have. She looked at him sleepily, then smiled, her eyelids drifting shut again only to pop open.

"Oh my," Samantha said, jerking to a sitting position. "You're awake."

Jake tried to lever himself up, his face grimacing in pain, and Samantha eased him back onto the blanket. He'd spoken to her before, of course, but he'd always seemed in some feverish haze. This time she didn't think he was, and not just because his skin felt cool and damp. He looked lucid and aware, and slightly amused.

How had she managed to lie down beside him, and why was she so flustered?

Samantha decided to get herself under control. "Would you care for something to drink, Jacob Morgan?" As she reached for the ladle, Samantha brushed her hand against the Rebel's sidearm in her apron pocket.

He drank greedily, stopping when she suggested he slow up, then lay back onto Samantha's pillow with a sigh.

"Where am I?"

"My farm." Samantha turned her back on him. "My name is Samantha Lowery." She glanced over her shoulder. He appeared perplexed.

"How did you know my name?"

Samantha dropped the ladle into the water pail, a lie forming readily on her lips. "You told me," she answered before squatting down beside him. If he didn't remember the time he caught her snooping in his saddlebags, she certainly wasn't going to remind him.

He seemed to accept her explanation readily enough, ,and Samantha quickly straightened his blanket, making certain to stay out of his reach. Now that he was awake, really awake, she was back to being afraid of him. She glanced toward the rope she'd used to tie him that first night. One end was still attached to the side of the stall, and Samantha wondered if she could wrap the other end around his wrists without him causing too much trouble. She caught his eye as he looked around the barn, and she decided she couldn't.

"How long have I been here?"

"Four days, almost five."

"And you nursed me all this time?"

"Yes. Actually my brother and I have . . . my big brother." Samantha's lie came easier this time. Captain Morgan was studying her, a wary expression on his face. And his wariness evoked the same emotion in her.

He looked at her steadily, his green eyes never wavering, and Samantha tried to match him in kind. But her hand crept into her pocket when he asked, "Is he the one who shot me, this big brother of yours?"

"No." That much was the truth. Samantha's hand tightened around the Rebel's gun, waiting for the next question. But he didn't ask if she had done the deed, or even who had, and Samantha's hand relaxed.

"How bad is it?" He angled his chin down toward his chest.

"I don't know," she answered honestly. "You've had a bad fever."

"Deliriums?" His eyes snapped back to hers and she glimpsed again that look of sadness before he masked it.

"Some." Samantha stood. "You rambled on a bit, but never about anything I could understand." This lying to him was second nature to her now. She was doing it without the slightest compunction—her father would roll over in his grave—and for no good reason. It even occurred to her that she'd like to ask him about being a doctor.

But it was better if she didn't know anything more about him. Samantha was honest enough—with herself anyway—to realize she'd formed an attachment to the stranger. It was one-sided, and obviously brought on by the intimate care she'd given him. But it couldn't go any further.

And she didn't want to talk about Lydia with him. Samantha wiped her hands down the sides of her skirt. "Well, you should be getting back to sleep. You need your rest." It was too dangerous to try and tie him now but she'd sneak back while he slept and bind him. He acted decent enough now, but he was weak, almost at her mercy. Samantha couldn't forget the first time she saw him — riding toward their cabin, sent by Landis Moore. He was bent on hurting Will and her then, and as soon as he was strong enough, he'd no doubt try again. What was she going to do with him?

"Thank you."

His softly spoken words stopped Samantha as she reached for the lantern. She didn't expect anything close to manners from one of Moore's men. "For what," she asked, yanking the lantern off the hook. Oscillating light splayed across him when she looked down. He really was a handsome man. She'd noticed it before when she compared her patient to the man in the daguerreotype, thinking that if he were cleaned up and shaved, he would be. But now she realized he just was, scruffy beard, scraggly hair, and all. Maybe those captivating green eyes made the difference.

He watched her now, a slight frown creasing his brow, and she remembered what he'd said, and that she hadn't responded. Clearing her throat, Samantha looked away. "It was nothing." She wished she weren't so aware of him as a man.

"Still, I'm grateful."

Samantha glanced back to see him smiling at her. His face was mostly in shadows but not so much that she couldn't make out his features. She'd once

51

thought a smile would transform his face and it did. Hurrying toward the door she left him in darkness.

Charity lifted head from paws, looked around, yawned, and rolled to her side as Samantha entered the cabin. She pulled the twisted string through the latch — not much protection from invaders — and glanced toward the loft.

The morning would be soon enough to tell Will about his new job. He would take care of their visitor from now on. Of course she'd see the bushwhacker good and tied first, but then Will could take care of his needs.

And she could get back to working the farm. A couple days of picking corn would purge this obsession she had with Captain Morgan. Then when he left, she wouldn't have to worry about it again.

But when she crawled under the quilt and fell asleep, she dreamed of the Rebel, waking up with her heart pounding and a strange warmth in her stomach. Clutching the quilt to her chest, Samantha looked out the one window in her room. The palest hint of dawn bleached the night sky with streaks of gray.

After thrusting her unstockinged feet into shoes, Samantha grabbed up Captain Morgan's revolver and headed for the stable. Charity trotted along into the yard, finally veering off toward the stream. The barn was dark, and Samantha waited for her eyes to adjust before moving closer to the captain.

He was asleep. One end of the rope was attached to a board separating the stalls. She laid the pistol on the ground well out of reach of the Rebel and carefully pulled the other end of the rope to his side. Quickly she tied it around his wrists, jumping out of the way and grabbing the gun when he jerked awake.

"What the hell are you doing?" She could make out his struggles in the dim light. Samantha watched as he seemed to realize his predicament. He quieted, straining to see her. "What's wrong with you? Are you crazy?"

"No." Samantha remembered she wore only her nightdress and backed farther into the shadows. "At least I'm not crazy enough to let you loose now that you're better." Charity started barking, that wild yelp she had when excited, and Samantha figured she'd flushed a quail.

"What's gotten into you, lady? And what the hell are you doing with my gun?" Jake gave one more tug on the rope, then flopped down on his back, exhausted.

"You needn't act coy with me. I know why you came here, and—"

"Why I came here! I'm here because some idiot shot me. Now untie this damn rope."

Samantha ignored his tirade as Charity ran yelping into the barn. The dog jumped on the captain, eliciting a grunt of pain, and bounced in front of Samantha still barking shrilly. "What is it, Charity?" Samantha felt a prickle of fear. The dog didn't act like this over a bird.

Then she heard the horses, and ran to the barn door.

"What is it, damnit?" Jake strained to sit up. Who's out there?"

The young woman turned toward him, and in the faint light from the open door, he could see the anger and hate marring her pretty face. "It's your friend Landis Moore."

Chapter Three

Why did she tell him that?

Samantha bolted through the door, chiding herself for her stupidity. Now all Captain Morgan had to do was call out and Landis Moore would know he was here. Wounded. And tied up. Oh, God!

Charity yelped and raced about, slowing Samantha's dash toward the house. Then suddenly the dog swerved into Samantha's path, tangling with her legs and the shoes she'd been too rushed to fasten, and sending her sprawling in the dust.

"Oh, get off me!" As if to apologize, Charity now leaped onto her mistress, lapping the dirt from Samantha's face with giant swipes of her tongue. "I'm not playing," Samantha spat between licks, but it was useless. By the time she managed to scramble to her feet, Landis Moore and two other men seated on their horses, not ten feet away, were watching her.

Samantha tossed back her braid, looking to the ground for Captain Morgan's gun. She couldn't find it! Somehow as she'd fallen or tumbled around with Charity, the revolver had disappeared. It was there someplace among the clumps of grass and weeds but she couldn't see it, and Landis Moore's voice reminded her there wasn't time to look.

"Seems you're having more than your share of troubles here, missy."

"What do you want, Moore?"

He leaned forward, resting his wrists across the saddle horn, and chuckled, the sound making goose flesh crawl down Samantha's back. "Now that's not a very neighborly question. I heard you had a problem out here the other day and thought I'd see if you needed any help."

"We're doing fine. And you're no neighbor of mine." Samantha took a step toward the house, only to have one of Moore's men sidle his horse that way, blocking her path.

"Not a neighbor?" His dark hooded eyes widened in mock surprise. "You must not of heard." Moore hiked himself up in the saddle, straightening the paunch that hung over his pants. Too much gluttonous eating and drinking, her father had said ten years ago when they'd first run across Moore. At the time he was in his twenties, a dark-haired, swarthy character, and a bully. But none of then realized then how dangerous he really was.

"Heard what?" Samantha hated to ask but then she didn't have much choice. The three horses kept inching forward, forcing her back closer to the barn. When was Captain Morgan going to call out to his friends? Maybe he couldn't hear them. She'd closed the barn door and there were no window slits in the front.

And Will. What was he doing up at the cabin? She hoped he didn't do anything foolish.

"I bought the Colt place. It butts up to yours, now don't it?"

"The Colts wouldn't sell to you! They wouldn't sell to anyone. They've worked too hard." Samantha paused for a moment, her eyes narrowing. "What did you do to them?"

"Why Miss Lowery, you wound me. The Colts and I transacted a business deal. We—"

"You lying bastard! The Colts came out here about the same time as my parents. They wouldn't have anything to do with you!"

"Now you're talking foolish, girl." Moore and his men made no pretense of hiding their actions now. The horses backed Samantha against the sod walls of the barn. Bits of dirt crumbled into her shoe. "Maybe you need to be taught some manners. What you think about that, boys?"

Both "boys" readily agreed, and Samantha tried to ignore their leering faces as she stared back at Moore. "Get off my property!"

He laughed harshly then leaned forward and grabbed Samantha's braid. "Big talk for such a helpless little girl." His tug pulled her against the side of his lathered horse. He bent down and Samantha could smell his sour breath as he spoke. "And one running around in her nightclothes. Some folks might say you was asking for it." He gave a savage yank, then let her loose. Samantha stumbled but stayed on her feet. Little comfort as the three men glared down at her.

Samantha's heart beat frantically and she clutched her hands together to keep them from shaking. She wouldn't show them how truly frightened she was. She wouldn't! No matter what they did.

"You think about it, little lady." Moore jerked his head to the side, and the two others turned their horses. "Moving might be the best thing for you, too. We'll be back."

Samantha collapsed against the dirt wall, locking her knees to keep from sliding to the ground. They were riding away. They were actually leav—

Moore was almost out of the yard when he reined to a stop, turning his mount in a tight circle. "Where'd you get that horse?" he yelled. Samantha's gaze shot to where he was looking, and her heart sank.

There in plain sight was the Rebel's horse. They'd put him in the small paddock beside the barn after Will fixed that stretch of fence. It seemed like a good idea at the time. But now the eastern sun shone off his chestnut coat and Samantha couldn't think of a single way she could have gotten a fine animal like that. Not to mention that Moore probably recognized it as belonging to one of his men.

Samantha wondered briefly why Morgan hadn't yelled out, but dismissed that thought as Moore trotted back toward her.

"Answer me, girl. Where'd you get him?"

"I traded." Samantha swallowed. "A stranger came through here last week needing food and clothing."

"And he traded that for a horse?"

Moore obviously didn't believe her, and why

should he? Her lie was stupid. The other two men were walking their horses up to join their boss. Samantha glanced toward the cabin and caught the glint of sun off a gun barrel poking through the paneless window. She hoped Will wasn't going to shoot. He'd never hit even one of them, and they'd be on him before he could reload.

"A horse for some food don't make much sense, girl."

"It does if you're starving," Samantha answered with as much certainly as she could muster. She must have been convincing, or maybe Moore had noticed the gun pointed his way by this time. For whatever the reason he signaled his men again, and they all cantered out of the yard.

"You think about it, little girl" drifted back to her across the prairie as they galloped away.

"Sam! Sam! You all right?"

She was and she wasn't. Samantha waved briefly toward Will as he raced across the yard. His shirttail was flapping behind him and his large flat feet were bare.

"I thought they were going to hurt you sure," he said skidding to a halt in front of her. "What's wrong? Oh no, what'd they do to you? I should have shot them." He grabbed his sister's shoulder.

"No." Samantha tried to say more but she was shaking so badly her teeth were chattering as if a winter wind had swooped down on them. "I . . ." she started only to be interrupted by yelling from the barn.

"What in the hell is going on out there? Someone

get in here!"

Samantha straightened, folding her arms across her chest and looking at Will. She'd totally forgotten about their visitor. But he wasn't going to stand for that now. He was hollering his head off, the sound ringing out loud and clear. Why hadn't he made his presence known before?

Following her brother into the barn, Samantha bumped into him when he stopped suddenly.

"Hell's bells, why'd you tie him up?"

"Because he's the enemy. And watch your mouth, young man. You're not too big for me to—oh my heavens!" One look at Captain Morgan, and Samantha forgot her brother's cursing. She dropped to her knees in the straw. "What have you done?"

"Ouch! Damn, would you be careful?"

"This isn't my doing," she yelled back, but her hands gentled on his wrist, where the rope had cut into his skin.

"I suppose I tied myself to this board." Jake gave his arms a jerk, yanking on the stall siding and sending the twined rope digging further into his torn flesh. He mumbled a string of curses he'd learned in the army, not giving a damn if she liked it or not. Stupid woman.

Samantha waited till he ran out of steam then went back to untying his wrists. Besides tightening the knot and cutting up his arms, he'd managed to pull the board loose from its support. "Something else to fix," she complained before blowing a strand of hair from her face.

Jake wasn't certain whether she was referring to

him or the board, but by the expression on her face when she looked at him, he guessed her sympathy lay more with the board.

"Oh, I give up." Samantha sat back on her heels. "Will, run and get me the knife. He's got this thing so wound up I can't untie it."

"My apologies," Jake murmured sarcastically as he watched the boy, Will, run out of the barn.

The woman shot him a look out of her blue eyes that had Jake wondering how he'd ever thought they were gentle. Then her gaze drifted to his chest and she clamped her lips together. "Would you look what else you've done? Your wound is bleeding again."

Jake shifted his head around and tucked his chin down to do her bidding. No wonder the thing hurt like hell. But it had hurt the whole time he'd tried to get himself untied, and it hadn't stopped him.

She stood, looking around, then tore off a strip of bedding hanging off the stall divider. Folding it, she sat down on her heels and pressed it against his shoulder. Jake sucked air in through his teeth.

"What *were* you trying to do?" She leaned into her hand to stanch the flow of blood, biting her bottom lip when he winced.

"Get loose," he snapped, then continued because she didn't seem to think that enough of an explanation. "I don't like being tied up, especially with the caliber of visitors you have around here. And maybe I—damnit would you watch what you're doing—thought you needed some saving," Jake finished through clenched teeth.

"Saving?" Samantha couldn't help laughing.

"That's real funny, Captain Morgan."

Funny? He hadn't found anything amusing since he'd been here — wherever "here" was. And he didn't think she had either. He looked up, not intending to remind her of what had happened — and how he'd seen saw her shaking when she'd come into the barn. But she met his stare with such defiance he forged ahead. "You weren't laughing much earlier . . . when those men were here."

"No," she agreed. "And I wasn't laughing last week when it was you."

"When what was me?" But she ignored him. Will had come back with the knife and she bent over him, intent on hacking through the twisted twine. Jake stared at the top of her head, thinking how familiar this seemed — her bending over him. But then she'd taken care of him so it was to be expected.

"Me what?" he repeated angrily. "What in the hell kind of woman are you to tie a wounded man up because he used to be in the Confederate Army? That's what you told the boy, isn't it?" Her lack of response angered him, made him struggle to lean on an elbow. "Well, isn't it what you told him? Don't you know the war's over? Or are you just too damn stubborn to admit it?"

She punctuated her order to hush by jabbing the knife toward him. Jake hushed — for the moment.

He watched her, trying to tap down his anger, as she sawed through the twine. Her hair was a golden color, combed back from a center part and braided into a long thick rope. There were bits of dirt and grass in it, some fell on his chest as she worked, but her hair smelled clean. He took a deep breath, trying to place the scent, but he couldn't. He just knew it was softer and prettier than soap.

Lydia had always smelled good. Jake smiled at the thought. Her perfume had been imported from Paris, and costly. But he'd never complained.

Jake studied the woman as she cut through the rope then began picking the slivers of string from his wrist. He doubted she sent off to any foreign country for her fragrance.

"Your name's Samantha, right?"

She glanced up, her eyes meeting his for only a moment. "Yes."

"I remember you telling me that."

Did he also recall finding her with his daguerreotype? Samantha glanced toward her brother, who leaned against a post watching Captain Morgan intently. "Will, I dropped a gun earlier, not far from the barn door. Go find it for me and take it in the house, please."

"Aw, Sam . . ."

"Just do it, Will."

"He your big brother?" Jake asked after Will shuffled from the stable. She was wrapping his wrist now, and Jake clenched his teeth to keep from crying out when she tied it off with less than a gentle touch. He decided questioning her while she had the upper hand wasn't very smart. Jake thought she wasn't going to answer him but she did, after settling down beside him. "Will's my younger brother. As any fool can plainly see."

Jake sucked in his breath as she pried off the

63

soiled, blood-soaked bandage from his chest. He thought she'd been lying about an older brother; now he wasn't sure. But if there was a man around here someplace, why hadn't he done something earlier when those men were taunting her?

She settled back on her heels, examining him critically. "This doesn't look too bad," she sighed before rewrapping his wound with clean bandaging. "But try not to tear it open again."

"I wouldn't have had to if you hadn't tied me up," Jake said reasonably.

She stared at him a moment, then pushed to her feet, brushing straw off the front of her bedraggled nightdress. "I'll send Will out with something for you to eat." She started toward the door.

"Wait a minute!" Jake pushed up to his elbow again. "Why *did* you tie me?" She glanced over her shoulder, the heavy braid of hair hanging down her back, but she didn't pause and she didn't answer. "Wait!" Jake repeated. "I'm Jacob Morgan and I—"

"I know *who* you are, and *what* you are." This time she stopped and faced him, her blue eyes angry. "You're lucky I didn't leave you out there"—she motioned toward the door—"for the wolves to feast on. All I want from you is to get well enough to ride that horse out of here, and leave us alone."

Her words, so embittered and impassioned, left Jake momentarily speechless. The war had filled a lot of people with hatred, but he rarely witnessed it firsthand—the results of that hatred, yes. The killing and maiming, but not the raw, look-them-in-the-eye-and-spit-on-them-if-you-could kind he saw now from this woman. She hated him, all right. She may be ministering to his wound. She may have fallen asleep in his arms. But she hated him.

Jake fell back against the pillow. Was all this because he'd worn a Confederate uniform? He stretched beneath the prickly blanket. He sure wasn't wearing it now. He was as naked as a jaybird. Jake wondered idly if the woman, Samantha, had anything to do with that, then got annoyed with himself for thinking such thoughts. But annoyed or not, he couldn't blot out the image of her taking off his pants and then lying down beside him. And he fell into a fitful sleep.

Jake jerked awake, feeling someone was watching him. He shifted, staring up into a slice of sun shining through the window cut through the sod, and saw the boy, Will. He leaned against the stall boards, a piece of straw stuck between his teeth, studying Jake as if he were a butterfly pinned to a board.

"I brought you some gruel," he said, motioning toward a pottery bowl he'd placed near Jake, using a turned-over pail as a table.

"Thanks." Jake moved, trying to ignore the pain as he reached for the bowl. Just the thought of food made his stomach growl. But before he could manage a sitting position, Will hunkered down in the straw, the bowl cradled in one hand, a pewter spoon in the other.

"Sam said I wasn't to get close to you but I don't think she wants you starving to death."

Jake wasn't too sure of that, but he gratefully accepted the gruel Will spooned out. It was warm, and sweetened with fresh milk. "What's she think I'm going to do to you," Jake asked between bites.

"Nothing, I suppose, or she'd a tied you up again. You ain't going to do nothing, are you?"

"Even if I wanted to, there's not much I could do like this." Jake took a deep breath. "Your sister realize the war's over?"

"Ain't us keeping things going." Will scraped the bottom of the bowl. "But then I don't need to tell the likes of you that."

Jake's hand stayed the spoon inches from his mouth. "What are you talking about, 'the likes of me'?"

The spoon plunked into the bowl. "I gotta get going now. Sam's waiting for me to help with the garden."

"No you don't." Despite the pain in his upper chest and the expression of fear on Will's face, Jake grabbed a handful of the boy's shirt and pulled him down in the straw. The pottery bowl landed on the straw-covered floor with a soft thud. "I want some answers. What do you mean, 'the likes of me'?"

Will's chin jutted out at an angle that reminded Jake of his sister. He didn't answer.

"Is it because I was in the Confederate Army? Is that what has you people so riled up?" Jake tightened his fingers in the cloth to fight a wave of dizziness.

"Like you said, mister. The war's over."

"Exactly. That's why I'm wondering what's going on here." He leaned back, releasing Will's shirt. "A strong dislike I could understand." Jake paused.

"You have anyone killed in the war?"

Will realized the Rebel no longer held him, and thought about bolting, but didn't. The man lying on the blanket seemed sincerely interested. "My brother was killed at the second Bull Run."

"I'm sorry."

Will's chin jutted out again. "Were you there?"

"At Manassas in '62? No." That had been the second summer of the war and he'd been home in Richmond, burying his wife and son. Jake looked back at the boy. "You thinking it might have been me that killed your brother?"

Will colored because he had been thinking exactly that. And even he knew how unlikely the chances of that were.

"Well, I wasn't there," Jake repeated. He'd rejoined Lee's army for their march into Maryland — not because of any burning desire to support the cause, but because he'd become numb after the death of his wife and son. He'd hoped helping others, doctoring, would give him some purpose. It hadn't. And now three years later he still floundered around without direction. The only difference was, now he didn't care.

Will seemed to take him at his word because he sat down, drawing his bony knees up under his chin. His bare feet were crossed. "Ain't you got no home?"

"What?" Jake had been fighting the memories again, and the boy's question hadn't registered.

"I was just wondering why you'd take up with the likes of Landis Moore, except that maybe you don't have no home to go back to. Least ways that's what Sam said."

"She did, did she?" Jake twisted around till he leaned against his saddle. His eyes narrowed as he studied Will a moment. "Landis Moore the fellow that was here this morning?"

"Yeah."

"He an ex-Confederate soldier? That why you think I'm with him?" Will shrugged so Jake continued. "Well, we Southerners aren't all alike, no more than you Yankees. And if what I heard this morning is any indication, Landis Moore isn't someone I'd like to know even if we did serve on the same side."

"You ain't riding with Landis Moore?" Will's voice cracked on the last word.

"Boy, I'm not riding with anyone. Just passing through on my way to Texas."

"Texas!" Will's pale blue eyes lit up. "You're going to Texas?"

"I suppose. Once this heals up, and I have enough strength to sit a horse again." Jake wished he could summon up a fraction of the enthusiasm Will had for his destination. The truth was he decided only recently to head for Texas. He couldn't stay in Virginia. He tried, but the memories were too strong there. And he didn't know where in the hell else to go.

Will skittered up closer to him, obviously forgetting his sister's warning to keep his distance. "I been thinking about going to Texas." His face fell. "But Sam won't even hear of it. She says there's nothing for us there and at least we have the farm here." He shook his head. "And there's no way I can leave her here all by herself."

"A man has to face up to his responsibilities." So much for her contention that she had an older brother on the farm.

Will grinned. He liked that the soldier, even if he was a Rebel, had called him a man. Sam was too often treating him like a little boy. "You got any responsibilities, mister?"

Jake swallowed. "Not a one."

They both looked toward the door when they heard Will's name being called. "I better go." Will scrambled to his feet, scooping up the bowl and spoon. "There's some water in that canteen if you want it." Will used his foot to scoot it over closer to Captain Morgan.

"Wait a minute. Who shot me? What's going on here?" Jake called out his questions but not one of them was answered as the boy loped through the door.

"About time," Samantha said as Will rushed from the barn, nearly colliding with his sister. She was carrying two pails of water toward the garden. Will felt guilty for staying with the stranger so long and making her do his share of the work. She smiled when he took one bucket from her. "I thought maybe I was going to have to come in there and rescue you."

"Naw. He didn't try nothing."

"Anything." Samantha didn't look up, just began scooping water over the plants they'd managed to save from Landis Moore's men. "I imagine he's too weak to do us much harm."

69

Will wasn't sure about that. The Rebel had seemed pretty strong when he'd grabbed him. But he agreed with his sister before adding, "Maybe he doesn't want to hurt us."

Samantha glanced over at Will. She wiped a damp curl off her forehead and arched her back. "Did he tell you that?"

Will trickled water down over the pumpkin leaves then remembered his sister said to wet the roots. "Yeah," he shrugged. "He did."

"Well, he'd be the first of Landis Moore's men to feel that way." Samantha moved the pail along.

"Says he's not one of Moore's men."

"Sounds like you and that Rebel had yourselves a right long talk, Will." Samantha crossed her arms. "I only asked you to take him some gruel."

Will kept working, thinking to make up for the time he'd wasted.

"I don't want you talking to him anymore." Of course the easiest way for her to make sure he didn't was to take care of Captain Morgan herself. But she didn't want to do that, and she didn't want to face up to why that was. "Did you hear me, Will?"

"Yeah. But I believe him!"

Samantha looked up at the sky and sighed. "Then what was he doing here, Will?"

"Say's he's on his way to Texas. You think he might take us with him if we asked?"

"Oh, Will." Samantha went to her brother, careful not to tramp on any of the plants. She squatted down beside him, grasping his hand when he reached

70

for the dipper. "Honey, there's nothing for us in Texas."

"I told him you'd say that."

"That's because it's true." Samantha knew how much her brother thought and dreamed about Texas, though she presumed a good deal of his infatuation stemmed from the hardships they'd endured here.

She sighed again. "Let's finish here so we can pick some corn. Fresh corn for dinner. Doesn't that sound good?"

"Yeah," Will admitted reluctantly. He worked diligently to water his half of the garden. Then together he and Sam went to the near cornfield. The ears were nearly ripe, and he imagined they'd soon have a huge job on their hands. But for now they picked only enough to feed themselves for a couple of days.

It wasn't until they returned to the cabin and Sam asked him to fetch more water that Will remembered the other thing he'd learned about the Rebel soldier. Will opened the door, the bucket swinging from his hand. "He wasn't at the second Bull Run," he said before stepping out on the porch.

Samantha paused, the knife she was using to slice the bacon slab poised over the meat. She wanted to call Will back, opened her mouth to do it, but in the end closed it again.

This wasn't about battles or Luke, or even the godforsaken war. Did Will actually think she'd hold something like that against a stranger? Samantha sighed, resuming her cutting. Maybe she would. Maybe all that had happened had affected her too deeply to look upon every man as her brother, the

71

way her father had preached. Maybe she did care that the man lying in the stable had fought for the Rebel cause . . . and worn a gray uniform.

But that wasn't the point here. "Ouch!" The knife slipped, slicing into her finger then landing on the puncheon floor with a dull thud. Samantha whipped her finger to her mouth, fighting back tears.

"Oh, heavens," she moaned, turning her back on the table and blinking her eyes. It's not as if her finger hurt that bad. She looked at it, hesitantly at first, and moaned again because it had already stopped bleeding. So why were tears rolling down her cheeks?

Samantha took a deep breath and wiped her face with her apron then returned to the bacon. She hacked off another few slices, started to put it up, then remembered the Rebel in her barn. Now that he was awake and his fever broken, he'd be eating what they did. She slapped the meat into the iron skillet heating on the stove. It began to sizzle, filling the tiny cabin with savory smells.

She'd feed the stranger, and send him on his way. In the meantime, she'd talk with Will. He needed to understand the battle they waged was for self-preservation. They couldn't afford to trust anyone, especially anyone wearing gray pants. And it had scarce little to do with differing ideologies.

Landis Moore wanted them out of Kansas, off their land. And he would do anything to accomplish it. He wasn't going to turn the other cheek. He wasn't going to go away. Samantha wadded her apron and used it to lift the hot skillet from the stove.

Will was too much like their father used to be. He trusted people, and believed the best. Well, she wasn't going to let what happened to her father happen to Will. She'd shoot the stranger again before she'd let it.

He had a lot of nerve telling Will he wasn't with Moore's gang. But she knew different. And she wasn't going to let the Rebel get to kindhearted, trusting Will. She'd just deal with him herself, she thought, slipping fried bacon onto a tin plate.

Chapter Four

He'd never slept so much. Jake stretched his legs and studied the dust motes swirling in the band of sunshine slanted across his makeshift bed. Sleep and eat, that's all he did. But he could feel his body healing and getting stronger. Sitting up didn't make him dizzy anymore.

Gingerly lifting the bandage crossing his chest, Jake tried to make a professional judgment of his wound. Then he remembered he didn't do that anymore. His doctoring days were over. But his wound was coming along fine. Healing despite the fact there'd been no doctor to look at it.

Closing his eyes, Jake wondered how many of the men he'd treated during the war would have recovered without him. Had he made a difference? Any difference at all?

Jake forced that thought from his mind. It was in the past. The war . . . being a doctor. Both gone forever. Like the rest of his life. Besides, he didn't need any special schooling to tell him his wound was healing. He knew he was getting better because he was damn tired of lying here in the straw.

Pushing himself up, Jake grabbed hold of the wooden partition between the stalls to steady himself. No one had fixed the stall divider he'd pulled loose over a week ago. It still hung from the one nail that held it. Jake jammed it back against the support with the heel of his hand, but it swung down again. Shrugging, wincing from the pain in his chest, Jake reached for his saddlebag. His pants were no longer draped over the stall divider.

"Just what do you think you're doing?"

Jerking around, Jake knocked against the loose board. "Ouch! Damnit, woman, what are you doing sneaking up on me like that?"

"I wasn't sneaking."

Her voice sounded strange and Jake glanced at her face, noticing the crimson blush that colored her to the roots of her honey-gold hair. Just as quickly he realized why and felt an unfamiliar warmth creep up his neck as he swept the blanket off the floor and wrapped it around himself.

He couldn't believe he'd stood there naked, *and* he couldn't believe it was making him blush. It wasn't as if he had anything to be embarrassed about. She'd walked in on him. It had just been a long time since he'd been undressed before a woman—hell, it had been a long time since he'd done anything with a woman—and this one seemed to constantly remind him of that fact.

Not that she did or said anything provocative. Her manner of dress lent itself to working a farm, not exciting the baser instincts in a man. And though she was pretty enough, she wasn't a great beauty. But more often than he liked, Jake found himself thinking about the line of her jaw when she cocked her head to listen to her brother, or the clear, serene radiance of her blue eyes.

Jake didn't want that. Feelings like the ones she unwittingly provoked were long buried beneath the cocoon he'd wrapped about his emotions—and better off remaining there.

And she made him angry too. Another vulnerable crack in his defenses. He hadn't seen her in days, but that didn't mean he forgot her accusing words—or that she'd tied him up. Just seeing her riled him.

She stood, hands on hips, watching him as he fumbled with the blanket.

"What *are* you trying to do?" she asked again.

"Get myself covered if it's all right with you." Jake tucked the blanket end around his waist, ignoring the straw that scratched at his skin.

"It makes no difference to me," Samantha said, hoping she sounded convincing. "It's not as if I haven't seen you before." True enough, but it was one thing to see him sick and feverish—and even that had left her flustered—and quite another thing to get a look at him standing, tall, broad shouldered and—

Samantha's face grew hotter, and she looked around for something to do. Last night's dishes lay in a neat stack in the straw. She busied herself gathering them up. "What are you doing up?"

"I'm sick and tired of lying down," Jake growled. He'd done more than his share of doctoring, but this was the first time he could remember being the one in need of mending. He didn't much like it either.

Dragging clothes from his saddlebag with one hand, Jake tried to keep the blanket up with the other. "I want some answers. Every time I ask a question around here, somebody makes themselves scarce." He looked up from his search, anger stamped on the masculine lines of his face. "And where in the hell are my pants?"

"Hung on the clothesline. I brushed them up for you." That, at least, she could answer with relative ease.

"So who asked you to?" Damn, he hated talking to her wearing nothing but a dusty old blanket. And the thoughts of her taking care of him when he'd been sick didn't do much to calm his state of mind either.

"No one that I recall." Samantha grabbed the saddlebag from his hands, startling him so much that he didn't resist. He just stood there, his expression shocked, groping for the blanket when it slipped. "Of course no one asked me to doctor your wound or feed you either, as I recall." She yanked a clean pair of butternut pants from the leather pocket. "Here," she said, thrusting them toward him before turning on her heel and heading for the door.

"Wait a minute." Jake expelled an exaggerated breath, then clamped his jaw shut before catching her eye.

"What?" Samantha paused, her hand on the latch. Why was it so disturbing to be close to him? When she'd handed him the pants, his scent, and the heat from his body had nearly been more sensual than she could handle. She needed to get outside in the fresh air.

"You're right. I do owe you some thanks."

Samantha swallowed. "You don't owe me anything. Just get yourself better so you can leave." She meant to stomp out of the barn, but an iron hand around her upper arm stopped her. She hadn't heard him move and had carelessly thought him incapable of such quick motion in his present state of health. With a sinking feeling in the pit of her stomach, Samantha realized she'd been wrong about a lot of things.

His grip was proof that the captain's strength had returned. The weight of his pistol bumped against Samantha's thigh. But could she reach into her apron pocket without his noticing and taking the gun? And if he caught her, what would he do? She didn't want to find out. Besides, the hand clamped around her arm didn't exactly hurt. It simply kept her from leaving.

Which seemed to be exactly what he wanted to do.

"Now that I have your attention, Miss Lowery, I want to know what's going on around here."

"What . . . what do you want to know?"

Jake lowered his nose to within inches of hers. "For starters, who shot me?"

Samantha hoped she didn't look as white as she felt. She could practically feel the blood draining from her face. But she met his eye. "What difference does it make."

"A hell of a lot to me!" Jake sucked in his breath

in agitation and immediately felt the makeshift tuck of scratchy wool loosen. His hands dropped to the blanket around his waist — and so did Samantha's gaze. She quickly pulled her eyes back to his face, but not before they traveled the length of his broad, hairy chest.

Turning on her heel, Samantha tried to leave, but again was stopped. "Not so fast. I asked you a question and I want an answer."

"When you ride with the likes of Landis Moore, you should expect violence and getting shot is part of—"

"That's no answer. Besides, I already told you I don't ride with Moore. And yeah, I know you don't believe me, but at this point I don't really care . . . Wait a minute." Jake's eyes narrowed. "Are you trying to say this Moore shot me?"

Samantha hid the relief from her voice. Why hadn't she thought of this before? "He could have, I suppose."

Those clear green eyes were little more than slits now as Jake studied her. "Could have?" The tone of his words expressed serious doubt. "Possible. But then that's not exactly the way I remember it happening. I heard gunshots and rode into a farmyard. I didn't see anyone. No gang of ruffians . . . nothing. The next thing I know a bullet slams into my chest and I wake up with you curled up beside me."

"I fell asleep."

Jake ignored her heated rebuttal. "It was your farmyard I rode into and your window I was facing when I got hit." Jake paused. "Did Will shoot me?"

The idea didn't sit well with him. He'd grown to like the boy. But Samantha's immediate denial convinced Jake he hadn't.

"No! Will didn't shoot you!"

"But then—"

Samantha jerked away so quickly Jake didn't stop her. Or maybe he was too amazed by his own deduction. Clearly he wasn't expecting this. But the surprise on his face turned to shock when she pulled the revolver from her apron pocket.

"That's right." Samantha cocked the gun, aiming it at a spot slightly lower than his bandage. "I shot you and . . . and I'll do it again if I have to."

"What in the hell for?"

"To keep you from hurting me. I—"

"Not now," Jake interrupted. "Before. I want to know why you shot me before."

"I told you." The arm holding up the gun trembled and Samantha steadied it with her free hand. "You're one of Moore's men and—"

"For the last time, I am not one of Moore's damn men!"

"Well, I thought you were at the time," Samantha conceded.

"Oh, that makes perfect sense. You just go around shooting everyone you suspect of riding with Moore?"

"Don't be ridiculous. They were shooting up my farm. You rode in right after and I thought you were coming after us." Samantha reached behind her to open the barn door. "That's all the explanation I intend to give."

"Well, I think —" Jake's advance toward her was cut short when she thrust the gun forward.

"You're obviously healed enough to be up. I want you off this farm by sundown." With that Samantha ran through the door, pulling it shut behind her. For long minutes she leaned into the rough planks waiting for her heart to stop pounding. Then when her head cleared and a semblance of calm returned, Samantha jerked away from the barn and trained the revolver toward the closed door.

Heat from the sun warmed the top of her head and sweat followed the path between her shoulderblades, but there was no movement from inside. Not so much as a sound.

For an insane moment Samantha considered peeking back inside. Perhaps he had collapsed. It wasn't that long since he'd suffered from a raging fever, after all. The touch of her hand on the latch brought reality slamming back to her. He was all right, and even if he wasn't, what did she care? All she wanted was him gone.

After listening a few more moments, Samantha pocketed the gun and trudged off to join Will in the cornfield.

Jake's first impulse was to explode through the door after her. He rushed forward, grabbing the latch before better judgment intervened. She was likely on the other side waiting for just such a move. Revolver — his revolver — in hand.

Not that dying terrified him. When he'd returned to the front, after burying his wife and son, he often

81

found himself wondering why he was being spared. There was so much death around him, so much suffering he felt unable to prevent. Thoughts of dying hadn't bothered him then.

But he sure as hell didn't like the idea of some green Kansas farm girl ending his life.

Besides, even if she didn't shoot him—again, what was he going to do? Shoot *her?* Hardly. Throttle her soundly? Tempting, but not something he seriously considered.

Jake let his hand drop and shook his head. There wasn't anything for him to do but get the hell out of here. Chalk this experience up to a continuation of the downward spiral of his life.

Glancing up from the slab of beef sizzling in the skillet, Samantha watched Will enter the cabin. She'd assumed he'd been down by the creek cleaning up, but he was covered with as much Kansas dust and corn silk as when he'd disappeared some thirty minutes ago.

"Smells good," he said before stepping back through the open door and rinsing his hands and face in the tin wash pan. He obviously noticed Samantha's expression.

"It'll be ready soon." Samantha pursed her lips to ask where he'd been, then thought better of it. She liked to go off by herself sometimes—why shouldn't her brother? She just hoped he had enough sense to stay close to the house and away from the barn.

Samantha hadn't told Will about her run-in with

the rebel today. She hoped it wasn't necessary. Surely Captain Morgan planned to leave, and what better time to head out than while she and Will were in the fields.

But it took only one glance toward the paddock as she and Will traipsed over the prairie toward the cabin to see the rebel's horse still there. Which meant the rebel was too.

"You know, I've been thinking, Sam."

Samantha suppressed a smile. He sounded just like their father, except he hadn't been old enough when Pa died to realize the resemblance. "What you been thinking about, Will?" She'd tell him about the rebel after supper.

"I'll bet Jake"—Will's eyes skidded to his sister—"I mean Captain Morgan would enjoy taking his meal sitting at a real table."

For a long moment Samantha said nothing. She was too busy containing her anger. Will's slip of the rebel's given name hadn't escaped her. She took a deep breath, concentrating on lifting the cornbread from the Dutch oven. "I thought I told you to stay away from that man, Will. Is that where you've been, in the barn?" Her eyes scanned him quickly.

"Aw, Sam."

"Don't 'Aw, Sam' me. I told you to stay clear of him, and you deliberately disobeyed me." She dropped the platter of meat onto the table with more force than necessary.

"I ain't a little kid no more for you to be bossing around!"

"Anymore, and don't use ain't."

"See what I mean?" Will stepped into the cabin, tossing the linen towel toward its hook. It missed and drifted to the puncheon floor. "You're always telling me what to do, and how to do it."

The intensity in his light blue eyes made Samantha swallow her caustic reply. Instead she moved toward him. "Will, you don't understand. He's a dangerous man. More dangerous than you know, and I don't want you—"

"He ain't dangerous and he ain't one of Moore's men."

"Will." Samantha tried to keep her voice calm. "Whether he is or isn't doesn't matter now. Please use the sense God gave you and—"

"That's it, isn't it? You think I'm just a dumb kid?"

"No." Samantha stepped forward, her hands reaching toward her brother. He looked dangerously close to tears, and Samantha felt a tightness in her throat looking at his boyish freckle-spattered face. "Will, I'd never think that. It's just that—"

"Every idea I have is dumb."

He sounded like a petulant child, and right now Samantha was in no mood to deal with one. Taking a deep breath, she tried to regain her calm. "Will, I don't think we should discuss this now. We—"

"What if I want to talk about it? What then, Sam? It's always what you want."

"That's the stupidest thing you ever said." Nothing was as she wanted. Nothing. Did he think for one moment she wanted to work this farm from sunup to sundown to scrape out a meager existence for them? Did he think she wanted to sew dresses for the women in town when she couldn't afford a decent one for herself? Did he think she wanted to deal with men like Landis Moore and Jacob Morgan?

Samantha was so wrapped up in her thoughts that she didn't notice Will's expression. But she couldn't miss the aggrieved tone of his voice. "That's it, Sam. You think all *my* ideas are stupid."

"I do not." Why had she used the word "stupid"?

"Like us going to Texas."

"For heaven's sake, Will. There's nothing for us there."

"And letting Captain Morgan eat his meals with us."

"I don't want to discuss that man." Samantha turned back toward the stove. "Now sit down and eat your supper." This conversation had gone far enough. Food was Will's weakness. But it didn't entice him this time.

"I *ain't* hungry," he wailed, and Samantha was sure he deliberately emphasized the "ain't."

"What do you mean 'not hungry'? Where are you going?" But Will grabbed up his hat and kept going through the open door into the twilight.

Jake stood in the shadow of the front porch as Will stormed out across the yard. He had come to the cabin for his guns. The boy had tried to get him to come up to the house for supper, insisting it was his sister's idea.

Jake knew better than that.

But he didn't really care what Miss Samantha

Lowery wanted. *He* wanted the rest of his belongings, and then he intended to get the hell out of here.

But right now he was standing on the porch looking into the lighted cabin through the open door — watching Samantha Lowery cry. Knowing at least some of the reason for her unhappiness was his fault. Not all, Jake assured himself. She'd done her part to make Will fly out the door, passing within ten feet of Jake and not even seeing him.

Jake thought about going after the boy, but didn't. Some time alone was probably what he needed right now. Probably what his sister needed too. But that wasn't going to get Jake his revolvers.

Mumbling a curse under his breath, Jake turned away. He'd come back for the guns after he saddled his horse. By then she'd have time to compose herself. Except the crying wasn't letting up. Jake backed off the porch, but he could still hear her crying, soft, sad sounds that sailed to him over the chorus of frogs and hum of mosquitoes.

He hesitated. The last thing he wanted was to get involved in this woman's life. Before he could stop himself, he peered back through the open door. Now her arms lay on the table cradling her head. The light from the lamp turned her hair to gold and her small body trembled.

"Miss Lowery."

Samantha's head jerked up and she quickly rubbed her palms down her face, hoping new tears wouldn't replace any she managed to scrub away. "What do you want?" she asked, embarrassed by the hiccup in her voice. But then she had worse problems than embarrassment. What was the rebel doing up and in her house?

Her eyes swerved to the revolver she'd put on the mantle when she started cooking.

Jake noticed her glance toward the gun — his gun — then back at him. Her voice, despite the small sob, was angry. Why hadn't he just gone back to the barn when he had the chance? Had he actually felt sorry for her? "You don't have to get that gun. I'm not going to hurt you."

Samantha froze. Since their meeting this morning, thoughts of his doing just that haunted her. He was unarmed, but now that he'd entered the cabin, she wasn't sure she could beat him to the mantle. Her voice was lower this time. "What do you want?"

"Not to cause any trouble. I told you I'm not one of Landis Moore's men."

"And I told you, I don't believe you." Samantha brushed back hair that had fallen across her face and watched a scowl darken his handsome face. Lifting her chin, she pushed back the chair and stood. She wasn't sure why she said that because she was beginning to doubt his involvement with Moore. But that didn't change the fact that she'd shot him — and that he knew it.

"Fine." Jake strode farther into the twilight-shadowed room. "I don't give a damn what you believe. Just give me my revolvers — and anything else you pilfered from my saddlebags — and I'll be on my way."

"You can't have the guns."

"And just why the hell not?"

Why not indeed? They were *his*. "I . . . I don't trust you."

Jake's brow arched. "I find that rather amusing coming from a woman who shoots first and asks questions later." Jake watched embarrassed color flood her face. "Are you planning to add thievery to your list of misdeeds?"

"I'm no thief."

When he didn't reply, Samantha examined him with narrowed eyes. He was watching her, his green eyes questioning . . . accusing. Would he take the guns and leave — or would he decide, once he had the upper hand, to mete out his own form of justice?

Samantha could feel the blood coursing through her veins as she studied him. He looked fit enough, if a little on the thin side. He was dressed in the gray pants of a Confederate soldier. In deference to the heat, he'd left off the jacket, and wore only a white, loose-cut shirt, buttoned to the neck. His suspenders dangled down over his hips — a reminder of the wound beneath the shirt.

The wound she'd inflicted.

The wound he might . . . *might* want to avenge.

But he wanted the guns and in the end she had no choice but to give them to him. He could certainly overpower her if she tried anything. And with Will off who knows where . . . Samantha swallowed. "I'll get them for you."

"If it's all the same to you, I think I'll do the getting." Jake moved toward the mantle.

"Well, you don't have to act as if I intended to — to . . ."

"Shoot me?" Jake questioned, sliding the revolver into the waistband of his pants.

"Yes." Samantha crossed her arms.

"Pardon my foolish suspicion. I can't imagine what caused it." Jake took a quick look around the room. "Where's the other one?"

Samantha ignored his sarcastic remarks. "In the pie safe."

The further arching of his brow made Samantha turn away as he headed for the pierced tin cabinet. Maybe he would just leave. He already had one gun and hadn't turned it on her.

The clatter of tin plates hitting the floor caused her to look back in time to see the captain grab hold of the pie safe door.

"What's wrong with you?"

"Nothing."

"You knock my dishes all over the floor and you say it's nothing?" Samantha took a cautious step toward him.

"That's right." Jake silently cursed the nausea and weakness that swept over him when he bent to search for the gun. "I said there's nothing wrong and I—"

"You're white as a ghost."

Jake shifted then straightened, fighting the light-headedness. He swallowed, refusing to grab hold of the pie safe again. This was the longest he'd been on his feet since being shot, and his legs felt like rubber.

Add to that the fact that his stomach growled with hunger—no one had brought him a noon meal. The smell of good food drifted about him, making his mouth water, and reminding him graphically of times during this last year of the war when he'd gone without. But he wasn't going to ask for food, and he wasn't going to take any more from this woman. He turned toward the door. "I'll be leaving in the morning."

"What about your other gun?"

Jake scowled then bent over to look inside. The moment he did, the weakness hit him again like a punch in the gut.

"Come over here."

Jake tried to shake off Samantha's hand on his arm but he was too busy trying to stay upright. "I'm all right, I tell you. I just want to — "

"Would you sit down before you fall?" Samantha shoved him toward the chair. "I dragged you once, and believe me, it's not something I want to do again."

Jake grinned. He couldn't help it. He felt weak, and embarrassed by the fact that he was close to fainting like some vapid female. But the vision that entered his mind of this little woman dragging his bulk anywhere was too amusing. He wondered if she could. She certainly didn't look like she could begin to handle his weight. She was small, almost delicate, and pretty. Not beautiful, Jake reminded himself. Not like Lydia, but pretty just the same.

"What?" Samantha blew a tangle of hair out of her eyes and planted her hands on her hips.

"Did you really drag me into the barn?"

"Will and I did." His grin broadened and Samantha found she wasn't impervious to its charm. He had a nice smile. But then she knew he would.

And he'd shaved. The beard was gone. Now she could see the squared chin with just a hint of a cleft, and the firm jaw. Samantha shook off her silly musings. "Now tell me what's wrong."

"Maybe I'm a little dizzy."

"Maybe more than a little." Samantha glanced at Captain Morgan. His smile faded, partly because she didn't return it, and partly because there really wasn't anything to smile about. He looked a little better now that he was sitting. Some color had returned to his face.

"Is your chest hurting you?" Samantha checked his shirt for blood, but saw none. Still, she didn't believe him when he shook his head.

"Well, it's obvious you can't leave," Samantha heard herself say as she took down a mug to pour him some tea.

By the expression on her face as she looked around at him, Jake could tell she was as surprised by her statement as he was. He took a deep breath. "I think it's best if I do."

She couldn't argue with that. Actually, she couldn't imagine what possessed her to reverse her order that he leave. But she also couldn't ignore that he could barely stand. And enemy though he was, she'd put a lot of energy into seeing him healed. Samantha didn't want all her work to be for naught — at least that's what she told herself. "Staying a few more days isn't going to cause any more of a problem than you already have."

Where had this woman learned her manners? She made him feel about as welcome as a weasel in a hen house. But then that's probably what she thought he was. Jake considered denying again that he had anything to do with the man who'd been here the other day, but decided it was useless. She believed what she wanted to believe. He wore a gray uniform; thus he was out to hurt her.

Besides, he couldn't keep his thoughts or his eyes off the plate heaped high with food on the table.

Samantha caught his gaze lingering on the tin plate with its rapidly cooling helping of meat and cornbread.

She didn't want him taking meals in her house. But then she didn't want him in her house period. Yet there was no denying he was already here. With a sigh, she pushed the plate toward him. "You might as well eat this. It doesn't look like Will wants it."

Jake hesitated only a moment. He knew she didn't really want him here, and before the war he'd never have accepted such an ungracious invitation. But the war changed a lot of things, including his willingness to skip meals. Jake thought about explaining that hunger was part of the reason for his weakness. But she probably didn't care.

If he had to guess, he'd bet she was thinking about her brother. She looked sad. He cut off a bite of beef, watching her a moment before he ate it. Was she going to cry again? Putting down his fork, he waited for her to meet his stare. "He's just feeling his oats a little is all."

Her eyes held his for a moment then she glanced away. "I don't want to talk about Will with you."

Damnit, she *was* going to cry. Jake took a swig of

tepid tea. If he had any sense, he'd pick up the plate and make his way back to the barn. Eating at a table wasn't worth this aggravation.

He never could stand seeing a woman cry. Lydia had discovered that about him even before they were married. And had become very adept at using that knowledge to her advantage. Not too often, though, he added to himself because it seemed disloyal somehow to think that at all.

But regardless of what his dead wife had done, this woman wasn't trying to manipulate him with her tears. If anything, she was doing her damnedest to conceal how close she was to breaking down.

"Listen," he said, ignoring his own advice to leave. "Rebelling against authority is something all boys do at his age."

She shot him a look clearly meant to say mind your own business. But then her expression softened. "Did you?"

Jake grinned. "Sure. Now I didn't have an older sister to bedevil. With me it was my pa mostly." The grin broadened. "I wasn't much older than Will when I decided to run away to sea."

"Really?" Samantha studied him a moment through narrowed eyes. He didn't strike her as a sailor. "Why?"

"Why?" Jake hadn't thought about why for a long time. "Partly, I guess, because it was something I knew my father wouldn't approve of. Don't get me wrong. We got along fine for the most part. I admired him greatly, and loved him. But"—he grinned again—"he did seem to have me on a short lead.

93

"Anyway, the sea beckoned. I'd met this boy, more a man really, and he took me down to the taverns by the docks. Gave me my first taste of something stronger than wine. Then sent me upstairs for . . ."

Jake stopped, realizing he'd almost told this woman, this stranger, about his first sexual encounter. That would hardly make her feel better about her brother, not to mention it wasn't something a gentleman discussed with a lady. "Let's just say he introduced me to some new and enjoyable pastimes, and I figured they'd all be mine for the asking once I went to sea."

Samantha swallowed. She hoped he couldn't tell the way her pulse raced and her stomach tightened. He was telling her a story about when he'd been young, not much older than Will, by his own admission. And she couldn't force certain images from her mind.

He'd been with a whore. When he was what, fifteen or sixteen? He hadn't said it, but Samantha wasn't completely naive. There was a house in town where whores lived. She'd seen them leaning out the windows. They wore bright colors and their hair hung down about their bare shoulders and they did everything they could to entice the men inside. Not that the men she saw go through the door looked as if they minded.

Captain Morgan had been to a place like that. He'd lain with one of those women, touching her and letting her touch him. When he was younger, his shoulders probably weren't as broad as they were now. There wouldn't have been the small lines radiating from the corners of his eyes, or the brackets around his mouth. But his lips were the same. They'd have been firm with the nice points on his upper lip like now, and his eyes—

Samantha sucked in air. He looked at her strangely, almost as if he knew her thoughts, knew how warm she felt inside. Knew she wasn't thinking about him making love to a whore, but remembering what it was like to wake up lying beside him, her head on his shoulder. Quickly she glanced away. "Did you go to sea?"

"No. My pa got wind of my plans and came down to the tavern. Yanked me out of there and whupped me good. At the time I was furious because I thought he ruined my life. And of course I thought myself too much of a man to take kindly to my father's—what's wrong?"

"Nothing." Tears were leaking out of Samantha's eyes faster than she could blot them on her napkin, and she jerked out of the chair and turned her back. "I think you better go."

"Now wait a minute." Jake was out of his chair before he thought about doing it. Her shoulder was warm and soft when he touched it. "He didn't really hurt me, you know. And I really wasn't cut out for a life at sea. I—" Jake stopped. She was shaking her head and sobbing in earnest now. He turned her toward him, and though she stiffened, she let him. "What's wrong?" he repeated.

Samantha pushed against his chest. "Go away."

Jake didn't know if she meant away from her, or from her farm, or off the face of the earth. But he

95

did know that right at this particular moment she didn't mean it. He pulled her to him. "Tell me," he murmured into her hair.

Samantha sobbed. She shouldn't be standing like this with him. But it felt so good to have someone to lean against. Someone strong. She buried her face in his soft cotton shirt and let the tears come.

Jake didn't think she planned to say anything. Except for her soft crying she was silent for a long time. He held her close, running his hand over her hair in what he hoped was a soothing motion. He could feel the dampness of her tears, her body move against his as she breathed, and he tried to keep his thoughts on comforting.

"He whupped you," Samantha mumbled into his shirt.

"I told you it didn't hurt much." Could she possibly be crying over a beating his father gave him over fifteen years ago? When she looked up at him, Jake knew how foolish that idea was.

"But he was there to do it. To keep you from making a big mistake." Samantha's breath caught on a hiccup. "No one's here for Will."

"You are," Jake told her realistically.

"But I can't . . . whup him . . . or do *anything* to make him listen to me."

Apparently this admission was too much for her because Samantha sagged against him, new tears dampening his shirt. Jake's arm tightened, and he rested his chin on top of her head. "You don't need to whup him to make him listen. Will loves you. He's just growing up, that's all."

96

She shook her head, the motion moving her body against his, and Jake felt his own stir with something more than the promise of comfort. She looked up at him again, her eyes large and crystal blue from tears. Her dark lashes were spiked with moisture, and her mouth was slightly open.

Jake didn't know why he did it — if he'd looked for reasons he certainly wouldn't have — but his mouth came down on hers. Gently at first for there were still thoughts of comforting mingled with the desire. But then he felt her warm breath, tasted her, and the passion exploded, blocking out all else.

He overpowered her. His arm locked her upper body to him, and his large hand cupped her head, digging into her hair and dislodging the pins holding her braid. His scent surrounded her, his taste filled her mouth, and she could scarcely breathe. Yet all she could think about was getting closer.

It was silly, she knew, but Samantha had an unmistakable urge to crawl inside him and let pure sensation pour over her. Her arms twined around his waist. She could feel him against her, rock hard, and she seemed to melt.

His mouth was hot and wet, intense, and it shattered her senses. Samantha wriggled against him, mindless of the open door, mindless of propriety. She only knew a coil inside her wound tighter, and only he had the power to release her from this maelstrom.

But he didn't. As abruptly as he started the kiss, he ended it. Samantha clutched at his elbows when he pulled away, needing support to keep from slipping to the floor.

"I apologize." Jake sucked air into his lungs. Samantha looked up at him, her expression as dazed as he felt. What in God's name had possessed him? He'd meant to offer comfort—though why he felt the need, he didn't know. But he'd ended up devastating them both.

Whatever happened between them was spontaneous and unexpected. Jake had been with his share of women. Even after Lydia's death, there were times when the tension got to him and he sought release. But none of those times left him feeling this shattered.

He wasn't sure he ever had. And that realization made him feel guilty as hell.

Stepping back, Jake glanced away, then steeling himself, looked back and met her eyes. "I really am sorry. I . . ."

Samantha shook her head and turned toward the stove. She didn't trust herself to speak, and when she looked back, she knew it wasn't necessary. The Rebel was gone. Crossing to the door, Samantha saw him stride into the darkness.

At one time she thought getting rid of him might be difficult. But Samantha had seen the expression on his face after he'd kissed her. He'd been thinking of the woman in the daguerreotype. And she had no trouble believing that he was sorry.

He'd be gone by morning.

Chapter Five

Samantha woke with a start. Again sunshine poured through her window, and she shook her head and moaned. She'd never been one to lie abed — with the farm demanding all her attention, it wasn't possible — and she refused to start now. But more often than not lately she slept till well past dawn.

Throwing her feet over the side of the bedstead, she scurried across the downy, cottonwood floor and splashed water into the bowl. The mirror was ornate and chipped, a long-ago casualty of the trip from Boston. Samantha glanced at her reflection and groaned. She looked like she hadn't slept a bit.

"Not far from the truth," Samantha mumbled as she scooped water onto her face. After Captain Morgan had left the night before, she'd sat in the rocking chair waiting for Will to come back. After an hour or so she decided he wasn't likely to show up with her sitting waiting for him. So she went to her room and latched the door, falling on her bed in an exhausted heap.

She thought she would cry. It seemed like a good

time. She was alone, and heaven knows she was upset enough.

But she couldn't keep her mind focused on the farm, or Landis Moore, or even Will long enough to summon up a tear.

All she could think about was Jacob Morgan and that kiss.

That's why she hadn't slept even after she heard Will come in and climb to the loft. That's why she tossed and turned till her curls were a mass of tangles. Samantha unwound her braid and swiped the brush through her hair.

There it was again. She cocked her head to the side. She hadn't been imagining the noise that woke her. Hammering. Will was hammering something. And he hadn't had any breakfast.

Samantha dropped the brush and twisted her curls into a bun—quickly. Not because brushing her hair reminded her of last night . . . of Jacob Morgan's fingers tangling in her—

"Stop it," Samantha admonished herself. There was no reason to think of him again. She was certain he'd ridden off at first light. Off to Texas like he told Will . . . or maybe back to Landis Moore. Samantha shook her head. She didn't think he'd go there. But he sure didn't want to stay here.

His rejection after that kiss was obvious. Samantha didn't have much experience with men, but she'd read that easily enough.

"Well, I certainly don't want him here," Samantha mumbled, ignoring the memory of his expression when he backed away from her. She pulled on a clean dress, stepped into her shoes, and started for the barn.

First she'd talk to Will. She was sorry about last night, and intended to tell him so. Maybe she did "mother" him too much; it was hard not to since she'd been doing it so long. But he was growing up, as Captain Morgan pointed out — she guessed she should be thankful to him for that.

She and Will would work out their problem. The fact that he'd got up early and started work told her he was willing to try.

Samantha stepped into the glaring sunlight. Morning glories webbed their way up the porch supports, filling the air with their fragrance.

Heading for the barn, sidestepping the chickens that cackled at her feet, Samantha smiled. The hammering sounded louder now, a firm steady beat, and she wondered what Will could be making. Whatever it was, she'd be sure to show her gratitude. Will did a lot for the farm — she certainly couldn't manage without him. She needed to let him know that more often. After she talked with Will, she'd fix him a grand breakfast of ham and griddle cakes with —

Samantha stopped short in the doorway. The inside of the barn was dusky, the muted light from the slits cut in the sod alive with dust motes. But not so dark she couldn't see plainly.

And what she saw made her chin drop.

Will was there all right. He was sitting on the milking stool, a startled expression on his face, and a piece of straw between his teeth. But he wasn't hammering.

101

Jacob Morgan was doing that. At least he was until he followed Will's gaze and saw Samantha standing in the doorway. Then he simply stared at her, his eyes following a path from her hastily arranged hair to her scuffed shoes and back.

Samantha swallowed, feeling heat creep up her neck and spiral in her belly. He wore the same pants as last night, snug gray wool. Again both suspenders dangled down his narrow hips. His shirt was white, damp from sweat, and unbuttoned to reveal his muscled chest — that is, what wasn't covered by his bandaging.

"Sam." Will stood, spitting out the straw. Apparently he'd taken their argument last night to heart — at least enough to be uncomfortable about being here with Captain Morgan.

But Samantha really couldn't think about Will right now. She couldn't take her eyes from their Rebel guest. She was remembering last night — not the row with Will but the kiss afterward, and by the expression on the captain's face, he was thinking of the same thing.

But it only took him a moment to regain his control. He shrugged toward the hammer in his right hand. "I took your advice about staying a few more days."

Had she told him to stay? Samantha remembered saying something about his being too weak to leave, but that was definitely before the kiss. He hadn't seemed to lack for strength then. Samantha pulled her mind back to the present. He was talking and she missed most of it. Something about fixing up a few things around the farm in payment for her treatment.

"That's hardly necessary." Samantha's voice sounded strange, and she cleared her throat, wanting with all her heart to turn and run for the cabin. She'd pull the latch string and hide in the room till he left, and— "I'm sorry. What did you say?" Goodness, she had to start paying attention. She was acting even more foolish today than she had last night.

"I said"—Jake shifted his feet—"it might not be necessary but I'd like to do it. There are a couple of things that need—"

"We manage fine."

What a prickly woman. What a damn prickly woman! Manage fine like hell. He saw the place. The garden was a mess, the fence near falling down, and how they kept dry during a storm was beyond him. The shakes on the roof curled and sagged.

And it sure wasn't as if he wanted to get involved with her problems. He could just as easily get on his horse and ride west, weak or not. And he would have already if Will hadn't come into the barn early this morning.

The boy had wanted someone to talk to—someone besides his older sister. And like it or not, Jake fit the bill. And it wasn't as if he really minded. If his own son had lived . . . Jake forced his mind away from that painful course. He liked the boy. He understood a little more about the woman. And she was a damn good cook.

Besides, she couldn't help it that he'd lost control of himself last night. Because deep down Jake knew that was the main reason he wanted to saddle up and move on. Not that it would happen again. He'd see to it that there'd be no more kissing. But she acted as if he'd thrown her to the floor and tossed up her skirts—and he was having a hard time keeping the whole thing from his mind.

Jake laid the hammer on the stool. "Look, if it's all the same to you, I'll stay on a few more days. And while I'm here, I'll do a little work to help build up my strength."

"Why?"

"Why what?"

"Why are you helping out?" She didn't trust him any more than she trusted any of Landis Moore's men.

Jake blew air out through his mouth. Maybe he should just saddle up and ride out. Forget about the boy, forget about the food. "Look," he said when he calmed down enough to turn back to her. The defiant thrust of her chin didn't salve his anger. "We seem to have our share of differences—starting with you shooting me down for no reason."

"I had my reasons!"

"Maybe you thought you did. But I doubt even *you* believe them anymore."

She couldn't argue because, Lord help her, she was beginning to think she'd made a mistake. But she couldn't tell him. She could only stare at him wide-eyed.

Jake shook his head and leaned back against the stall divider. Had he honestly expected an apology? Did he even care for one? He crossed his arms. There

104

was no reason to push for something he wasn't getting and wasn't sure he wanted.

"It's up to you." Jake met her gaze squarely. "I can stay on a few days. Trade some chores for meals. Or I can ride out now."

Samantha's hands tightened around the folds in her skirt. He'd left the choice to her. From the corner of her eye she could see Will leaning forward, his elbows resting on his knees. From the expression on his face it was obvious what he wanted her to say. The decision would be easy for him. But then *he* trusted the Rebel. Even If she did concede he wasn't a member of Moore's gang, could she abide a rebel?

Samantha swallowed. "I suppose you can stay for a few days. Two maybe," she added, wanting to set a definite time limit. "But . . ." Heavens, how could she say what she was thinking? What she'd been thinking about all morning. The answer was she couldn't.

Crossing her arms, her posture mirroring his, Samantha nodded toward her brother. "I'm going to fix some breakfast. Will—" But the boy was way ahead of her and raced out the door yelling something about getting water from the creek. Charity trotted along at his heels.

No longer having Will as a buffer between them made Samantha realize how much she wanted— needed one. Will may not have said anything during their discussion, but she'd known he was there.

Now the musky air ripe with animal smells hung heavily between them. She knew she should leave, but he was staring at her and she couldn't seem to break the spell. She could think only of last night and what it felt like in his arms. "I . . . I better . . ." Samantha straightened her shoulders. She was acting like an idiot again and she refused to continue.

Something needed saying—about the kiss last night—and she rushed ahead before she could think too much about it. "If you stay, there can be no repeat of . . ." She tried, but she hadn't gotten all she had to say out before she looked at him. He arched his brow, and she went tongue-tied. She tried again. "No repeat of—"

"I'm not interested in anything but some honest work, a few meals . . . and staying to myself."

"I see." Samantha folded her hands. He obviously knew what she was trying to say and he agreed. Readily agreed. Why did she find that annoying? Taking a deep breath, she pushed that thought from her mind. "That's good." She paused. "Well, I'll get to fixing breakfast." Glancing over her shoulder, she added, "You're welcome to come to the cabin to eat. If you want."

Jake almost laughed at her offhand invitation. He wasn't sure why she offered, but he was pretty confident she didn't really mean it. Strangely, that made him all the more eager to accept.

He turned, giving the nail one final whack before glancing over his shoulder. "I'll be up to the house directly." Then he watched as she trudged out of the barn.

Unconsciously rubbing the area around his wound, Jake leaned back against the stall. Samantha Lowery was a strange one all right. A woman who'd shoot a man then spend days and sleepless nights nursing him back to health. Who'd tell you she shot you, then ask you to eat at her table to hide her fear.

A woman whose passionate kiss could leave a man wondering and longing for more.

Jake cringed at that. She did more than just make him angry. A hell of a lot more. This feeling had been creeping up on him for days almost too subtly for him to notice. But last night it erupted. And it was still there. Even while the woman stared at him, distrust filling her blue eyes, it was there. How could he feel desire for her? How could he feel it at all?

But the fact that he did, contrary to all reason, bothered him as much as the gnawing guilt it caused. It also made him determined to control this lust, to prove to himself he could, before he moved on.

Anyway, she wasn't exactly warming up to him. She still acted as if anyone from the Confederate Army was the next thing to a criminal. Jake considered telling her why he'd joined the war, but decided against it. He didn't care if she liked his politics. He didn't care if she liked him at all. But even as Jake tried to convince himself of that, a little voice in his head questioned why he was staying.

Samantha burned the griddle cakes.

It wasn't the first time in her life it happened. But it was the first time she didn't have a good reason. The stove wasn't too hot. No other work distracted her. She couldn't even blame Will's chattering. For he'd brought in the water then left again to see to the cow.

No, the only excuse she had was not an appealing one. She'd been thinking about Jacob Morgan. Thinking about his clear green eyes, the breadth of his chest, and that kiss. Always that kiss. Why had she said he could stay?

But she must stop daydreaming, Samantha decided as she mixed up another batch of batter, beating at the lumps of cornmeal. He'd be here only a few more days and she would simply ignore him.

Not so difficult, she decided a short time later while she sat at the table across from Will and the Rebel. All she had to do was concentrate on her food. Cut a bite of griddle cake. Dip it in the puddle of syrup she'd made from sugar and water. And eat it. Simple.

It wasn't like she was being ungracious. She'd given Jake Morgan a stack of cakes and he had plenty of company. Will hadn't stopped talking to him since they'd finished the blessing.

And it was all about Texas.

"I've never been there myself," Jake said, wiping his mouth with the linen napkin.

"But you know how wonderful it is, right?" Will shot his sister a telling stare, which she pretended not to notice.

"Well, I know my brother liked it when he went there back in '46. Told me once he wouldn't mind going back." Jake took another bite. He could say one thing for the woman, she knew how to fill a man's stomach.

"Your brother fought against Santa Anna's

troops?" Will seemed near ready to burst with excitement.

"Yeah." Jake grinned.

"Is he going to Texas with you?"

"No." Jake lifted his eyes and met Samantha's blue gaze. "My brother was killed . . . at Gettysburg."

"Gee, Mr. Morgan, I'm sorry. I didn't know."

"Don't worry about it." His words were for Will, but his eyes never left Samantha. "That's what happens in wars. And I told you, it's Jake."

"Sure, Jake." Will took a big swig of milk, his swallowing the only break in the silence.

The Rebel was still looking at her, and Samantha wasn't sure what his expression meant. He had lost a brother and so had she. Did he think that gave them some sort of common ground? No, Samantha corrected herself quickly. He wasn't looking for common ground any more than she was.

Besides, the fact that their brothers fought on opposite sides just made their differences that much more pronounced.

Pushing back her chair, Samantha rose. "Does anyone want any more to eat? I can fix some more."

"No thank you, ma'am."

"Naw, Sam."

Both males at the table spoke at the same time. Will didn't surprise her. She'd seen him slip his last griddle cake to Charity, who devoured it in one huge canine gulp. And she was certainly used to his sloppy speech that resisted all her efforts at reform.

But she hadn't expected the Rebel's innate politeness. She expected him to be crude . . . like Landis

109

Moore and his men. Samantha paused as she scraped her plate into Charity's bowl. She was comparing Jake to Moore's men, but she no longer thought he was one of them. The dog nudged Samantha out of the way. She straightened, plunging the dish into the wash pan.

"May I speak with you a moment?"

Samantha whirled around. She heard chairs scraping along the floor and footsteps and assumed Will and the Rebel had left the cabin. But she was only half right. Will was gone. Jacob Morgan wasn't. He leaned against the door jam, watching her, his lips relaxed in amusement.

Samantha's soapy hands flew to her hair. She couldn't help the reaction, or the gray suds that splattered on her face. What was she doing? She didn't care what her hair looked like for him, or anything else about him for that matter. Lifting her apron she gave her cheeks a swipe. "What do you want?"

She certainly was full of vinegar. But then he'd startled her, even if he hadn't meant to. He'd just been too engrossed in watching her bend over to make sure she knew he was still inside. Jake shook his head. Watching her was the last thing he should be doing. The crease between his brows deepened. "I noticed some shakes piled in the barn."

Shakes? It took a moment for Samantha to realize what he meant. "Oh, yes," she said, picking up the Rebel's plate from the table and sliding it into the soapy water. He'd left no scraps. "My brother Luke bought those before . . . before he left. He planned to build a new barn and use them for the roof." She emptied steaming water from the iron boiler on the stove into the wash pan and began scrubbing at the dishes. It was easier talking to him if she didn't have to meet his eyes.

"You still aiming to do that?"

"Build a new barn?" Samantha shrugged. "Maybe." Actually she hadn't given it a thought in nearly four years. "Why?"

Jake straightened, and moved across the floor. He didn't like talking to someone's back. "Thought I might use some to patch the cabin roof."

It was on her tongue to say the cabin roof was fine. But it would only take a glance upward to prove that a lie. Daylight shone through the warped shingles, and the last time it stormed, she and Will had barely managed to keep the bedding dry. Still . . .

Samantha plunged her hands in the steaming water, her shoulder nudging a lock of hair off her damp cheek. Why did he have to come over here to talk? He was so close and so big. She'd thought him large and heavy when she'd taken care of him, but standing, he loomed over her. "Are you sure you're up to climbing on a roof?"

"I think I can manage it."

"What if you get dizzy and fall off?"

She would have to bring up his spell last night. Well damnit, he'd been weak from hunger, and he *had* been shot in the chest and delirious. "I won't get dizzy," he insisted, daring her to discuss it any further. He didn't think she would because that might lead to remarks about her crying, or what happened

111

when he tried to comfort her. No, he didn't think she'd push the issue, and almost grinned when she didn't.

"Suit yourself," Samantha said with a shrug. She almost added, if you want to get yourself killed, but stopped herself. Maybe he did want to do just that. When he was feverish, he'd said he wanted to die. Perhaps he planned to throw himself off the roof, and . . . Samantha looked around to tell him to be careful, but he was already gone.

It wasn't long till she heard something being dragged outside the cabin. Looking out the window, she saw Will and Jacob Morgan maneuvering the ladder from the barn into place. A little later he and Will were pulling a makeshift travois stacked high with shakes. Then she heard him climb onto the roof and call down to Will. Right then Samantha decided this wasn't a good time to sew Peggy Keane's new dress. She'd work in the garden. With a glance toward the ceiling, Samantha marched out of the cabin.

The day was hot for the end of September, and it wasn't long before sweat trickled down Samantha's back, pooling in the fabric at her waistband. Her broad-brimmed bonnet did little to shade her from the sun's rays, but she wore it anyway as she carried water to the withering plants. She'd neglected this chore for days and the brown-edged leaves were a vivid reminder.

"I should have worried more about my vegetables than some gun-shot Rebel," she grumbled as she checked the tomato plants. They were doing fine and she plucked a few red spheres from the vine. Then reluctantly her head tilted till she could see the cabin.

Captain Morgan may have started on the back of the roof, but now he'd worked his way to the front. He leaned into the slope, positioning an oak shake over the curled edge of another. Nails stuck out of his mouth at all angles, and Samantha could tell from here that he favored his left side as he swung the hammer.

"Darn fool shouldn't be up there doing such work this soon," she told herself as she moved on to her squash plants. Even taking care, he might tear open the stitches she'd painstakingly sewed in his chest.

Samantha stood, making no pretense of doing anything but studying her unwanted visitor. She squinted her eyes against the sun's glare and watched him shinny down a foot or two. He'd removed his shirt so she could plainly see the bandage wrapped around his chest. It looked startling white against his sun-bronzed skin. No sign of blood.

Still, he shouldn't be up there.

Grabbing the bucket, Samantha walked toward the cabin, scattering the chickens that strutted toward her. Charity lay on the porch, her head resting in the shade, and she opened one lazy eye as Samantha approached. Standing out far enough to see onto the roof, Samantha called up.

"Where's Will?" It wasn't exactly a useless question. She did wonder what had become of her brother. They had started this job together this morning . . . now there was no sign of him.

Jake braced his boot against a shingle and twisted

113

around. He took the nails from his mouth, back-handing the sweat from his upper lip, and glanced down. The woman stood in a small patch of grass, hand shading her eyes, looking up at him. He motioned toward the barn. "He went for another load of shakes."

"Oh." Not a very eloquent reply, Samantha decided, but then coming over to stand near the overhanging eaves wasn't the smartest thing she'd ever done. It wasn't that she had any complaint about his work. From what she could tell peering up through the shadow of her hat, he'd done a good job of patching the roof. It certainly looked better than before he started.

Jake shifted. Waves of heat from the relentless sun poured down on his bare shoulders. But that wasn't the reason his blood scorched through his veins. The damn woman had loosened the neck of her blouse. Two buttons. Two lousy buttons, but even from six feet above her he could see the delicate hollow at the base of her neck, and the gentle swell of her breasts. The sight played havoc with his senses. Where in the hell was her brother?

Lowering the brim of his hat, Jake examined the last nail he'd hammered into the oak shingle. "Will mentioned something about running to the creek for some fresh water."

"I see." Samantha turned away. Standing here beneath him was ridiculous. She stepped onto the porch then stopped. Rebel or no, he deserved some courtesy from her. "You're doing an admirable job, Captain Morgan," she said after backing up. He

114

seemed surprised to see her back in the yard, and shocked to hear anything complimentary coming from her.

He twisted, sending a shower of wood chips drifting to the ground. "Thank you most kindly, ma'am. It's a pleasure to work for such a lovely lady." Jake grinned. His gallantry amazed him and, by the looks of the hand that fluttered to Miss Lowery's throat, flustered her. At one time he was considered quite the ladies man. Richmond mothers paraded their daughters in front of him and he charmed them all. Of course that was before he married Lydia.

A fissure of guilt ran through him. Intellectually he knew his wife was dead. He'd come to accept that. But emotionally he didn't think he ever would. And that's why the Lowery woman bothered him. Looking at her made him think of soft Virginia evenings with the scent of magnolias drifting through the open parlor windows and the sound of sweet feminine laughter tickling his ear.

But that was ridiculous. The woman standing below him was nothing like the belles he used to know. They wouldn't have been caught dead dressed in a plain, sweat-soaked skirt and blouse, with their hair tangling out of a worn hat. Nothing but silks and satins touched their delicate skin.

As for sweet melodic laughter, if the Lowery woman knew how to laugh, he sure hadn't heard it. Not that he wanted to. He had no business trying to charm this woman. He gave the last nail an extra and unnecessary whack. When he glanced back down, she was gone.

* * *

Dinner was great. Jake didn't think he'd ever tasted better. There was stew made from a rabbit Will snared, savory and flavored with wild onions. The fried squash was crisp and the cornbread soft. And Jake was certain he'd made a pig of himself. He stood outside the barn thinking of the days he'd have sold his soul for a fraction of the meal he ate tonight, and shook his head.

Toward the end, outside of Petersburg, and then retreating toward Appomattox, there'd been few supplies. Parched corn began to look like a delicacy.

But she'd fed him a lot more than a handful of corn. A few more days of eating like this, and working outside, and he'd feel as good as new. Then he'd move on.

A flash of lightning shot across the darkened southern sky and Jake stuffed his hands in the pockets of his butternut pants. The wind had picked up, and by the looks of it, there'd be a storm soon. Slowly he made his way into the barn.

"It's going to rain."

Samantha looked up from the seam she was painstakingly sewing in the purple satin. When had Will stopped reading? She'd been too absorbed in thought to notice the lack of his sing-song voice. "Did you finish *Moby Dick?*"

"I'm tired of reading it. I know what happens."

"Only because I read it to you." Samantha shifted

closer to the light. "Now it's your turn." She pushed the needle through the fabric. "Is there something you don't understand?"

"Yeah. Why are we making Jake stay out in the barn during a storm?"

Samantha's lips pursed. "I meant about the book."

"I ain't interested in the book. Why'd some guy care so much about a dumb whale anyway?"

"The whale is symbolic." Samantha paused and looked up at Will. He didn't seem likely to appreciate a discussion of Melville. "Perhaps we have heard enough *Moby Dick* for tonight." Will shoved the book across the table as he jerked out of his chair. "But we'll read some more tomorrow."

"Aw, Sam . . ."

"I promised Ma you wouldn't grow up without learning to read."

"I can read."

"And appreciate good literature," Samantha added before going back to her sewing. She sighed. Getting this gown finished by Friday was another promise she planned to keep if she had to stay up all night. They sorely needed the cash money Mrs. Keane paid.

"So what about Jake?"

She loved her brother dearly, but he could be a persistent bother sometimes. Like now. Samantha regarded him where he'd flopped onto the settee. "What about him?"

"Sounds like it's going to rain pretty hard."

"It will be good for the garden."

"He's going to get awful wet."

117

"A little water won't hurt him." Samantha bit off a thread.

"We ain't talking about a little bit. The last time it stormed, the barn floor was sopping."

Samantha said nothing as she held the dress closer to the lantern to check her stitches.

"Did you hear what I said, Sam? Jake's going to get himself soaked to the skin and it don't seem right after he worked all day to fix our roof."

"Doesn't. It *doesn't* seem right," Samantha corrected, tossing the dress on the table. "And just what do you want me to do about it?"

"Ask him to come up to the house," Will stated sensibly.

"He's probably already asleep," Samantha countered quickly.

"I can still hear his mouth organ."

Samantha pushed herself out of the chair. She could hear it too. The plaintive melodies he played had haunted her all evening. "Oh, all right. I'll go get him."

"I can go."

"No. If he has to come up to the house, I'll be the one to ask."

Chapter Six

Wind whipped at her skirts as Samantha slammed the cabin door behind her. She didn't want to invite the Rebel into her house. It was bad enough he was here at all. He made her uncomfortable, and she couldn't explain why.

Oh, there was the obvious. He was a Southerner. And even if she hadn't been taught from the time she could remember the evils of those who lived below the Mason-Dixon line, the last few years would have been a worthy lesson. But there was more to it than his home state and the color of his uniform.

When she'd taken care of him — when he was weak and at her mercy — Samantha could handle his presence, but now . . . Now he was up and about and he intimated her. His shoulders were broad. He was tall. He was too male. Altogether too much of a presence on the small farm.

And that was even without the memory of that kiss.

Lightning forked across the horizon, searing the sky with white hot light. It made the tiny hairs on the back of Samantha's neck bristle, and she hurried across the yard toward the barn.

The strains of a harmonica, sad and soulful, floated on the blustery air. Samantha cocked her head, straining to hear, frowning when the peeling thunder smothered the sound. She didn't recognize the melody, but it instantly conjured up an image of lost love. Was he playing for Lydia?

Samantha gnawed on her bottom lip, steps away from the barn door, listening and wondering. What had become of Lydia? Had she died during the war? The angry wind tugged at her hair, and Samantha absently tucked a strand behind her ear only to have it come flailing out again to whip around her face.

Maybe Lydia wasn't dead. Maybe she had left him for another man. Samantha hugged her arms about her waist and shook her head. She didn't think Lydia—or any woman—would leave Jacob Morgan. And the idea of him leaving Lydia was ludicrous. Unless . . . unless he was simply going to Texas to find them a home and she was going to follow . . . with his son.

Samantha paused, staring unseeing into the black night. She never considered the possibility he was married. But now that she thought of it, Samantha had to admit it was possible—even probable. Except . . .

The kiss.

He wouldn't kiss her like that if he was married. Would he? Samantha sucked in her breath as big fat raindrops began plopping on her head. The answer to that question was simple. He was a Rebel, wasn't he? And Rebels would do anything.

And she hadn't done anything to stop him.

Jake looked up as the barn door banged open. The wind grabbed it, sending it slamming against the turf wall with a dull thud. Thinking to shut it, he bent his leg to rise and that's when he saw the figure in the doorway. Instinct made him reach for his gun. His blood ran cold till lightning flashed, silhouetting the figure. He recognized Samantha Lowery an instant before she reached back for the door and tugged it shut behind her.

He couldn't see her well. The tallow candle she'd given him burned on an overturned bucket, but threw out precious little light. He could tell she was wet, and her hair tangled about her head in disarray. The sight of her made his pulse quicken.

Jake shifted, lowering the hand-cupped harmonica from his mouth. He didn't know what she was doing in the barn at this time of night, but he knew it had nothing to do with the fantasies that kept popping into his head. He'd started playing to wipe them out, but it hadn't worked. The harder he tried to think of his dead wife, the more Samantha Lowery came to mind. And now she stood before him. And it was all he could do not to pull her down onto the straw-covered floor and finish what he'd begun the other night.

Instead he rested forearm on bent knee. "Did you forget to milk the cow?" Jake knew better. He'd seen Will leave the barn with a pail full of frothy white milk earlier. But the silence made him uncomfortable, and Samantha didn't seem ready to break it.

"No." Samantha stepped farther into the barn. She could barely make him out in the shadows. He sat with his back to the wall, one leg stretched out before him. He was hatless and coatless, and if he noticed the drop in temperature caused by the storm, he didn't show it.

But then, Samantha realized, she'd forgotten to grab her shawl before leaving the cabin. Her wet cotton blouse stuck to her skin, causing chill bumps to dance along her flesh.

Shivering, Samantha looked away, wondering if he was married . . . wondering why she cared. Finally when she could stand the heavy silence between them no longer, she met his eyes. "It's storming and Will . . . and I . . . thought you might be more comfortable in the cabin." Samantha paused. "Sometimes this roof leaks." As if to add credibility to her explanation, a glob of mud plopped onto the straw near the rebel.

Jake stared at her a moment. "You're asking me to wait out the rain in the cabin?" He didn't even try to hide his surprise.

"Yes," Samantha said quickly, her gaze returning to him. Then because she was basically an honest person, she added, "It was Will's idea."

He could believe that. Damned if he couldn't. Jake shook his head. Unconsciously he rubbed the wound that was aching him worse — maybe because of the weather. The woman stood watching him, and when she realized what he was doing, he let his hand drop. "Aren't you afraid I'll kill you if I get the chance? Or maybe you've an idea to finish the job on me."

He made her mad. Jake saw anger flash across her face before she turned her back to him and reached for the latch. "It's obvious human kindness doesn't work with the likes of you — you — " She managed no more before Jake grabbed hold of her shoulder and spun her around.

"Rebel! Is that the word you were searching for?" Anger and fear narrowed her eyes but Jake went on. "You're a fine one to be talking about human kindness. You have so much hate built up inside you that you go around shooting innocent people."

"Your innocence has yet to be proven." Samantha tried to wriggle out of his grasp but he held her firm.

"Is that why you agreed to let me stay a few days? Why you came out here all alone? Because you think I'm riding with that Moore fellow?"

He definitely had her there. Though she refused to admit it. Long before she'd let him stay on, Samantha knew she'd made a mistake when shooting him. But that didn't mean being around him wasn't risky. He looked dangerous now, hovering over her in the near dark.

Just because he acted forgiving today didn't mean he held no grudge against her for wounding him. She was foolish to come out here. Samantha took a steadying breath, trying to ignore the sizzle of his hands on her rain-soaked shoulders. "I thought you might be more comfortable in the cabin." Samantha forced her voice to remain calm. "But since you'd rather stay here, it's all the same to me."

"Ah, but I wouldn't." Jake suppressed a grin when

her jaw dropped. "I've spent too many days in the elements not to appreciate some comfort in a storm."

She knew he spoke of the rain, of seeking a dry, warm spot to wait it out. But when he mentioned comfort, all Samantha could think of was being held in his arms. She stood motionless, breathing in the smell of him, watching his eyes turn a smoky green.

"What's the matter, Miss Lowery? Didn't you think Rebels had feelings?"

His sarcastic tone infuriated her. Twisting out of his grip, she jerked open the door. Sheets of wind-whipped rain washed over her before she was pulled back and the door slammed shut again.

"I don't think either of us should try for the house just yet," Jake said.

Oh, Lord. Why had she come out here? Samantha squared her shoulders, feigning courage she didn't feel. "Perhaps you're right." He'd stepped away from her, which was a relief, but a moment later water drizzled through the thatch roof near Samantha. Before she could move, Jake gripped her elbow to guide her aside. His touch made her warm all over.

"It looks a little drier over here." Jake motioned toward the empty stall lit by the flickering candle. She followed and stood leaning against the stall divider.

Samantha wished he'd say something . . . anything. But all he did was watch her. She could feel his stare down to her sodden shoes. It made her skin hot and her breasts taut. And by the expression on his face, the clinging fabric of her blouse made her condition obvious.

"It's letting up some." Samantha crossed her arms. "I'm going back to the cabin."

What made her think the rain was subsiding, Jake didn't know. He could still hear the steady plopping on the roof, which seemed more sieve than protection. But it was obvious she didn't want to be here with him. He caught up with her as she yanked open the door. He threw the uniform jacket he'd grabbed over her head, then bundled her outside before she could protest.

Rain, silvered by near continuous streaks of lightning, pelted the yard. Samantha felt herself buffeted to the side, and her feet slipped in the slimy mud. Reaching out, she grabbed for the barnyard fence. All she managed to do was lose her grip on the wool jacket. It slid down to her shoulders and raindrops pounded her face as she started to fall. But before she hit the ground, she was hauled against something strong and solid.

The Rebel.

He tucked her under his arm then took off running across the yard. His shoulder offered some protection from the torrents and his strong arm steadied her when her feet slipped again. By the time they reached the porch, she was more being carried than running.

Will yanked open the door. Apparently he'd been watching their progress through the window. "Hell's bells, you two are wet!" he yelled as Jake propelled them into the cabin.

Samantha opened her mouth to comment on Will's cursing then snapped it shut. Somehow it seemed a very appropriate way to describe them. She was soaked to the skin. Her hair hung in sodden clumps, dripping fresh water onto her face and down her back.

Besides, she was too breathless to give a lecture. She was enveloped by Jacob Morgan and the sensations were simply too strong to ignore.

His warmth permeated her, not just where their bodies touched but throughout her entire being. She breathed, and it was him she smelled. Steamy like a summer storm, his scent made her stomach muscles tighten as the rest of her longed to melt into him.

Samantha pushed herself away, or he maybe just let her go. But the next thing she knew he was drawing the damp jacket from her head and maneuvering her toward the stove. Will pulled out a chair, and hands on shoulders, the Rebel lowered her into it.

"Please, Captain Morgan." Samantha sprang up. "I'm perfectly all right. A little damp, maybe. But I won't melt."

Jake grinned. "Believe me, Miss Lowery, I never thought you would." She might feel soft and sweet in his arms, but that's where Samantha Lowery's similarity to sugar stopped. Jake sidled closer to the stove, catching the towel Will tossed his way. *He* was wet and cold even if she wasn't. Damn, the woman was full of vinegar. Didn't she recognize a chivalrous act when she saw one? And what the hell was he doing being chivalrous anyway? The damn woman shot him!

But that didn't keep his eyes from straying to Samantha's wet bodice. The damp material clung to

126

her breasts, and the fabric was nearly transparent. She must have realized her predicament, or maybe his surreptitious glances were more obvious than he thought, for she grabbed up her shawl and swirled it around her shoulders.

"I'm going to change into some dry clothes," she announced before tramping off to her bedroom. Muddy footprints marked her path.

Samantha leaned against the closed door and took a deep breath. What in the world was the matter with her? She let the shawl drop to the floor. She wanted nothing more than to hide in her room, but she refused to let the Rebel run her from her own cabin. Stripping from her sodden clothes, Samantha found herself wet down to her pantaloons. After quickly towel-drying her hair and body, she pulled on a clean dress.

Her shoes were another matter. They were hopelessly covered with mud. She could clean them off, but not now. And there was no way she was going back out in front of the Rebel with her feet bare.

Grimacing, Samantha dug in the trunk that held the clothes her family brought from back East. Her mother had been raised with money. Just because she decided to marry a poor minister and move across the county with him had been no reason to abandon her pretty things. At least that had been her mother's idea before reaching Kansas.

But though most of the gowns she brought were useless in her new home, Samantha's mother kept them, and sometimes late at night she'd wear them for her husband. Samantha remembered lying in the loft listening to them talking and laughing, pretending her father had come to call.

Biting her lip, Samantha pushed aside a silk gown and found the shoes she sought. They were kid, brittle from age, but when she pulled them on over her stockings, they fit. Of course they'd be no good for outside work, but at least they covered her feet, and despite the ravages of time, they were pretty.

Samantha lifted her skirt, examining her feet. They looked a lot smaller and more feminine than they did in her work shoes. Dropping the sturdy cotton material, Samantha sighed. What did it matter what her feet looked like?

Before leaving the room, she brushed back her damp hair and tied it at her nape with a bow.

Rain still pelted the roof, but Samantha was pleased to see as she reentered the front room that no water leaked from the eaves. And then she saw the Rebel. He was standing near the window she'd broken out. Samantha had taken down the blanket, her original cover, and replaced it with a piece of tautly stretched cotton. He turned when she shut her bedroom door. His eyes met hers, then dropped to sweep over his clothes.

"Will said it was all right for me to wear this." His hand fell to his side and he wished to heaven he'd told the kid to forget it. There were worse things than being cold and wet, and this was one of them.

Samantha stared a moment longer at the Rebel dressed in her older brother's clothes, then nodded. It seemed strange to see once again those work pants she'd patched and the shirt with the blue stripe she'd

128

always thought made Luke look so handsome. She felt a twinge of sadness, but that wasn't the reason she turned abruptly away.

She was going to laugh. Samantha brushed her hand down the side of her skirt and crossed the room toward her sewing basket. Her shoes squeaked and she glanced back to see if the Rebel noticed. He watched her, his brow arched as if daring her to say anything.

A giggle escaped.

"Where's Will?" Samantha said, trying to cover up the sound.

"In the loft looking for a pair of clean socks."

Her gaze shot to his feet, and another noise erupted from her, this time more like a strangled guffaw. Samantha coughed, then cleared her throat. "I think there are some in the basket." Samantha's eyes met Jake's after a detailed journey up his body, and her composure crumbled.

Clear peals of laughter rang out. Samantha made one futile attempt to squelch her mirth, then tossed her hands up and gave in to it. She sucked in her breath, wiped tears from the corners of her eyes, and realized something.

She wasn't the only one laughing. The Rebel's deep rumble joined in. He paused, rubbing a hand across his jaw, and gave her a crooked, self-mocking grin. "Will was so certain they'd fit, I didn't have the heart to argue," he said before crossing the floor toward her. I bet I do look pretty ridiculous though."

"Not really," Samantha insisted before catching a glimpse of his disbelieving expression. "Maybe the pants are a little short," she observed, glancing down at the hairy legs and large feet sticking out from the trousers. And she had worried about coming out into the room barefoot. At least her feet would have been hidden beneath her skirts.

"Perhaps a tad." Jake lifted his leg, pretending to survey the hem that hit him midcalf. "But then I suppose the pants go with the rest of my ensemble pretty well." The shirtsleeves, unbuttoned at the cuffs, dangled well above his wrists. And even though the shirt was made loose and billowy, it still fit him tightly across the shoulders.

"You can't be comfortable in that."

"Oh, I don't know." Jake pulled a chair across the table corner from her and sat down. "At least they're dry." He glanced toward the clothes he'd draped over another chair close to the stove.

"True, but they're—"

"They're fine, Miss Lowery." Jake looked away then found his eyes drawn back to her. "You're beautiful when you laugh," he said, catching them both off guard. Her expression showed shock and disbelief, and Jake figured his matched. Why in the hell had he said that? True enough, he thought her pretty since he first woke to find her snuggled on his shoulder. But he hadn't seen her laugh, even smile for that matter, until now.

Merriment made her blue eyes alive with silvery sparks, made her face breathtaking. But that was no excuse for his saying it. And those sparkling eyes weren't laughing now. They were wide, turned up slightly at the corners, and staring at him in wonderment. And her mouth, that sweet mouth he had kissed into submission, was open—only slightly—but enough for him to see the tip of her tongue.

Jake leaned forward. He could swear she drew toward him too. And then Will came clambering down the ladder.

Samantha jerked, her body slamming into the chair back, the jolt knocking some sense into her scattered wits. Had she come close to kissing him . . . again? Taking a deep breath, Samantha reached for her sewing basket, nearly knocking it onto the floor. Jacob Morgan's fast hands kept her pins and threads from scattering.

He jumped up when he first heard Will, and now he met the boy before Will's feet hit the floor. Will turned, his expression apologetic. "Gosh, Jake, I thought they'd fit you better than that."

"Hey, Will," Jake said, tussling the boy's shock of wheat-colored hair. "It's all right. They're dry. How about those socks?" he questioned when Will still seemed concerned.

The heavy wool socks did nothing to improve his comical appearance, but they were at least warm. It amazed Jake how quickly the temperature had dropped with the onset of the storm.

Because he didn't know what else to do, Jake sat back down at the table. But this time he sat across from Samantha. She didn't look up, just kept stitching furiously at something she was making out of obnoxious purple silk. When Will flopped down, his attention was all for Jake.

"Did you bring your mouth organ in with ya?" he

asked, leaning forward expectantly.

"As a matter of fact, I did." Jake reached into his pocket. He'd retrieved it when he changed his pants.

"Could you play something for us . . . please?" Will added when Jake seemed to hesitate. "Sam and I heard you earlier, and really liked it."

"I never said I liked it . . ." Samantha's words trailed off as she realized how rude she sounded. She just didn't want the Rebel thinking she sat around listening to him play. She concentrated on her next stitch. "Of course, we'd love to hear you play, Captain Morgan."

The Rebel's grin told her he knew her first statement closer to the truth, but he sidled up on one hip and drew out his harmonica. After some tune-up trills, he began to play.

Some of his songs were festive and cheerful, some where full of longing, but he played them all with the same enthusiasm. And Samantha was enthralled. She followed the motion, the movement of his hands as he slid the harmonica side to side, her sewing forgotten in her lap. His clear green eyes were hidden, their lashes lowered, blocking any view of his emotions. But the music filled the gap, washing feelings of joy, sorrow, pain, and love over her.

Jake had never played for a more receptive audience. He usually only pulled out the harmonica when he was alone. He'd received it from an uncle when he was thirteen, had mastered the notes quickly, and just as quickly delegated the instrument to the box in his chifforobe where he kept useless bits of his childhood. An aggie he'd thought at one time

132

had magical powers, a musketball he'd found while visiting cousins near Yorktown (he was certain it was the last shot fired in the Revolutionary War), a rabbit's foot from an albino rabbit. Occasionally he'd take out his treasures, and never failed to give the harmonica a workout.

But then he'd gone North to school, leaving the harmonica in Richmond. When he married Lydia and moved to his own house, the box went with him. But his new wife wasn't partial to the sound, and after Andrew was born, she'd been afraid the noise would wake him. And Jake had been busy with his medical practice—too busy to indulge in childish habits like sitting in a quiet corner and letting the music seep into him.

He'd almost left it behind. When he joined the Army of Virginia, his bags were packed and he'd said his good-byes to Lydia and little Andrew. And suddenly he'd thought of his harmonica stashed in his treasure box. Taking the stairs three at a time he found it, slipped it in his pocket, and rode off to war.

He regretted a lot of things over those four long years, but never bringing the harmonica.

Jake tapped the harmonica in his palm. The last strains of "My Old Kentucky Home" still hung in the air. Will was sitting, elbows on table, chin in hand, waiting. Samantha leaned back in her chair, her eyes dreamy, her soft lips tilted in a smile. She stayed that way, her breathing soft, the pulse quivering just above where her collar buttoned beneath the hollow of her neck. Then her eyes focused and locked with

133

his, and she jerked ramrod straight in the chair.

"That was very nice," she observed, hastily retrieving her sewing and trying to appear busy.

"It was great!" Will chimed in, and Samantha admitted her brother's assessment was closer to the truth. "Play something else."

Jake shrugged. "I'm afraid that's about all I know."

"But Jake—"

"Willy," Samantha interrupted, then bit her bottom lip. Hadn't she decided to stop mothering her brother so much? She searched her mind for something to say to take the sting from her reprimand. Then found she didn't have to. The rebel picked up the copy of *Moby Dick* from the table.

"Who's reading this?"

Will made a face that eloquently said what he thought of the novel. "I am," he grumbled, his accusing eyes trained on Samantha. Had she thought this subject would be better?

"It's one of my favorites," Jake said, turning to the fly page.

"You like reading?" Will was obviously struck by disbelief.

"What?" Jake glanced up from perusing the page. Most of his books had been destroyed when Richmond burned. The ones left, those at his parents' house, he'd packed up and put into storage when he started West. He hadn't realized until now how much he missed them . . . even his medical volumes. "Yeah, I like to read."

"But reading's for sissies."

134

"Will!" Why had she decided to stop mothering him? He needed mothering! At least he needed his manners corrected. Samantha dropped her sewing to tell him so, but the rebel's laughter cut her off.

"Sissies, huh." Jake rubbed his chin, his eyes meeting Samantha's. She could see the humor shining in the clear green depths. "Guess I must be a sissy then."

"Naw," Will objected. "You ain't no sissy."

"I don't know." Jake leaned back in his chair. The wood creaked above the sound of the storm. Again his gaze found Samantha. "I must be because I sure like to read."

Will was speechless. His mouth gaped open. It was no secret to Samantha that Will had made the rebel into some kind of hero. And now he was left wondering. One thing for certain, Samantha had to agree with her brother. Jacob Morgan was no sissy. She imagined Will would come to the same conclusion. In the meantime, she'd give them all something to do.

"I'm going to make some tea," she said standing. "Would anyone like a piece of leftover pie from supper?"

Jake looked up at her. The apple pie from supper was some of the best he'd ever had. He was surprised there was any left. He'd thought he'd eaten all of it. He told Samantha as much and smiled at her blush. She wasn't nearly as tough as she liked to make him think.

"Hey, Jake." Will forced Jake's attention away from watching the Lowery woman prepare tea. "You really like this book?"

"Sure do." Jake picked it up again. "You ever read it?"

Will rolled his eyes toward his sister. His voice low, he admitted. "She read it to me, and now she's trying to get me to do it."

Jake kept his tone conspiratorial. "Does she listen to you?"

Will nodded. "Like a teacher. I'm too old for school."

Jake shrugged. "Maybe, maybe not. But in any case, how about if you read to me."

"Now?"

"No. Tomorrow when we're working. We'll take turns reading *Moby Dick* to each other. All right?" Jake's brow rose quizzically.

"All right."

Samantha sliced a piece of pie for Will. Did they really think she couldn't hear them? Samantha considered turning and informing the two males sitting at her table that they weren't pulling a thing on her, but she didn't. She wanted Will to read . . . to enjoy reading. And the Rebel was doing more to accomplish that than she ever could. She angled her knife to the left, cutting him off a larger hunk of pie than she'd originally planned.

By the time they finished eating, the storm's fury had abated. No longer did the wind howl or the rain pelt the roof overhead. Samantha stood gathering up the dishes. "The roof held," she said, smiling up at Jake, who'd followed her to the dry sink. "It's the first time in over a year we haven't had to place pots

136

around on the floor." She could give the devil his due. But when he was standing close to her like this, he didn't seem much like a devil—though he sure could tempt her.

"Good." What was it about this woman that had him constantly wanting to kiss her? Even now with her hands wrist deep in dishwater and her brother sitting five feet away, he had the strong urge to pull her into his arms.

Well, he had no intentions of making the same mistake he'd made last night. He'd stay one more day—as they agreed—then he'd ride off and never give Samantha Lowery another thought.

With that intention firm in his mind, Jake turned on his heel and left the cabin—in his stocking feet.

Chapter Seven

"I won't do it, and that's final!" Samantha gave her brother a determined look before bending down to pluck a ripe prickly pear. Thoughts of its sweet, strawberry flavor made her mouth water as she placed it carefully in the burlap bag tied at her waist.

She'd risen early that morning and had decided to go on a search for the wild fruit. Why she suddenly had the urge to pick fruit today, she wasn't sure, but it had nothing to do with avoiding the Rebel. She was certain of that.

A little solitude was all she was after. A chance to think. But apparently that wasn't to be. As soon as she started out of the cabin, with a hasty word to her brother about her destination, he fell into step beside her.

He was still there.

"Give me one good reason," Will persisted.

Samantha took a deep breath in an attempt to calm herself. It didn't help. Turning on her brother, she glared at him from beneath her straw bonnet. "I can give you lots of reasons. But all you need to know is that I am *not* going to ask Jacob Morgan to stay on."

"But Sam—"

"No arguments, Will." Samantha went back to picking prickly pears, but she should have known she hadn't heard the last from her brother.

"We need someone to help us with the corn."

He had a point there. The cornfield had rows standing straight and tall as sentinels. Samantha had checked it this morning. She'd smiled at the sight of their hard work come to fruition. Water droplets left over from last night's rain had sparkled like prisms in the early morning sun.

But though she and Will would need help to harvest the crop, it wasn't going to be the Rebel. "I'll talk to Jim Farley when I take Peggy Keane's dress into town. You remember him from last year."

"And you said he was slow as molasses in January."

Why did Will have to pick now to have a good memory? "Well, we got the job done, and that's what counts."

"Sam . . ."

"Will!" Samantha gathered the bag shut, deciding she'd had more than enough fruit picking for one day. "Captain Morgan is leaving today or tomorrow."

"I know." Will followed her up the path. "I heard you two talking last night after I went to bed."

Samantha paused. "Then you know he already has his plans made."

"He might change his mind if you talked to him."

"I don't think so."

"But he might."

"Willy, I'm getting very tired of this. We won't discuss it anymore." They climbed the slight rise the cabin was built on, and Samantha continued on through the door, leaving her brother kicking at a clod of dirt. She pretended not to, but there was no way she could miss his last grumbled words.

"He wouldn't be so anxious to leave if you were nicer to him."

Well, this was as nice as she was going to get, Samantha decided, slamming the door behind her. Maybe he wasn't one of Landis Moore's men — though she wasn't *absolutely* convinced of his innocence — but he was still a Rebel soldier.

He was still just passing through, and the faster he got on with it, the better.

But Will would miss him. Samantha sighed. She needed to be more understanding toward her brother. As surly as the Rebel was toward *her,* he'd been wonderful with Will. It was obvious Will liked him, and it was probably more than a matter of hero worship.

Her brother needed a man's influence. He needed to be around a man. But all he had was her. And there wasn't a thing she could do about it.

Samantha spent the rest of the day close to the house. She went to the garden once to pick the tomatoes bent close to the ground with their heavy ripeness. But the rest of the time she worked on Peggy Keane's dress. She'd promised to have it finished by the end of the week, and if she didn't keep at it, she'd miss the deadline sure.

Too much time had been spent taking care of the

rebel, Samantha decided. Caring and thinking about him, she amended honestly. But no more. She and Will needed the cash money she earned from her sewing, and she couldn't afford not to live up to her end of the bargain.

But more times than she could count, Samantha found her gaze straying from the purple silk toward the window. She'd lifted the stretched cotton to let in the air and allow her more light. Even though breezes sang through the wild sunflowers and riffled through the cottonwood leaves, the day was uncomfortably warm. As if wiped away by the storm, no clouds filtered the sun. It burned large and bright in the cerulean sky.

The Rebel worked on the barn roof. There weren't enough shakes to cover the entire structure, but apparently he decided a patch job was better than none at all.

In deference to the heat, he'd removed his shirt. There was no doubt about it, he'd gained some weight. That slightly hollow-cheeked, gaunt look he'd had when he first came was gone. His chest was fuller, the ribs less pronounced. His body was bigger, brawnier.

Samantha snorted. What could she expect the way he ate? She took a few stitches in the ruching around the collar of the gown, then let her eyes stray back to him. She couldn't begrudge him his appetite. It wasn't as if he was growing fleshy. To the contrary, his body looked whipcord lean, the muscles gleaming hard in the sunlight.

How long had he gone hungry to become as thin

as he was before?

He paused to backhand sweat from his brow, and Samantha watched him lean toward the edge. He yelled down something she couldn't hear, but when she allowed her gaze to stray from the Rebel, Samantha saw Will.

He straddled the fence, book in hand, and appeared to be reading out loud. Samantha couldn't keep from smiling. Will most likely didn't like it — Samantha imagined he'd much rather be on the roof helping the Rebel. But Jacob Morgan was keeping his word about the reading. And he'd keep his word about leaving too, Samantha decided.

Reluctantly she turned back to her sewing.

By late afternoon her back muscles burned from fatigue, but she was almost finished the gown. All there was left to do was hem the voluptuous skirt. But for now she needed to start supper.

Taking the slab of beef off its hook near the stove, Samantha began slicing off steaks. Apparently Captain Morgan planned to wait till after the evening meal to leave so she cut off several more hunks of meat. She'd let him indulge in one more big meal before he rode away.

Goodness, she couldn't understand why thoughts of him leaving bothered her. He was rude, angry most of the time, overbearing, and arrogant, and she should be happy and relieved that her association with him was almost over.

So what if he helped out around the farm. He owed her at least that much work for all the food she fed him. Samantha let her mind skim over the fact

142

that she shot him. There was no way she would ask him to stay on. She'd pick every darn ear of corn herself before she gave in to Will's suggestion. Grabbing up a potato, she started hacking away at the peel.

A noise outside made her glance through the window. Neither Jacob or Will were in sight. They'd finished the barn roof and headed out to the cornfield. Will had dashed in to tell her earlier. As he ran out the door, she warned him about trying to talk Captain Morgan into staying.

Samantha shook her head. She expected them back before now. Her eyes strayed across the flat landscape and her fingers stilled, knife in midshave down a potato.

A column of dust spiraled into the air, and it was coming toward the farm . . . from town. She supposed it was possible for any number of folks to be visiting from Hager's Flats, but Samantha couldn't shake from her mind her last group of visitors.

By the time Samantha dropped the potato and wiped at her hands, she could make out a man on horseback. When she realized who it was, she hurried to the pie safe to retrieve Captain Morgan's revolver.

Sticking it in her apron pocket, Samantha rushed to the door, throwing it open before Bundy Atwood could dismount. She didn't want him thinking he was welcome.

"What are you doing here, Bundy?"

The man paused momentarily, his right foot kicking free of the stirrup, and stared at Samantha from beneath his hat, his eyes dark and brazen. Then he slid off the dun-colored gelding. After giving his reins a negligent toss toward the fence, he sauntered toward the porch. "Now is that any way to greet an old friend, Samantha?"

"You're no friend of mine, Bundy Atwood. And I want you off my property."

Atwood braced his boot on the porch step. "Now I can remember a time you were right anxious for me to come calling."

She didn't answer him, but the awful truth was, she could too. He'd been new in the territory, handsome in a slicked-back, pretty sort of way. At least she'd thought so at the time. He'd visited the farm often. At first it was Luke he'd professed to be visiting, but after the third time he'd made it clear that Samantha was the reason for his frequent trips from town.

And Samantha was thrilled. She was a shy, inexperienced seventeen when he'd started courting. She hung on his every word, though later she couldn't imagine what he'd said that was so interesting. But she'd planned their life together.

When she first heard rumors that he was riding with Landis Moore, she couldn't believe it. They'd never really talked of politics, but Samantha was confident he had abolitionist sentiments like she did. After all, he came from Pennsylvania.

But when she dared to ask him about it, he laughed in her face. He didn't give a damn about some darkie living in Mississippi, and he didn't want her thinking about it either. And as for Landis

Moore, he was only trying to see that honest white men had the right to bring slaves into Kansas if they wanted.

He grabbed her when she started to walk away from him. She thought for too long about her father's lectures on the evils of slavery not to have strong feelings on the subject. But Bundy didn't seem to care how she felt. When she protested he shook her, then grabbed her up for a fierce kiss.

She'd always enjoyed the kisses he stole before. They were so sweet and pleasant. But what he did to her that day wasn't. Her lip split from the pressure of his teeth, and she gagged as he forced his tongue into her mouth. She fought and scratched and earned herself a ear-ringing smack for her efforts. But he let her go, with a warning that she better get used to things the way they were because he'd be back.

She refused to see him, sending a bewildered Luke to give Bundy the message the next time he called. She didn't tell Luke why she was breaking it off with his friend. She was too embarrassed. But when Bundy refused to take no for an answer, coming by, again and again, and finally catching Samantha alone, she hadn't needed to explain.

Luke returned from the fields, a towheaded Will by his side, in time to see Bundy tackle Samantha from behind as she ran from him. Bundy's fist was raised above Samantha's face, but he never landed the blow.

Luke grabbed Bundy by the neck and came close to strangling him before Samantha could pull him off. Bundy had ridden off with a warning never to return and an expression on his face that made Samantha's blood run cold.

The war started not long after that. Atwood and Moore were rumored to be with Quantrill in Missouri. But Samantha saw Moore's men one other time in 1861. The night they came for her father. She didn't know for sure if Bundy was with them. But she knew she didn't want him here now.

Atwood straightened, coming up on the porch with a lurch, and Samantha backed up, her fingers tightening on the revolver. "I'm warning you, Bundy." Samantha tried to keep her voice calm, but knew she'd failed. Sweat broke out on her upper lip, and she resisted the urge to swipe at it with her palm.

"Hell, Samantha." Atwood made an impatient motion with his hand. "The war's over. Can't we just let bygones be bygones? We used to get along pretty good." He gave her a grin that to Samantha's shame she had once thought beguiling.

She raised her chin, and stared him straight in the eyes. "I'm not interested in forgetting about the past. And the war's got nothing to do with it. Now get on your horse and ride away while you still can."

"You always was a little spitfire, Samantha. And a real looker when you was riled."

He moved so unexpectedly and quickly that Samantha had no chance to yank out the gun. His arms enveloped her, forcing hers down to her side. She could feel his hot breath on her cheek as his grip whooshed the air from her lungs.

146

"What do you have to say for yourself now, Samantha? What, no threats?" His hold tightened. "I think it's about time we took up where we left off before the war. Seems to me I had you on the ground and we was getting real chummy before old Luke stuck his nose in where it didn't belong."

"You make me sick."

His dark eyes narrowed till they were not more than fierce slits of glittering mica. "Any more talk like that and you might have more problems than a few drunken soldiers shooting up your place."

"What are you talking about?"

His grin was evil. "Just thinking what a shame it would be if something happened to that cornfield you've worked so hard on." His face began descending toward hers. "Now you be nice to me and I can see that things like that don't happen here." His hand closed painfully over her breast as his mouth slammed into hers.

"Get your hands off my sister!"

Bundy's lips stilled and he lifted his eyes, but kept them and his sneer trained on Samantha. "Shit, Will, ain't nothing wrong with a little kissing."

"There is if the lady doesn't want it."

That voice most certainly did not belong to a thirteen-year-old boy. It was deep and resonant, and more than a little gruff. Samantha shut her eyes and let the sound roll over her. Bundy loosened his arms, and while Samantha took a deep breath, she glanced around toward the man who'd spoken.

Jake stood beside Will, a restraining hand on her brother's shoulder. They'd been on their way from

147

the cornfield to the creek when they heard the commotion. He looked hot. His striped shirt was open at the neck and sweat-molded to his body. Standing, legs slightly apart and eyes straight ahead, he appeared strong and dangerous. Despite the lack of a sidearm.

Bundy's fingers tightened for a split second on Samantha's arm — a promise of things to come — and then he stepped away from her. His hand dropped in a seemingly casual motion toward the revolver strapped to his hip. But Samantha knew there was nothing unintentional about the move. He stroked the gun lovingly, but he didn't draw it. Instead he leaned against the porch post.

"Who says the lady doesn't want it?" His smile was cool and confident. "Samantha and I have been . . . friends for a long time. Isn't that right, honey?" With those words his hand snaked out and grabbed Samantha's wrist, yanking her toward him.

The movement was so quick and unexpected that Samantha was plastered against Bundy's side before she knew what had happened. She squirmed, fighting him, grasping for the gun in her pocket. Her mouth opened to tell him what she thought of his vile manhandling and even worse crimes, but then clamped shut.

From the corner of her eye she saw Will and the rebel moving toward her. And they both looked more than willing to protect her honor.

And they'd both get shot if they did. Samantha could feel the tension in Bundy's body as his hand tightened on the gun.

Samantha stopped struggling. "He's right," she said, her eyes on Jake Morgan. "We are old friends."

"Sam!"

Samantha ignored her brother's outburst. Of course *he* knew better. Will had seen Bundy that day years ago, and even though only eight, Samantha knew he remembered.

Samantha straightened. "Bundy's right," she repeated, her eyes on Jake. "We are old friends. But I've had a change of heart." Her gaze shifted to Bundy. "Would you please just leave?"

"Well now, I'm not real inclined to do that."

"You heard the lady." Jake took another step toward the porch. He wished he knew exactly what was going on here. Will seemed ready to bust a gut, and Jake purposely moved in front of him. As for Samantha, she didn't seem overly enthusiastic about the newcomer's attentions, but then she wasn't exactly resisting him either. The last thing he needed, Jake decided, was to get involved in some lovers' quarrel. Hell, he wasn't interested in getting involved with anything.

But this man didn't want to let it go. Turning on Jake, giving Samantha a little shove to the side, he stepped off the porch. "I don't believe I got your name."

"Morgan. Jake Morgan."

Bundy swept his eyes down Jake, while his hand rested on the gun cocked out from his hip. Finally he pushed back his hat and shook his head. "Well, Jake Morgan, I'm not sure I like you hanging around here."

"He's just passing through," Samantha injected. Jake stood perfectly still through Bundy's inspection, but now his gaze flew to Samantha. He clearly didn't like her answering for him.

"That right, Morgan? You passing through?"

Ignoring the man, whom he took at the very least for a bully, Jake looked skyward. While he watched a hawk circle lazily overhead, he tried to decide what to do. Nothing came readily to mind. The man was armed, angry, and apparently enough of a fool to mix the two. Jake had seen enough of his kind during the war to last a lifetime. They were the ones who usually got themselves along with anyone dumb enough to tangle with them killed.

Damn, he hated putting himself in that category. Taking a deep breath, Jake leveled his gaze on Will. "Help your sister fix some coffee."

"What for?" Will looked at Jake as if he'd suggested he attempt flying.

"Do it." Jake motioned toward the porch where Samantha stood, her expression as disbelieving as her brother's.

"Now wait a minute. I'm not fixing coffee for—" But her last words were cut off when Will reached her side. He grabbed her arm and turned her toward the door.

"Come on, Sam," he said, quieting her sputtered refusals. Will pulled the door shut behind him, and gave a glaring Samantha a shamefaced shrug.

"What do you think you're doing?" Samantha asked, her hands balled into fists at her hips.

"What Jake said." Will yanked on the window cov-

150

ering, letting the cotton flap down to block out the scene in the yard. It also had the effect of hiding what went on in the cabin. Quickly, Will went to the mantle and reached for the musket.

"What Jake said," Samantha mimicked. "Since when do we do what Jake says around here?"

"Aw, sis." Will checked the charge. "I didn't mean nothing. I just think Jake knows how to handle Atwood."

"Then why are you priming that musket?"

"Just in case." Will looked up to see Samantha reaching for the door. "Hey, what are you doing?"

Samantha shifted, revealing the revolver she'd scooped from her pocket. *"I'm* going to get rid of Bundy Atwood."

"Jake can handle it," Will insisted again.

"He should. They're both cut from the same cloth." Samantha stopped and bit her lip. She didn't really think that was true. "Look, Jake has no gun, and we both know how Bundy can be."

"I know how Jake can be, too. And he wanted us out of the way."

"Well, that's ridiculous. I'm going out th—"

But before Samantha could finish her sentence, the door opened, forcing her to step back, and Jacob Morgan entered. Alone.

Horse's hooves sounded through the opening, and Samantha stood on tiptoe to look past Jake. Bundy Atwood rode away toward town. Puffs of dust spewed into the air as he urged his mount to a gallop.

Samantha slanted Jake a look. His expression was

angry but calm. Not like someone who'd just faced an armed man. But then maybe he knew there was nothing to worry about.

Bundy rode with Landis Moore. If Jake did too . . . Samantha didn't have time to fully consider this before she noticed Jake's gaze lower to her hand. She still clutched the pistol—his pistol—and she watched as his dark brows rose. Without a word he held out his hand.

"When you leave." Samantha didn't like feeling totally helpless around him, regardless of the fact he'd done nothing to hurt her or Will. But he didn't seem to care how she felt about it.

"I want it now. I'll be leaving at first light."

Samantha met his stare, her own steady. With an exasperated sigh, Samantha laid the gun across his palm.

"How'd you get rid of him, Jake?" Will asked eagerly. "What did you say to him?"

"Yes," Samantha agreed. "Do tell us what you said to have him riding off so quickly."

"Not much." Jake leaned back against the door jamb. It was obvious the Lowery woman was annoyed with him, but he wasn't sure why. She didn't like giving up the gun, but she should have been resolved to that. Maybe she didn't like Will and him interrupting her little meeting with Bundy Atwood. That was Atwood's story. He implied Samantha was embarrassed by her brother showing up. Jake just wasn't sure.

"But what?" Will had pulled up a chair and now straddled it, his chin perched on the curved back.

Jake glanced toward Samantha. "I just suggested this wasn't the best time to go courting."

"Courting?" Samantha's hands flew to her hips. "He wasn't here to do any courting, and you know it."

"I don't know." Jake folded his arms and pushed away from the door. "That's what he said. Gave me quite a tale of woe about you giving him the heave because he fought for the South."

"That's ridiculous." Samantha grabbed a skillet off its hook and slammed it on the stove. The Rebel just raised his brows.

"Sam's right," Will piped in. "It didn't have nothing to do with the war. Luke and me, we caught him hurting Sam real bad one time. He—"

"That's enough, Will. I'm certain Captain Morgan isn't interested in our affairs."

But damnit, he was interested. Jake felt his gut tighten at the idea of Atwood hurting Samantha. But he forced himself not to ask. Instead he stuck the revolver in the waistband of his pants, then started for the door. "I don't think Atwood will be back," is all he said before leaving the cabin.

"He's not coming in for supper." Will stared at his own plate piled high with fried steak and boiled potatoes, then at Jake's empty seat.

"Maybe he left already." Samantha used her knife to slice off a small bite of meat.

"Naw, his horse is still in the paddock."

"Then perhaps he doesn't know it's time to eat.

153

Maybe you should run down and tell him."

"He always come before without no reminding."

Samantha bit her tongue to keep from correcting Will's grammar. There was no need to amend what he said though. Jacob Morgan seemed to have a sixth sense about when she was putting food on the table. "Well, maybe he simply isn't hungry."

Samantha met Will's incredulous gaze. All right, they both knew the Rebel was always hungry. And this evening's meal was good . . . real good. Without admitting it to herself, Samantha had made it special for him. As a kind of thank-you. For getting rid of Bundy today. For being kind to Will.

Samantha sighed and threw up her hands in an impatient gesture. "Why don't you take his plate to him. Maybe he's busy getting ready to go." A ridiculous assumption, Samantha admitted. All he had to do was saddle his horse and ride away.

Wood scraped wood as Will pushed back his chair. He grabbed up the cutlery and steaming pewter cup with one hand, the plate of meat, potatoes, and squash with the other. Halfway to the door he paused. "You know he might still stay if you asked him."

"Oh, Will." Samantha pushed her plate aside, her appetite suddenly gone.

"Well, he got rid of Atwood for you. He's handy to have around."

"Take him his dinner, Will."

Samantha sat staring out the door into the twilight long after Will had disappeared into the barn. His own dinner sat cooling on the table, but she didn't think her brother cared.

He wanted Jacob Morgan to stay. And there was nothing she could do to grant him his wish. Even if she wanted to.

Picking up a fork, Samantha pushed a potato around her plate. She hated to admit it but it was kind of nice having him around. Oh, he could be an aggravation, but he had fixed the roof, and more importantly, he'd got rid of Bundy Atwood.

Grabbing up her plate, Samantha emptied it into Charity's bowl, then tossed it in the dry sink. The pewter clattered against the tin lining. She hadn't told Will about Bundy's warning, but that didn't mean she forgot about it. He threatened to ruin their corn crop. She was certain he had Landis Moore's backing for that. But he also let her know she had one way to stop it.

Be nice to him.

Samantha cringed to think what that meant. She grasped the edge of the dry sink, her head bent back, and she smothered a sob. She wouldn't let anything happen. She wouldn't!

But how was she going to stop it?

"He's finished eating. Said to tell you it was real good."

Samantha straightened. She was so overcome by her worries she hadn't noticed Will coming into the cabin. Quickly she brushed away a tear that had seeped between her closed lids, and poured water into the sink. Charity came scurrying over to her bowl, obviously pleased by her windfall of steak. She gulped noisily.

"Bring your plate over and I'll warm up your dinner," Samantha said as she shaved lye soap into the pan. She wanted to ask what reason the Rebel gave for not coming to the house for supper, but didn't. Will seemed upset, and Samantha didn't want to talk about the reason. She knew.

After he finished with his warmed-over meal, doing little justice to it, Will climbed the ladder to his loft. She knew he blamed her for the Rebel leaving, but it wasn't her fault. He wasn't interested in sticking around here. Was he? Will seemed to think all she had to do was ask him, but Samantha didn't think that would work. Besides, she didn't want to.

Samantha reached into her sewing bag and started the task of hemming Peggy Keane's gown. The lantern cast iridescent shadows on the purple silk as she worked, trying to keep her mind from returning to her problems.

But the harder she tried not to think of them, the more they pushed to the forefront of her thoughts. Without the corn crop, there wouldn't be enough to eat or feed the animals over the winter. She and Will would be doomed. But she couldn't give in to Landis Moore, or Bundy Atwood.

Samantha paused to rub her sore eyes and realized how late it was. She should go to bed, but she knew she wouldn't be able to sleep. There was only one thing for her to do.

Resigned, Samantha stood. She might as well get it over with.

Chapter Eight

Carefully lifting the glass globe, she lit the lantern, watching the wick burst into flame. The moon was out tonight, round and bright, slanting a silvery glow through her bedroom window. She noticed it when she hurried in to find her shawl.

It wasn't chilly tonight, but then she didn't really need the lantern either. But having the tightly woven shawl wrapped round her shoulders and the black metal lantern made her feel better . . . stronger.

She didn't like going to the barn to confront Jacob Morgan.

Perhaps *confront* wasn't the right word. As he was quick to point out several times, the war was over.

But her personal war wasn't. And asking the rebel to stay was only one battle . . . skirmish, really.

Samantha opened the door, poking the drawstring through the hole so she could reenter without waking Will. Charity stretched, opening one, then both bleary eyes. She seemed relieved when Samantha told her to stay put.

The night was beautiful, clear-skied and balmy for

the first days of October. Samantha was eleven when her family left Massachusetts, twelve when they reached Kansas. Her memories of those times before the journey seemed surreal, almost magical. Samantha realized she built up the past in her mind, transformed the everyday to epic proportions. She hadn't really lived in a mansion, just a nice two-story frame house, with a parlor and dining room, and lacy curtains at the window. The church where her father preached didn't really have a steeple that reached the heavens. But it was neat and tidy, full of straight wooden pews and the smell of beeswax and flowers.

Samantha shook her head. It did no good to dwell on the past. Her family had lived a quiet, comfortable existence until her father, with his wife's whole-hearted support, decided he could best serve God by moving to Kansas and fighting the evils of slavery.

Glancing back at the cabin, Samantha felt a pang of regret. This was her life now. Without her mother. Without her father. Or Luke. Just she and Will, and a poor excuse for a farm in Kansas.

Squaring her shoulders, Samantha walked across the yard to the barn. One lonely whippoorwill sang in the cottonwood tree, and Samantha almost expected to hear Jake's harmonica join it in a duet.

But the rebel wasn't playing tonight. He was probably asleep; Samantha couldn't see any light coming from the barn. She almost turned around right then and there and marched back to the cabin. Who needed him anyway? She and Will had gotten along fine without him. Maybe not *fine,* but they had survived. They could do it again.

She could ride into Hager's Flats tomorrow and see if Jim Farley would come out for a week or so till they finished the harvesting. Suddenly Bundy's threat flashed into her mind. She'd stand watch with the musket if she had to. Besides, what did she think Jacob Morgan could do if Landis Moore and Bundy Atwood really wanted to hurt them? Nothing, that's what.

Her father certainly hadn't been able to stop them.

But she didn't turn back. Cautiously she inched the barn door open.

Jake lay on his back, one arm folded under his head. He watched the moonlight streaming in the slitted window and listened to the creaking door.

His pistol lay within easy reach, but Jake felt no need of it. He knew who was coming into the barn. The night was so silent, even the few animals in the barn were quiet. He was lying here with only the sound of his own breathing to keep him company when he heard the cabin door shut. The grass was dry and brittle, an easy way to mark someone's progress.

Coming from the cabin there were only three possibilities. The dog he eliminated immediately. No barking. Will would have moved more quickly.

That left Samantha.

Jake felt his groin tighten even as he wished she hadn't come. He stayed away from the house tonight because he didn't want to see her again. He'd made up his mind to leave so there was no reason to prolong it.

Warm yellow light overpowered the thin silver glow as she moved toward the stall where he slept. Jake lay still, listening to her come. Someone should warn her about sneaking up on people. If he didn't know who it was, he might be tempted to shoot first and ask questions later.

As it was, he waited until she reached the foot of the stall, then he lifted his head.

"I—I thought you'd be asleep." Samantha held the lantern high with one hand. The other she used to clutch the shawl at her breast.

"I'm not." Jake's eyes narrowed and he tried to make out her features. It was impossible. Her face behind the light was deep in shadow. His head fell back on the cushion of his folded arm.

It was a dismissal, pure and simple. Samantha shifted. Her arm was sore from holding the lantern aloft. She lowered it, her mind working frantically. Asking him to stay was not as easy as she'd supposed—and she thought it would be very hard. But he wasn't making things any easier for her.

She wished he were completely dressed, then realized she'd seen him wearing a lot less. That thought sent hot blood to her cheeks. Still it was disconcerting standing there looking at him. His long form filled the stall. He wore his gray pants and his feet were booted and crossed at the ankles. But his shirt was unbuttoned and open, the flaps spread revealing a wide expanse of hair-sprinkled chest—and no

160

white bandage.

"It isn't raining, is it?"

After the silence that stretched between them, Samantha was surprised by his question. "No. Why?"

"Just thought you might have come to offer me the comforts of your roof."

"No." Samantha felt waves of temper rising and squelched them down. They hadn't gotten on from the moment he regained consciousness, but he never was this rude. But then she wasn't exactly all manners either. She had come disturbing him and had yet to give him a reason. Samantha opened her mouth to tell him and felt her courage slip another notch. Her gaze snagged on his scar. "How is your wound?"

Jake shoved himself to sitting, his arm dangling between raised knees. "Have you come to play Angel of Mercy again?" he asked, just making out the scowl that crossed her face. "Sorry, I'm all better."

She turned on her heel so quickly, it took all Jake's agility to make it to the door before she did. When he did, he leaned his forearm against it, blocking her exit.

"I apologize." Jake dropped his forehead onto his arm. "That was uncalled for." And he wished he knew why in the hell he was treating her like this. Their relationship had never been easy, but he'd never been hurtful. Regardless of the fact that she'd shot him in the first place, he did owe her for saving him.

But mean or no, driving her away was the best way

161

to repay her. Because if she was feeling half the desire he was, being out here alone with him was the last thing she needed. He dropped his arm.

Samantha grasped the latch. Her knees were weak. She didn't think her legs would carry her back to the house. She took a deep breath, but that didn't help. The air smelled of him, rich and sensual. A lethargy crept into her limbs and she twisted her fingers in the knitted shawl to combat it. The lantern hung limply from her other hand, her skirt blocking most of the light, throwing his face into shadow.

But he was looking at her intently. Samantha could tell even though she could see nothing of his eyes but two glittering slits.

She hadn't told him why she'd come to the barn. The realization struck Samantha just as she thought maybe . . . maybe, she could force herself to move. She swallowed. "I need to ask you something."

"What?" His voice was low and huskier than she remembered.

Will was certain all she had to do was ask, but seeing him now, hearing him, Samantha's doubts rushed to the forefront. But she wouldn't give up without trying. That had never been her way, and now more than ever she needed to fight for what little she and Will had.

Her shoulders straightened, the languid mood of moments ago shoved aside. Lifting the lantern she studied his face. "I'd like you to stay on."

"No."

Relief from making her request was shortlived as

his succinct reply sunk in. She watched his retreating back. His dismissal was complete.

It took Samantha a moment to realize it. When she did, anger flushed out any remnants of desire she'd felt.

"Why not?" She followed him to the front of his horse's stall. His horse had eaten her grain and pastured in her paddock. And Lord knew, Jacob Morgan had consumed enough of her food to feed an army. She'd nursed him, for heaven's sake! He owed her.

Never mind that she'd shot him in the first place. Samantha's shoulders slumped forward. What was she thinking? Of course it mattered that she shot him. But that didn't mean he couldn't stay . . . just for a little while. But he wouldn't even explain why. He moved to the far side of his bay's head, rubbing her neck.

"I'm not staying," was all he said in response.

"But you don't understand. I . . . we need your help. Bundy Atwood—"

"Seemed pretty reasonable to me this afternoon." Jake leveled a look at her. "He's not the first man to return from war to find his intended has changed her mind."

"What?" Samantha couldn't believe what he was saying. She also was getting tired of holding the lantern. With jerky motions she hung it from a hook beside the stall. "What are you talking about?"

Jake gave a final rub to his horse, then turned toward his own stall. He wished she'd just leave, but he

163

didn't think that would happen until he explained himself. His wishes had a habit of falling short lately. Steeling himself he looked back over his shoulder. "I'm talking about a man being off to war for four years and returning to find there's nothing left."

"And you think that's what happened to Bundy Atwood?" Samantha swallowed. Was that what had happened to Jake? Pushing that from her mind, she took a step toward him. She didn't really care what had happened to him.

Jake shrugged, feeling a twinge of pain near his left shoulder. "That's what Atwood thinks."

"It's just not true." Samantha threw her hands up, resisting the urge to grab hold of his arm and shake some sense into him. "It didn't happen that way. And what's more, Bundy doesn't believe it did. He lied to you."

Jake shrugged again, then smoothed out the corner of his blanket-bed with his boot toe. He didn't look at her. "I'm going to sleep now. I suggest you go back to the house and do the same."

Another dismissal. Samantha heard her teeth gnash as she clenched her jaw. "And you're leaving in the morning?"

"I said I was." Jake shrugged out of his shirt. The honey-soft glow from the lantern brushed over his body, throwing his arms and chest into patterns of light and shadow. Samantha pressed on.

"He threatened me." Her voice started low, almost calm, but intensified as she continued. "He said if I were nice to him, he'd see that my corn crop wasn't destroyed."

Jake, who'd felt the urge to do more than threaten her a time or two, grimaced. "Maybe he just wants to take care of you. But if you don't want him, just tell him so and be done with it."

"Are you crazy?" Samantha gave up the battle and grabbed his arm. His eyes narrowed as he looked down at her hand but she didn't care. "Bundy Atwood is a liar. He makes a game of bullying innocent people and you . . . you believe him because he fought for the blasted Confederacy. Brothers in arms and—"

Samantha never had the chance to finish. Jake came at her so quickly, pushing her against the side of the stall, shoving the air from her lungs with his big body. His face was lowered, close to hers, and the vertical line between his brow deepened.

"Listen, I never asked to come here and get mixed up with you. And God knows I never asked you to shoot me. So why don't you just wise up and let me alone. I'm no hero who's going to come along and make everything right.

"Atwood threatened you. Well, I'm sorry for that, but it's not easy having everything you ever loved stripped away from you. Maybe he just wants to forget the war ever happened and start over." Jake paused. "Something you'd be smart to do too."

He stepped back, but was still close enough for Samantha to feel the imprint of his large body on hers. "He's the one who won't forget about the war.

165

He's—"

"Just tell me this." Jake cupped her shoulders with his hands. "Did you ever promise to marry him?"

"Yes, but I—"

"But you what?" Jake's scowl deepened. "You changed your mind, fine. You don't want him sniffing around your skirts. That's fine too. You tell him. But don't think keeping me here is going to help. Because unless I get out of here, I'm going to be doing a hell of a lot more than sniff at your skirts."

Samantha's eyes flew open. Jake's expression was hard, as if his face were chiseled in granite. Anger flared his nostrils, tightened the lines of his mouth. But in his eyes, Samantha noticed something more. The light of desire. It should have frightened her more than the anger, much more. Especially in light of his words. But she could only stand there, her back against the stall, her breathing shallow and filled with his scent, and stare.

He shocked her. Jake took one step back, then another, allowing her plenty of room to rush by him and make a beeline for her nice safe cabin. She'd pull the welcome cord, throw herself onto her bed, and hate him. And be a damn sight better off after he rode out.

But she didn't move. She just continued to stare at him with those big blue—Jake took a deep breath—beautiful eyes. "What's the matter? Don't you believe me?"

Samantha tried to swallow but couldn't. She opened her mouth to answer him, though she had no idea what to say. But it didn't matter. Before she could focus on a clear thought, he grabbed her, crushing her against his chest and pulling her up to taste her mouth.

His lips were hard, unyielding, but the tongue that stole into her mouth was satin smooth and sensual. Samantha's head swam. Occasionally a thought would drift by that she should stop him — or at least try — but then he'd shift his mouth, reaching farther with his tongue, and she lost any desire to do anything.

She was drowning in him. Her hands clasped his elbows to keep her from falling. No longer were her knees just weak; they seemed nonexistent.

And that was made all the more real when he pushed her away. His movement wasn't rough or even harsh, but Samantha's palms flattened against the stall side to keep her from falling. It was so sudden, this move from glorious sensations to the cold aloneness she felt now.

His breathing was shallow, nearly as ragged as hers as Samantha stared up at him with startled eyes. She should be shocked. She should force her legs to motion, send them running from the barn in virtuous haste. He wouldn't follow. She knew that as surely as she knew she couldn't flee.

"Now do you understand?" Jake made his voice gruff. She still only stared at him. He told himself to turn away. If she couldn't leave, he should. A walk in the balmy air might help, might soothe his aroused state. But like her, he seemed rooted to the spot.

And then her hands, those same small hands that had nursed him so gently, came up, hesitantly at first, then with greater resolve, and locked around his neck. She rose on tiptoe, her breast pressing against his chest, and pulled him down to her.

Even as he succumbed, moving slowly toward the softness of her mouth, warning bells rang in his head. *Don't do this to her. She may think she knows what you're about, but she doesn't.* But the sweetness of her lips obliterated the caution, and as his fingers locked in the tangle of her braided hair, only a faint buzzing rang in his ears.

Had it been this way before? God help him, he couldn't remember. All he knew was the warmth and passion of her as he moved his mouth across hers. And then only touching her there wasn't nearly enough.

Her neck was warm, her shoulders rounded as he followed a path down her body. His hands spread, curving around her ribs, finding the underside of her unfettered breasts with his thumbs. The swell beckoned, and as he crested the swollen mounds, Jake heard her sensual moan.

How he'd missed that sound, as pure and sweet as sunshine.

But there was more he'd missed, much more.

Jake's lips skimmed across her cheek, nibbled the tip of her ear, then rushed back to taste again the honeyed mouth. And his fingers fumbled with the small bone buttons that ran from the starched collar to the tapered waist of her dress. Trembling fingers that had ofttimes been praised for their sharp, precise work now found so simple a task as unfastening difficult.

Her skin was petal soft beneath the plain calico gown, and pale as moonlight. Jake touched her tentatively, pulling away to watch her as his fingers trailed along her collarbone. Her golden-tipped lashes lifted slowly, seductively, and Jake sucked in his breath at the expression of longing in her eyes. Eyes gone dark with passion.

He knew then she wouldn't stop him. If he didn't call a halt to this madness, they would end up in the straw making wild, shattering love. But he couldn't stop. Lord help him, he couldn't.

Samantha ran her tongue lazily across her bottom lip. It felt tender and swollen and it tasted of him. She should have been repulsed. But she wasn't. Oh my, how could she feel this way about a stranger . . . a Rebel. She knew almost nothing about him. He was a man who spoke of one thing while in the clutches of fevered sleep, and of something else again while awake. Yet she could no more stop what was happening than cause the endless prairie wind to cease.

His fingers dipped lower. They skirted the upper swell of her breasts, then hastened to undo the remaining buttons. His knuckles abraded her skin, then the threadbare cotton of her chemise. Her nipples tightened almost painfully and Samantha arched toward him.

The sudden yank of the dress and shift down over

her shoulders made Samantha gasp. But one glance at his face as he stared at her bared breasts and she lost all thought of protest. The clear green eyes were nearly black, and the heavy lids made him appear more dark fantasy than man. His gaze scorched her. Her nipples hardened and thrust out as if begging for his touch.

His finger grazed the taut tip, then his tongue, and Samantha came close to swooning onto the straw-covered floor. His hands grasped her hips, and pulled her flush to his lower body as his head swooped down. His mouth surrounded her nipple with fiery, moist heat and Samantha cried out. Her head rolled to one side then the other as he feasted on her breasts.

Samantha longed to touch him but her arms were caught, held fast at the elbows by the fabric of her gown. She moaned his name and received a long, open-mouthed kiss in return. And then he was moving down her again, past the thrust of her breasts to the downy skin below. His lips skimmed across her; his bristle of whiskers sent tingles up her spine and she sighed.

He dropped to his knees, his hands clutching her buttocks, his hot breath searing through the skirt and single petticoat covering her. And then her legs did give out. Slowly she sank, sliding down his body until he cupped her face and kissed her again.

He seemed to sense her need to touch him, for he pulled at her sleeves, freeing her arms.

His skin was smooth and sleek with sweat.

Samantha couldn't get enough of running her hands over him. Her breasts were pressed to his naked chest, her thighs to his, and the rock-hard evidence of his desire for her nudged her soft stomach.

Jake shifted and she writhed, and together they tumbled toward his blanket. Instinctively Jake twisted to absorb the brunt of the fall on himself. Pain replaced passion as white hot agony shot from his wound. "Damn," was all he managed to grit between his clenched teeth as he rolled onto his back.

"What is it?" Momentarily bewildered, Samantha lay atop him, her pale breasts mounds of creamy softness pressed against his darker chest. The sides of the stall threw them in shadow but Samantha could make out the lines of pain around his mouth. "Oh, my heavens. Your wound. How could I have forgotten?"

"Most likely the same way I forgot," Jake countered. The pain was beginning to subside into a dull ache.

"Did you open it? Is it bleeding?"

"No."

"What can I do?"

Jake shifted, trying to keep his expression sober. She was staring down at him so seriously. "If you could move just a little."

"Oh my. I'm hurting you." Embarrassed color flooded Samantha as she glanced down to see herself sprawled, half naked, on top of him. "Let me get up."

"No." Jake grabbed her arm. "Just wriggle over

171

this way a bit."

"But —" Samantha's words were cut off by a kiss so deep and thorough that she forgot to protest. By the time it was over, his right hand was above her stocking, stroking her thigh, and her legs were spread over his hips.

Jake rolled to his side, taking Samantha with him. She tumbled onto the wool blanket. The last pins securing her hair fell out, spilling golden curls that fanned out, framing her face. And then he was atop her, supporting his weight on the elbow of his right arm.

Her skirts had risen, tangled with her legs, and Jake pushed them higher. His hand splayed across her bare hip then, seeking a more intimate haven, delved between her legs. Her eyes sprang open when he touched her, gently stroking the tender flesh that ached for him. And then she moaned as his finger became bolder and fiery desire washed over her.

Jake wasn't certain how he managed to unfasten the buttons of his pants. All he knew was one moment he was watching her eyes flutter shut and the next pressing into her moist heat. She was tight but wet with desire and he came into her with one strong thrust.

Her cry of pain rang in his ears, and Jake stopped, forcing himself to be still until sweat broke out on his forehead. He hadn't thought about her being a virgin. Bundy Atwood's remarks this afternoon implied a relationship that went beyond handholding and chaste kisses. He found Atwood's references to

Samantha annoying, and the man himself contemptible, but now Jake realized he'd believed his lies. Maybe he just wanted to believe them.

But now it was obvious they weren't true.

Jake shifted. He could barely make out her features. "Are you all right?"

"Yes." Her answer was little more than a breath of air. And then she moved, fractionally at first, but as Jake took up the rhythm, more smoothly. She reached for something, her mind, her body, her soul, all strove for the crest of the wave. She slipped and slid, meeting the hard intensity of his body, straining toward something she couldn't define.

His control vanished. Her heat, the moist movements of her body, obliterated all but the most primal need. Jake tried to stem the tide rushing through him, to prolong the pleasure, but too long his body had endured the ache of abstinence. Jake exploded inside her, thrusting deep and convulsively.

He rolled away quickly. The dull pain he'd felt around his wound didn't seem so dull anymore. And supporting himself on one trembling arm was impossible. His breathing was ragged and a sudden deep lethargy swept over him. He tried to focus his mind on what had happened, but couldn't. All Jake knew was that he hadn't lost control like that in a very long time. Not since his randy youth.

Turning his head, he studied the woman beside him. She lay on the farthest corner of the blanket. He hadn't heard her move. Her eyes were closed, and her breathing shallow. Jake watched the erotic rise

173

and fall of her breasts before forcing his attention back to her face. She looked small and fragile, and Jake felt guilt flood him. He should have been gentler with her . . . hell, he should never have touched her.

"Samantha." His hand reached out to where hers lay limp on the blanket.

She jerked it away. "Don't say anything." Samantha sighed and sat up. Why hadn't she noticed how itchy the blanket was before, or how strongly it smelled of straw?

He expected her to be meek, even weepy. She looked so vulnerable lying there, and Jake had lots of experience with that reaction. But she wasn't crying, or even whimpering. She just stared at him, disbelief shadowing her blue eyes.

"I'm sorry." The words seemed banal, and Jake regretted them the moment they were out of his mouth. Besides, he had no idea what part of it he was apologizing for.

Her eyes widened for a fraction of a second before she turned away. "It wasn't your fault. I shouldn't have come out here." Samantha bit her bottom lip. If she didn't get away from here, she was going to cry, and cry hysterically. He'd already witnessed her bawling once. She didn't want him to see her again. Especially with this . . . this . . . whatever it was, as the cause.

Twisting about, Samantha tried to find a sleeve. Her dress was wrinkled and littered with straw, and for the life of her, she couldn't find the right hole.

174

"Let me help you."

"No!" Samantha's eyes closed as she pulled her arm away from his fingers. "I can do it." Pushing to her feet, she scurried behind the stall side, crouching down to hide herself from his eyes. She squirmed and struggled, tearing the worn cotton, but finally managing to shove her arms into the sleeves. Her fingers trembled as she buttoned the front as quickly as she could. She didn't want him coming behind the meager partition to offer any more assistance.

He didn't.

By the time Samantha managed to right her clothes as best she could, she'd also managed to fight back the desire to cry. Or worse, to throw herself into his arms and beg him not to leave her.

She stood, straightening her skirts, and started toward the barn door without looking toward the stall where they had made love. She almost made it out of the barn before his voice stopped her.

"Are you sure you're all right?"

Samantha turned. He was standing, leaning against the post, his arms crossed loosely. He'd pulled up his pants, but was still shirtless. Samantha swallowed, remembering how his tawny skin felt beneath her fingers. Determined, she pushed that thought aside. With her chin raised, she looked him squarely in the eye. "I'm fine. Good night, Captain Morgan." It sounded ridiculous, calling him by so formal a title after what they had just done, but at least her voice was firm. And her legs were strong as they carried her across the yard.

He'd responded to her words, but as Samantha crept into the cabin she realized that he'd said not good night, but good-bye.

She couldn't sleep. Not even after scrubbing herself with the water in the pitcher and putting on her night rail. Samantha spent the night in the rocking chair, her knees tucked under her chin.

Near dawn she heard Will climb down the ladder from the loft. He made his way across the parlor, calling to Charity before going outside. Less than five minutes later he was back, bursting through the door and shouting.

Samantha shut her eyes as he called to her from the other room. "Sam! Sam! He's gone."

Chapter Nine

Flames sizzled and smoke spiraled into the morning sky as Jake poured dregs from his coffeepot on the small campfire. How could he have forgotten in three short weeks how terrible his coffee tasted? And his cooking was even worse. Scraping the congealed beans from the skillet, Jake tried not to compare his meager fare with the tender biscuits Samantha would be pulling from her Dutch oven about now.

No doubt about it, that woman could cook.

"It's not her culinary skills you can't get off your mind," Jake mumbled to himself as he rolled his blanket. He stood, stretching the kinks from his body — still favoring his left side — and hiked the saddle over his horse. He stopped a little past midnight thinking to make camp and get some sleep before heading south.

He might as well have stayed in the saddle for all the rest he got. He tossed and turned, cursing the hard ground, the droning mosquitoes, even the mournful call of a lonesome wolf. In short, everything but the real problem.

He'd treated her badly.

Never mind that she'd shot him; that she hated the sight of his uniform; that her acrid tongue could sometimes slice as neat as a knife. He'd treated her badly.

Jake tried to soothe his conscience by telling himself she wanted him too. But it didn't work. Jake tightened the cinch. He was older, certainly more experienced, and he should have stopped it.

But the truth was, he hadn't wanted to stop. So he'd used her, and now he couldn't get her or what they did on his itchy wool blanket out of his mind. And worse, to his way of thinking, Jake knew guilt wasn't the only reason he couldn't let thoughts of her go.

"Howdy."

Jake grabbed for his revolver, twisting toward the sound of the voice in one fluid motion. His horse pawed the ground and Jake cocked the gun, squinting into the early morning sun. Damn careless of him to let someone come riding into his camp without even hearing it. Another reason to put Samantha Lowery firmly from his mind.

"Ain't no call for that. I'm a Reb, like you." The man sitting on the spotted mare did sport several pieces of a Confederate uniform, but during four long years Jake had learned not every Southerner was a friend.

He kept the gun leveled. "What do you want?"

"Nothing much. Saw smoke from your fire." The man climbed down from his horse, seemingly oblivious to the loaded gun pointed his way. Jake couldn't decide if he was brave or crazy. "Thought you might like some company. I like company."

Jake watched through narrowed eyes as the stranger

squatted by the drowned fire that offered nothing in the way of heat. The man was short and squat, pudgy in a soft doughy way. His face was broad and guilelessly open as he looked up at Jake.

"Well, do ya?"

"Do I what?" He couldn't explain why, but Jake was finding it hard to keep a gun trained on the man.

"Like company?" he said as if he was asking the most natural thing in the world, and Jake was remiss in not answering.

"I suppose. But I'm not really after any right now."

"I'll wait," the man said and settled back on his haunches, presumably to do just that.

The words were so innocently delivered that for a moment Jake could only stare. Noticing the revolver still trained at the man's back, Jake reholstered it. "Listen friend—"

"Abner. Abner Moore. But you can call me Ab. All my friends do."

"Sure, Ab." Jake hunched down beside him and looked into his eyes. He'd run into people like this before, when he was practicing medicine. Even though Abner Moore had the body of a—Jake made a quick survey—forty-year-old man, his mind had settled in at a much younger age. "I'm Jake."

Shifting, Jake took a look around. There didn't appear to be anyone with Ab. He was unarmed from what Jake could tell from looking at his too large, dirt-streaked clothing.

"Jake," the man repeated, then gave an open smile showing the absence of several teeth. Then just as quickly his expression turned serious. "You ever kill you any of them Yankee bastards?"

A sudden vision of prisoners who'd died under his care flashed into Jake's mind. "Yeah, I suppose I did," he said, knowing his answer didn't address what Ab meant. But then he wasn't sure Ab knew what he meant. His conversation reminded Jake of someone a good deal younger than Will. Especially when he let out a shrill Rebel yell and flopped back on his rear.

"I knowed it. I just knowed you was one of us." He was grinning again, and Jake shook off the uncomfortable feeling that gave him. "I never got me any of them blue bellies myself, but Landis said there's still time."

"Time?" Jake managed a glance about him to assure himself that no one else was around.

"Yeah, you know. Maybe there's still time for me to kill me some."

The words would have been bad enough spoken with malice, but Jake didn't feel there was enough understanding in Ab for that. It was as if he was parroting something he'd heard. "The war's over," Jake said calmly. Every time Ab trained his expressionless eyes on him, Jake felt the hackles at the back of his neck bristle.

Ab made a sound through his lips which Jake took to show disagreement. He didn't wipe away the spittle. Landis says ain't never gonna be over. Landis says we gotta show—"

"Who's Landis?"

"My brother." Ab's expression seemed to indicate he thought Jake should know that. "He takes care of me. He and Bundy, and—"

"Bundy Atwood?" It was more than the back of his neck that was prickling now.

"Yeah." Ab backhanded his mouth. "He's my friend. Killed hisself a lot of damn bluebellies, he did. Now he's going to kill more. Gonna take care of his woman too, bloody bitch."

Ab delivered his obscenities with the same causal tone he talked of killing. The lack of emotion was unnerving. Jake tried to match his tone. "What woman is that?"

Again the expression of disbelief. "Damn Samantha Lowery, the bitch." He spoke the phrase as if they were all part of Samantha's name. Jake supposed he'd heard it often enough to believe it. "But Bundy's going to take care of her. Said I could help. I like that, sticking my poker in women. You like to do that, Jake?"

It took a moment for Jake to control himself enough to answer. He had the strongest desire to plant his fist squarely in Ab's flabby jaw, to pull his revolver and plug him full of holes. Instead he forced himself to remember whom he was dealing with. He was spared answering as Ab went on telling how Landis took him to town to see Miss Betsy sometimes. But he thought he was going to like doing it to the Yankee bitch more, 'cause she was prettier.

"Course, Bundy, he says everyone will get his turn. Bundy's nice. He's my friend."

"Listen, Ab." Jake stood. "I'm going to be on my way now."

"I'll come with you."

"No. I don't think you should."

"But Landis says I ain't to go nowhere by myself. He

181

says I might get into trouble."

Jake stared down at the hulk of a man and felt something close to pity. An emotion the situation didn't warrant, he assured himself. "Where's your brother now?"

"That way." Ab pointed one ham hock of a hand in the direction he'd come. When Jake followed the motion, he noticed a small group of mounted men coming down the road, headed in their direction.

Reaching for his gun was second nature.

Ab noticed the reaction. He rolled over to his knees, following Jake's gaze. A big grin spread across his face. "It's Landis," he said, hefting himself up. "You ain't going to need that. You're my friend."

Jake was unprepared for the shove Ab gave his hand, but he managed to hang on to his revolver. He also decided holstering it might be his best course at the present. The mounted men had seen his camp and were wasting no time descending upon it. And Ab was ambling off to meet them. Jake slid the gun down his hip and waited.

"Landis!" Ab reached up, grabbing the bridle of the lead horse, and Jake got his first look at Landis Moore. He was small-framed, especially in comparison to his giant of a brother, with gray-washed black hair curling down his neck and a broad pockmarked face. His eyes were blue, pale, almost silvery in the early light, and they were leveled in anger at Ab.

"What the hell you think you're doin', boy, running off like that?"

"I weren't running, Landis." Ab's head was bent close to the horses, and he continually rubbed the reins

182

nervously. "It's just that I was up early and went out ridin'. And I found a friend."

Ab swirled around toward Jake, and for the first time Landis seemed to notice him. Not that Jake had gone unobserved during the conversation between the Moores. Jake had seen the scrutiny of the two other riders.

But now Landis Moore's eyes were on him, cold and steady. Jake met his stare and couldn't help thinking of the fear Samantha felt for him. That icy glare would frighten anyone.

"What's your name, stranger?"

"His name is Jake, Landis, and he's my friend." Ab's head was bobbing up and down as if it sat on a loose spring.

"That right?" Landis demanded.

"What? That my name is Jake, or that I'm Ab's friend?" Jake kept his eyes on Landis, but he could sense the two other men, neither of whom he'd ever seen before, moving toward their leader.

Landis studied him a moment, and then a smile crossed his face that in no way softened the frigid stare. "Both."

Jake shifted, his hand resting against his gun. "I'm Jake Morgan. Your brother here wandered into my camp this morning."

"He's a Reb, Landis!"

"I can see that, Ab."

Jake had pulled on his gray tunic to help fight off the chill of the previous night. When Jake had ridden off from Appomattox at the end of the war, it hadn't occurred to him to toss out his clothes. Pants and coats had been hard enough to come by during the four years of war. They weren't something to be taken lightly. Nor, Jake had discovered, were they something to be worn lightly.

"He killed him a lot of Yankee bastards. Told me so," Ab continued.

"Did he now?" Landis rose up in his saddle and glanced around. "Where's your horse, Ab?"

"Left him back there, behind them trees."

"Go get him."

"Sure, Landis." Ab shuffled to the side. "Where's Bundy and Jimmy?"

"Off looking for you, Ab." Landis kicked his foot free of the stirrup and dismounted. "We weren't sure which way you'd gone."

"Sorry, Landis." Ab dropped to his knees in the dust at his brother's feet. "It won't happen again."

"That's what you said last time." Landis stepped aside as Ab shielded his head against a blow. "We'll finish this later," Landis admonished, bringing a derisive chuckle from the other two. "Right now I want to talk to Jake here."

"He's my friend."

"I know. Now go get your horse."

Jake watched Ab scurry off, followed by one of the men who were still mounted. The other sat, his hands crossed on the pommel, and waited.

Landis Moore glanced back toward where his brother had disappeared through some bushes, then back at Jake. "He's slow." He tapped a finger to the side of his head. "Been that way since he was born. Nothing to do about it but keep an eye on him. But sometimes he makes that hard. I appreciate what you done for him."

"I didn't do anything." Jake walked toward his horse and unlooped the reins.

"Now there's where we differ in opinion." Landis moved between Jake and his horse. "No telling what might have happened if you hadn't been here."

Jake cocked his head and waited. Landis Moore was hard to read, but Jake was pretty sure there was more going on here than a simple thank-you.

"Where you headed?"

"Why?"

Again came that smile that seemed more like he was baring his teeth. "It's not just idle curiosity, let me assure you. I'm Landis Moore." He paused as if he thought Jake should recognize the name, but when there was no reaction forthcoming, he continued, "I'm sort of the unofficial head of the Reb soldiers in these parts."

Jake shrugged. "I'm just passing through."

"Too bad. We could have used someone like you. The South needs every man she can get."

"Like I said—"

"Yeah, you're just passing through."

Jake gathered up the reins and nudged Moore aside. It was all he could do not to question the man about Samantha and Will. But he knew it wouldn't be a good idea to reveal what Ab had told him. Nor did he think he'd get anything resembling the truth for an answer.

Settling into the saddle with a soft creak of leather, Jake urged his mount forward. After a few steps he pulled back on the reins. "You know, Moore," Jake said, twisting around to face the man. "I was under the impression the war was over."

"Not by a long shot, boy. Not by a long shot."

"Is everything satisfactory?" Samantha folded her hands in her lap, squeezing her fingers till they were white. She didn't like dealing with Peggy Keane, but there was no help for it. Still, she didn't like the way the woman was examining the tiny stitches on the sleeve of the dress Samantha just brought her.

Peggy looked up, her brown eyes focusing on Samantha as if she'd forgotten her presence. "I suppose it will have to do," she said after a moment's hesitation. She stood, holding the gown up to her ample bosom, and twisted, letting the skirt float around her. "I had hoped for a more pronounced bustle."

Samantha bit her tongue to keep from suggesting she had more than enough of her own. Peggy Keane's waist was tiny, but unlike Samantha she was well endowed in other areas. Areas that Peggy had once assured Samantha appealed to men. That had been before the war, before Samantha's father's death. The girls had attended school together, and though they hadn't actually been friends, they had known each other.

Peggy was two years older, eons more mature, and thanks to the war, much, much wealthier. As Samantha looked around the parlor now, it was difficult to believe that Peggy used to live in a soddy. But Peggy had married a man twenty years her senior. And Thadeus Keane had grown rich delivering corn and other grain to the soldiers during the war. Rumor had it he didn't much care which side he sold to as long as they paid in gold.

Samantha sat forward on the horsehair sofa. It was a deep royal red that matched the heavy curtains hanging at the windows, blocking the meager air. The room was stifling, and Samantha tried not to show her impatience. She'd made enough dresses for Peggy to know that this was as much a part of the selling process as making the dress. But Peggy paid well, when she finally got around to handing over the money. And she and Will sorely needed the money.

But today Samantha wasn't in the mood to watch Peggy preen about, moving gingerly between the heavy pieces of furniture. She'd brought the wagon wheel to town, strapped on the side of the mule, and she wanted to get it to the smithy in time for him to fix it today.

She'd considered stopping there first, but even though Samantha had carefully wrapped Peggy's gown in sheets, she didn't want to take any chances on soiling it.

"Well, what do you think?" Peggy obviously was tired of waiting for Samantha's compliments. "Won't this be the most beautiful gown at the town ball?"

"Yes." Samantha swallowed her pride and smiled. What Peggy really meant was won't I be the most beautiful woman at the ball. Not really a ball, Samantha reminded herself. The town of Hager's Flats wasn't the place for a ball. But they did have dances now and then, which Peggy seemed determined to call balls.

Samantha had to admit she probably would be the

187

prettiest woman there. At least the men would think so. But then Samantha never went so she really didn't know.

A sudden vision flashed into her mind. She was dressed in a gown of shimmering silk, soft as a whisper, with her hair piled high. She was dancing, her head thrown back in laughter, her eyes on only one man, her partner.

Jake.

A smiling Jake, like in the daguerreotype.

Samantha grimaced. She'd worked so hard to purge him from her mind, and there he was, tall and handsome, and . . . Samantha felt tears sting her eyes and glanced toward the clock ticking loudly on the mantle. She would forget about him. She would!

"I really need to be getting on my way. So if you'd — "

"You aren't staying for tea?"

"I can't." Samantha lowered her lashes. Peggy was angry and would likely pay less for the gown because of her snit. Samantha rushed on to explain. "I need to take a wheel over to the blacksmith's and have it fixed before I go home. Will's there alone, and I don't like leaving him too long." She didn't mention Landis Moore or Bundy Atwood. Samantha had spoken to Peggy about them once before and been chided for exaggerating.

"Oh, pooh. Will's near grown." Peggy flopped down in a plush chair, tossing aside the gown Samantha had spent so much time on. "I counted on you visiting for a while."

"I'd like to, really," Samantha said to convince Peggy. "But I can't. Not this time."

"When are you coming back to town?"

"I don't know," Samantha answered honestly. "We have to be harvesting soon, and . . ." That was something else she had to do today. See if Jim Farley would come out and help with the corn.

"All you ever do is work," Peggy complained.

There was nothing to say to that, so Samantha only stared. She couldn't help feeling a twinge of pity for Peggy, though Lord help her, she didn't know why. The women of the town seemed to avoid her, even though she had the biggest and only brick house, and her clothes were the finest. And it couldn't be much fun married to old Thadeus. But then Samantha had heard talk that Peggy didn't let a little thing like marriage keep her from her flirtations.

Be that as it may, Samantha had things to do, and limited time to do them. She walked over to where Peggy sat pouting in the chair. "I really do have to go."

"Oh, all right." Peggy flounced up and yanked out a drawer in the dark oak secretary. "Here's the money for the dress." She plunked some coins into Samantha's outstretched hand.

Samantha closed her fingers, too proud to count it. "Thank you. Let me know if I can make anything else for you."

"I don't know." Peggy tossed her sable ringlets. "I've been thinking of sending to St. Louis for my clothes."

Samantha only nodded as she saw herself to the door. She didn't really think Peggy would go through with her threat. She enjoyed flaunting her wealth in front of Samantha too much. Still, it would be nice if

189

Samantha could get some more steady custumers for her sewing. The trouble was, most of the women sewed for themselves.

The sun bore down on Samantha as she descended the steps from the Keane home. Glancing over her shoulder, she decided it really was pretentious. Especially with the rest of the town so primitive by comparison. Samantha shook her head as she untied Prudence, the mule, from the fence post and led her down the dust-choked street.

She shouldn't be so hard on Hager's Flats. There was a hotel, two churches, and a school. Not to mention the bank and mercantile. Several saloons, quiet now in the middle of the day, opened onto the main street. Hager's Flats had definitely grown since she'd come here as a child of twelve. Samantha caught sight of the sheriff leaning against the hotel porch post. He touched his hat in greeting, and Samantha nodded. Sheriff Hughes didn't work at hiding his Southern sympathies. But most people didn't realize how strong they really were. If it hadn't been for her father's death, Samantha wouldn't either.

The blacksmith shop was empty, and Samantha searched out back to find Linc Jones the Smithy. After looking at the wheel, he assured Samantha he could fix it. And that it wouldn't take very long.

Which gave her time to see about hiring Farley. Samantha knew he kept a room over the newspaper office, but after walking there and climbing the rickety stairs, no one answered her knock. Inquiring downstairs didn't help either.

"We don't see much of Jim here," Walt Doolittle, the

paper's editor, informed her. "He's not much of a reader." This comment set off a guffaw from Walt's assistant, as Samantha expressed her thanks and headed back outside.

The saloons seemed the next logical place to look, but Samantha didn't like the idea. Still she and Will needed the help. Taking a steadying breath, she pushed open the door of the one closest to the newspaper office.

The few patrons glanced up, but none of them was Jim Farley, so Samantha moved on. She tried two other establishments, each time with no success. Samantha wiped the back of her hand across her brow. She was hot and tired, and prickles of hair escaped the tight bun at her nape, making her feel more uncomfortable. A drink of water would taste wonderful, but Samantha wasn't about to ask for one in a saloon, and she wasn't in the mood to visit with any of the townspeople she knew, much less return to Peggy Keane's house.

Instead she trudged up the street toward another saloon. She doubted Jim was there. It was considered by the townspeople as the best of the lot. The place was frequented by the town's more respectable people. And Jim Farley wasn't in that category. But who knew what he might do. Maybe he'd wandered into it by mistake.

Passing the hotel, Samantha noted that Sheriff Hughes no longer thought it necessary to hold up the building by leaning on it. She wasn't interested enough to speculate on where he might be, but as she walked by his office, he surprised her by stepping out the door.

"Miss Lowery," he called when she continued past him. "I need to speak with you a minute."

"I'm looking for Jim Farley," Samantha gave as an excuse for not engaging in any discussion with the sheriff. She never forgave him for his reaction when her father died.

"Haven't seen him." Ralph Hughes's mouth quirked with irritation. "But I want you to come in here."

"I really don't see—" Samantha tried to jerk her arm away from the sheriff's hold as he propelled her through the doorway.

"Do you know this man?"

"Sheriff, I—" Samantha's protest died on her lips. Her eyes may not have adjusted to the dim light in the dingy office, but she'd recognize the form, the height, and the broad shoulders anywhere. "What are *you* doing here?"

"I'm charmed to see you again, too," Jake said sarcastically. It had been a long day, and it wasn't even close to over. And now he'd broken his own newly formed rule about minding his own business—and apparently for nothing.

"Can I take that as a yes?" Hughes rested his considerable girth against the paper-littered desk.

Samantha tore her eyes away from Jake. She wasn't prepared for the consuming emotions that engulfed her. "Yes, I know him."

"Well, he rode in here today, telling me some disturbing things about you, Miss Lowery."

Her gaze flew back to meet Jake's, but his expression was unreadable. There was only one disturbing thing he could have told the sheriff, and she should

MORE PASSION AND ADVENTURE AWAIT... YOUR TRIP TO A BIG ADVENTUROUS WORLD BEGINS WHEN YOU ACCEPT YOUR FIRST 4 NOVELS ABSOLUTELY *FREE* (AN $18.00 VALUE)

Accept your Free gift and start to experience more of the passion and adventure you like in a historical romance novel. Each Zebra novel is filled with proud men, spirited women and tempestuous love that you'll remember long after you turn the last page.

Zebra Historical Romances are the finest novels of their kind. They are written by authors who really know how to weave tales of romance and adventure in the historical settings you love. You'll feel like you've actually gone back in time with the thrilling stories that each Zebra novel offers.

GET YOUR FREE GIFT WITH THE START OF YOUR HOME SUBSCRIPTION

Our readers tell us that these books sell out very fast in book stores and often they miss the newest titles. So Zebra has made arrangements for you to receive the four newest novels published each month.

You'll be guaranteed that you'll never miss a title, and home delivery is so convenient. And to show you just how easy it is to get Zebra Historical Romances, we'll send you your first 4 books absolutely FREE! Our gift to you just for trying our home subscription service.

BIG SAVINGS AND FREE HOME DELIVERY

Each month, you'll receive the four newest titles as soon as they are published. You'll probably receive them even before the bookstores do. What's more, you may preview these exciting novels free for 10 days. If you like them as much as we think you will, just pay the low preferred subscriber's price of just $3.75 each. *You'll save $3.00 each month off the publisher's price.* AND, your savings are even greater because there are never any shipping, handling or other hidden charges—FREE Home Delivery. Of course you can return any shipment within 10 days for full credit, no questions asked. There is no minimum number of books you must buy.

4 FREE BOOKS

TO GET YOUR 4 FREE BOOKS WORTH $18.00 — MAIL IN THE FREE BOOK CERTIFICATE T O D A Y

Fill in the Free Book Certificate below, and we'll send your FREE BOOKS to you as soon as we receive it.

If the certificate is missing below, write to: Zebra Home Subscription Service, Inc., P.O. Box 5214, 120 Brighton Road, Clifton, New Jersey 07015-5214.

FREE BOOK CERTIFICATE

4 FREE BOOKS

ZEBRA HOME SUBSCRIPTION SERVICE, INC.

YES! Please start my subscription to Zebra Historical Romances and send me my first 4 books absolutely FREE. I understand that each month I may preview four new Zebra Historical Romances free for 10 days. If I'm not satisfied with them, I may return the four books within 10 days and owe nothing. Otherwise, I will pay the low preferred subscriber's price of just $3.75 each; a total of $15.00, *a savings off the publisher's price of $3.00.* I may return any shipment and I may cancel this subscription at any time. There is no obligation to buy any shipment and there are no shipping, handling or other hidden charges. Regardless of what I decide, the four free books are mine to keep.

NAME _____

ADDRESS _____ APT _____

CITY _____ STATE ____ ZIP _____

TELEPHONE (____) _____

SIGNATURE _____
(if under 18, parent or guardian must sign)

Terms, offer and prices subject to change without notice. Subscription subject to acceptance by Zebra Books. Zebra Books reserves the right to reject any order or cancel any subscription.

have expected it. The fact that she hadn't — had almost forgotten the extent of their differences — made his betrayal seem worse. "You bastard," was all she could say before turning away. She missed the questioning lift of Jake's brow.

"Now see here, missy. I won't have talk like that in my office and certainly not from some snip of a — "

"I don't know what he told you," Samantha said, swirling around. "But I shot him in self-defense. At least I thought it was self-defense at the time." The low chuckle to her side made Samantha toss a look over her shoulder. "Well, I did," she insisted, scowling at Jake's amused grin.

"Hold on. Did this woman shoot you?"

Samantha heard the question the sheriff addressed to Jake but didn't understand what was going on, any more than she understood Jake's shrugging answer. "If she says so."

Both men were staring at her now, and Samantha felt color flood her already flushed cheeks. "Isn't that what he told you," she asked though she already knew the answer.

"I don't know nothing about no shooting, but I'll be asking Mr. Morgan here if he wants to press charges." Hughes emphasized these words by crossing arms over his barrel chest. "This Morgan fellow came in here today telling me you was in danger and that I should go out and arrest Bundy Atwood."

"Bundy Atwood." Samantha didn't know what to think. She looked from one man to the other, but neither of their expressions was telling her anything. Jake no longer appeared amused. A vertical line creased between his brows, and his sensual mouth was firm.

"Told him that was ridiculous, what with you and him being sweet on each other." Hughes's tone conveyed his wonderment at Bundy's taste. "But then I guess the war does change things, especially being the way you are. But murder? I can't buy that."

The way she was? What did he mean by that? Samantha pursed her lips. What did she care? But murder? She knew Atwood might be capable of it, certainly, but would he murder her? "I don't understand."

"I ran into one of Atwood's friends this morning," Jake mentioned matter-of-factly.

"After you left the farm?" Oh, why did she bring that up? Jake's eyes shone vivid green as they bore into hers. He knew she would be thinking about last night.

"Yes. After I left the farm." Jake cleared his throat. "Anyway, he started talking and said that Atwood planned to kill you."

"Just like that he told you this." Maybe she was right about his association with Landis Moore's men. Certainly no one went around bragging of murder to a stranger.

"He took me for a friend because of my uniform."

"It was Ab Landis," Hughes said in disgust. "Ab Landis."

"But he's . . ."

"An idiot," Hughes spit the words out.

"Slow-witted," Jake corrected. "Look." Jake forced air out his mouth. "He told me what Atwood planned for you. I thought the sheriff should hear about it so I let him know."

"And I'm just going to forget about it," Hughes

said, pushing away from the desk. "Now are you going to do something about this shooting thing or not?"

"No." Jake headed for the door, yanking it open and disappearing into the sunlight.

All Samantha could do was watch him leave.

"Now listen here, young lady, I don't want any more trouble from you."

"From *me?*" Samantha's expression was incredulous as she looked at the sheriff. "What about Atwood and Moore?"

"What about them. Don't tell me you're taking stock in something old Ab said." Samantha didn't answer and Hughes continued, "Even you should know he doesn't have a brain in his head."

"You know as well as I do that's not what I'm talking about." Samantha turned on him, hands on hips. "My farm was shot up a few weeks ago."

"I heard and I'm sorry."

"Sorry? That's all you can say. You're sorry?" Samantha sighed in disgust. "Moore did it."

"Did you see him?"

"No. But—"

"Recognize anyone?"

"No! They wore scarves over their faces."

"Then I'm afraid you're just going around accusing people without call, like you always done. You better watch that, Samantha. You hear me, girl?"

But Samantha was already out the door, stomping down the boardwalk toward the smithy. She should have known better than to waste her breath on Hughes. She should have learned that lesson long ago.

No one was going to help her. She thought briefly of

Jake Morgan going to the sheriff. After his insistence that he wasn't going to get involved, it surprised her. Of course, it did no good. And he certainly left quickly enough when he realized it.

Well, she'd take care of Will, and the farm, and herself!

Samantha was so deep in thought that she didn't notice the hand that shot out of the alley. It grabbed her arm and yanked her between the two buildings before she could utter more than a strangled cry.

Chapter Ten

"Ouch! Damnit. Watch your elbow!"

Samantha gasped and stopped in mid-kick. She knew that voice. Twisting around, she watched wide-eyed as Jake rubbed the area around his wound.

"What are you doing?"

"Nothing." Jake flexed his muscles, grimacing as pain shot through his chest.

Samantha took a step toward him, then backed off, smothering her instinct to tend to him. "I meant, why did you pull me in here? You scared me to death."

"You should be scared." At her confused expression, Jake sighed deeply. His hands rested on his hips. "I want to talk to you."

"You want to . . ." Samantha threw up her hands in disbelief. "So you drag me off the street? Did you think I'd refuse to speak with you any other way?" Samantha tried pushing thoughts of last night, of what they'd done, from her mind. They resurfaced anyway. Knowing no other way to escape her disturbing emotions, she turned on her heel and headed back toward the street.

A strong arm crossing in front of her chest stopped her. With no semblance of dignity she was flattened against the side of Horace Matthew's mercantile. "I want to talk to you without anyone else knowing." Jake gritted the words between clenched teeth.

He had her undivided attention now. Her breath came in shallow gasps, and blue eyes seemed to take up half her face. Jake watched the tiny pulse in the hollow at the base of her neck. Slowly he lowered his arm, sucking in his own breath when his forearm brushed her breasts.

"Listen," he said, his voice husky. Jake stepped away from her and cleared his throat. "What I said back at the sheriff's office was true. Now, I know you put no stock in what Ab Landis has to say," Jake hurried on when she seemed about to interrupt him. "But I was there, and I believe him. He may not have understood everything he was saying, but he was repeating what he heard. And that was that Bundy Atwood plans to kill you." Jake paused. He wasn't certain how much he should tell her. Finally he continued, "And he doesn't plan to do it in a very pleasant way."

"I know." Samantha leaned back against the building.

"You know?" Jake forced himself to keep his voice down.

"Well, I don't actually *know* what he plans, but

I've been around him, and I've seen what Landis Moore is capable of, so—"

"So what are you going to do?"

Samantha sighed. "The only thing I can do. I'm going to go get my wheel, and go home and harvest my corn, and—"

"Are you crazy? No, don't answer that. I already know the answer." Jake shoved back his hat in disgust.

"I'm leaving now." Samantha straightened her skirt.

"At least go back to the sheriff and—"

"He didn't believe you, and he's even less likely to believe me. The sheriff and I . . ." Samantha hesitated, deciding how much to tell Jake. She finally decided he didn't really want to know any of it. "Let's just say Sheriff Hughes and I have tangled before. And it does no good." Samantha started toward the street then stopped and looked over her shoulder. "Thank you for the warning."

Samantha hurried toward the smithy. Her wheel was fixed, and she payed for it and watched as Linc tied it to Pru.

"That should do you, Samantha," Linc said, giving the mule a friendly pat on the rump.

"Thank you." Linc Jones had been in Kansas almost as long as Samantha's family. He wasn't an abolitionist, and hadn't come to help the territory enter the Union as a free state. To be honest, he'd abhorred some of the methods used by the free-soilers. But neither had he ever been a proponent of slavery. He'd pretty much remained neutral during the bloody years of '56 and '57, and through the long years of war.

But he knew everyone, and most everyone in town or the surrounding farms needed his services at one time or another.

Samantha gathered up Pru's reins. "I heard the Colts sold out and moved back East."

"Yea, Zeb Colt had me do some work on his wagon before he left."

"It's kind of surprising, isn't it?"

"In what way?" Linc started back toward the open door of the smithy.

"Well, they've been here so long." Samantha shrugged. "And endured so much. You'd think they'd stay."

"I don't know." Linc leaned against the door. "Zeb said Suzanne had had all of Kansas she could take. You know she'd had a bad experience with some ruffians."

"Border ruffians?" Samantha stepped forward.

"Aw, I don't think there's any of them still around. Nah, these were just some rough men." Linc pushed away from the door. "Guess that had something to do with their decision." He shook his head. "You be careful out there at your farm, Samantha."

Careful, indeed.

Samantha could think of little else as she made her way home. It was slow going. Pru wasn't inclined to move quickly — Samantha guessed she took exception to the wheel bouncing against her side.

But the thing that made the trip seem so long was the fear Samantha experienced. She'd been afraid before—lately it seemed more times than not. But this was far worse. Several times she had a prickling feeling that she was being followed. But when she looked around, no one was there.

When the cabin came in sight, Samantha heaved a sigh of relief. Everything looked normal. The chickens were clucking around, scratching for seeds. Charity was lying in a patch of late afternoon sun, her nose buried in her paws.

Samantha slid from Pru's back just as Will came bursting through the door. He ran toward her, full of excitement and grabbed for the mule's reins.

"I thought you'd never get home," he said. "Guess who's back?"

"Back?" Samantha's mind flew to all sorts of possibilities, Bundy Atwood and Landis Moore heading the list. But when her gaze followed Will's pointing finger, she caught sight of Jake Morgan leaning against the open door frame. Her breath left her in a rush. "What are you doing here?"

Jake's brows lifted. "At the moment wondering what's for supper."

Didn't this man ever think of anything but his stomach? Samantha pushed a reluctant Will toward the barn. "Take care of Prudence," she told him before marching toward the house. As she approached the porch, Jake stepped aside to let her enter the cabin. And then he followed her in and closed the door.

Samantha took a deep breath, allowing herself time to settle down. She hadn't expected to see him again, and certainly not casually leaning against her door. "I don't recall asking you to supper," she said, turning to confront him.

Jake crossed his arms. "I'm not staying without being fed." He cocked his head to the side. "You do remember asking me to stay, don't you?"

How could she ever forget that, or what had happened after he refused. "Yes." Samantha clutched the chair back. "But I also remember your reply."

"I've changed my mind."

"Why?"

"Listen, Samantha. I still think you're crazy to stay here. But I can't leave, knowing what I know. I told myself I could. You can believe me when I say I want to. But I simply can't."

"This isn't your problem." Samantha gave up her death grip on the chair and took a bowl off the shelf. Better to keep her hands busy than to let him know how upsetting his presence was. After scooping cornmeal from the bin, she added water and began mixing with a carved wooden spoon.

"I know that." Jake watched her a moment, her head bent in concentration as she whipped the spoon around. "And when the war was over, I told myself that never again would I get mixed up with something that wasn't my concern, but —"

Samantha glanced up. "Is that the way you felt, that the war wasn't your concern?"

"No." Jake ran his fingers through his hair. "It was my concern. It was everybody's concern. Maybe it just wasn't my fight."

"Then why did you do it?"

"Why?" Jake shook his head. "I don't really know

202

why. It seemed the thing to do at the time."

"Like this does."

"Maybe."

"Well, your help isn't necessary this time." Samantha placed the corn batter in the Dutch oven.

"What I said in town about Bundy Atwood is true."

"And I believed you . . . still believe you." Samantha turned to find him standing near her. She hadn't heard him move. Brushing past him, she put the dirty bowl in the dry sink. "That's why I sent a telegram before I left town. To the military commander at Fort Scott. I asked him to send some troops."

Yankees, she meant. She'd contacted the Yankees. Jake had a moment of apprehension before he remembered the war was over and he had a parole, and life went on. "That's good," he heard himself say. "Do you think they'll come?"

"Probably . . . hopefully," Samantha amended. "The commander was an old friend of my father's. He used to be devoted to helping the families sent here by the New England Emigrant Aid Company."

"Is that how you got here?"

"Sort of. We weren't exactly part of that group. My father decided we should come here to a place that needed us more, rather than settle in a bunch. He believed in spreading the word."

Jake lifted his brow inquisitively. Already the sweet smell of cornbread filled the cabin. "What word was that?"

"Abolitionism. My father . . . my entire family felt strongly that slavery was an unholy institution."

"I see." Jake hooked a chair leg with his boot and scraped it across the floor. After straddling it, he faced Samantha. "I guess I'll only be staying a short time then."

"I just told you, there's no reason for you to stay at all."

"Till the army gets here, there is."

"I won't lie with you again."

Jake's head shot up, his eyes locking with hers. He'd have bet she'd convinced herself their intimacy never took place. "I didn't expect you would."

"Good." Samantha folded her hands. "Because if you think by staying that . . . What I mean is . . ."

"It was a mistake," Jake finished for her.

"Yes. A mistake," Samantha agreed. "And if you think by staying here—"

"That we'll repeat that mistake?"

"Yes . . . I mean no. I mean we won't." Samantha swallowed. Just looking at him brought back vividly how it felt to be held by him, to be kissed, to have him deep inside her.

"I know we won't." But he wanted to. Just looking at her—hair curling out of the bun she'd put it in, soft mouth pursed—he wanted to. Jake took a deep breath, trying to suppress his wayward thoughts. "Something's burning."

Did he know what she was thinking? "What?" Samantha felt embarrassed color tint her cheeks.

"Burning," Jake repeated, heading for the Dutch oven on top of the stove. "The cornbread."

"Oh no. Oh, my goodness." Samantha grabbed a

204

dish towel and reached for the lid, but Jake beat her to it.

"Ouch, damnit!"

"I won't have cursing in my house either!" Samantha pushed him aside and dragged the oven off the stove.

"I burned myself, damnit!" Jake scowled at Samantha and fanned his hand back and forth, cursing under his breath.

"And whose fault was that?" She pried the lid off. "It's ruined."

"What about my hand?" It didn't take a doctor to know that his burn wasn't serious, but it hurt. And damnit, she should care something about it.

"Oh, let me see." Samantha blew hair out of her face. She gave one last wistful look at the charred cornbread, and turned her attention to Jake.

Her hands were gentle as they opened his fingers. She traced the burn carefully. "It doesn't look bad."

"It hurts." Jake grimaced at his words. He sounded like a whiny kid. But he wanted sympathy. From her. As ridiculous as it seemed. As foreign to his nature as it was, he'd liked it when she gave it to him before. And he wanted it again.

Samantha studied his expression. He didn't act like this, even when his wound was at its worst. He gave her a boyish grin and she shrugged. After dragging the pottery butter crock off the shelf, she placed it on the table.

"Let me see it again," she said, stepping between Jake's outstretched legs. Her skirt brushed against his pant legs, and Samantha tried to ignore the fleet-

205

ing sensation that ran through her.

The butter felt warm and slippery on her fingers as she slid them across his broad palm. His hands were rough, she remembered that well from the night he'd touched her, but the butter softened his calluses.

Samantha tried to keep her touch impersonal as it traced the angry reddened ridge traversing his palm, but she could not dismiss his nearness.

His hand wavered and she used hers to steady it. Her hands were used to work, to the sun and soil of a Kansas farm, but they looked small and pale, almost dainty compared to his.

Taking a steadying breath, Samantha dipped two fingers into the crock for more butter. Jake shifted and his thighs tightened on either side of hers. Samantha swallowed hard and glanced at Jake. He was looking down at their hands. Her standing to his sitting put her slightly higher than he. She couldn't see his eyes, just his lashes, long and gold-tipped as he watched the slow movement of her fingers over his palm.

Breathing became difficult, and Samantha's knees felt weak. She cleared her throat. "Does it feel better now?" Her voice sounded husky.

Jake lifted his eyes. He couldn't explain what was happening here, but from the expression on Samantha's face, she felt it the same as he.

She professed to want no part of him physically; he readily agreed. Yet the urge to possess her, to feel again those slender legs wrapped around him, was almost overpowering.

He leaned forward. The abrasion of her skirt

against the V of his legs was as powerful as a caress. Lord, her eyes were blue, soft, sweet and innocent, and locked on his. And her lips were parted, ready to be kissed . . .

"What's that smell? Is something burning, Sam!"

Will burst through the door, breaking the sensual spell surrounding Samantha. She jerked away from Jake—had she just come close to kissing him?—and grabbed up the butter crock. Sliding it on the shelf, she kept her back turned to Jake and her brother. But it only took so long to replace the crock, and in the end she had to turn around. Taking a deep breath, then letting it out slowly, Samantha faced her brother. The glimpse she caught of Jake showed him still sitting, though he'd twisted his chair to position it toward the table.

"Nothing is burning," Samantha said matter-of-factly, though she noted a slight breathless quality to her voice. "I simply overcooked the cornbread, and—"

"How come?"

"I beg your pardon."

"How come you *burned* the cornbread? You never burn anything."

True enough. Her father had considered waste a sin. And burning food, especially in those early years, was undeniably a waste. Samantha had learned early on—almost as soon as her mother died and the responsibility for cooking had fallen on her—not to burn the meals.

She set about scraping the charred cornbread into the slop pot. "Well, I burned this."

"Your sister was filling me in on the . . . responsibilities for my new job," Jake interjected. "I guess we both forgot there was something in the Dutch oven." Jake pushed off from the table and stood. "There's a lot to get done. What do you say we get started?"

"What about supper?" Will seemed genuinely shocked by Jake's suggestion.

And Jake could hardly blame him. His stomach and the chirping of twilight crickets were enough to convince him that it was past time for supper. But there was nothing to be done for it. Besides if Samantha felt half as bewildered as she looked, a little time alone wouldn't hurt.

Grabbing his hat off the table, he linked his other arm around Will's neck. "Let's see about putting that wheel back on the wagon."

"In the dark?" Will trailed along reluctantly.

"There's still plenty of light."

Will's response was lost as the door shut behind them.

Samantha straightened, dropping the knife she'd used to scrape the cornbread into the iron pot with a thud. What in heaven's name was wrong with her? Her hands were trembling, and with no conscious effort, she could recall the way it felt to touch Jake.

Moving toward the window, pushing aside a section of stretched cotton, Samantha glanced outside. Sure enough, Jake had set Will to lighting the lantern and fetching the wheel. He himself was straining against the wagon, shifting it into a better position to work on it.

She could tell he still favored his left side, but he

used his right hand as normally as if he hadn't burned it. Samantha shook her head, wondering just how sore it could have been. As she watched, Will brought the wheel up, and after a few words from Jake, he rolled it into place beside the axle. Then Jake hunched over, straining against the wagon's weight. Samantha could see the bulging of his muscles and the grimace on his face as he lifted. It reminded her again of just how strong he was. And how much she enjoyed watching him.

With a sigh, she turned away from the window. His staying here was never going to work. But he didn't seem likely to leave until the army arrived in Hager's Flats. Samantha could only hope they'd come—and come soon.

She was still hoping that the next day, but not so desperately. Oh, she still wanted the soldiers to arrive and take care of capturing the gang harassing the settlers, but she decided she could handle Jake's presence.

Supper last night hadn't been nearly the ordeal she'd expected. She'd fried up ham and potatoes and made fresh biscuits—not quite ready to face another batch of cornbread after cleaning up the first. By the time Jake and Will came in, they were dirty and hungry . . . and tired.

They all ate quickly and quietly. When Will excused himself without even finishing his apple pie to climb slowly into the loft, Samantha knew a moment of panic. Once again she was alone with Jake. And history had taught her where that could lead.

But this time it led nowhere. Jake rose, thanked

her for the meal, and left, — she assumed, to sleep in the barn.

And she was glad. She really was!

This morning after devouring a huge stack of flap-jacks, and surreptitiously massaging his wounds Jake motioned for Will to follow him into the yard.

"Wait a minute," Samantha yelled when they hitched up the wagon and drove it past the cabin door. Between hurriedly cleaning up the breakfast dishes, she packed them all a lunch.

"No need for you to come along," Jake said after gracefully bounding from the seat. "Will and I can handle the corn. Isn't that right, Will?"

"Sure is, Jake."

Samantha looked from one to the other. Will was obviously thrilled by the idea of spending the day with Jake, even if it meant picking corn, and Jake . . . Jake was staring at her, his expression un-readable. Samantha pursed her lips. "I always help with the harvesting." Which wasn't exactly true. Before Luke left for the war, she hadn't.

"Well, this time you don't have to."

"But I—" Samantha stopped herself. Jake didn't look as if wished to argue the point. He also didn't seem willing to concede it. Samantha had gone into the cornfields when they hired Jim Farley because he was basically lazy. She knew Jake didn't suffer from that malady.

"All right," Samantha said, folding her hands. "I'll stay here."

"Good."

"It's not as if I don't have plenty of work to do."

Embarrassed by the lift of the corners of Jake's mouth, Samantha glanced away, but looked back when he reached into the wagon bed.

"I want you to keep this with you." *This* was one of his revolvers. "I happen to know it fits nicely in your apron pocket."

Samantha scowled when he slid the gun in, making the calico apron sag around Samantha's waist. Apparently he'd known all the time that she carried the gun in case she needed to use it against him.

"Now, I don't want you shooting at anything if you can help it. You've a penchant for hitting innocent people." He punctuated that remark with an exaggerated flexing of his shoulder. "But if you need help"—his expression grew serious—"if anyone comes here, I want you to shoot."

"A signal?" Samantha asked, and he nodded.

"I'll be here right away." It was then that Samantha noticed Jake's horse tied to the back of the wagon.

And she felt safe. Safer than she had in years. Ridiculously safe when you considered that just two days before someone had threatened her—and more, that she was placing her trust in a Rebel.

Samantha glanced out the window. She'd rolled up the cotton to let in the whispery breeze that sifted through the tall grass south of the cabin. The sun was working its way toward its zenith. Samantha had spent the morning cleaning the cabin—something she'd put off too long. She'd fed the chickens and watered the garden, and now decided to launder Will's and her clothes—another neglected chore.

211

Carrying water was not a task Samantha relished, but the creek did seem particularly pretty today, the water splashing over the brightly colored pebbles.

She didn't intend to tarry, but by the time she made her way back up the path, Samantha realized she had.

She also realized someone was in her cabin.

Sloshing water over her skirts, when she dropped the pail, Samantha ran the rest of the way. There were half a dozen horses in the yard, and she recognized some of the riders. That and the knowledge they weren't Moore's men kept her from firing the gun.

One horse was riderless, and as Samantha rounded the cabin's corner she saw Sheriff Hughes amble out her front door.

"What were you doing in my home?" Samantha demanded as the burly sheriff caught sight of her.

"There you are, missy. Been lookin' for you."

"Which gives you absolutely no right to trespass in my cabin."

"Now, maybe it don't but then again, maybe it do." Sheriff Hughes pushed back his sweat-stained hat and scratched at his scraggly beard. "Got word from a Colonel Adams over Fort Scott way. Sent a telegram sayin' he's sending some troops to help protect the populace." Hughes spit on the porch. "Now this strikes me odd seeings how *I'm* the one's suppose to be doing it."

"Maybe he thinks you need help." Samantha's chin rose.

"And maybe he's been hearin' tales from some

snip of a girl who don't know when to mind her own business."

"Listen, Sheriff"—Samantha's response was cut off by the pounding of a horse's hooves. Whirling around toward the cornfield, she saw the Rebel galloping toward her. He brought his mount up close enough for her to smell the scent of lathered horse, and slid off. Without giving Samantha a glance, he greeted the sheriff.

"Any trouble here?"

"Not that I can see. Thought we'd seen the last of you, Morgan."

"I thought I'd stay on awhile. The lady needs some help with her corn." Jake handed his reins to Samantha. She was so surprised by the action, she took them. He just rode in and took over, and Samantha wasn't sure she liked that. But she had to admit that, with his hat low over his brow and his sidearm strapped around his lean hips, he looked able to handle most anything.

"So, what brings you out here, Sheriff?" Jake crossed his arms lightly.

Hughes stared at Jake a moment while the bees buzzed around the morning glories and the horses shifted fretfully. Finally he shrugged. "Been a stage holdup. The posse—" he motioned toward the men still mounted—"and me, we're doing some trailing."

"It was Landis Moore, I'll bet you." Samantha stepped forward.

"Now that will be enough of that talk out of you, missy. No one saw anyone's face. And I don't like the idea of you going around bad-talkin' a citizen of this here town without good cause."

Jake ignored Hughes's reprimand as well as the furious expression on Samantha's face. "Tracks lead this way, do they?"

"Not far from here."

Jake nodded, then rubbed his chin. "We haven't seen anything, have we, Samantha?"

"No." She still didn't like the way Jake took over. "Of course I doubt you're doing much serious tr—"

"Samantha and I will keep our eyes open and let you know if we see anything," Jake interrupted, giving Samantha a hard look that she returned.

"You just do that." Sheriff Hughes hitched up his pants, then sauntered down the steps. Grabbing hold of the saddle pommel, he pulled himself astride. He twisted the horse's head with a jerk of the reins and led the men off without another word.

Samantha watched them scatter the chickens then turned on Jake. "What was that all about?"

"What?" Jake pulled off his hat, combed fingers back through his hair, and resettled it on his head.

"Cutting me off like that. Hughes isn't trying to catch Landis Moore. He never has. He's just out here trying to harass me."

"Maybe."

"Maybe? You sound like the sheriff." That got a rise from him. Jake shot her a steely look before stomping into the cabin.

Samantha followed, startled when he turned on her. Her hand fluttered to her throat.

"Why in the hell didn't you fire the pistol like I

told you to?"

"What?" Samantha hadn't been expecting this shift in the conversation."

"You heard me." He was right there. He was so close to her there was no way to help but hear. "I gave you the revolver and told you to shoot it if someone came. But did you do it? No."

"I have to look up and see a cloud of dust moving along the road to know something's going on. What in the hell would have happened if I hadn't looked up?"

"I would have taken care of it. And would you please stop cussing?"

"Like you almost took care of it there at the end? You push anyone—even Sheriff Hughes—too hard and they're going to push back. And don't correct my speech. I'm not Will."

"I know that well enough. And it's not your speech I'm correcting. It's your penchant for profanity. And as long as you're in my house, I most certainly will voice my opinion of it."

"Well, don't expect me to obey." Jake folded his arms and leaned against the ladder to the loft.

"I don't." Samantha mimicked his pose. "And do you have any idea why Sheriff Hughes came out here?"

"He said he was—"

"He got a telegram from the army in Fort Scott. They're sending troops and he's running scared."

Jake straightened and shook his head. "I'm not so sure about the running scared part. But I can tell you one thing, Samantha. If he is, you don't want to get caught in his retreat." He stalked toward the door, his movements full of animal grace. "Just try to keep your opinions to yourself and stay out of his way. And fire the damn gun if someone else comes." With that warning, he slammed out the door and Samantha wondered if his help was really that helpful.

Chapter Eleven

The dream made Samantha's blood run cold. Even in sleep she had a vague awareness she hadn't relived this particular horror in a long time. It used to be so common to imagine the shots, to wake up trembling. But that was years ago. That was when . . .

Samantha's eyes flew open and her breath caught tightly in her chest. This was no dream. The gunshots shattering the night quiet were real.

Samantha tore through her bedroom door. She screamed and her heart pounded loudly in her ears when she slammed against something hard and human.

"Sam! It's me, Will."

"Oh, Will." Samantha gave him a quick hug before a fresh volley of shots made her shove him toward the floor.

"What's going on? Who's out there?"

"I don't know." For one terrifying moment memories of another night washed over her. She'd awakened then to gunshots and screams. The smell of something burning. The recollection seared through her body. It was strong. It was paralyzing. And it took Will clutching at her foot to break the spell.

Sucking in her breath, Samantha hunched over and rushed toward the far wall. The room was black as pitch but she found the rough, gravelly surface of the hearth and followed it up with her palms. She was standing when her fingers closed around the musket stock.

"What are you doing, Sam?"

"Hush. Just stay down." Crouching down, Samantha made her way to the front window. The night was cloudy with only a pale filtering of moonlight to see by. Horses. She could make out horses and riders prancing about in her yard.

The gunshots stopped.

The yelling began.

Whoever was outside was calling her names, names so vile Samantha had to fight the urge to drop the musket and cover her ears.

They didn't like her telegraphing for federal troops. That much was obvious. Samantha tried to separate herself from what they were saying and concentrate on the voices. Did she recognize any of them? Was it Landis Moore? Bundy Atwood? She couldn't tell for sure.

Part of her problem was that the voices kept blurring and fading, merging with the taunts and bellows from long ago.

"Come out, you yellow-bellied coward," they'd called to her father. "Come out and see what we do to the likes of you. Nigger lover! Nigger lover," they'd yelled while she cowered beneath her quilt.

Shots rang out again and Samantha pulled herself back to the present. This was no time for reliving the past. She could hear Will's heavy breathing as he scooted over to her. She could just make out his form in the shadows.

"I think that's Jake," he said, leaning closer to whisper his words. "Listen. They're the ones being shot at now."

Samantha tried but she couldn't tell the difference, except that now the men in the yard did seem upset. She even heard one yelp in pain before someone yelled for them to head out.

Samantha slumped against the wall, listening to the fading hoofbeats as the men rode away. Will struck a match, the sulphur exploding with a hiss. He touched the burning Lucifer to the lamp wick and settled the globe, illuminating the room just as there came a pounding on the door.

"Samantha! Will. You two all right?"

It was Jake and relief swept Samantha from head to bare toes. Will rushed to let him in, yanking the door open with more force than necessary.

Reholstering his revolver, Jake stepped into the cabin. "Everything all right here?" He scanned the room till his eyes locked with Samantha's. She was kneeling on the floor, leaning heavily into the wall. The musket lay on the floor beside her and her face was white as the night rail buttoned high at her delicate neck.

He knelt beside her. "Are you hurt?"

"No." Samantha swallowed, trying to pull herself together. She knew nothing had happened this time—that the other had been long ago—but it didn't help. She wished Jake would look away so she could compose herself, but he seemed intent on watching her as if she might shatter at any moment.

Will finally gained his attention long enough for Samantha to stand. "I think you got one of them. What do you think, Jake?"

"Could be." Jake caught Samantha under the elbow and helped her to a chair. He had the urge to gather her into his arms but decided it most likely wouldn't be welcome. But seeing her pale, her blue eyes dark with fear, did strange things to the pit of his stomach. She scraped her chair in toward the table, and Jake leaned back against the wall.

The pale peach shade was returning to her face, and she made a feeble attempt to smile that tore into Jake's heart.

Will was babbling on in the background, speculating on who may have participated in the nighttime raid, and what part of the anatomy Jake's bullet had struck. Jake listened, shaking his head and shrugging at the appropriate times, but his eyes never strayed from Samantha.

"Listen," Jake said, interrupting Will's assertion that he'd never really been scared. "I think I should sleep in here for the rest of the night."

"No." Samantha's voice might be softer than her brother's, but *her* answer was the one Jake heard over Will's enthusiastic agreement. "That won't be necessary." What little color she'd regained quickly drained from her cheeks.

"I think it is," Jake said. "I'll just bed down here

by the door with Charity." The dog who'd been barking frantically a short time ago didn't even look up when Jake said her name.

"Here? In the parlor?"

Jake would hardly call this room a parlor, but he couldn't help grinning at the expression on Samantha's face. "Will." He turned toward the boy. "Run to the barn and fetch my blanket, will you?"

"Sure. But you can sleep in the loft with me. There's plenty of room."

"Thanks, but this is fine." Jake watched Will run out the door before turning back to Samantha. "Where did *you* think I planned to sleep?"

"I'm sure I didn't give it any thought."

Jake's chuckle sent rosy color to Samantha's cheeks. It also made Jake uncomfortable. What was he doing teasing her like this? So they both thought of the same thing regarding sleeping arrangements. After what happened the other night, that was only natural. But that didn't mean they were going to do anything about it. Samantha glanced up, her blue eyes, shining dark in the lamplight, and Jake almost groaned.

Grabbing a chair, he straddled it to face her. "What happened here tonight?"

"I . . . I don't know what you mean."

"Those men, coming in here shooting and hollering up. They scared you."

"They'd scare anyone."

"True enough, " Jake admitted. "But not like they did you. You're still shaking." He reached out and covered her hand with his. "And remember, I've seen

221

you face scary situations before."

"I don't know what you're talking about." Samantha pulled her hand from beneath his, and immediately missed the warmth.

Jake didn't believe her, but he lost his chance to pursue it when Will came bounding in, rolled-up blanket in one hand, saddlebags in the other. "Thought you might want these," he said, tossing them toward Jake.

Samantha rose and made her way toward her bedroom. It suddenly hit her that she was dressed in nothing but her well-worn night rail. Though it covered her from chin to toes, there was nothing restricting or starched about it. And looking at Jake, who'd only managed to pull on a pair of pants before tearing into the house did strange things to her insides.

She shut the door and leaned against it, the wood feeling sturdy against her back. She knew it wouldn't keep Jake out if he wanted to come in. But he didn't want in. He had laughed at her reaction to his staying in the house. It was laughable. Why would he want her when he had someone as beautiful as the woman in the daguerreotype?

Samantha shook her head and pushed away from the door. What was she thinking? She didn't care if Jake wanted her. She . . . she was the one who didn't want him. A Southerner. Was she crazy? She'd just put him out of her mind for good.

There were only two problems with that, Samantha realized as she lay huddled in her bed. One, he refused to leave. And two, the only thing that filled any void he felt was thoughts about the night they hanged her father.

She must have finally dozed. When her eyes opened again, it was morning—well past dawn by the looks of the lemony sun filtering through the dust-streaked windowpane. How could she have missed the cock's crow again? Samantha dressed hurriedly, splashing water into the bowl and dousing her face, then rebraided her hair with practiced quickness. Her dress was of brown sprigged calico, and she buttoned it high beneath her chin. Her dash into the main room stopped abruptly.

Jake sat at the table grimacing into a pewter mug. He was alone. "Where's Will?" Samantha asked, and her question made him look up and smile. Samantha steeled herself against the flutter of excitement that caused.

"He's doing his chores. I offered to help, but . . ." Jake shrugged.

"But what?"

"He said I should fix us something to eat."

Samantha glanced around the kitchen area. The cracker barrel was open, and there were coffee grounds around the mill. "Why didn't you just wake me?"

"After last night I thought you could use the rest." Jake went to the door and tossed the remains of his coffee into the yard, scattering some chickens who hung around waiting to be fed.

"Those gunshots woke everybody up." Samantha

223

grabbed an apron off the hook and wrapped it around her small waist. She told herself she would not look at Jake, but it only took a few seconds of no response from him before her eyes sought his. He looked at her as if he knew there was more to it than she was saying.

"Captain Morgan." She gave the ends of her apron ribbons a tug, tying them on. "I've lived out here for nearly ten years. I'm not some hothouse flower that needs protecting and cosseting."

"Fine."

"I can take care of myself."

"Good." Jake watched as she grabbed the Dutch oven and clanged it on the stove. Even when she banged the heavy iron about, she looked fragile. Golden hair escaped the severity of her braided bun and curled about a face whose finely wrought features looked as if they should be painted on porcelain. Her body was small, delicately boned, and soft. If ever there was a woman who looked like she should need protecting, it was Samantha Lowery.

But looks could be deceiving. And with Samantha he knew they were. She might need some help now and then. But she could take care of herself and her brother.

Unexpectedly a vision of another woman came to his mind. A woman who *had* needed taking care of. A woman he'd failed.

Pushing to his feet, Jake turned toward the door. "I think I'll see if Will needs any help."

"Fine," she said, mimicking his earlier word. Samantha brushed coarse coffee grounds into her

224

palm with the curve of her hand. "Feed those chickens while you're at it." Samantha tossed the order out without looking around, and she waited for the protest she figured would follow. It was a menial task that even Will gave her trouble about doing, but Jake said nothing as he left the cabin, feed in hand.

Samantha let go of the dasher and stood, rubbing the small of her back with her knuckles. She wasn't in the mood to churn butter. And that was surprising. Normally she enjoyed the peace and solitude the chore offered. She could sit in the shade of the porch and enjoy the beauty of her home—the quiet, ofttimes hidden charm she rarely had time to appreciate. But today, neither the delicate yellow sensitive plant nor the tall sentinel sunflowers held any appeal. She ignored the lingering scent of morning glories and the chubby quail waddling out beyond the barn.

Nothing appealed to her today. Not since Jake had told her after breakfast that he wanted to do some visiting this evening.

"It's a waste of time," Samantha murmured, resuming her seat on the bench tucked under the sloping porch eaves. Taking up the wooden dasher, she pulled the churn between her spread legs and continued her up-and-down motion. Her eyes scanned the prairie.

Fall flowers peeped through the undulating grasses as the relentless wind whipped across the land. A white crow circled lazily overhead then came to roost in the stand of sycamores to the east of the cabin.

What did he hope to accomplish by asking her neighbors for help?

He'd get nothing more than her father had. They'd talk a good show, agreeing with his assessment that something needed doing. But when push came to shove, they'd back down and hide in their homes, their tails tucked neatly between their legs.

And the most amazing part was that Samantha couldn't blame them. Not a one of her neighbors. They'd done the wise thing. They were still alive. Only her father lay in a grave because he resisted. And for what? The war had taken care of the slavery problem. So he accomplished exactly nothing.

The jingling of a harness stirred the late afternoon silence and Samantha squinted, searching the distance for the wagon. She saw it coming from the direction of the cornfield, shimmering in the waves of October heat. It didn't take long for her to make out Will sitting on the seat, driving, and Jake walking along beside. Behind her brother, the wagon bed was heaped with ears of corn.

Pushing to her feet, Samantha went into the cabin and, after storing the butter, set to work making biscuits. The stew she'd started earlier that afternoon filled the cabin with rich warm scents. Samantha was certain Will and Jake would appreciate the hearty meal.

And maybe after the long day he put in, plus eating a good dinner, Jake would be too tired to worry about visiting neighbors.

He was, but Samantha could tell Jake wasn't going

to let a little fatigue stop him. She watched as Jake pushed away from the table and stood. "I'll go hitch up the wagon."

"Jake, I—"

"I know you don't want to do this, Samantha, but there's no other way."

"We could wait for the army." It was no good. She was offering the same arguments he'd already rejected. Showing patience she never expected, he sat down across from her. She thought he'd take her hand, but instead he folded his on the table.

"You have a hell of a lot more faith in the Union Army than I do. Maybe they'll come. Maybe they won't. But in the meantime something has to be done." Jake shifted.

Her mind knew that—even agreed with him—but it was hard to fight the demons from her past. In the end she didn't try. Pushing away from the table, Samantha scooped up her plate and piled it atop Jake's and Will's. "No one goes visiting in the evening around here . . . especially during harvest."

Samantha poured steaming water into the dishpan. "This isn't Richmond." She turned to catch his eye. "That is where you're from, isn't it?" Seeing his nod, she went on. "Folks around here are exhausted by sundown. Best to let this wait till Sunday."

He seemed to accept her logic with a shrug, but he still stood and reached for his hat.

"Where are you going?" Samantha voiced her question before she could stop herself.

"Where I should have gone first thing this morning. Into town."

"But—"

"I know you don't put much store in the sheriff." Jake blew air through his teeth and gave his head a shake. "And frankly, from what I've seen, I don't either. But damnit, Samantha, someone was out here last night shooting up this place, and I'm pretty sure I wounded one of them. And I'm going to see that the sheriff knows about it."

He could have saved the time and effort, Jake thought again as he waited for Samantha to come out of the house early Sunday afternoon. The sheriff had listened to him, rubbing his bristly beard and watching Jake with pale, washed-out eyes imbedded in fleshy folds. He even promised to look into it— soon. But he didn't seem overly concerned.

"Just some of the boys lettin' off steam," he said, leaning back in his chair and crossing scarred boots on an equally scared desk. "You should know how that is, boy."

Should he? Jake didn't think there was any steam left in him to escape. Of course, he'd decided there wasn't much of anything left in him until Fate had dumped him on this farm in the middle of nowhere. Now he was lusting after a woman, getting attached to a kid, and fighting for a cause he didn't completely understand, and that sure as hell wasn't his.

Will banged shut the barn door and skipped across the chicken-pecked yard, Charity trotting along at his heels. The boy was dressed in what Jake guessed were his best clothes. For once you couldn't see a couple inches of leg sticking out of his pants. Dressed to go visiting, Jake thought, then looked down at his own pants. He'd made some changes too.

"You bringing your mouth organ with ya?" Will stopped to lean against the wagon just as Jake was doing.

"Hadn't thought to." Jake looked at Will from beneath the brim of his hat. "This isn't exactly a social call we're making."

Will shrugged. "Still couldn't hurt."

"Maybe you're right." Jake wondered, not for the first time, about the boy's existence. Far as Jake knew, neither Will nor his sister did much of anything but work the farm. Samantha had gone to town once since he came, but he figured she didn't do much but work on that trip.

It didn't seem right, them stuck out here their whole life doing nothing but hard work. But then he guessed with just the two of them—a young woman and a boy—to run the place, it took most all their time.

Still, it was easy to tell from the expression on Will's freckled face that he was excited about their upcoming visits, no matter what the reason for them.

Removing his hat and backhanding the sweat off his brow, Jake turned toward the boy. "You want to run and get the harmonica for me. It's on the ledge over the—"

"I know where it is." Will was halfway to the barn when he called back over his shoulder. "I seen where you put it."

"All right." Jake settled the hat back on his head. "And then, how about seeing what you can do to hurry your sister up."

"Sam! Sam!" Will halted in front of the barn door and hollered toward the house. "We needs get moving, Sam!" With that he disappeared into the barn and Jake just shook his head.

Samantha quickly tied the ribbons of her best — but hardly new — bonnet under her chin and sighed at her reflection in the mirror. She was running behind, and she didn't need Will's shouting to let her know. She heard the harness jingle when Jake first brought the swept-out wagon from the barn. But the pies she'd baked this morning took longer than she thought and then her hair didn't seem to want to stay in the upswept do that fit best under her bonnet. Hurrying out of her bedroom, she grabbed a large basket off a hook and carefully fitted the still warm pies into the bottom, covering them with a checkered napkin.

Jake straightened, slipping the harmonica into his pocket as the cabin door opened. He shifted, turning his head to comment on how long he'd been waiting, but the words never came out.

He was certainly used to seeing her — for over three weeks now he'd run into her most every day. Hell, he'd even lain with her, though the darkness had veiled all but a tantalizing peek of smooth shoulder or long moon-kissed thigh. But he'd never seen her dressed in anything but wash-worn calico dresses. Drab things that did nothing but hide the sweet

230

curves of her body.

Not today. Today she wore a gown of blue—not light or dark, but bright like her eyes. The dress wasn't fancy, not by Richmond standards, but it fit her well. And Jake would wager his harmonica she wore a corset under the soft material.

The bonnet, trimmed with the same blue fabric, wasn't going to afford much protection from the glaring Kansas sun, but it sure did make her look pretty. Beautiful.

Jake wasn't sure how long they stood there staring at one another but Will's voice interrupted his thoughts.

"What kind of pies did ya bake, Sam?"

"Ah, apple." Samantha hurried to the wagon and placed the basket under the seat. Her face felt hot and her blood seemed to strum through her veins. She knew she looked different today—in truth she'd tried to fix herself up. But she hadn't expected the reaction she received from Jake.

Whatever he was thinking, he didn't say anything, and to look at his expression now, you wouldn't think he'd noticed a thing. He helped her into the wagon, then climbed up himself. After checking to see Will hurdle himself into the wagon bed, Jake let loose the brake and "clicked" the horses into motion.

The farm lane was no more than wheel ruts with tufts of prairie grass sprouting in tracks down the center. Samantha held tight to the seat to keep from jostling too much, and to keep from bouncing against Jake.

Now that she sat under the hot sun, her body stiff

and uncomfortable in the confining stays, Samantha wondered just what had been in her mind when she'd dressed that morning. Oh, she always wore something better than work clothes to visit, but this she did for Jake Morgan. And he hadn't said a word.

If his expression was an indication, he didn't like her looks at all. Well, that was fine with her. She didn't even want to be making this silly trip. It wasn't going to do any good. Samantha cast a quick glance to her side. Her eyes opened wider in surprise. She'd been so busy watching for his reaction to her, she hadn't noticed him. She did now and a frown formed on her lips.

"It's not going to help, you know."

"What's not?" Jake flicked the reins.

"Getting rid of your Rebel uniform. They're going to know anyway."

"What, do I have a giant R carved in my forehead?" Jake twisted to stare at her from beneath his hat.

Samantha ignored his sarcasm. "Word gets around. They'll know. And they'll wonder why you're worried about protecting anyone from Landis Moore."

"Maybe you should do the talking then."

"That wouldn't be much better," Samantha mumbled.

Jake shifted when his knee brushed against hers. She appeared not to notice, just continued to stare off toward the horizon. Fields of wild sunflowers swayed in the breeze, their large heads bowing, but Jake didn't think she even noticed. He didn't know

232

why she was so against talking to neighbors about their common enemy. To Jake it seemed the logical thing to do.

But then, he wasn't an expert on logic of late. It certainly didn't make sense for him to still be here.

Hadn't he decided one night when the cries of the wounded precluded any sleep that there were no righteous causes? Yet here he was on his way to meet with a bunch of hardened Yankee sympathizers to push for a cause that wasn't his. And worse yet, the person whose cause it was didn't want him doing it.

He guided the horses off the main road, thanks to a nudge from Will. Samantha hadn't said a thing, and Jake was sure she'd have let him drive right past the Nelson farm.

Like the Lowery place, Nelson's buildings were crude by Virginia standards. But their house was larger than Samantha's, having several additions fanning out from the main structure. They weren't big, though Jake guessed one to be a kitchen and the other an extra bedroom.

Before Jake halted the wagon, a woman with a young child perched low on her hip and another tugging at her skirts appeared on the porch. She fanned back limp strawberry blond hair and used the same hand to shade her eyes.

"That's Loni Nelson," Samantha volunteered as she reached under the seat for one of the pies. She smoothed a napkin over the golden crust. "She lost her younger brother in the war, so I'd—"

"I'll watch my step," Jake grumbled before vaulting off the seat.

"How are you doing, Loni?" Samantha twisted away from Jake's hands the moment her feet hit the packed earth.

"Doing fine, Samantha." Loni brushed at an older child who peeked from behind her skirts. "Run and get your pa. Tell him we got company."

Samantha held out the pie, her smile tentative. "I did some baking this morning and thought—"

"We don't want no trouble. We just . . ." Loni's voice trailed off as her eyes caught her husband coming toward the house.

"I don't want trouble either, Loni." Samantha paused and turned to follow the older woman's gaze. "Hello, Seth. This is Jacob Morgan."

To this point Jake had been standing, his hat hanging by his side, wondering what was going on. Obviously Samantha knew these people and they knew her, but there was none of the friendly hospitality he'd expected.

Jake stuck out his hand toward Seth Nelson and tried to ignore the slight hesitation before he took it. "I heard Samantha had herself someone working her place."

"For a while anyway," Jake responded, then nodded toward the woman.

"Well." Samantha was getting mighty tired of holding the pie in front of her like some sort of offering. "If we could come in for a bit . . ."

"Suit yourself." Loni Nelson's invitation was hardly gracious but she did move herself and her brood away from the door.

"It was my idea to come," Jake began after the

234

adults were seated around a scarred oak table.

Will was in the corner by the rocking chair, his own piece of pie forgotten while he helped the two youngest Nelson children with theirs.

Samantha looked up, her fork poised, when Jake spoke. "It wasn't entirely his idea." Her eyes met Jake's. "I mean . . ." She couldn't lie with him looking at her like that.

"Samantha . . . Miss Lowery has been having trouble with some raiders." Jake pushed his pie aside. "She thinks it's Landis Moore. And we've heard you might have a similar problem."

Jake leaned forward, his elbows on the table, and watched Loni and Seth exchange a slow glance. "Now what I'm thinking is that we should get together and go to the sheriff, and if that doesn't work, we could band together and fight this—"

"We don't want any trouble." Seth Nelson echoed his wife's words from earlier.

"And I'm not proposing any." Jake shifted back, trying to keep his tone conversational. But he could feel the tension in the air and a quick glance around the room showed him that all the Nelson children old enough to talk were listening to every word. "Seems to me, trouble's already here."

"Maybe." Seth rose, grabbing his platter with large, raw-boned hands. "But I'll not be making it any worse."

"How can you say that when he rides in and shoots up your place? He does do that, doesn't he? Because that's what he does at Samantha's."

"What goes on at my own farm is no concern of

235

yours." Seth dropped the plate back on the table. "I have chores to do."

Samantha watched him stalk through the door. She knew it would be like this, but a tiny part of her had hoped differently. That same part turned her toward Loni, reaching for her sleeve with her fingers. "He has to see we can't let Moore go on this way. He forced the Colts out. He owns their farm now."

Loni jerked her arm away. "All I see is that if there's trouble brewing, you seem to be in the twix of it."

"That's not fair." Samantha let the hand she'd used to touch Loni fall to her lap.

"Lots of things ain't fair out here." Loni pushed back from the table. "Now I'll be thanking you for the pie . . . and asking you to leave." Her light hazel gaze fell on Jake. "And take him with you."

Three more pies; three more less-than-enthusiastic welcomes.

His reception he could understand. He was a stranger — and one who'd embraced a different side in a war freshly over. But Samantha? What could have happened for her to receive the animosity of her neighbors?

By the time Jake had unharnessed the horses and fed them, shades of purple faded the sky into the horizon. He didn't expect much in the way of supper but even Samantha's warmed-overs were tasty. Still, Will headed for the loft before he did the stew justice.

The day had been tiresome and disappointing. On the ride home, Jake hadn't mentioned any of what

236

had happened, but he wasn't going to let more time go by without getting some answers.

He suspected Samantha knew why he hung around after she cleared the table. Taking a deep breath, she sat in the chair across from him and folded her hands on the table.

Her eyes were direct; his question the same. "What aren't you telling me?"

Chapter Twelve

What aren't you telling me? Such a simple question with such a complex answer. Where should she begin? Taking a deep breath, Samantha decided on the beginning.

"I don't know how much you know about Kansas history."

"I read the papers." Jake rubbed his fingers across his jaw. "Listen, Samantha, I'm not interested in a school lesson. I want to know why your neighbors treat you like you're carrying the plague."

"Because to them I am!" Samantha stood so quickly she had to grab the back of her chair to keep it from tipping over. She turned away from Jake's astonished stare and paced to the stove. "Do you want some coffee?" she offered, lifting the battered enamel pot with her balled-up apron.

"No."

Of course he didn't. He wanted answers. Samantha set the pot down and returned to her chair. "I need to give you a little background."

"I'm listening."

"My family came here in '55. We . . . my father was an abolitionist." Samantha shook her head. "I told you this before, but I want you to understand. To my father, abolition wasn't just a theory. He truly believed in the evils of slavery and was willing to sacrifice . . ." Samantha paused and her gaze collided with Jake's before focusing on a spot behind his left shoulder. "Much," she continued. "He was willing to sacrifice a lot.

"At first it seemed like an adventure. Kansas was nothing like our home in Massachusetts, but . . . Luke was thirteen and I was twelve, and Pa said we came to stop the spread of slavery. He was going to vote in the elections to make Kansas join the union as a free state."

She was taking her time getting to the point, but Jake tried to be patient. He watched her lovely face sadden and leaned toward her. But she didn't seem to notice.

"Then my mother died." Samantha's voice was low. "She never did adjust to this place, to living without . . . comforts. When she took sick, there was no doctor and she was just too weak and fragile to fight."

Like Lydia, Jake found himself thinking, then forced his mind back to what Samantha was saying. She straightened, seemingly making an effort to shake off her grief.

"Pa changed after that. He no longer seemed content to fight slavery with his vote or even the sermons he gave to our neighbors." Samantha rose and retraced her steps to the stove. She was reaching for the coffee pot when she remembered Jake didn't

239

want any.

"Pa started traveling all over the territory, even into Missouri, preaching against slavery." Samantha rubbed her hands down along her skirt. "People started thinking he was crazy or something. But he wasn't." Samantha turned to stare at Jake. For some reason it was important for him to understand. "He just got carried away out of grief."

"Who took care of the farm while he was off . . . abolitioning?" Jake had a suspicion he knew but he wanted to hear her say it.

"Luke and me. Will wasn't much more than a baby."

Neither were you, Jake wanted to say, but didn't. He wished Samantha's father were here so he could tell him what he thought of his going off and leaving them. But that wouldn't change what had already happened. He should know that better than anyone.

"How does Landis Moore fit into this?" Jake wanted to know.

Samantha shook her head. "He mixed with my pa like oil and water. Landis lives across the border in Missouri. There were five boys . . . brothers, counting Ab. He's the one you met on the road. Kind of dull-witted.

"Anyway, at first Moore didn't take my pa very seriously. But the more they crossed paths, the worse it got." Samantha sank into her seat. "I tried talking to Pa. Luke did too. But it didn't do any good. Pa wanted to unite the farmers around here." Her eyes met Jake's. "He wanted them to fight this evil . . . and its disciple, Landis Moore.

"Most of them ignored him. They had enough to

do just getting their crops in and harvested without worrying about abolishing slavery. But a few of them listened, even came to the rallies my father held."

"Each of those families had something bad happen to their farms. The Andersons' cow turned up dead . . . shot. The Hazards' garden was destroyed. And the Nelsons' barn burned to the ground.

"When the war started and Luke went off to join up, I thought things would get better. Word was that the Moore boys, except for Ab, had enlisted in the Confederate Army."

"What happened?" Jake unconsciously lifted his hand to comfort Samantha, but stopped when he realized what he was doing.

"One night." Samantha's voice sounded distant. "Luke was gone. Will and I were asleep. The noise woke me. Shooting and yelling . . . awful things." Samantha swallowed.

"Like the other night." A sudden vision of her huddled by the window, face stark white, eyes huge and dark, came to him. He knew she was frightened . . . more than frightened when he burst through the door. But he didn't know she was reliving a horror from her past.

She looked at him now, her bottom lip caught between small white teeth, and nodded, then trying to keep her voice steady, she continued, "They came through the door and grabbed Pa. I tried to get to the gun, but I couldn't. Someone knocked me against the wall and dragged Pa out.

"The next morning I found him down by the creek . . . dead. They'd cut him . . . and hanged him."

Samantha took a deep breath and hurried on before Jake could say anything. "The sheriff didn't want to believe it was the Moore brothers. I didn't get a good look at them. They wore kerchiefs over their faces," she explained. "But I knew.

"Sheriff Hughes made a halfhearted attempt to find Pa's killers. But he wouldn't cross over into Missouri."

"So that was the end of it," said Jake, then pushed away from the table and strode to the window, staring out into the darkness. He remained calm because she was. But he wanted to pound his fist into the wall and curse the Fates that would allow this to happen.

And he wanted to hold her and let her sob and weep as she had a right to. He'd wrap his arms around her, stroke her beautiful golden hair, and tell her he'd never allow anything bad to befall her again.

But he had no right to do that. When he left, he'd have no control over what happened to her. Hell! He most likely didn't have any control now. Not if today was any indication.

It was hard to comprehend all she'd been through. The war had affected him, but her problems hadn't ended after four bloody years of war.

"Not exactly," Samantha replied suddenly.

"What?" Her words broke through the haze of memory.

Samantha waited for Jake to look over his shoulder. "You said that was the end of it. But it wasn't. I went back to the neighboring farmers. To the same ones my father tried to organize and I pleaded for them to help me go after Moore.

"I can't blame them for . . . for turning me away. Not really. They'd all suffered at Moore's hand, and now they had all the more reason to fear him.

"So you see." Samantha held out her hands, palms up. "Maybe they were justified in acting the way they did today." Samantha sighed. "I knew they would. I should have told you why earlier."

"Why didn't you?"

Her hands fell to her side and her shoulders rounded in defeat. "I don't know." Samantha studied the tips of her shoes. She wore the pair that belonged to her mother. No one had noticed.

Wrapping her arms protectively around her waist, Samantha looked up through her lashes. "I do know why I didn't tell you. At least part of the reason." She waited for him to ask why. No words were spoken but the expression on his handsome face broached the question. His dark brows drew together, deepening the crease between.

"I wanted you to stay. But I was afraid you wouldn't if you knew." The tight set of his firm lips didn't change and Samantha rushed on. "I wasn't positive the farmers wouldn't help. Rumor in town is that someone's harassing more than just me." Samantha's voice dropped and Jake stepped forward to hear her. "But I guess they all figure things could be worse . . . and siding with me is a pretty sure way to make that happen."

Samantha moved toward the stove. "You certain you don't want some coffee? I could use some about now."

"Sure." Jake took two mugs from the sideboard and held them out as she started to pour.

"I want you to know," Samantha began as she set the sugar and a small pot of skimmed cream on the table. "I won't blame you if you leave . . . and I don't think you're one of Moore's men."

"That's a relief." Jake gave her a lopsided grin as he splashed a healthy dollop of cream into the steaming liquid in his cup. Before the war, he'd drunk his coffee black. Now he did what he could to erase the memory of gulping down the bitter brew the mess had passed off as coffee.

"Actually, I haven't thought that for a while now," Samantha admitted. She wrapped her hands around the mug, trying to warm her icy fingers. How could parts of her be so cold when the night was warm? The air around her seemed thick and alive, like it did sometimes before a thunderstorm. But there'd be no storm tonight. She'd seen the stars splattered over the velvety sky.

Jake didn't say anything, only stared at her. Overhead he could hear the shuffling of dried grass — Will fidgeting in his sleep. The clock on the mantle ticked, a steady backdrop for the croaking of frogs from outside. "I'm not leaving."

She looked up and Jake was struck again by how many different shades of blue her eyes could be. Prismed sky blue when the sun caught them. Deep, velvety periwinkle by candlelight. He stopped himself from thinking about the deep indigo of her passion.

"I won't blame you if you do."

"So you said." Jake shook his head and combed fingers back through his hair. "But I won't." The words came out on a breath of air. "I said I'd help

244

you get this crop harvested, and I will. By then the Federal troops will probably be here."

"Hopefully." Samantha didn't know whether to laugh or cry. She only knew she felt like doing both. She also felt like moving toward Jake and putting her arms around him, leaning into his strength. But she didn't.

He'd listened to her story and he still planned to stay. But that didn't mean he sympathized with her, or felt anything but obligation for that matter. He'd said he'd do something, and he was going to do. Regardless of his feelings in the matter.

And how could he help but be somewhat appalled by what she'd said? He was from Virginia . . . the South. He most likely had slaves of his own.

He'd asked for an explanation and received one. There didn't seem to be any reason to hang around. It was late; the cock would crow plenty early tomorrow morning. But Jake was having a hard time making his body do what his mind knew it should.

He'd made one mistake with this woman. He'd made love to her. Nothing could change that. But she'd made it abundantly clear she wanted no repeat of that. So why couldn't he accept that?

He didn't stay on at her farm because he desired her. If anything, that was reason enough for him to move on. But there it was deep in his gut like a gnawing ache, a desire that wouldn't go away.

He looked at her buttoned up in her prim dress. And he wanted her.

He saw her cooking over the stove, the heat of the day amplified by the radiating metal. And he wanted her.

He lay abed on a layer of straw, listening to the cow chewing her cud. And he wanted Samantha Lowery.

But tonight it was more than lust that drove him.

He felt a kinship with her. A kinship that was hard to explain. They'd been on different sides of a conflict that had scarred both their lives, maybe too deep for them ever to be whole again.

Hardly a pleasant thing to have in common with someone. But in Samantha's case he felt the pull nonetheless. It made him pause, his hand on the latch, and say something trivial about getting an early start tomorrow.

It made him wish he could take her in his arms and carry her to her bedstead. And make love to her the way he should have the first time.

First and last time, Jake reminded himself as he swung out into the night. First and last.

Air whooshed out of Samantha's lungs—air she didn't realized she was holding until the door shut, closing Jake off from her view. She'd thought he was going to kiss her . . . and more. Right before he left the cabin, he looked at her the way he had that night in the barn. The night they'd made love.

Desire flashed in his eyes, tightening the planes of his face, and making her want to melt into him.

She didn't, of course. Samantha could never allow a repeat of what had happened that night in the barn. Never.

But as she climbed into her lonely bed, Samantha couldn't remember exactly why not.

* * *

By morning the reasons were abundantly clear. She spent a restless night dreaming about Jake. The images that swam through her head were erotic and sensual. But they all ended with him leaving her. Alone and longing for him.

She'd been left too many times to risk it happening again. Jake would leave. There was nothing she could do to stop that. But when he did, he wasn't going to take any more of her with him than he already had.

Samantha refused to speculate about how much that was.

And she refused to let him get any closer to her. She'd told him all he needed to know about her family and he was still staying to help. But she didn't have to treat him any differently than she'd treat any hired hand. And she didn't intend to.

After two days of seeing him only at meals — and even then he ate quickly and excused himself — Samantha realized Jake felt the same. He didn't want to sit in the evening and talk of books, or play the harmonica. He wanted to be left to himself.

Or more to the point, he wanted to separate himself from her. Will was another story. They spent long days in the fields together. And to hear Will tell it — which of course, was all she had to go by — he and Jake joked and talked all the time.

"Did you know Jake and his brother once tied their cousin's pigtails in knots while she slept and it was so bad she couldn't get the tangles out? And they had to cut some of her hair off."

Samantha settled into her chair and squinted into the lantern light to thread her needle. A smile blossomed on her face when she imagined a young Jake doing something so devilish. She noticed Will's eyes on her and sobered her expression. "I doubt the *cousin* thought it was very funny."

"No sirree. She was angry and crying. And Jake said it made him sorry he did it," Will admitted. But Will was still chuckling over the story.

Samantha took a few stitches in the red silk. Peggy Keane sure did like bright colors. "You and Jake sound like you're having a grand time."

"Sure are." Will leaned back, a copy of *Leatherstocking Tales* forgotten in his lap. Mistaking his sister's silence for disapproval, he jerked forward. "Course we've been getting all our work done too."

"What?" Samantha pulled her fluttered thoughts back and smiled at her brother's earnest face. "Oh, I know you have, Will. You . . . you and Captain Morgan are doing a wonderful job." She didn't need Will to tell her how hard the two of them were working. She saw plenty of evidence herself. Piles of corn filled the crib.

They'd be finished soon. And then Jake would leave.

Samantha turned her attention back to Will. He was telling another of his "Jake" tales, this one about the war. Tensing, Samantha wove the needle into a gather of fabric and looked up at Will.

He was rattling on about a Union patrol and Samantha cleared her throat. "You know, Will," she said, interrupting his description of the soldier's surprise, "now I know you enjoy talking to him, and he's been nice to you. But you . . . we must remember that Captain Morgan fought on a different side

248

during the war . . . the enemy side."

Samantha's gaze slid to the leather-bound book she hadn't even suggested Will read—she owed the Rebel for that. But that didn't mean she'd allow him to influence Will unduly. She took a deep breath. "I just don't think it's a good idea for you to listen to him glorifying the Confederacy. You know it stood for a lot of bad. For things your father and brother died to stop." Samantha turned back to her sewing. She couldn't honestly say her father's death had meant anything.

"He don't . . . doesn't do that, Sam." Will's pale blue eyes collided with Samantha's and his freckled face flamed. He knew she noticed him correcting his grammar and he didn't want to see his sister gloating. But she didn't say a word, just went back to her sewing.

Will sat a little straighter. "The stories he tells me are funny ones. Like the time the cook got startled and poured too much salt in the stew. And everyone was yelling for water. Or the time—"

"I just don't want him glorifying war to you, Will."

"He hates war." Samantha looked up from the seam she sewed and Will went on. "He says it's nothing but killing and suffering . . ." Will stopped. "I think something awful happened to him in that war. Something he . . . doesn't want to talk about."

She'd sensed the same thing. When he was sick and feverish. Then she'd glimpsed the war he lived through—the hell.

That's when she'd decided he was a doctor. Funny, she'd almost forgotten that. He never mentioned it.

He didn't look like any doctor she'd ever known. But then Samantha had only seen old Doc Shelton, and he was more likely drunk as not.

She took another stitch. He didn't work like a doctor either. He worked like a field hand, sweat-slick muscles gleaming in the bright sun and broad shoulders straining.

Samantha realized the wayward tangent of her thoughts and drew in a deep breath. Will was watching her, his expression puzzled. She straightened her back. "I'm certain terrible things happen to most everyone in a war." Look what we went through and we weren't even fighting, she finished silently.

"Now I think you should . . ." Samantha stopped herself and tried to rephrase her suggestion. "I'm tired," she said, carefully folding the crimson fabric into her sewing basket. "Tomorrow morning will be here before we know it. And if this evening is any indication, it will be a warm one."

"You're right about that." Will pushed away from the table and headed for the loft ladder.

"And Will." Samantha leaned over the lamp and, cupping her hands, blew out the flame. Smoke curled up around her. "If Captain Morgan doesn't want to speak of the war . . . well, it would probably be better if you didn't ask him."

"Sure, Sam." Will let go of the rung and gave his sister's shoulders an awkward hug as she walked by him.

Samantha resisted the urge to envelop him the way she had since he was three years old when his care became entirely hers. He was growing up; she had to let go. But it was hard. So very hard.

Samantha closed the bedroom door behind her. Light from the moon poured through the window, limning the meager furnishings. Will was lucky to have Jake Morgan here during this time of his life. The thought struck Samantha, even surprised her, and she couldn't let it pass.

She might wish for someone else to be the man Will looked up to. Someone who hadn't been in the Confederate army. But the more she discovered about Jake, the more she had to admit he was a good man.

And the more she admitted, to herself anyway, that she was attracted to him—powerfully. Yet there was still so much she didn't know—so much he kept to himself.

Samantha stripped down to her shift and lay on the cool sheets. It was a long, draining day, and sleep should be easy to find. But the longer Samantha lay, twisting this way and that, hoping for a comfortable position, the more she realized slumber was a long way off.

Finally she sat up, staring out the window, listening to the lonely wail of a faraway wolf.

The barn was dark. No lantern light shone through the slits Luke and Pa had cut through the sod. She could imagine Jake asleep, his long, lean body stretched out on the pallet, his arm thrown up over his head.

Closing her eyes, Samantha shook her head, willing the vision to disappear. But it wouldn't. She'd seen him like that before. She'd lain with him. He was a Rebel and he was leaving. And she couldn't get him out of her mind.

Enough.

If she couldn't sleep, she refused to waste her time mooning over some Confederate soldier. She'd do something useful. Pulling her wrapper around her and tying the belt at her, waist Samantha went back into the parlor. She lit the lantern and set about mixing flour and yeast to make bread. She wouldn't bake it tonight; the stove was out. But she would knead it and let the dough rise.

The slice of moon was high when Samantha covered the sweet-smelling mound of dough with clean linen and brushed off her floury hands. She felt better. Cooking and baking always did that for her. But she still doubted she could sleep. If anything, her body tingled, more awake than ever.

Samantha wasn't sure where the idea for a bath came from, but once she had it, there was no letting go. It had been a while since she'd an honest-to-goodness, dunk-down bath. Sometimes she went wading in the creek, but she hadn't even done that since the Rebel had showed up. Most of the time she had to make do with a scrubbing from the china bowl in her bedroom.

But not tonight. There was not a soul to see her; everyone was asleep. And she intended to luxuriate in a tub—even if it was a cut-down barrel.

After carrying five buckets of water to the old barrel behind the house, Samantha remembered why she didn't do this often. But thoughts of what it would feel like sinking into the swirling liquid kept her going. Satisfied that there was enough water to cover her bottom, Samantha went back to the house for some clean clothes, a towel, and the soap she'd made—the batch she'd added the essence of prairie flowers to.

The tub was small, but if she folded her knees up under her chin, Samantha managed. The water lapped up her shins and the curve of her hips as she threw back her head and stared at the wondrous black sky and the myriad spattering of stars. Why hadn't she ever thought to do this before?

Jake tried, but he couldn't keep up. Orderlies kept carrying litters into the tent and dumping their grisly baggage of bloodied humans at his feet. Their twisted tangled limbs fell to the straw-covered floor and they clawed at him with bony fingers.

Jake lunged for the man nearest him, lifting him onto a makeshift table made from the parlor door they'd stripped from its hinges. Was he in a parlor? Jake swept a quick look around him. Yes, he was in a house, a field hospital, but he couldn't fathom where. Or what battle was being fought.

All he knew was it was bloody, and no matter how hard he worked, how hard he tried, how hard he prayed, he could not do enough.

The man before him groaned and Jake quickly examined him, looking for the cause of the blood and gore that covered his body. Flies buzzed brazenly around, hovering close to the man's foul-smelling leg.

Jake reached for his saw and a scream came from the man . . . or was it from Jake? It sounded again, this time closer.

Jake jerked awake and lurched to sitting. His

breath came in painful gasps and he could feel the rapid pounding of his heart against his ribs. Jake closed his eyes and forced his mind to accept the obvious.

He wasn't in a field hospital. The war was over. He was in Samantha Lowery's barn with sweet-smelling straw for his bed and a handful of animals for company.

His racing heart slowed, his breathing calmed as reality sank in. It had been a dream—a dream he'd lived—but a dream all the same.

Jake stood and peeled the sweat-dampened shirt from his body. He hadn't had the nightmare in a while—was hoping it, too, was a thing of the past. Taking a deep breath, Jake leaned against the stall. At least he hadn't relived the awful night his wife had died . . . or the day he'd buried his son. Jake rubbed his hands down his bristly chin.

No doubt about it, dreaming of Samantha Lowery was preferable to this. Even if it did have him waking with a painful erection and guilt.

He needed to get out of here. Off this farm. Out of Kansas. The crop was almost harvested. In a few days he'd have fulfilled that part of the bargain. But he couldn't leave Samantha and Will alone, knowing what he did about Atwood's threats.

Jake socked his fist into the stall, startling his horse. Where was the Union Army when you needed them? Where was the damn Union Army now?

Pushing away from the splintery wood, Jake gave up on the notion of getting any more sleep. His blanket was hot and twisted, and he felt restless.

He'd go down to the creek, cool off a bit. No need

to light a lantern, he knew the way. Without bothering to pull his boots on, Jake left the barn. The moon lit the way as he tramped across the yard.

The cabin was dark and Jake let his imagination wander to what lay behind Samantha's bedroom window. She'd be stretched out, covered by nothing but a thin sheet, her breasts rising and falling with each breath she took.

The urge to head for the front door was strong. Just to get a peek at her, he told himself, but knew he was lying to himself. He wanted to make love with her—like before.

Only this time it would be different. This time he'd take his time and please her as much as she had him. He knew last time his release had come too soon.

It had been too long since he'd been with a woman and his desires had run too hot and frenzied. But whatever the reason, it wasn't fair.

Jake rounded the cabin and stopped, his heart leaping into his throat and his skin prickling hot. Samantha stood in a tub, her back to him, one hand high over her head. She held a cup and slowly poured the trickling water over her moon-pearled skin. Jake's mouth went dry as he watched her.

And then as if she sensed she was no longer alone, she turned her head, slowly, sensually, until her eyes met his.

Chapter Thirteen

For long moments Samantha forgot to breathe. She stood, pale and motionless as a marble statue. Her hand still held the empty cup as the last of the water skimmed over her skin. She could see Jake's gaze follow the path of shimmering droplets down to the small of her back, then over the firm swell of her buttock. And she could swear the moisture sizzled on her flesh.

A respectable woman would cover herself. Or shriek and shrink away. Samantha knew that. But she couldn't. All she seemed capable of was standing in shin deep water and watching the heat and passion in his stare. His green eyes shone like polished jade in the moonlight. And like a lodestone they drew her.

Air, thick and expectant, now rasped into her burning lungs. Samantha wet her dry lips and swallowed. He hadn't moved since she glanced over her shoulder and saw him standing in a patch of moonlight. He wore only his gray pants, no shirt, no shoes.

There was no white bandage to mar the broad perfection of his gleaming, hair-sprinkled chest. But she could definitely make out a puckered scar below the hollow of his shoulder.

Was it seconds or minutes since he'd interrupted her bath? Samantha couldn't say. Time seemed measured by the pounding of her heart, the deepening of her desire.

Slowly, fluidly Samantha began turning toward him. Odd as it seemed, she didn't realize she'd moved until she saw the flame of white hot passion that lit his eyes. It spurred her on, till she faced him squarely.

Jakc's eyes narrowed as he took first one, then another step toward her. She was more beautiful than he could ever remember a woman being. All glowing and ivory white in the moonlight. He almost feared if he touched her she'd vanish.

But she wanted to be touched. Her breasts were full and rose-tipped, her nipples hardened and thrust toward him. He itched to feel them beneath his palm. His eyes slid down her flat stomach to the delta of golden curls and his mouth went dry.

His movement toward her was no more designed than her turn to face him. Some things cannot be stopped, cannot be altered. Jake reached her in half a dozen strides. The hands that clasped her to him were not tentative or even gentle. This was no time for a mild-mannered kiss.

His lips took hers open-mouthed and hungry — and she could do naught but respond in kind. Her skin was water-slick as he lifted her from the tub, holding her high against his hardness. Jake wanted to take it slow this time, but he honestly didn't know if he could. Already he throbbed, his desire near ready to explode.

She wrapped her arms around his neck, her fingers pressing insistently into the damp curls at his nape. His chest abraded her breasts, her toes barely touched the ground, and Samantha thought she'd surely melt. His big hands clasped her buttocks, his tongue invaded her mouth, and Samantha wriggled and moaned with the ecstasy of it.

Only the need for air made them break off the kiss. Samantha threw her head back and Jake skimmed his lips down her neck and across the ridge of her collarbone. He was more aroused than he ever remembered being, and he didn't want to lose the feeling.

Slowly her lowered her until she stood in front of him. He saw the bewilderment on her face as he stepped back. But before she could question his action, his hand cupped her breast, his thumb rubbing over the sensitive peak and she swayed toward him.

Leaning forward he scooped her into his arms, lifting her high against his chest. She seemed surprised at first with this new arrangement, but Jake shifted, settling her more comfortably. "I want you long and slow," he mumbled. "And all to myself."

He gave her no time to protest, though that was the farthest thing from her mind, as he carried her toward the barn. Ripe musky smells assailed Samantha as he pushed through the door. It was nearly black inside, but Jake found his way to the makeshift pallet in the stall. He lowered her carefully, sucking in his breath when she let her fingers trail down through his chest hair and catch at his waistband.

Jake yanked off his pants and lay down beside her, touching her, trying to slow his racing pulse. His lips found hers again, and this time he took the time to explore. His tongue followed the generous curve of her upper lip, then sucked the lower into his mouth.

"I've wanted to do that for so long." His whispered words filled the silence around them. Straining to see her, Jake could distinguish only a vague pale outline. But he knew she was pleased. He could feel her smile.

The darkness cocooned them. Unable to see more than the faintest shadow of Jake, Samantha luxuriated in her other senses. The feel of his hard muscles, the smell of his manly body, the taste. She was drowning in a sensual sea, and had no desire to save herself.

When he shifted on top of her, Samantha's legs opened to accommodate his body. It was like the last time . . . only somehow different. His kisses, his hands on her flesh, were driving her wild.

Samantha arched, reveling in his gasp when she brought his shaft near her moist heat. His fingers skimmed down her body and her own breath caught. She thought the pleasure couldn't go any higher. She was wrong. His flesh slid across hers, dipping and stroking, and the tension intensified.

Her legs spread shamelessly, her body bowed, and a maelstrom of ravishing sensation spread through her. Flashing lights appeared where before the darkness had reigned. She trembled, convulsed, clutched at the corded strength of his shoulders. And she knew what she'd missed the other time.

But he didn't give her an opportunity to sort out the earth-shattering feelings that had rocked through her.

"Are you all right?" Jake whispered on a raspy breath.

"Yes. Oh, yes," Samantha gasped. And then he entered her.

There was no pain this time; only the sweet, sensual slide as he drove into her. His power and size expanded her body; filled her completely.

And once again Samantha felt herself whirling, her head and body spinning like the core of a tornado. She clutched him. She met his fiery kisses with urgent hunger. And as his thrusts became deeper, lightning fast, thundering into her, she sparked, and then exploded. Waves of ecstasy rolled over her, then lashed back to him. Jake shuddered and groaned. Then unable to hold out a moment longer, he had his own tumultuous climax.

Thoroughly spent, Samantha collapsed onto the woolen blanket. Jake still rested between her legs. His face was buried in her silken curls. He shifted closer, his breath fanning across her ear. "I must be heavy."

"No," Samantha sighed. "Not really."

She felt his smile this time before he rolled away.

Samantha expected him to settle beside her and stirred at the sudden lack of heat when he didn't. "Where are you going?" Did he really plan to leave after what they'd shared? Eventually he would. Samantha knew that. But so soon?

"I'm over here." Samantha raised on elbow to stare into the darkness toward the sound of his voice. "I want to see you this time," he explained, a moment before a blossom of light bloomed in his hand. He cupped the flame that threw stark, erotic patterns of shadow and brilliance across his big body.

Samantha tried to look away, but couldn't. She watched unabashedly as he touched match tip to wick and spread a pale glow over all but the eves and far corners of the barn. The cow and horses didn't seem to notice Jake as he moved back to the stall where Samantha lay, but she was aware of nothing else.

Suddenly shy, Samantha took a deep breath and glanced around for something to cover her nakedness. She could find nothing. Her clothes, even the towel she'd planned to dry with, were in the yard near the tub. It was too late to do anything but burrow into the straw. Jake stood over her, the tin lantern held high. Then he turned and hung it on a hook.

"I . . . I really should go back to the cabin." Samantha tried to seem as unaffected by their lack of clothing as he was.

"I know." Jake settled down beside her. She went quite readily into his arms as he lay down, her body contradicting her earlier statement.

Jake closed his eyes. He had no business cuddling her to him or tangling his fingers in her thick blond curls. But then he had no right to do most of the things he did with her. And it hadn't stopped him.

She wriggled closer, letting her fingers drift toward his scar. "Does it still hurt," she murmured.

"Not much." Jake took a deep breath as her hand continued to skim over his chest. Light, feathery stokes that made his body quicken. He felt himself grow hard and tucked his chin to see if she noticed. At first he thought her unaware of what she did to him but then she tilted her head and he saw the teasing sparkle in her blue eyes.

"Jake?"

He tried to keep his breathing steady. "Hmmm?"

Her fingers found and followed the line of chest hair that arrowed southward. "What did you mean when you said you wanted to see me this time?"

Jake's burst of laughter came almost as quickly as his movements as he flipped her beneath him. "What did you think I meant?"

But Samantha was too busy laughing to answer. Jake settled into the cradle of her body, weight resting on his elbows. He grinned at her good humor then splayed her hair out on the blanket. It shone like gold against the gray wool.

"You're very beautiful." He dipped and brushed a kiss across her lips to hide some of the emotion surging through him. He loved to see her laugh—to see her happy. But when he moved to look at her again, her expression had sobered. "What is it?" Jake touched her cheek.

Samantha's breathing brought her breasts in contact with his chest. "You don't have to say that. I know the way things are."

"Then tell *me*." Jake searched the depths of her cerulean eyes.

Samantha wanted to look away, but the pull of his intense gaze was too great. She swallowed and began. "We have . . . nothing permanent. You will leave soon. And I can accept that," she added quickly. "This . . ." Samantha's hand lifted, then fell as if in defeat. "Just happened. Neither of us wanted it to." She took a deep breath and her voice firmed and she shocked him to his core with her next statement. "But I don't want it to stop."

Samantha lowered her lashes. How could she have said something so . . . so brazen. If he didn't think her a hussy before, he most certainly did now. Heat raced through her body, and it had nothing to do with the feel of his hot flesh pressed to hers.

"Samantha." Jake's finger caught under her chin. He waited for her eyes to meet his before he continued, "I don't want it to stop either."

With a skim of his hand down her body, he began to show her how he felt.

Samantha sighed and rested her head on Jake's shoulder. This last time they made love only deepened her resolve to take what happiness she could before he left. But it also frightened her. He'd been so loving, still was, as his thumb made gentle patterns on her arm. And Samantha found there were some things she simply had to know.

"Jake?" Her body felt drowsy and replete, but there was an underlying tension in her voice.

"Hmmm?" He was going to have to get up in a moment and take her back to the cabin; otherwise they'd both fall asleep. For all Samantha's assurances that she could handle this turn in their relationship, Will couldn't if he found them asleep like this come morning.

"Who is the woman in the daguerreotype?" Samantha had tried to forget she ever saw it, or that he called out a name in his delirium, but found she couldn't. Her heart lurched when she felt Jake tense.

"My wife." Jake twisted his head to catch a glimpse of Samantha. "She was my wife. She died." His words were crisp and succinct.

"I'm sorry." Samantha could sense he didn't want to talk about this, but something kept her going. "And the boy?" Samantha knew she couldn't stop now until she heard it all.

"My son." Jake's words were whispered on a breath of air. "He's dead too."

"I'm so sorry." His words were full of pain, and Samantha felt tears well up in her eyes. "How tragic for you. But sometimes—"

"I don't want to talk about this." Jake shifted to look at her, then turned away. "I've heard all the platitudes, and—"

"What?" Samantha asked when he didn't go on. Jake's eyes narrowed and he looked at her in a way that she'd seen before. When he found out who'd shot him.

"How did you know about the people in the daguerreotype?"

Samantha forced herself not to flinch. Why hadn't she thought of this when she asked about his wife? Because she was too worried that he might still be married, Samantha reminded herself. She took a calming breath that didn't really help. "I . . . I saw the daguerreotype."

"You saw it? But it was in the pocket of my jacket." He paused, then his voice quieted. "Did you go through all my things?"

"Yes, but . . ." Sitting up, Samantha glanced back over her shoulder. "I thought you were with Landis Moore, so—"

"So you assumed that gave you the right to pilfer my things."

"I didn't pilfer! I wanted to know who you were."

Jake shook his head. "I guess I can't blame you for that. At least no more than for shooting me in the first place."

Samantha sucked in air. How could she forget all the differences between them? In his arms she had. But apparently he hadn't. Or maybe it was just that she wasn't in his arms now. "I better go in."

"I'll walk with you." Jake reached for his pants.

"No." Samantha scooted out of the stall. "I

know the way." Before he'd more than stood, she closed the barn door behind her. She went behind the cabin, yanked on her shift, and emptied the tub . . . and tried to keep from thinking of all that had happened.

Jake sat with his saddlebag across his knees. It had been a long time since he'd looked at the picture. It always felt like he was uncovering a fresh wound. But he knew he had to see it tonight.

Reaching in among his clothes, he found the scrolled frame. The moment his hand closed over the familiar metal, Jake realized he had seen it recently. When he was feverish from his wound. He'd looked at it then. Samantha must have given it to him.

Viewing it now brought pain, as it always did. Except Jake found he didn't have the urge to bury his head and cry. Though he didn't usually give in to it, the desire to clutch the likeness of his family to him and express his grief was always there.

But not tonight.

Tonight he studied the three people posed beneath the protective glass and almost smiled. He trailed his finger down the center of the gown Lydia wore. It was green . . . no, blue, he remembered, a deep shade of sapphire blue. She worried it wasn't becoming enough. Jake said she looked beautiful, but she questioned him, seeking reassurance it was the perfect dress for their sitting.

Jake's gaze drifted to his son standing proudly beside his mother. You'd never know by seeing him there, that he'd fidgeted and squirmed just moments earlier. He wanted to play with his lead soldiers.

The daguerreotype was made before Jake left for the war. His son was five. He'd be nine if he'd lived. Almost as old as Will.

Jake's breath caught on a sob. Samantha was right. It was tragic that they were dead. Tragic that so many were dead.

Jake extinguished the lantern and lay down on his blanket. He couldn't see the picture any more but he held on to it. His mind flew back through the years touching first one memory, then another. They'd been pleasant, happy times before the war. Each remembrance made his heart lighter.

Until he recalled the day he buried Lydia. Their son had died a week earlier. As he walked down the hill from the cemetery, his father had touched his sleeve. He offered some words of sympathy then he began talking about Lydia and Andrew's death.

"I don't want to talk about it," Jake had said then, the words echoing the ones he said to Samantha. He meant them three years ago and he thought he meant them tonight. But lying here alone, his memories and guilt to keep him company, Jake wasn't sure.

Breakfast was strained.

Samantha stayed at the stove making griddle cakes as long as possible. She didn't want to sit at the same table with Jake. Not with last night so fresh in her thoughts.

She'd lost her mind.

That was the conclusion Samantha had come to the night before when she could no longer keep memories of her behavior at bay. She'd lost her mind. But she had it back now. And she wasn't going to allow a repeat of what had happened. But she couldn't say that because she already had—after the first time they'd made love. And she let it happen again.

She couldn't tell him. But she sure didn't want to face him. Jake and Will were discussing their plans for the day. They'd be finished eating soon and then they'd leave and—

"What do you think, Sam?"

"About what?" Her hand stilled, the ladle of batter inches from the hot skillet.

"Do you think we should start harvesting the east field?" Will asked, his face showing surprise she wasn't following the conversation.

"Oh." Samantha turned to face the table—she couldn't help herself—and her eyes locked with Jake's. She swallowed. "I don't know." His expression was strange . . . unreadable, and Samantha quickly jerked back toward the stove.

She wasn't going to worry about what he was thinking. He let her know last night he didn't want her getting close to him. Oh, physically close was fine. Fine with *him*. But let her ask a question about his past—about his wife—and he wanted no part of her.

He could pretend his anger the night before had

come from her looking through his saddlebags. But Samantha knew differently. He retreated within himself the moment she asked about the woman in the daguerreotype.

As chair legs scratched over the wood floor, Samantha nodded her acknowledgment of Jake and Will's thanks for breakfast. The door opened and closed, and Samantha let out her breath. How was she ever going to manage until Jake left the farm? She seemed constantly to whirl around — wanting him to stay; wanting him to leave. Well, today she definitely wanted him to — "

"Samantha."

The spatula clattered to the floor as Samantha twisted around. "I . . . I thought you left with Will."

"He has a few more chores to do before we go out to the field." Jake stepped closer.

"Oh." Samantha scooped up the spatula and took it to the dry sink. He was still in the cabin. She could hear him breathing, could smell his scent. She grasped the edge of the dry sink.

"Samantha, I — "

"Do you want more to eat?"

"No."

"Well, then." Samantha poured water into the dishpan, hoping he'd read the dismissal in her actions.

"They died of typhoid fever. I was away, down on the Peninsula, when I got word they were sick." Jake kept talking as Samantha turned toward him. "I rode for Richmond as fast as I could, but by the

269

time I arrived they were both . . . gravely ill."

Samantha realized her hands were dripping and wiped them down the front of her apron.

"My son, Andrew, died first. He was six. I always thought he was so strong, but . . ." Jake took another step. "Lydia, my wife, died later the same week." His hands came up in surrender. "I always felt there was something I should have done. Something to save them."

"Jake." Samantha touched his sleeve. "People die. There was nothing you could do."

Jake looked down upon her sweet upturned face. Her blue eyes shone with compassion . . . compassion he wasn't sure he deserved. "I knew the war would be difficult for her," he said by way of explanation.

"Jake, war is hard on everybody."

"But not everyone dies from it." Jake lifted his hands to Samantha's shoulders. "Look at you. Trouble and hardship have plagued you since you were a little girl. Then the war, being on your own. You survived." His fingers trailed down her arms and he looked away.

"The thing is, I knew how she was. Hell, we'd been married for eight years. And before that." Jake glanced over his shoulder. "I'd known Lydia near all my life. If anyone understood that she wasn't the type of woman to survive on her own, it was I." His shoulders rounded. "But I left them both."

"You had no way of knowing they'd get typhoid fever. You're taking too much on yourself."

Samantha searched for the words that would make him understand he wasn't responsible. But by the defeated expression in his pale green eyes, she knew she wouldn't find them.

"The truth is, I wanted to go." Jake shook his head. "I thought I could make a difference."

"I'm sure you did."

Jake's laugh was cynical. "Hardly. All I accomplished was deserting my wife and son when they needed me."

"Stop that." Samantha batted at his arm. "I'm tired of hearing how their deaths were your fault. Did your wife . . . did Lydia beg you to stay with her?" If she did, she was weaker even than Samantha assumed.

"No." Jake shook his head. "She wanted me to help defend Virginia."

"Well, see?" Samantha's hands folded at her waist.

"She didn't know what war was. She thought of it more as one big parade, with fancy uniforms and plumed hats."

"Did you?"

"Did I what?" Jake backed toward the door. He'd wanted to tell Samantha about his wife, but this conversation was getting them nowhere. Why was she arguing with him? He knew what happened. He knew he deserved to feel guilty.

"Did you know what war was like before you went?" Samantha moved between Jake and the door, daring him to push past her.

"Of course not. No one does."

"Yet you blame yourself because Lydia didn't." Samantha took an aggressive step forward. "You're forgetting I saw her likeness. And yes, I went through your saddlebags to find it. While you were feverish, I studied it a lot." Samantha paused for breath and to see if he'd berate her again for invading his privacy. When he said nothing, she went on.

"Your Lydia was a grown woman." Samantha planted her fists at her waist. "If she said she wanted you to join the army, she probably meant it. And apparently she took care of herself and your son for a while after the war started, so you shouldn't be thinking she didn't know how. As for the typhoid fever . . ." Emotions had made her voice louder than she intended. Shaking her head, she lowered her voice. "As for the typhoid fever . . . you had no way of knowing *or* controlling anything about that."

"Are you finished?" Jake stood glowering down at her.

Samantha sucked in her lower lip and nodded. What had gotten into her lecturing him like that?

Jake crossed his arms. "You're right."

"What?" Samantha's eyes opened wide and her hands fluttered down to her side.

"I said you're right." Jake watched the play of emotions across Samantha's face. Her expression finally settled on bewilderment.

"But . . ."

"I'd never considered that she handled things for over a year. But she had. She kept the house going

272

and food on the table. And in her letters she never really complained."

Samantha straightened her shoulders. "Well, there." She nodded. "You see."

"Of course, I still wonder if I might have saved them if I were home."

"But you don't know that for sure." Samantha cocked her head to the side. "And you never will. So you really should stop punishing yourself for it."

"You think that's what I've been doing?"

Samantha's smile was sweet and understanding. "Yes, Jacob Morgan. I think you have."

"But you think I should stop." Jake's hands cupped her shoulders. His warm breath fanned her face.

Samantha felt her grip on reality loosening, but she forced herself to say, "It's about time."

She heard him agree with her just before his lips, warm and pliant, closed over hers. Samantha's arms went around his waist and she melted toward him.

The kiss deepened. Tongues stroked and Samantha moaned deep in her throat. Had she less than an hour ago decided she would never let him touch her again? Now that was all she wanted.

Time and place seemed to disappear as he pushed her against the door, wedging his body against hers. Samantha's legs opened, her skirts spreading and she could feel the hard evidence of his arousal. He groaned when she moved against him, a deep hungry sound that Samantha loved.

But there was something else. Another sound. And it just barely skimmed the corners of her consciousness.

Jake heard it too because he pulled back, giving her a dazed look which Samantha knew matched her own. Not that both of them didn't recognize Will calling from the yard. It was more than either could understand how they forgot he'd be back for Jake any minute.

"I better go." Jake's voice was husky and low.

Samantha could only nod. She felt totally disoriented and light-headed. She watched Jake reach for his hat and finger-comb his sun-streaked hair before settling the hat over his head. And still she stood leaning into the door.

"I'll be back late this afternoon." Jake bent, planting a quick kiss on her lips. "In the meantime, don't forget to fire the gun if you need me."

She still had one of his guns. But since the sheriff's visit, she'd had no reason to fire it. Samantha was beginning to think that maybe Landis Moore had moved back to Missouri and forgotten about his old vendetta with her family.

At least that's what Samantha hoped as she watched Jake amble across the yard to meet Will. He ruffled the boy's hair and led the way into the barn.

Fire the gun if you need me, he'd said. Samantha shook her head and laid the back of her hand against her cheek. She had a powerful need for him at this very moment. But as she began clearing the breakfast dishes, Samantha laughingly decided that was not what he'd meant.

The morning and afternoon dragged. Samantha threw herself into her work — weeding and watering the garden and baking bread. She finished another dress for Peggy Keane and baked a cobbler. Anything to keep her mind off why she couldn't wait for Jake to return.

"You're being silly," she told herself time and time again. Worse than silly. Wanton. That was an excellent word for her behavior. But she just couldn't bring herself to care.

Samantha's hands stilled on the sheet she was dragging off the clothesline, and she squinted toward the west. The late afternoon sun turned the sky into a splash of peach and crimson, and she wondered when Jake and Will would return.

She was so busy daydreaming that she didn't hear the man walk up behind her. Didn't even realize he was there until rock-hard arms swooped around her. A scream started low and lodged in her throat as warm lips pressed a kiss to the side of her neck.

Jake.

He twisted her around in his arms, transferring his mouth to hers and pulling her up against him.

"You scared me," Samantha breathed when he lifted his head.

"Sorry." Jake's mouth skimmed down her cheek, and his hand covered her breast. "I thought you heard me."

"Hmmm." She was gradually hearing nothing but the excited beating of her own heart. His lips nibbled hers, and she lost almost all sense of time. Just like this morning. "Wait a minute." Samantha pushed lightly on his shoulder. "Where's Will?" They were, after all, standing in the yard.

"Down at the creek." Jake punctuated his words with another kiss. "We stopped there to get cleaned up."

Samantha now realized his hair and shirt were damp. She ran her fingers down his chest. "I hurried," he mumbled before his open mouth took hers.

But they both knew it was only a matter of time before Will came strolling into the yard, so with a mutual deep breath they pulled apart.

Jake took another breath. "You have something burning in the stove?" he asked after draping his arm around her shoulders. It would be a shame if supper were burned, but he'd have no one to blame but himself. And if forced to choose between food or kissing, he guessed he'd take the kissing.

"No. I took the bread and pies out."

"Pies." Jake's grin was lecherous. "What kind?"

"Apple . . ." Samantha wrinkled her nose. "I smell it too."

So did he. Jake jerked around, his eyes narrowing at what he saw. A huge cloud of black smoke.

"My God!" Samantha cried as Jake took off running across the yard. "The cornfield."

Chapter Fourteen

By the time Samantha reached the barn, Jake was barreling out the door, his arms full of bundled blankets. His eyes met hers only an instant before he took off toward the far cornfield.

"Find Will," he yelled back over his shoulder. "He's down by the creek. So's the wagon."

Samantha didn't wait to hear everything. Gathering up her skirts, she raced down the path, screaming for her brother. A chubby quail scurried out of her way as she rushed past the wagon, but the slow mules hardly gave her notice.

"Will!" Samantha skidded to a halt by the pebble bottomed creek. Her heart pounded painfully, and an ache in her side made her double over. But she scanned the area, yelling her brother's name again and again. Her only answer was the hypnotic drone of insects and the peaceful babble of water.

Samantha jerked around. The column of smoke spiraled higher into the cloud-spattered sky. Grabbing the bucket off the wagon, she scooped it quickly through the water and looked around for something else to fill. Realization that there was nothing came quickly. With a sigh of frustration, Samantha climbed into the wagon seat and turned the mules toward the field.

Smoke stung Samantha's eyes as she pulled on the reins and bounded from the wagon. She wiped tears from her eyes and called for Jake, but the fire had a voice of its own and she could barely hear herself.

Grotesque black billows defiled the air, making breathing difficult and seeing nearly impossible. Samantha covered her mouth and nose, trying to filter the air with her fingers as she hurried around the perimeter of the fire.

When she spotted Jake, her heart raced with relief. He was covered with soot, his face heat-singed, and he was coughing between gasping breaths. But he kept up a rhythmic slapping of the flames with a cinder-burned blanket.

He didn't notice her until Samantha grabbed his arm.

"Other . . . blankets?" She managed to wheeze out the question when he jerked around toward her.

"Get . . . out . . . of . . . here!" His words were muffled by the piece of shirt he'd torn off and tied around his lower face. But his eyes, when they flashed toward her, demanded compliance.

Compliance he wasn't going to get from her. Grabbing a handful of skirt Samantha yanked, then wrapped the rent fabric around her mouth and nose. "The blankets," she bellowed after again clutching his arm. "Where are they?"

Jake glared at her then jerked his hand toward the edge of the field. At first Samantha thought it was just another command to leave but when she glanced around she could make out a crumpled pile of wool near a tangle of weeds. Whirling around she seized the gray wool and soon she was by Jake's side slapping at the orange flames.

Her lungs burned and her back ached savagely but Samantha kept going. It was like fighting a battle, she imagined. Going beyond what you ever dreamed you could do. But unfortunately, this enemy seemed to be winning.

Jake dropped his smoldering blanket and ran to the wagon for a shovel he'd tossed in that morning. Now he bent his back to digging, throwing dirt toward the flames, and knocking the next row of corn out of the fire's path.

Samantha, reading his strategy, threw down her blanket and rushed to clear away the fallen stalks. But still the fire gained on them.

Determined to fight, Samantha bent over a tangled pile of stalks when she felt her feet knocked out from under her. A heavy weight descended, knocking even the oxygen-starved air from her lungs. For one frightening moment as she realized the weight was Jake, Samantha thought he had lost his mind. Then he began slapping at her skirt and she stared down in horror to see her dress smoldering.

Tears rolled down Samantha's cheeks as she lay on the packed ground. Too tired and discouraged to know if they were from the smoke or her own disheartened spirit, she let them flow.

"You . . . all right?" Jake's words snapped Samantha out of her lethargy and she scrambled to her feet, ignoring his hand. What would happen if they lost the crop from this field? She didn't want to think about the answer to that.

"It's no use." Jake pulled at her arm.

"But we can't just—"

"This field's gone. We can try to save the—" Jake stopped and squinted through red-rimmed eyes toward the sky.

"What?" Samantha looked up. A fat raindrop splattered on her face, cooling her cheek. She gasped, taking the next one in her mouth. Jake's expression told her he felt it too.

"It's raining," she whispered, almost afraid to say it too loud. If the storm gods heard, they might stop even the hope of a miracle. But today the spirits seemed generous, for before Samantha could wonder if the occasional drops would have an effect on the fire, the heavens opened up, pouring torrents of rain on the blaze.

Lightning streaked across the sky, giving the whole scene a surreal aspect. Samantha looked out across the field and watched the once hungry flames sizzle and die.

She glanced toward Jake. He glanced toward her. And grins broke simultaneously across their wet, soot-streaked faces. Samantha was in his arms before she realized either of them had moved. Jake wrapped himself around her, lifting her high and swinging her around. Samantha's tattered skirt clung to her legs, plastered there by the drenching rain. Her arms flew around Jake's neck and Samantha threw back her head and laughed.

Then Jake started laughing and twirled her again and Samantha wondered when she'd ever been so happy.

"It's raining," she sang out. "We needed a miracle and we got it."

Jake had pretty much given up on miracles. But with Samantha saying it, with her blackened face dripping wet and streaked, and still so beautiful it took his breath away, he wondered. He liked her to be happy.

Samantha kissed him. At first when she bent her head down to brush his mouth with hers, she meant it as a shared celebration. But as soon as their lips met, they both knew it was much more.

They pulled back and stared, their breath mingling for only a moment before Jake let her slide slowly down his body. Their rain-soaked clothes felt slick, and sensual, as she rubbed against him.

And then they were kissing again. No light tentative kiss, but something deep and hungry and as satisfying as the rain smothering the remaining smoldering cinders.

"God, Samantha, I want you." Jake dug his fingers into Samantha's sopping hair. He gave her no

281

chance to answer before crushing her lips again.

And she wanted him. Samantha molded herself to him as the rain sizzled around them. Though her mind rebelled, Samantha forced herself to keep a modicum of reality. "What about Will?"

"Will?" Jake clamped his hands on Samantha's shoulder, peeling her away from his body. "Where is he?"

"Why he's . . ." Samantha glanced around, seeing the fire-ravaged patch of field; the tall stalks that hadn't been touched. But there was no sign of her brother. "I thought he was with you." Samantha watched Jake shake his head and a sinking feeling began in the pit of her stomach. "But he has to be. He wasn't by the creek." Her voice took on a frantic edge. "There's no way he could miss this fire and I know he'd come to help."

She explained this to Jake as he jogged to the edge of the burned-out area. He cupped his hands and yelled her brother's name into the storm.

"What?" Samantha ran to him across the spongy ground. She scrubbed the wet hair out of her face. "What do you think happened to him?"

"I don't know." Jake yelled again for Will. "Go back to the house." He turned toward Samantha. "Check the cabin and the barn."

"But I . . ."

"Just do it, Samantha. And the creek, too. Maybe he . . ." Jake shook his head. There was no explanation as to where Will was—at least no good one. "Go on now." Jake touched her cheek because he saw in her eyes that she was just as worried as he. And because it made him feel better. "I'll look around here."

Samantha hesitated only a moment before heading off toward the cabin on a run. Panic made her heart beat crazily. Where could Will be? She tried not to think about where Jake was looking.

"Will! Will!" The steady sheets of rain muffled her screams.

The cabin was empty. Samantha rushed through, knocking over a chair without even noticing. Water streamed off her clothes as she climbed to the loft.

The barn was empty except for the cow, who looked up lazily as Samantha threw open the door.

By the time she plodded through the muddy bank by the creek, found nothing, and made her way back to the cornfield, Samantha was frantic. She couldn't lose Will. She just couldn't!

The rain had slowed, a sad, cold drizzle that spoke of loneliness and despair. She pushed that thought away and called out to Jake.

"He's not back . . . I didn't find him."

"Me neither." Jake stopped his systematic search through the corn rows and studied Samantha. She looked as if there wasn't much holding her together but she didn't hesitate to come over to him.

Straightening her shoulders, she asked, "Where have you looked so I don't waste time repeating."

Jake hesitated. "Back that way," he finally said, nodding back over his shoulder. He'd searched through the charred debris from the fire, looking for any sign that the blaze had destroyed more than corn. "No sign of him," he added.

Samantha swallowed down the bitter taste of fear and nodded. Jake seemed to think the cornfield was the place to look, and thank heaven he hadn't found Will's body in the burned rubble.

"Any chance he could have gone into town or to a neighbor's," Jake called across to the other end of the row that Samantha was searching.

"I don't think so." Samantha straightened and rubbed the small of her back. The rain had stopped but she hadn't noticed until now. "He'd more than likely take a horse to town. And they were in the paddock. And even if he did decide to go visiting, he wouldn't do it so close to supper-time. You know how he is about— "Oh, no," she cried. "Oh, no!"

"What is it?" Jake raced along the row, batting at the sharp edged corn leaves that drooped into his path.

"Will's hat." Samantha held up a muddy, broad-brimmed straw hat for Jake to see, then clutched it to her chest. "It's Will's hat and he wore it this morning when he left. I know. I saw him put it on." Samantha's eyes were filled with tears when she lifted them to Jake.

"This doesn't necessarily mean anything," he cautioned, though he started beating through the corn stalks close to where she'd found the hat. After a moment, Samantha joined him.

But though they covered the area thoroughly,

there was no sign of Will.

"This is close to where we finished up working today," Jake finally said. "Maybe he dropped his hat this afternoon."

"Maybe," Samantha acknowledged, but she didn't stop looking.

Twilight was making it harder to see in the shadow of the tall cornstalks. Jake figured they had perhaps another half-hour of light before it became impossible to see. But though he renewed his efforts, they found no other clue to Will's whereabouts.

"We need lanterns," Jake finally said, when he could barely see his hand in front of him.

"You go get them, I'll keep looking," came a voice to his left.

Jake rubbed his jaw, then arched his back. "Come on," he said, moving toward the sound of her rustling through the stalks. "You need to go back to the cabin and get some dry clothes. You're going to get sick out here in this cold." As the sun set, the air had taken on a decided chill.

"I'm fine. You go back if you want. I'm going to keep looking."

Jake grabbed Samantha's arm, pulling her against him so he could see her face. "Listen. We're going to keep looking for him. But we won't do him any good thrashing around in the dark, and making ourselves sick."

What he said made perfect sense, but something in Samantha couldn't accept it. "I can't stop," she said, her face turned up toward his. "I can't."

"Samantha." Jake wrapped his arms around her, holding her close, trying to give her some of his warmth. "We'll find him, honey."

"Oh, Jake, I'm so scared." Samantha sobbed the words into Jake's damp shirt. "If something's happened to Will, I don't know what I'll do."

"Shhh." Jake's fingers caught in her tangled hair. "You'll be able to keep up the search better—we both will—after some hot coffee."

Jake turned, keeping his arm around Samantha's shoulder, and when he did, his boot knocked against something hard. Reaching down and feeling for the obstacle he discovered a boot.

"What is it?"

Jake let go of Samantha and pushed aside cornstalks. "There's somebody here."

"Will?" Samantha knelt down in the soggy field.

"I can't tell." Jake worked his way up to the head. "Yeah, it's Will," he said as he leaned over to listen to his chest. He touched something wet and sticky, with an all too familiar smell.

"Is he . . ." Samantha rustled through the stalks till she knelt across from Jake.

"He's alive," Jake answered and could feel her relief.

"Oh, Will." Samantha leaned over him, her hand tracing his cheek with its soft peach fuzz whiskers. "What's wrong with him? He feels so cold."

"I don't know." Jake scooped down under the boy and lifted him high against his chest. "We need to get him into town. To a doctor."

"No!"

Jake stopped tramping through the field and glanced back at Samantha even though he could make out nothing but a shadowy form. "Samantha, he's unconscious and Lord knows what's wrong with him. He needs a doctor and I intend to see he gets one." He started off again. "Run ahead and pull the wagon as close as you can."

Samantha surged to Jake's side. "I don't want to take him to Doc Shelton."

"Well, if he's the only doctor in town, he'll have to do."

"There's you." Samantha heard Jake's sharp pull of breath and rushed ahead before he could say anything. "I know you're a doctor and I want you to help Will."

"You don't know what you're saying."

"Don't I?" Samantha dogged Jake's heels as he pushed forward, out of the cornfield, carrying Will. "I heard you rambling when you were feverish. I know you're a doctor."

"*Was,* Samantha. I *was* a doctor. But I gave that up at Appomattox Court House." He'd reached the wagon and settled Will onto a pile of corn cobs. Samantha climbed in after him. After pulling off his shirt, Jake balled it up and pressed it against the side of Will's head. "Hold this," Jake told Samantha. Looks like he's cut and it's going to be a bumpy ride."

"I don't want to argue with you." Samantha

brushed wet hair from Will's face. "But we're not taking my brother into town. If Doc Shelton isn't drunk, he's well on his way, and I won't have him butchering up Will. If you won't do it, I'll just have to take care of him myself." The sob at the end of her speech was annoying but Samantha didn't care. She said what she thought, and if the Rebel didn't like it, that was too bad.

"Oh, hell!" Jake jerked himself into the wagon seat. "Hold him steady." With a slap of the reins, Jake turned the wagon, heading it toward the cabin.

No sooner had Jake pulled the mules to a halt than he jumped off the seat and climbed into the back, scattering corn into the mud. Samantha moved away so Jake could lift her brother. "Light as many candles and lanterns as you have," he ordered as he carried Will through the door.

Samantha yanked back the quilt on her bed and then hurried about the cabin, doing as Jake asked. By the time she returned to her bedroom, a lamp in one hand, candles in the other, Jake was stripping Will out of his clothes.

"What happened to him?" She held the lamp over Jake's shoulder.

"I'm not sure."

Jake knew the exact moment Samantha saw the extent of her brother's injuries. At the sound of her gasp, Jake glanced toward her. She appeared so fragile and vulnerable, he had the strongest desire to hold her and assure her Will would be all right.

288

But he didn't have the time—or the confidence—to tell her that.

"I'm going to need water . . . hot water. And something to use as bandages. And more light," he added as she rushed out of the door. He'd operated plenty of times in worse conditions than this, but whatever he could do to tip the odds in Will's favor, he would. Besides, the next best thing to holding Samantha was to keep her busy and out of the room.

"The water's heating." She was back in the bedroom within minutes, carrying a pile of linens and two additional candles. Jake turned from examining the bump on Will's head.

"Good. Now if you'd just—"

"I'm staying right here," Samantha responded as she set another candle aglow. "I can help."

Jake's eyes met hers. Though he could tell it took all her control to keep from breaking down, she held his gaze. "All right, stay."

As it turned out, Jake brought in water from the kitchen while Samantha tore linens for bandages.

"There's so much blood." Samantha tried to keep her voice steady.

Jake gently wiped the side of Will's face. "I think it looks worse than it is. He has some cuts, but this is the only bad one." Jake pressed a bandage to the side of Will's head, beneath a goose-egg-size knot, then motioned for Samantha to hold it. "I'll need to stitch that up."

As he spoke, Jake trailed his hands down Will's

ribs. "There are plenty of bruises but everything feels like it's fine inside."

"What do you think caused this?"

Jake shook his head. "Something hard and sharp hit his head. And his leg . . . in several places." It looked to Jake as if he'd been trampled by a horse, but he didn't say that to Samantha. He just continued his examination. He worked quickly and efficiently and Samantha tried not to think. Tried not to worry about anything beyond the skillful movement of Jake's fingers.

"His right leg's broken." Jake looked up when Will moaned. For the first time since the war, Jake wished he'd brought his medical supplies with him. He'd left them packed away in Richmond, vowing he'd never use them again.

But he'd have used them in a minute if they'd been here.

After Jake cleaned away the blood from Will's leg he caught Samantha's eye. "Stay with him."

"Where are you going?" Samantha twisted to watch Jake as he headed for the door.

"I need to find something to use as splints."

When Jake returned, he carried two shakes. Sitting down, he used a knife to whittle them to fit around Will's lower leg. "There's some horsehair boiling on the stove. Can you get it for me? And bring in your sewing basket too," Jake called over his shoulder.

"What are you going to do?" Samantha set the things he'd asked for on the bedside table.

"Stitch up this cut on his shin first." Jake threaded the softened horsehair through a needle. "Then I'll set his leg." His eyes met hers. "I'm going to need your help."

Will was showing signs of waking up and Jake told Samantha how to keep him still while he worked. She put her weight into holding her brother down, all the while biting her bottom lip to keep from bursting into tears. By the time Jake had finished stitching the cut on his leg, Will had passed out again.

The bandage Jake slid under Will's leg was fringed on both sides with cut strips or "tails." After showing Samantha how to flex Will's leg, Jake reduced the fracture. He wrapped the bandage around Will's leg, weaving the tails in and out to form a tight, smooth fit. Then he pressed the splints in place and wrapped those snugly.

The cut on his head required only a few stitches and Jake took care of those quickly. "We used boiled horsehair in the war when the blockade runners couldn't get us surgical thread," Jake explained to Samantha. "It works pretty well." Jake straightened. "Now all we can do is keep him warm."

There was nothing he could do for the knot on Will's head, and he hoped he was right about no injuries to the boy's organs.

"Is he going to be all right?" Samantha pulled the quilt around her brother's shoulders.

"I think so," Jake began, but honesty forced him to add, "but I can't be positive. I—"

"Why not?" The tears she'd held at bay while there was something to do now rolled down Samantha's cheeks. "You're a doctor. You should know things like this!" She clutched Will's hand, refusing to let go when Jake first tried to turn her away.

"Samantha." Jake's voice gentled her as he squeezed her shoulder. She tensed, resisting him for a moment before burying her face in his chest.

"Who would do this?" Her words were muffled. "He's just a boy. Will never hurt anyone."

Jake had no answer so he just held her as Samantha cried. After a while she quieted and he ran his hand through her damp hair. "I want you to change into something warm and dry."

"No, I'm just going to sit here with—"

"Will's going to need you in the next few days. You won't be any good to him sick." Jake pulled back and looked down at her. "Now I'm going to the barn to change, and I want you to do the same while I'm gone. When I get back, we'll take turns sitting up with him."

Jake hurriedly changed his wet clothes for dry ones and unhitched the mules. Before he went back to the cabin, he picked up his revolver.

She'd put on a pot of coffee while he was gone. Jake poured two cups and knocked lightly on the bedroom door. Samantha sat by the bed. She'd pulled on a clean dress and put her golden hair back in a hastily tied ribbon. When Jake came in, she glanced up, accepted the coffee, and immediately placed the mug on her bedside table.

"I keep watching his chest," she said. "Looking for the movement as he breathes." Her own breath came out on a sob. "It's the only way I know he's alive."

Jake put his own coffee down untouched. "Will's young and tough," he said, pulling a chair over beside hers.

"Tough . . ." Samantha repeated the word and a sad smile curved her lips. "He doesn't look very tough now." She trailed her finger along his ashen cheek.

"Why don't you get some rest. I'll watch him for a while." Jake wasn't surprised when Samantha shook her head.

"I couldn't sleep." Samantha folded Will's hand in her own. "Will was only three when Mother died. He doesn't remember much about her." She slanted Jake a look. "I've told you this before, but I . . . I feel so . . ."

Jake moved his chair toward her. "Samantha, don't do this to yourself."

Samantha straightened her back. "You're right." She sniffed. "I'm looking for the worst. Will's going to be all right." Samantha settled the quilt higher around his neck, trying not to notice the freckles that stood out so against his pale skin.

"You've taken care of lots of hurt people, haven't you? During the war, I mean."

"Yes."

"And they got better, didn't they?"

Jake heard the plea in her voice, but he couldn't lie. "Some of them."

"Some?" Samantha knew what he said was true but it didn't keep the words from causing a sinking feeling in her stomach.

"I was a doctor, Samantha. Not a miracle worker. Not by a long shot." Jake pulled himself from the swirling memories invading his mind. "But I think Will has a good chance. His leg should be all right, and he already woke up once." He didn't say that the boy had lost a lot of blood or that lying in the cold mud and rain hadn't helped him.

Samantha seemed to accept his words at face value for she settled back into her chair to wait.

And Jake settled into his memories. Had he really thought he'd escape from anything by traveling west? Jake rubbed his jaw. He tried not to think about all the men and boys he'd seen wounded and crying in pain. He tried not to recall how many of them had died. But tonight, seeing Will lying motionless on the bedstead, he couldn't help himself.

The memories seemed to suck him in, making him feel once again the pain of being ineffective . . . useless before the onslaught of war.

"Jake."

Jake sat up abruptly, looking first at Will, then toward Samantha. He could tell by her expression that she'd called him several times before he heard.

"Why didn't you ever tell me you're a doctor?" Samantha had wondered about that ever since he'd wakened from his fever.

"Because I'm not. Not anymore."

"Is it something you can turn your back on?"

Jake's only answer was to stand. "Do you want some more coffee?"

"No." Samantha stared at the hands folded in her lap. "I didn't mean to pry."

"Didn't you?" Jake paced to the doorway and stopped. Turning, he pierced her with his green gaze. "You want to know why I gave up being a doctor? I'll tell you." His fingers shot back through his rumpled hair. "I didn't care anymore. Soldiers would be brought to me and I'd perform surgery or I'd saw off their leg . . . their arms . . . and I didn't even look at their faces. They weren't like people to me. They'd live or they'd die and I didn't care. I couldn't feel . . . anything," Jake finished softly.

"I don't believe that."

Jake's bark of laughter was self-mocking. "You don't want to believe it."

Samantha pushed back her chair. She expected him to leave when she started toward him, but instead Jake held his ground, his expression defiant. "You're right," she said. "I don't want to believe it. But there's more to it than that. You can't tell me you didn't feel something when you took care of Will. I watched you."

"Will's different."

"Is he?"

"Yes." Jake bit off the word.

Samantha shook her head. "No. I saw your face when you took care of Will. You cared . . . and not just because you know him."

Jake raised his hand to touch her hair, then thought better of it. His eyes were sad. "You don't know anything about it."

"Then tell me." Samantha did give in to the desire to touch. Her fingers rested on Jake's sleeve.

Jake's gaze held hers. The line between his brows deepened before he looked away. He was shutting her out. And Samantha wasn't certain why that hurt so much. But standing here with her brother, the only person she had in this world, hurt, she needed to know. "Tell me," she said again and held her breath as he began to speak.

"It's like I lost a part of myself." Jake paused, shaking his head slowly. "That sounds stupid, doesn't it?" He went on before she could answer. "Being a doctor was all I ever wanted to do." He looked down and smiled. "Even when I tried to run away to sea, I wanted to be the ship's doctor."

"When fighting broke out, I knew I had to help. Believe it or not, there was a moment of indecision about which army to join. I'd gone to school in the North, in Philadelphia."

"Then why did you join the Confederacy?"

Jake shrugged. "Richmond was my home. My family lived there . . . my wife's family. And I felt loyalty to Virginia. Besides, I didn't see the differences as clear cut as you did . . . do."

"But I—"

Jake held up his hand in surrender. "I know how you feel about slavery. But I didn't own any slaves. That issue wasn't so clear for me. And there were other matters, states' rights, and . . . well anyway, I decided it didn't really matter which side I joined as long as I . . . helped relieve suffering."

Will moaned and Samantha rushed to the bedstead. Joining her, Jake touched the boys cheek and checked his head wound for fresh blood. Satisfied that everything was going as well as could be expected, Jake sat down. "He's not running a fever. I really do think he's going to be all right."

Samantha's smile was broad. "Thanks to you. You helped him and you can help others."

Jake leaned his chair back, balancing it on two legs. He didn't want to argue with Samantha, but he didn't think she was right.

Chapter Fifteen

"Sam?"

Samantha jerked awake, almost tumbling off Jake's lap. She'd fallen asleep huddled in his arms in the rocking chair her parents had brought from Massachusetts. Jake's hand clasped around her waist, righting her, and their eyes met briefly before she leaped up. She crossed the few feet to the bed . . . and Will.

"How are you feeling, honey?" Samantha brushed strands of wheat blond hair off his forehead, careful of the knot on his head.

"Thirsty," Will countered with a voice rusty from disuse. "And hungry, too."

Tears stung Samantha's eyes as she glanced down to where Jake had pulled back the quilted cover and was examining Will's leg. He glanced up and winked and Samantha forced herself not to hug first Will and then Jake. Instead she smiled, blinking back tears of happiness. "I think I can fix you something. And as for being thirsty . . ." Samantha cradled Will's head and gave him a drink from the tin cup beside the bed.

Several times through the night, Will had awoken, and she and Jake had taken turns offering him sips of water and tea. But though he'd moaned about the pain then, he'd never seemed alert the way he did now.

"Sam." Will grabbed her wrist as she moved away from the bed. When she turned back around, he continued, "It was Moore."

Samantha didn't speak for a moment. She could feel Will and Jake watching her. Through the long night, worry about Will's recovery had kept thoughts of who'd done this at bay.

She'd suspected Landis Moore, of course, but somehow she couldn't accept that even he would hurt Will like this. Her father had openly challenged Moore and she'd defied him and his friend Bundy Atwood. She had no doubt either of them would hurt her if they could. But Will?

"Oh, Will, are you sure?"

"I heard him, sis." Will succumbed to a fit of coughing and Samantha's gaze flew to Jake. He piled pillows under Will's head and suggested Samantha give him another drink. The sip of tea seemed to help, but Will still looked pale.

"Don't talk now, Will. There's plenty of time to —"

"No!" Will's voice was frantic. "You've got to know."

"Then tell us, Will." Jake moved a chair over close to the bed and motioned for Samantha to sit down. "Just take it slow and we'll listen."

"All right." Will took a deep breath. "After you left the creek, I remembered my hat. I left it in the cornfield. So I went back. That's when I heard them."

"Heard who, Will?"

"The men." Will strained to sit up and Jake gently pushed him back onto the pillows. "They were talking about burning the field. Said that would show you." Will's gaze shifted to Samantha. "Maybe you wouldn't be so high and mighty then."

"Oh, Will." Samantha reached out toward him. "They were trying to hurt me and they got you instead. I'm so sorry."

Jake's hand clasped over her shoulder. "No one's blaming you for this, Samantha."

"What Jake says is true, Sam. This was my own fault."

"Will, I don't think—"

"I tried to stop them, Sam."

"Will." Samantha's voice was full of exasperation.

"I know I shouldn't have. I shoulda' come for you and Jake. But—"

"You certainly should have. You're just a boy. You could have gotten yourself killed!" Samantha bit her bottom lip to keep from falling apart. It didn't help as much as the strong arm Jake draped around her shoulders.

"Aw, I'm sorry, Sam."

"Hey, we've all done things in the heat of the

moment that weren't the brightest," Jake said, then grinned at the expression of relief on Will's face. "Just remember that people like Landis Moore aren't the sort any man should go up against alone."

"I know that now, Jake."

"Good." Jake pulled a chair forward, straddling it. "Now tell us what happened next."

"I stepped into the clearing by the cornfield. They were surprised to see me, that was for sure. Even though they had scarves pulled over their faces, I could tell they didn't expect to see no one. They just kind of sat there on their horses lookin' at me. Till I called out Moore's name, that is."

"What happened then?" Jake rested his chin on the arm slung over the chair back. His stance was as relaxed as his voice — for Will and Samantha's sake — but inside he was seething.

"Nothing really. He didn't say nothing anyways, just kind of nodded to his men. They started coming at me." Will paused. "It was real scary, with them on horses and some of them holding up burning brands. . . . But I didn't hightail it yet."

" 'I know it's you, Landis Moore,' I said. 'And you too, Ab. And Bundy.' I recognized his bay from the other week when he was here," Will said, turning toward Samantha.

"I thought about running for the cabin, but by this time they had me surrounded except for the cornfield at my back. There were maybe six of them. I didn't get a good count. But I did hear

Landis tell Ab to take care of me so I lit out through the rows. I've always been a pretty fast runner, haven't I, Sam?"

Samantha clasped his hand. "Yes, Will, real fast."

"But I wasn't fast enough this time. Ab's horse caught me real quick. He kept bumping into me. Then I fell down. The last thing I remember is looking up and seeing hooves coming down toward me." He shrugged. "I know it's not much, but . . ."

"You remember enough though, Will." Jake stood. "Why don't you get some rest now. Samantha and I will fix you something to eat." Jake held out his hand to Samantha, and after a moment's hesitation, she accepted it. They were almost to the door when Will's voice stopped them.

"Did they burn the cornfield?"

"No." Jake turned around and grinned. "It rained."

Samantha allowed herself to be pulled through the front room and out the door of the cabin, but as soon as it closed, she dug in her heels. "Where are we going? I thought we were going to fix Will some breakfast."

"We will, actually you will. Hell, you know I can't cook. But first I want to talk to you."

"If it's about what Will told us, I suspected Landis Moore from the beginning. I just never thought he'd hurt a boy."

"Well, now we know." Jake leaned against the morning glory-wrapped porch post. "I'm going to

302

hitch up the wagon, and after we eat, I want you to pack what you need."

"What I need for what?"

Jake's expression was incredulous. "A stay in town."

"Town." Samantha's hands rested on her hips. "I'm not going to town."

"The hell you're not."

"Listen, Jacob Morgan. This is my farm and I'm not leaving it. We've seen what Moore tried to do to the corn crop. Besides"—Samantha hung her head—"we don't have money to spend for a room in town."

"Now you listen to me." Jake pushed off from the post and advanced on Samantha, finally looming over her. "What we saw is what Moore's capable of doing to you or Will. Now when he finds out Will survived the fire, he's not going to feel very secure." Jake paused. "And I have money for the room."

"Perhaps I should take Will," Samantha admitted. "But I'll find a way to pay for it myself."

"You're going to town too. And I'm paying."

"What about the farm?"

"The hell with the farm. Besides you can't begin to protect this place by yourself."

"By myself?" Samantha swallowed. "But what about you?" She knew he wasn't staying forever, but after he'd pulled her into his lap last night and held her so gently and protectively, she hoped . . . But his next words proved her wrong.

"I won't be here."

"I see." Samantha turned toward the cabin.

"I don't think you do. I—"

"No. You don't have to explain. I know this isn't your fight. You said you'd stay to help with the harvest, but apparently you see things differently now. And I can certainly see why you want to be on your way."

"Oh, for heaven's sake, Samantha, I'm going after Moore and his men."

"You're what?" Samantha didn't like this much better than she liked the idea of his deserting them. "You can't do that!"

Jake threw up his hands. "Why not? I thought you'd want him brought to justice."

"Well, of course I do. But you yourself said not ten minutes ago that Moore wasn't the kind of man you went after alone."

"That was different," Jake said, a scowl darkening his face.

"How?" Samantha challenged. "You heard Will. Moore has a half-dozen men." She touched his sleeve. "Jake, I don't doubt you can handle some of them, but the odds are too much. Besides, he knows the territory and you don't. You'd never find him."

Jake took a deep breath. "Maybe I'll get some help."

"I think we should wait until the army gets here."

"And when is that going to be, Samantha? After

304

Moore succeeds in killing someone?" Jake raked fingers through his hair and settled his hat down low over his forehead. "I'm not waiting for any damn Union Army!" With that he stalked off the porch. "Get your things together," he called back over his shoulder before disappearing into the barn.

Samantha stomped her foot, but she went inside and did what he said. She didn't like leaving the farm but Jake was right about getting Will into town. They were so vulnerable out here — especially if Jake left. And he seemed determined to go after Moore.

Samantha stopped folding Will's shirt. It fell from her trembling fingers. Somehow she'd made it through last night without the nightmares hounding her. But here, in the light of day, she couldn't stop them.

Moore had dragged her father away and hanged him. Samantha closed her eyes but could not shut out the sight of her father's body hanging from the cottonwood tree.

And now Will. He'd come so close to meeting a similar fate. How could she let Jake go up against Moore?

"I've seen worse." Jake stood in the doorway of Samantha's hotel room and glanced around. Truth was, he'd seen better too. A lot better. But this was the best hotel room the town of Hager's Flats had

305

to offer. The mattress sagged, the dresser had a broken handle, and the porcelain pitcher on the washstand bore chips from past occupants.

Samantha shrugged. "It will have to do until we can get home." She pulled a dress from her carpet bag and shook out the wrinkles.

"How's Will doing?"

"He's asleep next door." Samantha turned back toward Jake and their eyes met. "I think the ride tired him out some."

Jake leaned against the door jamb. "I took care of the horses and your cow down at the livery stable."

"Thank you." Their trip into town was slow because Samantha had insisted upon bringing Faith with them, tied to the back of the wagon.

"Sure." Jake pushed his hat off his forehead. "I came to tell you I'm going over to the sheriff's."

Samantha dropped the gown across the bed. "Whatever for?"

"Hell, Samantha! Someone came out to your farm, left your brother for dead, set fire to your field, and you wonder why I'm going to see the sheriff."

"You needn't yell." Samantha crossed her arms. "I just thought you learned your lesson the last time you met with our illustrious Sheriff Hughes."

"This time I have a witness." Jake strode in the room, kicking shut the door behind him. This wasn't the kind of conversation he wanted everyone in the hotel to hear. "And as you so rightly pointed out, I need help to go after Moore's men."

"I hope you don't expect it from him. Excuse me." Samantha brushed past Jake.

"Well yes, as a matter of fact I do. And I intend to see he does something about this. What are you doing?"

"Putting on my hat. If you insist upon seeing Mr. Hughes, I'm going with you." Samantha settled a faded blue bonnet over her pinned-up braid.

"There's no need for that."

She patted the bow after tying it under her chin. "I'm going, Jake."

"Suit yourself. But that's going to leave Will here alone."

"Mrs. Tew will watch him. She owns the hotel. The Tews came to Kansas back in 'fifty-five, same year as my parents. She'll be glad to do it."

"All right. Let's—" Jake's gaze caught on the silk gown spread across the bed. Its deep blue color shimmered in the light streaming through the dust-caked window. He trailed his finger down the fabric. "I never saw you wear this before."

"It's not mine. It was my mother's," Samantha answered the unasked question in his eyes. "I thought I'd make it over for Peggy Keane. I'm not certain she'll like the color, but it's the best I can do."

"Make it over for yourself." The absolute last thing he should be thinking about right now was Samantha Lowery's wardrobe. Still he hated to see her give up the gown. Though she seemed to find

307

the idea of her keeping it amusing.

"I don't have anyplace to wear a dress like this. Besides . . . I need the money."

"Damn. We aren't going into this again, are we?"

"We most certainly are." Samantha's chin rose a notch and she folded her hands about her waist. "I said I wouldn't be beholding to you and I meant it."

"I told you before to forget it." Jake followed Samantha out of the room and down the narrow, ill-lit hallway.

"And I told you I have no intention of doing any such thing. I should be paying you for the work you do." She picked up her skirt before treading the steep stairs. "Not the other way around."

"Paying for your hotel room is not the same as paying you."

Samantha stopped in front of the oak desk in the lobby, smiling when an apple-cheeked older woman looked up. "Mrs. Tew, Will is asleep upstairs, and—"

"How is the dear boy?"

"Resting comfortably. I wonder if you could stay with him until I get back. I won't be long. And it's important or I wouldn't ask."

"Don't give it another thought, Samantha." Mrs. Tew called into the back room for her husband. "You and your young man just do whatever it is you have to do."

Samantha opened her mouth to deny that Jake was her "young man," then thought better of it.

308

Mrs. Tew would believe what she wanted. Instead, after thanking Mrs. Tew, Samantha led the way out into the bright Kansas sunlight.

Turning up the street, they walked along the boardwalk past the false-fronted buildings toward the jail. As they crossed in front of the mercantile, smells of apples and vinegar mingled with the pungent odor of horse droppings drifting from the street.

Jake glanced down at Samantha's straw bonnet and plain brown dress and, in spite of himself, thought about the blue silk draped around her lovely body. "About that dress—"

"Oh, no."

"What?" Jake felt Samantha stiffen as he took her elbow to guide her across an alley.

"It's Peggy Keane," Samantha sighed. "She . . . well, she's a talker and I don't have time right now."

"Who? The woman in purple coming toward us?"

"Yes," Samantha said around a grimace. "And for heaven's sake, let go of my arm."

"Samantha. I didn't know you were in town." Peggy Keane's words were for Samantha but her eyes never left Jake.

Samantha's smile was forced. "There was some trouble at the farm. Will was hurt," she added, wondering if that would stop Peggy's visual feast of Jake. It did.

"Hurt? My goodness, is he all right?"

"Yes." Peggy's concern seemed sincere and Samantha had a pang of guilt for purposely worrying her. That is, until she saw Peggy's gaze slide back to Jake. "He can't walk. For a while anyway," she added when Peggy gasped. "We're going to see the sheriff . . . Jake and I."

Still nothing but silence as Peggy gazed up at Jake. He'd taken his hat off and the midday breeze played with strands of his sun-lightened hair. Samantha had to admit he made a handsome picture standing there in his loose checked shirt and snug pants. But Peggy's reaction was ridiculous. And Jake, judging from the crooked grin he was sporting, didn't seem too anxious to move on.

Sighing, Samantha began the introductions. "Peggy, this is Jake Morgan. He works for me . . . as a field hand," she added, stretching the truth a bit.

"And Jake, this is *Mrs*. Peggy Keane." Samantha hadn't realized she'd emphasized the *Mrs*. so much until they both looked at her with equally astonished expressions. Samantha gave them both a small smile. "I guess we should be on our way."

"Of course. I didn't mean to keep you. Are you going to be in town long, Mr. Morgan?"

"I'm not sure." For someone who'd insisted he let go of her arm a minute ago, Samantha sure was pulling on his.

"Well, if you're here Saturday night, you'll have to come to the town dance. . . . Oh, you too, Samantha." Peggy let her hand drop on Jake's sleeve. "I always try and get her to come, but . . . you know Samantha."

"Actually he doesn't know me. At least not very well." Again both sets of eyes were on her. "I'm sorry, Peggy, but we really are in a hurry. I don't want to leave Will for too long." With that, she hauled Jake along the boardwalk.

"What's gotten into you?" Jake forced Samantha to slow her pace.

"Nothing."

"Nothing. You act like the whole Confederate Army is after you."

Samantha slanted him a look. "Very funny." She paused. "I thought you wanted to talk to the sheriff and then go after Moore."

"I do. But you know I was thinking. That's where you could wear it."

"Wear what?" Samantha stopped in front of the pine-planked jail. Several posters fluttered in the breeze and she caught a whiff of Sheriff Hughes's foul-smelling cigar seeping through the boards in the door.

"The dress. You could wear that blue dress to the dance."

"The dance?" Samantha reached for the latch, then let her hand fall. She faced him, her eyes as large as saucers, and again Jake was reminded of the blue silk. "My brother's been hurt, I've abandoned my farm, not to mention the fact that I need money, and you want me to go to a dance?"

"Hell, it was just a thought. Besides there's noth-

311

ing you can do now but sit and wait."

Samantha stepped back as if she'd been slapped. She wasn't used to doing nothing, and she didn't much like the idea. "I can earn money," she countered. "Altering and selling that dress to Peggy Keane."

"Fine." Jake turned toward the jail. Their conversation seemed to be attracting some attention from passersby. Samantha's hand on his arm stopped him.

"You want to go to that dance, don't you?"

"No." Jake tucked his chin and stared down at her in surprise.

"You needn't pretend otherwise. After all, Peggy Keane invited you. There's no reason in the world that you shouldn't go." Samantha shrugged. "And have a wonderful time."

"Well, there sure is one that I can think of." Jake faced her, hands on hips.

"What?"

"I'll be off hunting Landis Moore and his men."

"Oh. That's right." Samantha bit her bottom lip, feeling embarrassment flow through her. What was she making such a fuss about? "I don't know what's wrong with me." Heat rose across her cheeks. "It's just—"

Jake held up his hand. "It's all right. Like you said, a lot's been going on lately. It's enough to make anyone cranky. Let's just talk with the sheriff?"

"I wasn't exactly cranky," Samantha argued as

she walked through the door Jake opened for her. Except that cranky was how she'd acted. Samantha had said she didn't know what was wrong with her, but she had to admit it felt a lot like jealousy. And she wasn't happy to be feeling it about the Rebel.

Well, now that she recognized the emotion, she could fight it. Because whether Jake Morgan thought so or not, she had important things to do. Squaring her shoulders, Samantha faced Sheriff Hughes, who still sat, his booted feet propped on the desk.

He eyed her first, then Jake, a scowl darkening his pock-scarred face. His sigh was noisy. "What do you two want?"

"A posse for starters," Jake responded, crossing his arms and returning the sheriff's stare.

"What in the hell for?"

"To bring in Landis Moore." Samantha noticed that her pose, arms folded tightly under her breasts, mirrored Jake's, and she dropped her hands.

"Aw, not that old shit again." Hughes tucked in his chin and shook his head. "Lord, how long am I going to have to put up with this grudge you've got against Moore? Every time I turn around, you're in here complaining and I'm getting damn tired of— Hey! What the hell you think you're doing?" Hughes tottered on the back legs of his chair, trying to right himself after Jake had shoved his feet off the desk.

"I'm getting your attention." Samantha gasped

when Jake grabbed the sheriff by the front of his gravy-stained shirt, hauling him to his feet. On tip-toes he was still a half-head shorter than Jake, but that didn't stop his sputtering threat.

"I've half a notion to lock you up for this, Morgan."

"Moore's the one you'll be locking up. That is, after you help me find him." Jake let loose of the sheriff, watching his face turn red as an October apple. He sputtered and swore, his hand inching down toward the revolver strapped to his fleshy hip. But his eyes moved faster, saw the way Jake fingered his gun, and though his anger was strong, discretion won out.

Hughes straightened his vest, and turned toward Samantha, obviously considering her the easier of his opponents. "All right, what trumped-up complaint you got against Moore this time?"

"He hurt Will and broke his leg."

"Your brother, Will?" When Samantha didn't deign to answer that, the sheriff went on, "Aw, Will probably done tripped over his own feet."

"The boy was trampled by a horse ridden by Landis Moore's brother and Landis ordered it. This was before he set fire to one of the Lowery cornfields." Jake took a menacing step toward the sheriff. "Now what do you intend to do about it?"

Hughes's ferret eyes skittered about, but there wasn't much for him to see except Jake Morgan's wide chest. "I suppose we could get some men together tomorrow and ride out to Moore's place.

314

That is, if you're sure about this," he added in an attempt to save face.

"We'll start today, and we'll check out more than the old Colt place. Moore's from Missouri. We're not over a couple miles from the border."

"Now see here." Hughes lifted his flabby jowls but had to back down when Jake didn't give an inch. He tried reason. "I don't have no jurisdiction across the border."

"Then we'll ride over there and find someone who does." Jake turned and took Samantha's elbow, leading her toward the door. "An hour." Jake threw the words over his shoulder before he slammed the jail door.

Samantha blinked and shook her head. "I can't believe it."

"What?" His stride was long as Jake started back toward the hotel, and Samantha struggled to keep up. She'd seen him angry before—the time he found out who'd shot him came to mind—but she'd never seen him like this. His jaw was clenched and he flexed and unflexed his hand as if he longed to throttle someone. Samantha had a pretty good idea who that someone was.

"I can't believe the way you got Hughes to go along with you."

"He hasn't yet," Jake replied, glancing down at Samantha and slowing his pace.

"But I think he will. He seemed too scared not to." Jake shrugged, and Samantha went on, "I wish to goodness you'd been around when my father was killed." Samantha stopped short, realizing what she'd just said. Her father had died during the war at a time when Jake was in the Confederate Army. The last thing she wanted then was another Rebel.

"Why's that?" They reached the hotel and Jake followed Samantha across the threadbare carpet in the lobby.

"Maybe the sheriff would have done something about Moore then."

Jake faced Samantha at the bottom of the stairs. "Well, let's see what we can do about bringing him in this time."

Chapter Sixteen

The posse rode out of town, ten strong, on Monday afternoon.

Samantha stood on the boardwalk watching the Kansas dust swirl around the horses' hooves as they pranced, ready to leave, wishing she could go along. What a pleasure to hunt Landis Moore, to see him sweat when he knew defeat, to see him finally brought to justice.

Her gaze swept over the men. She knew less than half of them, and by their looks, she considered herself lucky. They were a motley group, dirty and foul-smelling—except for Jake. While the others shifted about, spitting into the street, joking about what they'd be missing tonight, Jake sat, his jaw clenched, waiting for the sheriff.

When Ralph Hughes came out of his office, tugging at his pants, and mounted, the group rode off. Jake's nod as he gathered up his reins was the only sign that he noticed Samantha's presence.

Samantha retraced her steps to Tew's Hotel. She couldn't help the wave of sadness washing over her.

Jake was gone, and he'd barely acknowledged her. But then what did she expect? Was he to reach down in front of everyone and drag her to him for a passionate good-bye kiss?

She hardly wanted that. Yet he hadn't kissed her at all. Not when they reached town, or in the hectic moments when he packed his gear, or even before he started out to the street. There was no sign . . . none, that he cared for her. No sign they'd made love in each other's arms. No sign he'd pulled her into his lap and held her through the night while they waited to see if Will would be all right.

With a sigh, Samantha climbed the hotel stairs to the room Will and Jake shared, bracing herself for a long wait.

The posse rode out on Monday afternoon, ten strong. By Wednesday morning they were back. Nine of them.

Samantha was sitting in Will's room, reading to him. The leg was healing nicely. Old Doc Shelton had stopped in after Mrs. Tew had told him of the injury. His hand trembled only a little and the words were not too slurred for understanding as he declared the boy on the mend.

"Nice even stitches you took there, Samantha," he'd said, examining Will's head. "See you used horsehair."

"Yes, but I didn't . . ." Samantha paused. If Jake didn't want it known that he was a doctor, it wasn't her place to tell. In the end she thanked Doc Shelton and sent him on his way.

"So what did Gulliver do then?" Will fidgeted in

his seat, reaching out to rub his broken leg. It was propped up on a chair and covered with a woolen blanket.

"Do?" Samantha realized she'd stopped reading and scanned the page to find her place. She was glad Will was showing more interest in books—and she knew she had the Rebel to thank for that—but right now she didn't feel like reading. And when she heard the commotion down on the street, she wedged a crocheted bookmark into the page and shut the book.

"What's going on?" Will inquired, turning his torso toward the open window.

"It looks like the posse's back." Samantha pulled her head inside the room and smoothed the cotton curtains.

"Do they have Landis Moore?"

"It doesn't appear so."

"Any of his men?"

"No." Samantha pulled down the sash, leaving only about a two-inch opening to allow a stirring of air.

"Well, I hope Jake comes up here quick to tell us what happened."

Samantha checked the pistol Jake left for them, handing it to Will. "Jake isn't with them."

"He's not?" The gun fell on Will's lap. "Where do you think he is?"

"That's what I intend to find out." Samantha wrapped a shawl around her shoulders. "You going to be all right?"

"Sure." Will slid his fingers around the gun butt.

"I'll ask Mrs. Tew to look in on you." With that, Samantha marched out the door and down the street.

The sheriff had already left his office, if in fact he'd gone there at all. Samantha scanned the street and spotted the sheriff's roan, among a group of horses tied in front of the States' Rights Saloon. Squaring her shoulders, Samantha headed down the boardwalk.

She'd never darkened the door of this particular establishment . . . and not just because of its Rebel-sounding name. But she did so now, pausing only a moment when her entrance caused conversation to cease. After all, embarrassment was the least of her problems.

"Sheriff Hughes." Samantha moved next to him at the polished mahogany bar. "I see you returned empty-handed."

Hughes turned, squinting over the rim of a shot glass filled with amber liquid. "What are you doin' in here, girl?"

"I might ask you the same. Didn't you leave town with the intention of finding Landis Moore?" Samantha could feel the attention of the other men standing at the bar, but she tried to ignore them.

"Couldn't find him," Hughes offered before up-ending his glass and noisily gulping down the spirits.

"I see." With arms crossed tightly under her breasts, Samantha continued, "And may I inquire where you looked?"

Hughes straightened, backhanding the liquid from his thick lips. "Well, little missy, I don't usually answer to anyone about how I do my job, but I'll give you this in hopes you'll stop chewing on this bone. We checked out the old Colt place, and then rode over Missouri way. Talked to some of his kin . . . an uncle."

"Said Landis and Ab set out for Tennessee just that morning." The sheriff puffed out his considerable chest. "Also said Landis and his brother was home last Sunday night. Says he'll swear to it."

"Then he's lying," Samantha countered. "Where's Jake . . . Mr. Morgan?"

Hughes's eyes narrowed until she could hardly see them in his cauliflower face. "Funny thing about that man of yours. He just rode off. Don't rightly know where he was off to. He tell any of you men?"

Samantha glanced around to witness a general shaking of heads and negative grunts from the members of the posse, who seemed to hang on Hughes's every word.

"Well, there you have it, missy. If you ask me, you and your brother should—"

But Samantha didn't wait around to hear what Sheriff Hughes suggested. Head high, she swept out of the saloon, not stopping for anything until she reached the quiet haven of her hotel room. She closed the door behind her, leaning into it and wringing her hands.

Her emotions were near the boiling point and she couldn't even decide what it was she felt. Anger, of course, at the potbellied, ignorant sheriff and his contention that Landis Moore was innocent of

321

shooting Will. But there was more.

Jake Morgan.

What could have happened to him? Did he really ride off without a second thought to Will . . . to her? Samantha bit her lip to keep the tears from pouring over her lashes. It made sense. Why would he want to hang around here? He made it clear from the beginning that he was only passing through. What better time to continue his trip to Texas than when he could accomplish it with no drawn-out good-byes or explanations?

Samantha sniffed and moved farther into the room, feeling guilty because Will was next door wondering what was going on and she didn't have the courage to face him.

She sank on the bed and another thought came. What if Jake didn't leave? What if he was still looking for Landis Moore? By himself? Or worse, what if something had happened to him and the sheriff didn't tell her?

She jumped up and paced to the window, then back to the bed. How could she find out the truth? And what could she do about it even if she knew?

A thump sounded, then another, and Samantha stared at the wall separating her room from Will's. He was using the crutch she'd purchased for him at the mercantile — and not the way she'd intended.

Sighing, Samantha opened the door and walked to the adjacent room, wondering what in the world she was going to tell Will.

* * *

Nearly three days passed and still there was no word of Jake. Samantha returned from selling milk she got from Faith to Sam Jenkins at the restaurant and knocked on Will's door. His voice sounded crotchety when he said to come in. He was hobbling around on his crutch, bumping into the washstand, then turning to knock into the bed.

"You seem to be getting the hang of it," Samantha offered, then settled down in a chair by the window when he only scowled at her. She picked up the blue silk gown and began stitching the bodice . . . more for something to do with her hands than anything else.

She'd decided not to remake the dress for Peggy Keane. Too many things bound her to the gown to sell it. Instead—and she really couldn't come up with a sensible reason for doing it—she was altering the dress for herself.

"I told Mr. Kelsy at the livery we'd be leaving tomorrow." Samantha looked up from her stitching to watch Will lower himself into the other chair in the room.

"I'm still not sure we should go back to the farm just yet. Jake said—"

"What Jake said or didn't say no longer matters." She rammed the needle through the ruffled silk. "He isn't here. Landis Moore is supposedly off in Tennessee and we're running out of money. Besides"— Samantha glanced up and smiled. "I still have a corn crop to harvest. I spoke with Jim Farley about coming out to help and he—"

"Jake wouldn't just run off and leave us like this."

Samantha's lips pruned. She'd ended up telling Will everything because she hadn't known what else to say. No great surprise to her, Will chose to believe that Jake was off looking for Landis Moore by himself.

"But the point is, Jake didn't come back." Samantha didn't see any reason for Will not to face reality. "And we need—"

"You have more money. Jake gave you some."

"Yes. But I'm not going to use it. It's bad enough he had to pay for our hotel rooms and food. "I'll pay that back. And—" Samantha held up her hand to quiet Will's next objection. "If he doesn't come back, I'll hold it for him. Maybe someday, when he gets settled, he'll write, and I'll send it to him."

"I still say he'll be back."

"Then he'll find us at the farm." Samantha bit off a thread. "The sheriff said Moore's off somewhere in Tennessee, so I don't think he'll cause us any more trouble." At least she hoped not. Though she definitely felt safer in town, she couldn't leave their only source of livelihood for too long.

"Can we at least go to the dance?"

"The dance?" Samantha looked over into Will's face, noticing a touch of color seep into his cheeks.

"Yeah. There's a town dance tonight. Didn't you know?"

Of course she knew. Peggy Keane made sure she did—or rather that Jake did. "Yes. I saw them laying the dance floor out in front of the school. But Will, what do you want to go to a dance for? You can barely get around."

"I can watch. Being stuck in this room is awful. Besides, you could wear that blue dress you've been sewing on."

What was it with this dress? Did everything else she wore look so bad that people longed to see her in the blue gown? Samantha didn't want to answer that — even to herself. But for heaven's sake, she had a farm to run. That didn't leave much time for gussying up.

But what would it hurt for one night? Will had had a rough time of it. They both had.

"All right. I'll see if Mr. Tew will help you down the stairs, and we'll go for a little while. But we're not staying late," Samantha cautioned when Will's face blossomed in a smile. "We have to get an early start for the farm tomorrow."

The gown was lovely. Samantha took another turn in front of the mirror nailed over the washstand, and smiled. The skirt swirled around, then floated down on the one petticoat Samantha had. It might look better if the skirt stood out more, but there was no help for it.

Samantha fingered the short puffy sleeves and the ruffled silk adorning the off-the-shoulder décolletage and wished Jake were here for yet another reason. She'd like for him to see her in the gown, but . . .

Tapping at the door made Samantha turn from the mirror. Mrs. Tew stood in the hall clutching an ornate bottle. "Just thought you might like to splash on some of this," she said as she entered the room. "Mr. Tew brought it all the way from St. Louis for me when he went to visit his sister last year."

"Oh, Mrs. Tew, I couldn't."

"Poppycock. Of course you could. Here, smell." She stuck the opened bottle under Samantha's nose and watched as a slow smile spread across her face.

"Roses," Samantha said, looking up. "My mother used to smell like this."

"And you shall, too. Now bend closer."

"But really, I can't take your toilet water. Besides, it was enough that you fixed my hair." Samantha patted the curls the older woman had pulled back on the sides and let trail down her back.

"Just a little." Mrs. Tew dampened her finger and touched it to Samantha's neck, then her temple, and finally the undersides of her wrists. Mrs. Tew leaned back, smiling her apple-faced grin. "Now you're ready."

Samantha gave Mrs. Tew a quick hug then went next door for Will. He was waiting for her, leaning on his crutch, and sporting a clean shirt. His chin dropped when he saw her. "Gee, Sam . . . I mean Samantha. I never saw you looking like that."

"Do you like it?" Samantha spun around, listening as the silk rustled around her ankles.

"Well, yeah. I mean it's real pretty. You're real pretty."

"Thank you."

"It's just . . ."

"What?"

"I wish Jake was here."

The smile faded from Samantha's face. "Well, he's not." She probably wouldn't mind so much if she hadn't been thinking the same thing. "Are you ready?"

The Ladies' Guild and their hard-working husbands had transformed the area in front of the schoolhouse. As they maneuvered through the crowd, Samantha heard comments that this wasn't the Guild's best effort, but to her and Will it looked magical.

"Let me see if I can find us a seat. Samantha walked in front of Will, clearing a path. "Are you doing all right?"

"Sure am." Will swung his broken leg up to meet the crutch he'd planted firmly on the ground. "Would you look at those paper lanterns? Ain't they grand?"

A string of Oriental-looking lanterns hung between one corner of the schoolhouse and the sycamore tree in the play yard swung gently in the chilly air. Samantha turned around, taking in the lights, the crowd all dressed in their Sunday best, and the excited gleam on Will's face, and was very glad she came.

"Let's go over there, Will." Samantha pointed to a spot close to where the musicians warmed up — Tommy Morton, the undertaker and cabinet maker, who played the fiddle passably well; old Eli Greenwich, his chaw of tobacco puffing out his cheek, who lovingly strummed the strings of his banjo; and Amanda Phillips, the minister's wife and piano player, who was trying to get the two men to follow her lead. "You can sit on the stump till I find you something more comfortable. And I think you can see everything pretty well from there."

By the time Samantha and Will made it through the crowd lining the perimeter of the wood plank dance floor constructed for the event, the stump was occupied by Miss Hannah Criswell. The elderly lady gave Samantha and Will a howdy-do, and even questioned Will about his leg. But she didn't give up her seat.

"Wait here." Samantha leaned toward Will's ear after Miss Hannah returned to watching the dancers square off for a reel. "I'll find you something to sit on."

The dancing started and Samantha cut a wide berth around the townsfolk as she headed for the open doors of the schoolhouse. Inside, under the hungry eyes of some of the town's children, the women of the Guild were setting out rum cakes and cookies, and sandwiches piled high with beef and ham. The punch bowl sat on planks they'd placed with one end on the teacher's desk and the other on a pile of wooden crates.

"Excuse me." Samantha stopped in front of Mrs. Weston, who was arranging oatmeal cookies on a platter.

"The cookies are three for a penny, but I get to pick which ones you get," the woman said without glancing up.

Samantha's gaze dropped to the cookies, noticing when she did, the charred edges on some of them, then back up at the woman. "I don't want any cookies. But do you think I could take one of these school benches outside?"

The woman looked up, her mouth pursed. "You're that Lowery girl, ain't you?"

"Yes, ma'am." Samantha had never had much contact with Mrs. Weston, whose husband owned one of the saloons, but she knew the Westons had sympathized with the Confederacy during the war.

"You look fit enough to stand," Mrs. Weston said, continuing with her task.

"The bench is for my brother, Will. He has a broken leg." Samantha tried to keep her tone pleasant but her jaw hurt from clenching it.

"Yes, I heard about that." Mrs. Weston paused. "From the sheriff. Heard you had him running off after Landis Moore."

"I'll take *that* bench," Samantha said, staying only long enough to watch Mrs. Weston's flabby jaw drop. The older woman recovered quickly though, and before Samantha had lifted the unwieldy bench, she was admonishing her to bring it back when the dances were over, her tone frigid as the threat of sleet.

Biting her tongue to keep her caustic retort from slipping out, Samantha struggled through the door. She didn't get three steps outside before again being confronted about the bench.

"Hey there, pretty lady. What you doing carrying such a heavy thing? Here, let me take it."

Before Samantha could object, the bench was hauled out of her arms and up against a burly chest. A boyishly handsome face above that chest smiled down at her. "Where do you want this?"

"I can take it really."

"Don't be silly. You just lead the way, little lady, and Amos Smith will follow."

Thus Samantha was introduced to Amos, a farmer new to the area, and her first partner for the evening. For once he'd deposited the bench, and helped Will settle into it, Amos refused to take any thanks except to lead Samantha around the dance floor in a lively waltz.

Once begun, Samantha seemed unable to stop the flood tide of men, young and old, who asked her to dance. She admitted to herself a liking for the attention, but after a few hours, her feet were aching and her conscience bothering her even more.

After nicely but firmly rejecting the next man who asked her, a tall skinny redhead who bobbed his head several times before weaving off through the crowd, Samantha made her way to Will.

"Oh, I'm sorry for leaving you all alone," Samantha said, squeezing onto the bench beside her brother.

"That's all right. I've plenty to see. Besides you look like you're having a good time."

"I do?" Samantha used her hand to fan her face. "Well, I suppose I am. But I have to tell you my feet feel like Pru's been clogging on them." This brought a laugh from Will, and Samantha stood. "Are you hungry? The Ladies' Guild is selling some nice-looking cakes in there." Samantha motioned toward the schoolhouse.

After being reminded by Will—a needless precaution—that he didn't like raisins, Samantha reentered the building. She carefully counted out the few remaining coins she brought from home, refusing to use any of the money Jake had left her. She bought Will two iced cakes and a cup of punch. Balancing her purchases, she stepped through the door, almost running into Peggy Keane.

"Why Samantha Lowery, I didn't know you were still in town."

"I am." Samantha bent down and licked a glob of icing off her hand. "But I'm going back to the farm tomorrow."

"Well, I'm glad you stayed for the dance. You look so pretty. Wherever did you get that gown?"

"Thank you. It was my mother's. And as for the dance, Will wanted to—"

"Is that handsome Jake Morgan with you?" Peggy's eyes scanned the crowd. "I do declare, I don't know why you hide him off at your farm."

"Actually, I didn't hide him anywhere. And no, he's not here." Samantha shifted to step around Peggy. "I have to take this to Will," she began, but Peggy drowned out her words.

"Well, there he is. What's the idea telling me he isn't here?"

"Who?" Peggy had stepped in front of her again, the icing was dripping, and Samantha didn't know what the other woman was talking about.

"Why Mr. Morgan, of course. Did you really think I wouldn't see him?"

"Jake?" Samantha murmured, then turned to look in the direction of Peggy's stare. Sure enough, taller than most of the crowd, Jake Morgan was moving toward her. Their eyes met and held, and Samantha felt her pulse begin to race. She honestly thought never to see him again; had tried to accept that he had left them to ride after his own dream. Now as excitement coursed through her, she knew she hadn't accepted anything.

"Is one of these for me?" He took one of the cakes out of Samantha's hand while she stood stock-still, staring. "I haven't eaten since noon, and I'm real hungry."

Samantha watched as he ate the sweet in three bites. When he reached for the second cake, she found her tongue. "Where have you been?" She pulled her hand back. "This is for Will."

"Missouri and I'll buy him another one." This cake disappeared in two bites.

"But the sheriff said you—"

"May I have a drink of that?"

Samantha gave him the punch and stood hands on hips while he drank it. "I thought they usually perked this stuff up a bit with spirits."

"I told you, I bought it for Will. Now will you tell me what you've been doing for the last four days?"

"Oh Samantha, don't be an old fuddy duddy," Peggy scolded her. "Can't you see this is no place to be talking about riding all over the countryside." Peggy smiled up at Jake and brushed a cake crumb off his chin. "Besides, they've just started a waltz, and Mr. Morgan, I find myself without a partner."

"She didn't find herself without a partner for long," Samantha mumbled to herself as she approached Will. He was leaning forward on the bench, his elbows resting on his knee. He barely noticed the three pieces of cake she set beside him — cake she'd bought with Jake's money.

"Jake's back!" Will's voice was full of excitement. "Did he find you?"

"Yes, he found me. Aren't you going to eat your food?"

"Yeah, sure." Will took a dutiful bite. "I told you he'd be back, didn't I?"

Samantha nodded. "Did he tell you where he's been and if he found Moore?"

"Nah. He just asked how my leg was feeling and said he wanted to talk to you. Where is he anyway?"

Samantha pointed to the couple she hadn't been able to take her eyes off. "Over there."

When the music stopped, Peggy — and Jake — disappeared into the schoolhouse, and Samantha flounced down beside Will. "Hey, what's wrong? You almost sat on my cake."

"I'm sorry." Samantha examined her skirts for icing.

"I'da thought you'd be happy now that Jake's back."

"I am."

"Well, you sure don't act like it."

Samantha made no comment to that, keeping her eyes on the doorway. Amos Smith asked her to dance again and she refused, earning herself another questioning look from Will. She was so busy ignoring his stare she didn't notice Jake was headed her way until he stood beside her holding two cups of punch.

"I drank yours earlier," he said, handing Will one of the cups. "And this one's for you. I figured you might be thirsty after all that dancing."

"Thank you." Samantha accepted the punch and took a sip. "How do you know I've been dancing a lot?"

"Makes sense." Jake's eyes raked over her, taking in the ivory smooth shoulders, full breasts, and tiny waist. "The men in this town aren't stupid, and you're the prettiest woman here."

Heat flowed into Samantha's face and she stared down into her punch, mumbling a quick thank-you.

"*I* told you she'd been dancing her feet off," Will interjected, as if Jake had forgotten where he really got the information.

"There was that, too," Jake admitted, his grin lopsided. He laughed, Samantha joined in, and Will's expression showed he didn't know what was the least bit amusing. "I hope you're not too tired to dance with me," Jake said, holding out his hand.

"Why no . . . I . . ." Samantha felt herself stammering so she just gave up and took his hand. She'd danced with nearly a dozen men this evening and none of them had affected her a bit. Why was this so different?

From the moment Samantha stepped into Jake's arms, her breath came in shallow gasps. The music was loud, but she was sure he could hear her heart pounding. She was so aware of him as a man she was certain her feet wouldn't follow his lead.

She cleared her throat, anything to take her mind off being held in his strong arms. "Did you find Landis Moore?"

Jake held her out from him and looked down into

334

her face. "No. I tried, but . . ."

"The sheriff said he went off into Tennessee."

"That's what his uncle said."

"But you didn't believe him."

Jake shrugged. "Let's not talk about this now." He held up their joined hands when she started to protest. "I promise I'll tell you everything later. But for now . . . it's been a long time since I danced with a beautiful woman. I want to enjoy it."

His words filled her with happiness but she couldn't help giving him a small reminder. "But you just finished waltzing with Peggy Keane."

The expression on his face before he laughed and pulled her closer made Samantha feel warm all over. And she discovered her nervousness had disappeared. She floated across the plank boards, feeling safe and protected, and positively marvelous . . . in Jake's arms.

After the melody had faded into the night, she wanted to hear about Landis Moore, but Amos asked her to dance again. Jake said he'd go keep Will company as if he expected her to accept Amos, so she did.

Shortly after that, the dance ended and all three of them walked back to the hotel, Will in the middle, complaining about how tired he was. They parted at Samantha's door, Will leaning heavily on his crutch, and Samantha sighed as she went in her room and turned the key.

She wanted to hear about Landis Moore, Samantha thought as she flopped on the edge of her bed. But here in the loneliness of her room she admitted something to herself.

More than to learn the fate of that bushwhacker, she wanted to be with Jake Morgan.

Samantha walked to the mirror and looked at her reflection. The woman before her seemed almost a stranger. A stranger that longed for Jake.

She was so deep in thought, trying to analyze this new development, that she didn't hear the footfalls in the hall. The rap on her door made her whirl around, her hand plastered to her racing heart.

Chapter Seventeen

"Who is it?" Samantha's voice quavered. She knew whom she wished were on the other side of the door, yet common sense told her to reach for the revolver Jake had left her.

She needed no gun. Yet the sound of Jake's voice brought on a new worry. Should she let him in, knowing what happened every time they were alone? Samantha closed her eyes and tried to think logically, but all she could feel was the wonder of being in his arms.

He'd turned away by the time Samantha opened the door. When he glanced back over his shoulder, Samantha saw the same indecision in his eyes that she felt. "I never got a chance to tell you about my trip to Missouri."

"No, you didn't." Samantha stood in the wedge of her open door. As he turned, she studied him in the light from the single oil lamp hanging three doors down the hallway. He was still dressed in gray pants that molded his muscular thighs, though he'd removed the sack jacket he wore at the dance.

The top buttons of his white shirt were loosened and Samantha could see the beginnings of curling chest hair.

"On second thought, it's probably better if I tell you in the morning." His grin was boyish. "This wasn't one of my better ideas." He held up his hand and gestured toward the quiet intimacy of the hallway, the greater seclusion of her room.

He moved back toward Will's doorway, and Samantha gripped the brass doorhandle till her fingers hurt. She was afraid. Afraid of what she wanted to do. Afraid that her sense of propriety would keep her from it. Would keep her from experiencing the happiness Jake brought her—if only for a short time.

He reached for the latch and the battle inside her ended. "Jake." He glanced toward her and Samantha couldn't help smiling at the surprised expression on his face. "Come tell me now," she whispered.

"Samantha, I don't think—"

"Please, Jake." Samantha opened the door wider in welcome, spreading the triangle of light from her room over the flocked wallpaper in the hall.

He'd never had an invitation more inviting or one that caused him more unease. Sitting on the side of the bed he shared with Will, he'd listed all the reasons—numerous, strong reasons—why he shouldn't go to Samantha's room. He couldn't come up with one decent reason why he should—except he wanted to with all his heart. But he was a grown man who knew a little of life, and wanting

338

to was not a good enough excuse to do something he knew was wrong.

But that didn't stop him from leaving his room and knocking at hers. When she didn't open the door straightaway, Jake thought he was given a reprieve from himself, from his own desires. But the respite was over, and Jake knew what he was going to do before his footsteps carried him into her room. But he still had a mind to resist this pull between them. He crossed to the window and peered out onto the darkened street.

"Is Will all right?" Now that Jake was in the room, Samantha felt shy and unsure.

"He's asleep." Jake fingered the fringe on the window curtain then turned around quickly. Samantha stood with her back to the door, as if she, too, knew distance was their only hope.

"Listen, Samantha—"

"Jake—"

They both spoke at the same time, then stopped, Samantha with a nervous giggle, Jake with a self-effacing grin.

"You first," he offered.

"No you."

Jake paused a moment then took a deep breath and leaned against the sill. "I did a lot of thinking as I rode across Missouri after Moore—who, by the way, I found no trace of."

Samantha folded her hands and studied the tips of her mother's kid shoes. "I figured as much."

"His uncle says he went off to Tennessee. But then he also swore Landis and his brother were home last Saturday night, which we know wasn't true. I rode around asking questions but no one—"

"What were you thinking about?" Samantha stepped toward him. At this moment she didn't care a fig about Landis Moore.

Jake looked up at her question. He paused a moment then blurted out, "How unfair I've been to you."

Samantha's head tilted. "I don't understand. I'm the one . . . I mean I shot you and pulled you into this. It's not your fight, but—"

"Samantha, I made love to you—twice—and Lord knows, I want to do it again."

"You do?" Samantha's eyes were wide.

"Hell, yes, but—"

"Then why aren't you?" She took another step, then another.

"Samantha I—" Jake held up his hands, palms out. "Now you just stop right there. One of us has to be rational and look out for your best interests." God, he wished she didn't look so beautiful to him. And her fragrance. He could smell the heady scent of roses and her.

"Jake, I—"

"No." Jake straightened. "You just stay where you are and listen. I'm no good for you. I'm passing through and you deserve a hell of a lot more than that. Now Samantha, I said not to move."

"I can't help it, Jake."

"This is exactly what I'm talking about. We don't seem to be able to fight this attraction we have for each other, so I think the best thing would be—"

"If we stopped trying." Samantha moved again, pressing herself to his long lean form.

"That's not what I was going to say," Jake murmured as he gave in and bent his lips to hers.

Samantha melted against him, her arms wrapped about his middle. His cotton shirt was smooth and she dug her fingers into it when Jake's tongue eased into her mouth. The kiss was deep and sensual, and by the time Jake lifted his head, his breathing was shallow.

"Oh God, Samantha, I want you so." Jake speared his fingers through the golden curls, sending the tortoiseshell combs Mrs. Tew had lent her flying. He angled her face toward him, catching her gaze and holding it with the intensity of his own. "But you deserve more."

"Let me decide what's best for me."

Jake touched his mouth to her cheek, her eyes, the tip of her nose. "Lord knows I care about you, Samantha. But I can't promise —"

"Shhhh." Her fingers sealed the lips she'd found so captivatingly sensual from the first. "I don't want your promises."

What she did want was to feel his strong arms around her, his hard body pressed to hers. And after only a moment's hesitation, he gave that to her. Samantha snuggled against his chest, listening to the steady beating of his heart, and knew this was worth it. Even if he rode out tomorrow and she never saw him again, she'd have this night, these memories. They'd stay with her always, because she loved him.

She smiled at the thought and wrapped her arms tighter. The fact that she loved him didn't surprise her. What did is that it had taken her this long to realize it.

"I'm glad you kept the dress." Jake spread his hands, fanning his fingers across her ribs. The silk felt smooth and warm like the skin beneath. He was fully aroused, eager to lay Samantha on the bed and watch passion fill her blue eyes. But he didn't want to rush this time . . . and he loved just holding her. Seeing the soft, rose-blush color of her cheeks, he nibbled her earlobe then told her how beautiful she looked.

"That's something else I thought about too when I was riding back from Missouri." The tip of his finger skimmed across the gown's décolletage and Samantha's breast filled and arched toward him.

"What? What did you think about?" Samantha clutched at his elbows to keep from sliding to the floor.

"You in this dress." The words were little more than a growl, and Samantha felt the heat of his breath as he bent to follow his finger's trail with his mouth.

Samantha moaned and her head dropped back. Her lower body pressed against his, and even through the gown and petticoat, she could feel his throbbing heat.

"God, when I saw you tonight . . ." His words trailed off as his tongue dipped, wetting the valley between her breasts. "It was all I could do not to drag you off behind the nearest building."

"Oh, Jake." He wooed her with his words and his hot, hot mouth, and all she could do was melt under his magic. Her hands road on his hips as his chin, erotically whisker-rough, nudged her gown's neckline. His fingers tangled in the curls hanging down her back, his rock-hard staff drove against her womanhood, and the silk inched lower.

Samantha's breathing stopped and a moan of joy lodged in her throat when the silk abraded over the extended tips of her nipples. But then his mouth was there, warm and soothing, assuaging the ache.

Her fingers flexed spasmodically as his tongue lathed her freed breasts. And then she could not stand the feel of cotton and wool beneath her hands. She yanked at his shirt, tugging it from his pants and greedily rubbing her palms over the sleek, satin skin covering his ribs. He groaned, his lips plundering hers, his fingers fumbling with the tiny pearl buttons marching down her spine.

Samantha grabbled with buttons, spreading the shirt halves just as he shoved down her bodice. Her breasts were firm and full and Jake adored them, first with his eyes, then his hands, rubbing his rough palms over the tight tips, then with his mouth.

How she loved the feel of him. Samantha touched his chest, reveling in his heat. Then she followed the arrowing strip of hair that traversed his body. She met the border of wool and didn't stop. He tensed, sucking in his breath when she encountered the large bulge and ever so gently squeezed it.

His mouth ground down on hers. Jake groped with the remaining buttons and tapes and sent her gown and petticoat billowing to the floor on a soft whisper of air. Her pantaloon ties proved stubborn, and their fingers met as Samantha tried to help. Finally in frustration he gave the string a yank and the worn cotton slipped down over her hips. His large hands followed.

Jake stroked and cupped, rubbed and smoothed. And all the time Samantha's desire grew to such dizzying heights she thought she'd explode.

Then abruptly he gathered her into his arms and strode the few steps to the bed. Gently he laid her down, taking a quick moment to strip off her shoes and stockings, then stood, silhouetted by the glow from the lamp and stared down at her.

Cool night air sifted across Samantha's body but the heat of Jake's gaze kept her boiling with need. She reached up to touch and he stepped closer. His skin was slick, covered with a fine sheen of sweat, and she trailed her fingers down his chest. This time when she reached the confining wool, she paused. Without taking his eyes off her, Jake unfastened his pants and shoved them down. He jerked around and shucked his boots before climbing onto the bed.

He loomed above her, blocking the light, filling her vision with his broad-shouldered body. His breathing was erratic, as was hers. His powerful arms, their muscles corded and bulging, bracketed her head. Samantha watched in anticipation as he leaned toward her, kissing first her mouth, then her chin.

His mouth was all that touched her, but Samantha could feel the sizzle of desire arc between them as he moved down her body. First one, then the other nipple received the erotic torture of his tongue.

He trailed a ribbon of dampness down the valley between her breasts. Samantha's breath caught as he slid lower. His breath fanned the golden curls at the apex of her legs, and Samantha moaned, her body arching toward him of its own volition. The heat of his mouth nearly drove her over the edge of the giant precipice, where she wavered taut as a bow string.

Then he moved, sliding up her body and impaling her with one quick, powerful lunge and she toppled into some great yawning void where sensation splintered reality. Her body quivered, drawing him deeper, tightened, and convulsed for long moments that seemed an eternity.

Samantha lifted her lashes and gazed into Jake's eyes. They were smoky green and searching. "Are you all right?" He brushed a lock of hair from her cheek.

Nodding and responding in kind to his quick smile was all she could manage. She felt drained and replete and believed herself totally incapable of moving. But when Jake shifted, imbedding himself even farther, Samantha knew a quickening of desire.

Her legs wrapped around his lean hips and she met each new thrust with growing need. Samantha clutched his muscled buttocks, boldly bringing him nearer, and the spiral of ecstasy erupted again.

This time when Samantha climaxed, Jake soared with her, his hoarse cry blending with hers. They collapsed in a tangle of arms and legs onto the mattress. After a moment, while Jake summoned what strength he had left, he rolled onto his back.

He slanted Samantha a look; he found her doing the same to him, and grinned. "Come here." Jake stretched out his arm and gathered her to his side. "Are you cold?"

"I . . . I don't think so." Samantha snuggled closer. Just seconds ago she thought she'd burn to a cinder.

Jake chuckled. "Let's pull the quilt up anyway."

After he settled them comfortably, Samantha's head resting on his shoulder, his arm around her, Jake turned and pressed his lips to her forehead. "I shouldn't stay." He paused. "Hell, I probably shouldn't have come."

Samantha leaned up on her elbow, giving Jake a wide-eyed innocent stare. "But you had to tell me about Landis Moore."

A bark of laughter shook his chest and Samantha grinned down at him. "Landis Moore was the last thing on my mind when I came in here." His head jerked up for a quick kiss before he pulled her back down. "But I guess we do need to talk about him."

Samantha sighed. "The sheriff thinks he's off to Tennessee and won't come around these part again."

"He also believes he was in Missouri last week when we know he was burning your cornfield."

"And hurting Will."

Jake tightened his grip on her shoulders. "And hurting Will," he agreed. "I don't know where he is but I still think we should keep an eye out for him—at least for a while."

He said "we." *We* should keep an eye out for him. Samantha knew he meant to leave soon. But maybe not right away. And the thought made her happier than she could say.

"Are you asleep?" Jake tucked in his chin to see Samantha's face. She didn't say anything about Moore, and that wasn't like her.

"No. And I agree with you. We should be watchful."

Jake sifted his fingers through her golden curls and wondered at his contentment. But even as he enjoyed it, a little voice reminded him it couldn't last. Not this night with Samantha. Not the happiness he found with her.

"Jake."

"Hmmm?" He was staring at the whitewashed ceiling thinking he really needed to get up and go to his own room—and wishing he didn't have to when she spoke his name.

"Where in Texas are you headed?"

"I don't know." Jake shifted around to face her. "Haven't really given it much thought. I didn't decide on Texas until recently."

"Oh." Samantha rolled her head to look at him. His arm was beside her, elbow bent, and he used

347

his hand to prop up his head.

"Why?"

"No reason. I just wondered." Not for anything would she tell him she wanted to know where he'd be so she could picture him there after he left.

"Mmmm." Jake lazily followed the curve of her breast with his finger. "Maybe Southeast Texas. Thomas . . ." Jake paused then glanced down and explained. "He was my brother. Anyway, he said it was pretty down there."

"I'll bet there are lots of towns that need a doctor too."

Jake's finger stilled. "My doctoring days are over."

"They don't have to be."

Jake flopped onto his back, throwing an arm across his eyes. "They just are, that's all. I don't want to talk about it anymore."

"But why?"

Jake peeked from under his arm. "You are a pestery woman, you know that?"

Samantha leaned up on her arm. "Maybe. But I still want to know. Is it because of what happened to your wife and son?" She couldn't imagine what possessed her to force the issue like this, but Samantha couldn't seem to help herself.

"It's not Lydia or Andrew, or even the war." Jake scrubbed his hand over his chin. "It's me. I just don't think I have anything to offer anymore."

"But that's not true. Look what you did for Will. Doc Shelton said he'd never seen so fine a stitching job."

348

This remark was met with silence, such complete silence that Samantha leaned closer. "Did you hear me?"

"Yes I heard you." There was a twinge of annoyance in his voice, and he took a deep breath. With a quick movement Jake tugged on the arm supporting Samantha, sending her sprawling across his chest. "Listen, I know you're trying to bolster my confidence." He positioned her better on top of him. "But the fact is, I don't want to be a doctor anymore."

"I don't be—"

Samantha's response was cut off when Jake's hand cupped her head, pulling her down for a deep, probing kiss. Her tongue met his for a sensual dance that heated his blood. But when he loosened his grip, she rested her elbows on his chest and looked him squarely in the eye. "—lieve you," she finished. "I don't believe you."

"Oh, yeah," Jake chuckled. "Looks like I'm going to have to use stronger measures than a kiss to end this conversation."

"Jake." She drew the word out. "Don't do that. I think we should talk."

"Not now, Samantha."

Samantha tore her mouth away from his next kiss before she was completely lost in a sensual haze. "I know what you're trying to do."

"Good." Jake grasped her buttocks and slid her up over him. "Then why don't you help?"

There was nothing she could say to that; besides, Samantha really didn't want to talk when they could be making love.

She moaned in acquiescence when he urged her down for another kiss. Her hair curled around them, a shimmering veil of gold that held the world and its troubles at bay—at least for the moment.

Her breasts pressed against his chest, her entire body, soft and smooth, molded to his hair-roughened flesh as he held her. Samantha's thighs spread and he arched, teasing her for only a moment before he thrust, filling her with his heat.

Samantha gasped as each movement she made created a surge of tension within her. She wriggled and his hands clamped on her hips.

"Take it slow or I can't be responsible," he murmured as she threw back her head.

She found a rhythm, exalted in it, and kept it up as Jake's body tensed beneath her. Then he slid his thumbs over her taut nipples before slipping his hand to where their bodies met. Deliberately, provocatively, he searched for the treasure buried deep in her tight curls.

He stroked and she writhed, her control gone, her body jolting to meet his wild, powerful thrusts.

Samantha collapsed on Jake's chest, her skin as slick as his, her body as spent. Jake gathered her close, rolled them to the side, and they both fell asleep, still intimately joined.

It was the commotion on the street beneath his window that woke Jake up. He shifted, smiling when he felt Samantha's warm, soft body cuddled with his. Just as quickly, his eyes popped open and the smile disappeared. "Damnit," he said, throwing back the quilt.

"What's wrong." Samantha drifted up from a marvelous dream to find it reality. She was entwined with Jake, though he seemed bent on changing that.

"I fell asleep in here." Jake rolled to the edge of the bed, then thought better of his haste and leaned forward, pressing his lips against Samantha's. "Good morning," he said when she wrapped her arms around his neck.

"Mmmmm" was Samantha's only response.

"I have to go." Jake unfolded her hands at his nape and guided them to his mouth. "I never meant to stay here last night. Maybe Will isn't awake yet."

"Is that what you're worried about? Will finding out?"

Jake yanked on his pants. "Not for myself. But I thought you might care."

"I do, I guess. At least I think I should." Samantha pulled the quilt up to her chin and leaned back against the wooden headboard. "But I doubt Will's still asleep. Not with all that noise outside. What is it anyway?"

Jake stomped his foot into the boot and strode to the window, sliding back the cotton curtains. He peered through the grimy glass then closed his eyes. Turning toward Samantha, he met her stare. "The army's here."

* * *

351

"I don't know why you're being so obstinate about this."

"I'm not obstinate." Jake wiped his mouth on the homespun napkin and stood.

"What do you call it then?" Samantha pushed back her chair without waiting for Jake to do it.

"I call it, not seeing any reason for me to meet with the army lieutenant."

"Because it's the Union Army."

"Maybe." Jake lowered his voice when he noticed Will regarding him strangely. The three of them had just finished a late breakfast in Hager's Flats' only restaurant. Now Samantha was pestering him to go with her to the sheriff's office, where the army had set up a temporary headquarters.

"The war is over, you know."

"Ha!" Jake flattened his palms on the table between plates of leftover pancakes. "Look who's talking, Miss Shoot First Ask Questions Later."

"I thought that was behind us," Samantha said, leaning forward herself.

"It is." Jake straightened, glancing around the room, glad to see they were the only patrons remaining in the place. "But that doesn't change the fact that I don't want to go have a sit-down chat with some Union officer, nor do I think it's necessary. Will and I can hitch up the wagon and have everything ready for you when you're finished."

Samantha gave an exaggerated sigh. "Well, if that's the way it has to be." She gathered up her reticule.

"It is." Jake bent over to help Will. "You don't

need me, Samantha."

Need him or no, she wanted him, Samantha thought, as she headed down the boardwalk toward the sheriff's office. Soldiers milled around in front of the false-fronted building. They moved aside as she came to a stop and then went in the office.

Her entrance produced a scowl from Sheriff Hughes, who was bent over his desk explaining something to the man sitting in his seat. That man, an officer in his early thirties, looked up and smiled before jerking to his feet.

"Lieutenant Matthew Farrow at your service, ma'am. How may I help you?"

"Lieutenant." Samantha sat in the chair he offered. "I'm Samantha Lowery."

"Ah." Farrow touched his dark mustache. "The lady that sent Colonel Adams the telegram. I had no idea you'd be so lovely."

Samantha felt her blush all the way to her toes, especially when she heard Sheriff Hughes's grunt of disbelief. Apparently the lieutenant heard it, too, for he turned on the man, an expression of disdain on his face. "I believe I'm finished with you for the time being, Hughes. I'll let you know if I have any more questions."

Hughes bristled at the dismissal. "But . . . but this is my office. I'm the law in Hager's Flats."

"Not as long as the army's in town. I have the authority to make that official if you'd rather."

Hughes grabbed his sweat-stained hat from the hook near the door and retreated in a muttering mass.

"Bunch of Southern sympathizers," Lieutenant Farrow said after the door slammed shut. "What an ordeal it must be for you."

"There have been moments," Samantha admitted, then smiled because Matthew Farrow was smiling at her. "I imagine everything will work out now that you're here."

"I should very well hope so. Now tell me all that's happened."

For the next half-hour or so, Samantha related everything she could think of, including her father's hanging, vandalism on her farm, Jake's conversation with Ab Moore, and Will's attempted murder. Matthew Farrow was an attentive listener, seldom interrupting, and then only to ask pertinent questions.

When Samantha finished, Lieutenant Farrow assured her she would have no more problems from Landis Moore. "I intend to clamp down on this town, especially the Rebel element."

"They aren't all bad," Samantha countered, only to have her hand patted by the lieutenant.

"I know what I'm doing, lovely lady. Don't worry your pretty head over it. Now"—the lieutenant stood when Samantha did—"please allow me to escort you home."

"There's no need."

"But I insist. You shouldn't be roaming about the countryside alone until we've brought Moore to justice."

"I truly don't believe he's in the area." Samantha thought of Jake's futile search for him. "Besides, I have my brother and . . . and a man I've hired to help harvest the corn with me."

"If you're sure you'll be all right then . . ."

"I'm quite sure." Even though he was a Union soldier, Samantha didn't think she cared for Matthew Farrow. He seemed nice enough, and he was certainly willing to be of service to her. And with his straight dark brown hair and deep-set brown eyes, he was handsome, but . . .

"You will allow me to call on you once I've taken care of things in town, won't you?" Lieutenant Farrow reached for her hand.

"Yes . . . I suppose so."

"Excellent. I'll look forward to it."

Samantha nodded in agreement. But she was more than happy to leave the sheriff's office and see Jake and Will waiting with the wagon at the end of the street.

Chapter Eighteen

"What are you singing about?" Jake came up behind Samantha as she scooped water from the creek into a wooden bucket. He took it from her as she straightened.

Samantha brushed hair from her eyes. "Was I singing?"

"Sure were. Sounded mighty pretty too." Jake draped his arm around Samantha's shoulders and gave her a quick kiss. "I'm leaving for the field now. Will's going along again to keep me company. We should finish up today."

Finish up. The day Samantha dreaded. The day there was no real reason for Jake to stay on. "That's good," she said, hoping her true feelings weren't too obvious.

Apparently Jake didn't notice any trepidation in her voice for he went on in obvious good humor. "If we get done this morning, I'm going to ride into town and see about getting that wheel fixed again. You need anything else?"

"Not that I can think of." Samantha smiled up

at him. Jake didn't act like he was aching to leave. He seemed happy and lighthearted. In the five days since they'd returned from town, Samantha and Jake and Will had gotten on fine.

There was only one occasion when Jake seemed out of sorts, and that was when he and Will returned from the fields to find that Lieutenant Farrow had come calling.

"He only stopped by to see if everything was all right," Samantha insisted when she stepped outside for some evening air and Jake followed. He'd been acting like a bear with a thorn in his paw all evening. He did little more than grunt at her explanation.

"Now just what is that supposed to mean?" Samantha kept her voice down so Will wouldn't hear them arguing and come to investigate. She could hear him in the house blowing into Jake's harmonica, trying to play a tune.

"It means, I don't know why he's not out trying to catch Landis Moore."

"He thinks Moore's long gone."

Again a disapproving noise, this one more like a snort than a grunt.

"You said very nearly the same thing when you got back from Missouri. What's making you change your mind now."

"Nothing. Who said I had? I just don't like him coming around here when there's no need."

Samantha peered at him through the gathering dusk, and a spark of understanding flashed in her mind. At first she couldn't believe it, but the

357

longer he scowled at her, the more likely it seemed. "Why Jacob Morgan!"

"What?" Jake rested his hands on his hips.

"You're jealous."

"Jealous?" His voice thundered between them and Will temporarily stopped screeching on the mouth organ.

"Yes, jealous," Samantha whispered after Will started playing again.

"That's the most ridiculous—" He clamped his mouth into a straight line and folded his arms. "I just don't want to see you get hurt," he informed her with a knowing nod.

"I know how to take care of myself." Samantha's stance matched his.

"Fine." Jake started off the porch. "I'm just not crazy about Union soldiers is all," he mumbled as he headed for the barn.

That was three days ago and since then neither Samantha nor Jake had mentioned the discussion or any of its implications. For all intents and purposes, it might not have taken place.

"I shouldn't be long in town," Jake was saying as they approached the barn. "But don't hold supper for me if I'm not back. I'll grab something when I get here."

"I'll save you something."

"Thanks." Jake ducked behind the barn and plopped down the bucket, splashing water over his boots. Before Samantha could ask what the devil he was up to, he'd reached out and pulled her into his arms.

"What are you—" His warm mouth cut off Samantha's protest as he lifted her up and twirled her around.

"Do me another favor," Jake said when they were both dizzy from kissing.

"What?" Samantha wrapped her arms around his neck.

"Come out to the barn tonight."

"But—"

"I know all about Will sleeping on a pallet in the parlor and you not wanting him to know, but damn I've missed being with you."

Samantha bit her lip then blurted out what she was thinking. "Oh, I've missed you too."

Jake grinned then twirled her around till her skirts whirled out and she giggled with glee. "Then you'll come?"

"Goodness. Put me down."

"Not till you say you'll come to the barn."

"All right," Samantha laughed. "But don't you be real late from town tonight."

"No ma'am. Wouldn't think of it." Jake punctuated his words with a kiss that had Samantha's head spinning almost as much as when he'd whirled her around. When he finally lowered her to the ground, they were both breathless and grinning at their silliness.

Jake touched her cheek and bent to kiss her again, but he stopped within inches of her lips.

"Jake! You coming, Jake?"

Straightening, Jake blew air out his mouth.

"Sometimes that brother of yours can be awfully pesky."

"It's only because he idolizes you." Samantha reached for the pail but Jake beat her to it.

"He does not. He just likes having a man around."

So do I, Samantha thought, but she didn't say it as they ambled from behind the barn.

"Coming, Will. Just helping your sister get some water."

"She gets water all the time, Jake," Will admonished from his seat in the wagon bed. "If we don't get to the field, we'll never get done. You don't want that, do you?"

"Lord no." Jake climbed onto the seat. "I'm aiming to get my work finished early today." His wink made Samantha smile as he started the mules off toward the field.

Apprehension wasn't exactly it.

Still Jake couldn't come up with a better word to describe his feelings as he rode into Hager's Flats that Friday afternoon. Would there ever come a day when he could face a town full of Yankees and not experience a flood of memories?

Jake shook his head. He'd experienced firsthand the destruction the Union Army could do, but then Confederate guns could shoot a man just as dead. It wasn't the armies so much as the war itself that had caused all the death and destruction.

Still, Jake kept a sharp eye out as he rode down

the main street of town toward the smithy. Blue-garbed soldiers loitered along the street, leaning against the wooden buildings or standing in small groups chewing the fat.

Lieutenant Farrow didn't seem to run a very tight company, for all his personal military polish. The soldiers were a straggly-looking lot with unkempt uniforms and dusty boots. But Jake imagined they hadn't sent an elite corp down from Fort Scott to tangle with a few outlaw border ruffians.

After dismounting, Jake unhooked the wheel and rolled it into the three-walled smithy.

"Howdy." Linc Jones looked up and let his beefy hand slip off the bellows. "What can I do for you?"

Jake nodded in greeting. "I'm doing some work for Samantha Lowery and she's still having trouble with this wheel."

Rubbing his hands down his leather apron, Linc approached Jake. "I fixed that thing once, didn't I?"

"Think so. But I'd like you to take another look at it."

Linc crouched down beside the wheel. The muscles in his wide arms shone with sweat. "How's Samantha doing? Heard there was some trouble out her way."

"She's fine. So's Will, now. Things should be better now that the army's here," Jake added because he knew that was how Samantha felt.

"The army." Linc spit on the packed ground floor of the smithy. "I don't hold with honest citizens like Samantha and Will Lowery being hurt. But I sure as hell don't like the army coming in here and taking over."

"Has there been trouble?" Jake leaned against a high bench.

"Not so long as you abide by what that Lieutenant Farrow says there isn't."

"What's he say?"

Linc straightened, spearing Jake with an icy stare. "Lots of things, but I just mind my own business. It's going to take me a while to fix this."

"Sure. I'll check back in a bit."

The first thing Jake noticed when he stepped outside was the group of blue-coated soldiers hanging around his horse. Taking a deep breath, he headed toward the hitching post.

"Excuse me, gentlemen." Jake shouldered his way through two of the men, but the soldier standing directly in front of the post didn't budge. He had a campaign hat pulled low over his eyes and cheeks that settled into his bull neck.

Jake met the private's stare. "You're in my way."

"Is that so?" The burly soldier transferred his chew from one cheek to the other, twisted his head, and let loose a stream of tobacco juice. After backhanding his mouth, he crossed his arms. "You a Reb, boy?" His eyes locked on Jake's belt buckle with its raised CSA.

Jake took a deep breath. "I was in the Confederate Army. But that doesn't change the fact that you're blocking my horse."

The private chortled. "You hear that, boys?

Johnny Reb here says I'm in his way." The "boys" all seemed to think this highly amusing. There were five of them in all, counting the two who'd moved for him—who now had closed in behind Jake.

"Listen." Jake kept his voice pleasant by sheer will. He had the strongest desire to bash the private's nose into the back of his skull. "I'm not after any trouble. Just want to get my horse and—"

"Your damn, lily-livered Reb horse, you mean," the private sneered then spit again, this time dangerously close to the toe of Jake's boot.

Jake's smile was chilling as he shook his head. "Anybody here smart enough to realize the war is over?"

"What you saying?" The private puffed out his chest and gave a sharp look toward the one soldier who had snickered at Jake's remark. "That we ain't as bright as some no-'count, lice-eating slime of a Reb?"

Jake blew air through his teeth. "Yeah. I guess that's about what I'm saying."

He expected the first blow and easily feinted away from the private's massive right. What Jake didn't expect was the two men behind him grabbing his arms and pinning them back in a painful squeeze.

Jake felt pretty confident about beating the private in a fair fight. But there was nothing fair about this. A fist landed in his midsection, doubling him over. Then something hard and heavy hit Jake's head.

He tried to fight back, and knew a moment of satisfaction as his boot connected with a shin. "God damn, Reb. Hold the bastard still while I teach him what we think of his kind in these parts."

Pain exploded in his gut, his head. The men pinioning his arms yanked tighter and Jake fell to his knees. They were going to kill him, Jake thought. He'd survived the war to be beaten to death in some 'one-horse' Kansas town.

And he'd never see Samantha again.

'Where do you think he is?"

"For the last time, Will, I don't know." Samantha wove the needle into the skirt she was hemming and dropped the dress into her sewing basket. She hadn't taken more than three stitches in the past half-hour anyway. "Would you stop pacing. That can't be good for your leg."

"But it ain't like Jake to miss a meal."

Samantha didn't bother to correct Will's grammar. "I told you Jake said he might be late tonight."

"But it's almost nine-thirty."

"I know. Perhaps the wheel took longer to fix than he thought." She shrugged, trying to appear unconcerned for Will's sake. "Maybe he stayed in town for the night when it got late."

Will stopped in front of Samantha, his crutch resting at his armpit. "You don't believe that no more than I do."

Of course she didn't believe it. Especially not after the way Jake had acted that morning about getting home early. But things do come up. Problems arise. And the only way Jake had of letting them know he'd be late was to send a message or come himself, so they'd just have to wait.

Besides, as much as she worried, there was a bright point. "Remember, Will, the army's in town so nothing really bad could happen."

"Yeah, I guess you're right, Sam." Reluctantly Will clomped over to his pallet and lowered himself.

"I know I am. Just go to sleep and I'll bet first thing in the morning Jake will be here."

But he wasn't.

Samantha watched the sun creep over the horizon and turn the sky a wash of mauves and pink. And still Jake hadn't come back. She wasn't able to sleep, finally gave up trying, and dressed by the light of a single candle.

The familiar clomp-clomp of Will's crutches sounded behind her, and Samantha turned on the porch and drew her shawl tighter. "You want some breakfast?"

"I guess." Will squinted in the direction of town. "Still not back, huh?"

"No." Samantha had already been to the barn in case he'd come in last night and she'd somehow missed him. "Well, I better get started on fixing something to eat."

"Sam." Will caught her arm as she moved past him. "I'm worried."

Samantha paused a moment, then touched his hand. "So am I, Will. So am I."

Neither of them ate many of the eggs Samantha had gathered, and she scraped them off the plates into Charity's dish. The dog gobbled them up before Samantha straightened.

Samantha glanced toward the clock then walked back to the table and sat down. Even if Jake had waited till morning to come back to the farm, he'd be here by now. "I'm going into town," she said when Will looked up.

"I'll go with you."

"No." Samantha folded her hands. "We can't take the wagon because Jake has the wheel and I don't think you're ready to sit a horse for that long a time."

"Aw, Sam."

"Don't 'Aw, Sam' me. You know what I'm saying is true." Samantha rose and went toward her bedroom. "You just stay inside and I'll be back as soon as I can." She paused, her hand on the latch. "And Will, I'm leaving you Jake's revolver."

"You think Moore's around again?"

"No," Samantha hurriedly answered. "No, I don't. But just in case."

By late morning Samantha rode into Hager's Flats. She'd stopped along the way at the Nelsons' farm to see if Jake might have spent the night there. The Nelsons hadn't seen him. They did offer their best wishes for Will's quick recovery.

"It's a sorry thing when people like Landis and Ab Moore can get away with crippling up a young

366

boy," Seth had said, and Samantha had stared down at him from her mare's back.

"It's a sorry thing when we do nothing and let him get away with it," she'd replied and watched as Seth colored beneath his sun-darkened skin.

"Now see here, Samantha. I'm nothing but a farmer. Besides, the army's here now to take care of us."

Samantha had ridden away without another word.

Seth Nelson had been right about one thing, she thought as she rode through the town. The army was definitely here. Soldiers seemed to be everywhere. But though she scanned the street from under her bonnet, she saw no sign of Jake or his horse.

Linc Jones greeted her warmly as Samantha climbed off the mare. "There you are," he said. "Wondered what I was to do with that wheel." He motioned toward the wagon wheel leaning against the shed.

"So Jake did come here," Samantha mumbled. "Do you know where he went after he left here?"

Linc pounded his hammer down on a horseshoe wrapped around the anvil. Sparks sprayed out and the loud clang made Samantha think she'd misheard Linc's answer.

"What did you say?"

"I said, I reckon they hauled him off to jail."

"Jail." Samantha stared at him wide-eyed. She hadn't heard him wrong the first time. "Whatever for?"

"Don't rightly know for sure," Linc began but Samantha turned and started out of the smithy. "Some sort of ruckus in the street from what . . ." His words trailed off as Samantha marched down the boardwalk toward the jail.

What on earth could have happened to get Jake thrown in jail? He knew better than to tangle with the sheriff—Hughes really wasn't worth the effort. Besides, Lieutenant Farrow would surely take care of any problem that arose.

Samantha banged open the jail door, startling the soldier who lounged in the chair, his feet stretched out on Sheriff Hughes's desk. He jumped up, reaching for his gun, then laughed self-consciously when he saw who it was.

"Sorry, ma'am. Didn't know it was you."

Samantha recognized the young soldier from the time she'd met with Lieutenant Farrow. "That's all right," she said, smiling at him. "I've heard a rumor that my hired hand is . . ." Samantha's gaze drifted to the cell and her hand flew to her mouth, stifling a scream. "Oh, my God, Jake!"

She ran to the cell door, clutching the bars and staring at the bruised and battered man inside. "Jake! Jake, can you hear me?" She jerked her head toward the young soldier. "Open this cell at once."

" 'Fraid I can't do that, ma'am."

"What?" Samantha was incensed. "This man is hurt. He could be dying." Her voice caught on a sob but she continued. "I demand—"

"What's going on in here, soldier?"

Samantha whirled around at the sound of Lieutenant Farrow's voice. "Oh, thank heavens you're here. This . . . this person refuses to unlock the door and Jake needs my help." Samantha looked into the cell when she heard Jake's moan.

"I'm afraid he's just following orders, Miss Lowery."

"Who's orders?"

Matthew Farrow removed his hat and hooked it on the peg behind the desk. "Mine."

Samantha's eyes shot up to meet his. Her voice was tight and she spoke slowly. "Then order him to unlock it." Her stare didn't waver, but then neither did the lieutenant's until he shifted his gaze to the young soldier watching the scene with undisguised interest.

With a slight jerk of his head, Farrow silently commanded the soldier to do Samantha's bidding. She rushed through the space as soon as the bars shifted open, dropping to her knees by the cot where Jake lay.

She touched the purple lump on his cheek and his eyes slitted open. "Samantha?"

"Yes, it's me, Jake." She wanted to hug him, to kiss him, to thank God he was alive, but she didn't want to hurt him anymore. His sensual bottom lip was split and Samantha trailed her fingertip over it in a soothing caress. "What happened to you?" Her voice was choked with tears.

"He refused to give up his gun. It's a new ordinance I've established for ex-Confederate soldiers," Farrow explained when Samantha glanced up at him. "And he resisted arrest."

"The hell I did!" Jake pushed himself to sitting, fighting Samantha's attempt to keep him prone. "His soldiers jumped me. Came close to killing me." Jake shoved to his feet and started toward the open cell door.

"Jake!" Samantha caught his arm. "Stop it." Though Lieutenant Farrow had retreated a step when Jake started after him, he now stood firm, his revolver drawn and aimed at Jake's midsection.

"See what I mean? You can't trust any of these Rebs."

Samantha stepped between the men. "Well, you can trust this one. If he says your soldiers beat him up without provocation, you can believe it."

"Samantha . . . Miss Lowery," Farrow amended when she raised her brow. "I questioned all five of my men and—"

"Five! Five soldiers pummeled an innocent civilian and you did nothing to them?"

"Now, there's no reason to get hysterical."

"Hysterical!" Samantha yelled, fearing she was becoming just that. "I'll show you hysterical." She gripped Jake's sleeve and tried to calm down. "I want this man released immediately."

"Samantha, I can take care of myself," Jake began but she ignored him.

"If he isn't, I shall send a telegram to Fort Scott and report this to Colonel Adams. My good friend, Colonel Adams." The good friend part was stretching it—though Colonel Adams *had* known her father—but at this moment Samantha realized

370

she would do anything for Jake. A small lie seemed insignificant indeed.

The tension in the small dusky room was palatable. Samantha stood, fists balled on hips and stared at Farrow. She imagined she could hear him thinking, deciding the best way out of this corner she'd wedged him in. She could feel Jake beside her, felt his anger and knew it was close to erupting. Dust flecks danced in the thin stream of sunshine that penetrated the grime-covered window as the seconds ticked away.

Finally when Samantha thought she could bare it no longer, Lieutenant Farrow cleared his throat. "I'm keeping his gun."

"Now wait a damn m—"

"That's fine." Samantha's arm coiled around Jake's.

"And I want him to get out of Hager's Flats . . . the whole area. And stay out."

Jake snorted. "We have no difference of opinion there."

Lieutenant Farrow's eyes narrowed. "If I catch him around here again, I'll lock him up. I can't have my soldiers being—"

"Where's his horse?" Now that the decision was made, Samantha wanted to get Jake out of there as quickly as possible. And she didn't want to listen to any lecture given by Matthew Farrow.

"At the livery." Farrow obviously didn't like the turn events had taken. "Samantha . . . Miss Lowery." He reached out his hand to her. "You don't have to trouble yourself with him. I can have the doctor take a look at him, then send him on his way. He's nothing but a Reb."

Samantha could feel the tension of coiled muscles in Jake's arm as her hand tightened. She gave the lieutenant the coldest of stares. "Please step out of our way."

Jake and Samantha garnered their share of inquisitive glances as they walked down the boardwalk toward the livery. Jake pulled his hat brim low over his bruised eyes. "Seems like word spreads quickly in Hager's Flats."

Samantha didn't answer but she straightened her back, raised her chin, and kept walking.

After they had gathered the horses—Jake's from the livery, hers from in front of the smithy—Samantha tightened the bow on her bonnet, then hesitated. "Are you able to ride? I can help you if you like." He'd walked all right, his tread firm and steady, but he looked so awful, his shirt torn and splattered with blood. And his poor face.

But Samantha knew the moment she offered that she shouldn't have. His pride had already suffered enough of a blow without her unwittingly adding to it.

"Damnit, Samantha." Jake's voice was tight as a wound spring. "I can sure as hell get on a horse by myself." Which he managed despite some difficulty. "Don't mother me."

Neither spoke on the ride back to the farm.

For Samantha's part, she was wishing she'd kept her mouth shut, and that she'd never let Jake go to town in the first place. But then it hadn't been her place to stop him, she reminded herself. If only the solders hadn't beaten him. If only she hadn't sent for them. If only there hadn't been this awful war. Because she knew what was going to happen now. There was no doubt in her mind.

"Samantha." Jake drew up his horse as they neared the twin cottonwood trees marking the edge of her farm.

The sound of him saying her name, coupled with the inevitable statement she knew was coming, made Samantha blink back tears.

"Aw, now don't go crying on me." Jake dismounted and went around to Samantha's side. His hands circled her waist and she slipped down into his arms. "I'm sorry about what I said. I had no call blaming *you* for anything." He touched the golden hair that trailed down her back. "If truth be known, I thought you were pretty wonderful back there."

"Oh, Jake, I'm so sorry they did this to you." She buried her face in his shirt, loving the feel and smell of him . . . pulling back abruptly when he winced. "I've hurt you."

"No. No. Never you." Jake enveloped her against him. "It's just that one of those soldiers had damn sharp knuckles." Jake looked down into her face. "That's supposed to make you laugh."

"I can't, Jake." Samantha stared up at him through tears that turned her eyes to crystal blue prisms. She reached up and touched a spot on his cheek that wasn't discolored. "I can't."

Jake pulled her close again and stood holding

her in the middle of the road. The horses whinnied softly and wandered off to the side to graze on the grass and still they stood, the wind whipping her skirts at his legs, absorbing the strength of each other.

"Samantha." Jake lifted her chin with his thumb and brushed his lips across hers. "I can't stay any longer."

She knew it was coming, yet forewarning didn't make his announcement any easier to bear. She swallowed, closing her eyes against the pain and regret she saw in his.

"There was a time when I thought . . . well, maybe there was a place for me here."

"Jake . . ."

"Shhh." His fingers touched her lips. "I care about you, Samantha. But it just isn't going to work."

"I know," Samantha whispered, wondering how the words got past her tight throat. And how she could stand here in the middle of the road surrounded by the scent of wildflowers while her heart was breaking.

Will did most of the talking at supper that night. He was righteously indignant for Jake's sake when he heard what had happened.

"I'll bet you put up a real humdinger of a fight," he said, shoveling a forkful of grits into his mouth.

"Will, there were five of them," Samantha chided as Jake shook his head laughing.

"You know, Will, what fighting I did do probably only made matters worse."

"Well," Will said proudly. "I'm sure they know better than to tangle with you again."

"And vise versa," Jake assured him, giving Samantha a crooked grin.

She smiled back and stood to reach for the pan of bread pudding. Jake had looked a lot better since he'd cleaned up. His fresh shirt covered the purpling on his ribs, and without the dried blood, his cuts weren't so noticeable. Still, his eyes were bruised, one nearly swollen shut, and his bottom lip was split. And she still thought he looked incredibly handsome.

Samantha dipped out the bread pudding—an extralarge helping for Jake, who once confided it was his favorite dessert—and sat down at the table, waiting patiently for Will to go to bed. But it was Jake who stood first.

"A mighty fine meal, Samantha," he said, reaching for his hat. He was sure as hell going to miss her cooking. But then he was sure as hell going to miss her. And Will. And the sense of belonging they'd both given him. But he didn't belong here. The Yankee lieutenant had made that perfectly clear.

Jake turned toward the door. "I think I'll turn in early tonight."

"Do you need anything?" Samantha was beside him in an instant, her hand on his arm, where he'd rolled up his shirtsleeve. His flesh felt warm and strong and she didn't want to let go.

"No. I'll be fine." He stared down into her blue eyes and could barely resist the desire to take her in his arms. But Will was sitting at the table finishing his dessert, and Jake and Samantha had decided to wait until morning to tell the boy he was leaving. So instead he reached for the latch and walked out the door.

Samantha looked around at the tin dishes on the table and her brother sitting beside it. He must have sensed her gaze, for he glanced up.

"What's wrong," he asked.

"Nothing." Samantha reached for the shawl folded on the pie safe.

"Then where are you going?"

"To the barn," Samantha answered honestly. "To be with Jake." She wrapped the knitted material around her shoulders, aware of Will's surprised expression and the questions he wasn't asking. "If I'm not back when you go to bed, don't forget to lower the lamp wick."

The soft glow of a candle pushed aside the darkness as Samantha opened the barn door. Jake turned, his hands on the shirt he was stripping down his arms when she entered. He stared at her a moment across the musky space and shrugged the shirt back over his shoulders.

"This probably isn't a good idea," he said, dropping his hands to his side.

Samantha shrugged, letting the shawl slip off her body. "I thought I had an invitation. At least I did yesterday."

"A lot of things can happen in twenty-four

hours."

"Does that mean you don't want me anymore?" Samantha's question was as brazen as the tilt of her chin.

Jake spiked fingers back through his hair. "Hell, you know better than that. But I'm leaving," he explained. "This will just make it harder."

"It can't be any more difficult than it already is." Samantha's fingers started a lazy journey down her bodice, leaving unfastened buttons in their wake. Her breathing was shallow as she spread the calico fabric, baring her flesh and simple shift to his gaze.

Slowly she lifted her lashes, and her legs trembled at the expression of unbridled passion in his eyes. "Make love with me," she murmured, moments before he rushed forward and crushed her in his arms.

Chapter Nineteen

Dawn came too quickly.

Samantha tried to ignore the insistent crowing of the cocksure rooster and snuggled closer to Jake. His arm tightened and he mumbled something in his sleep that made Samantha smile. She reached up and brushed a strand of light brown hair from his forehead, careful not to bump his bruised face. The innocent gesture filled her with longing and she curled her fingers and bit her lip to keep from crying.

He was leaving today—really leaving. They had talked last night after making love. He couldn't stay here. Not with the army out to get him—and Samantha had no doubt they were.

Jake didn't deserve such treatment. He'd remained as long as he had because of her—to help and protect her. But she didn't need his help anymore. And he had to leave.

Samantha could tell it hurt him to say it. He cared about her . . . she knew that. But apparently the painful memories of his wife and son, and of the war, made it impossible for his feelings to run as strong and deep as hers. She loved him pure and simple. She'd always love him.

But when he woke up, he'd mount his horse and ride away . . . and she'd never see him again.

Samantha took a deep breath, inhaling the smell of hay and animals and Jake.

He hadn't asked her to go with him.

Closing her eyes, Samantha relived their conversation last night as they lay on the twisted army blanket. Never once had he suggested she give up everything and follow him. Never once.

But she hadn't really expected him to. He was a Rebel, a drifter, wandering off to who-knows-where. And she had responsibilities. Will. The farm.

She stared at the cobweb-laced rafters and let her mind take flight. She imagined him asking her . . . begging her to ride off with him. What would she say?

"You look pensive this morning. What are you thinking about?" Jake rolled onto his shoulder and traced her profile with the tip of his finger.

"Nothing," Samantha lied. She shifted toward him, forcing herself to smile. "How do you feel this morning?"

"Like a cannon rolled over me," he teased, then grinned when her expression grew concerned. "No, really, I don't hurt too much. Like I told you yesterday, nothing's broken."

"That's what you said, but then you also don't seem to trust the doctor in you, so . . ."

"Now, Samantha. I told you I'm not interested in practicing medicine anymore."

The blanket pooled around her waist as Samantha

sat up. "You said you'd give it some thought."

"Did I say that?" Jake leaned forward to kiss the valley between her breasts.

Samantha sucked in her breath and her head fell back. "You . . . you certainly did. Last night."

"I must have been distracted." Jake lowered Samantha down on the gray army blanket and settled on top of her. He kissed her eyes, cheeks, and the tip of her nose, then settled in for a very distracting assault of her mouth. When he lifted his head, they were both breathing heavily. His fingers caught in a tangle of golden hair and his green eyes grew serious. "I'm going to miss you, Samantha Lowery."

It was in her mind to plead with him to stay — or take her along — anything so they could be together. She opened her mouth to say it when the clucking and fluttering of chickens drifted in through the barn's window holes. "Will," she moaned. "Will's up."

Jake gave an exaggerated sigh, kissed her again, then rolled onto the blanket. "Maybe it's better this way." He scrubbed his hands down across his face, wincing when he rubbed the area around his eyes. "I could stay here and make love to you all day but it wouldn't change the way things are."

He shook his head then turned to her. "Why don't you get dressed and I'll go have a talk with Will. I imagine he'll have some questions after last night."

Samantha nodded and watched Jake pull on his pants and shirt. After stomping into his boots, he reached down and pulled Samantha up beside him. His kiss was warm and deep . . . and it was a kiss of good-bye.

He left the barn then and Samantha heard him call to Will, suggesting they walk down toward the creek. "These bruises could use a soak in cold water." Samantha imagined him giving Will's hat a tug and her brother scurrying to keep up with Jake's longer stride. Will wouldn't be happy when Jake told him he was leaving.

Dejectedly Samantha pulled on her clothes and made her way to the house. In the quiet of her bedroom she stripped off her wrinkled dress and washed with the chilly water in the pitcher. Her skin puckered and goose bumps covered her arms but Samantha was so miserable she hardly noticed. She brushed out her hair, donned a clean dress, and went out to start breakfast.

Will had already stoked the stove so she took a large pottery bowl off the shelf and mixed up a batch of griddle cakes. It helped some to stay busy and she hoped she'd be able to hold herself together until Jake left. After that, she really didn't care what happened.

When she heard footsteps on the porch and the door opening, she started ladling batter onto the hot skillet. "Breakfast will be ready soon," she said without looking up.

"That's real nice of you, Samantha, but neither of us is going to stay around to eat it."

The bowl slipped from her hands, splattering batter and pottery shards all over the floor as Samantha whirled around. "What are *you* doing here?"

"Now is that any way to greet your old true love?"

"You were never my true love, Bundy Atwood, and you know it. Now get out of my house!"

He snorted and stepped forward and Samantha made a mad dash for the musket hung over the hearth. "Oh no you don't, you bitch." He grabbed her about the waist, lifting her off the floor and stopping her struggles with a savage yank of her hair. "Did you really think I'd ride off and leave you all safe and happy? Huh?" He tugged on her hair till tears streamed down Samantha's face. "Did ya?"

"Let me go," Samantha sobbed, her hands trying to fight his painful grip on her scalp.

"Sure I'll let you go. After I'm done with you. And Landis is. And Ab. And anyone else who wants a piece of a lying, nigger-loving whore."

"I still don't understand why you have to go, Jake. Don't you like us no more?"

"That's not it at all." Jake splashed clear, cold water onto his face. "I'm real fond of you." Jake took a deep breath. "And Samantha. It's just not as simple as that." Jake glanced back to where Will sat on the bank, his crutch by his side.

"It's 'cause of what those soldiers done to you, isn't it?"

"That's part of it," Jake admitted. "But not all. What happened in town just reminded me that I don't belong here."

"So you're heading for Texas. Just like that."

"It isn't just like that, Will. That's where I was going when I stopped off here. Remember? I'm only finishing the trip."

Will snapped off a stalk of grass and stuck it in his mouth, chewing on it a second before looking up and meeting Jake's eyes. "Did Sam know you was leaving before she went out to the barn last night?"

Jake stood, raising his face to the blue sky that reminded him so much of Samantha's eyes, then looked back at Will. He met his stare man to man. "Yes she did, Will. You have to understand— Now where are you going?"

Will struggled to standing, balancing precariously on one leg while he positioned the crutch. "You're no better than Bundy Atwood. Taking what you want then not caring a hang about her."

"Now wait a minute." Jake reached for Will but he jerked away. "For one thing, Samantha and I both knew what we were doing. When you get older, maybe you'll understand." Jake dropped his hand. "I care about Samantha very much."

Will's expression was disbelieving. He turned and started up the path, Charity trotting along beside him.

"And for another thing, Bundy Atwood never took anything from your sister."

"Yeah, but you sure as hell did, didn't you, Jake?" Will stumbled, then righted himself, and hobbled as quickly as he could toward the cabin.

"Shit." Jake mumbled the word under his breath as he kicked a rock into the creek. So much for explaining things to Will man to man. Maybe it didn't work because Will wasn't a man yet. Or maybe . . . Jake shook his head. Maybe it didn't work because Jake didn't have good enough reasons for what he did . . . for what he was going to do.

If that was the case, then what in the hell was he supposed to do? Jake took a deep breath and tossed a stone into the creek.

* * *

Will stumbled again and nearly fell when Charity darted in front of him, but he found his footing and kept going. He was heading toward the cabin but he didn't want to see his sister. He didn't want to see anyone.

He'd liked Jake from the first; loved him as only a boy could love a man he admired. He thought the feeling was mutual.

But somehow some man-woman thing between Jake and Sam had messed things up. That and the soldiers beating Jake. All these forces he had no control over were making Jake leave. Just like Luke.

Will took a moment to lean against the corner of the barn. His leg was aching and he rested his cheek against the sod, breathing in the familiar scent of earth and grass.

A noise off in the distance caught his attention. Will wasn't sure he'd heard anything till he looked down and saw Charity perk up her ears. She trotted around the side of the soddy, then suddenly let loose with a peal of sharp barks before racing across the yard.

Will pushed away from the barn, rounding the corner as fast as his broken leg and crutch would allow. His eyes widened in shock at what he saw. "Let her be," Will screamed as he part skipped, part scrambled toward the stand of trees where Bundy Atwood was tossing Sam over a horse.

Lying across the saddle, she was struggling, hitting out with her hands and kicking at Atwood as he mounted behind her. Atwood threw one thigh over

384

her legs and shoved her head down before gathering up the reins.

"Wait till we get you to Missouri," Will heard Bundy yell at Samantha before he turned his horse.

Atwood was riding straight at Will, thundering toward him across the yard's packed ground. The chickens scattered, flapping their wings in protest. Will knew he should run, but his feet seemed rooted to the spot. Charity barked and yelped, digging in her front paws and snapping her jaws, and still Will didn't move.

He saw the gun and Samantha's hair streaming like a banner. Then she squirmed about, arching her back and clawing at Bundy's arm. Bundy fired wild then erupted into a stream of cursing as he dropped the revolver.

Will leaped toward it just as Atwood jerked on the reins, forcing his mount's head up. Then seeing Will clutching the gun, he turned, galloping out of the yard in a cloud of dust.

"Jake! Jake!" Will screamed as Jake exploded around the cabin. "He's got Sam!"

"Who?" Jake rushed toward him, kneeling down in the dirt. "Who's got her?" Jake had heard the shot and come running.

"Atwood . . . he took off with her." Will clutched Jake's shirt. "He's taking her to Missouri. I heard him say."

Jake's jaw clenched and he jumped up. "Are you all right?"

"Yeah. Yeah." Will pushed to sitting. "But Sam!"

"I'll get her." Jake raced toward the barn. Within

minutes he emerged, leading two horses. He'd also strapped on his other gun.

By this time Will was back on his feet, leaning heavily on his crutch.

"I need you to do something."

"Anything, Jake." Gone were the differences of ten minutes ago. "You want me to go with you?"

"No." Jake lifted Will into the saddle, shoving and pushing till the boy was settled. "I want you to go to town. Tell Lieutenant Farrow what you saw. Tell him Atwood is probably taking Samantha to his uncle's place. He did say Missouri, didn't he?"

"Yeah." Will's splinted leg stuck forward. "Missouri, that's what he said. But Jake." Will grabbed up the reins. "Bundy said 'we.' 'Wait till *we* get you to Missouri.' Moore must be with him."

"Get the army, Will."

"Don't let them hurt Sam."

"I won't." Jake gave Will's mare a smack on the rump. The next moment Jake was in the saddle riding off toward Missouri.

Samantha's head pounded and the strong scent of lathered horse filled her nostrils. Every step the horse took compounded the ache in her stomach, and the nausea was like a cloud enveloping her.

She'd never known such physical agony.

Yet the end of the ride promised an even worse fate. Bundy Atwood made it abundantly clear what he and Moore's men had planned for her.

The blood rushing to her head dulled her reasoning, but still Samantha tried to plan an escape.

Nothing came to mind. And soon she only wished for a swift death to end the misery of the present, and the unthinkable future.

Samantha didn't know how far they'd traveled. She seemed to swim in and out of consciousness. But the horse was slowing, and when it stopped, she felt herself being shoved feet first off the winded animal.

She tried to catch herself, but her legs crumpled under her and she sprawled unceremoniously in the dirt.

"See you got her."

Samantha cringed when she heard that voice, even though she knew what Moore had planned for her.

"Said I would." That was Atwood, and Samantha cautiously brushed hair out of her face to see who else was about. She counted eight men including Landis, his brother Ab, and Atwood. And they were all looking down at her with feral expressions on their unwashed faces.

"You'll pay for this . . . all of you." Samantha's voice was weaker than she wished but at least it was firm.

Moore's snort of laughter told her he wasn't impressed by her words or the evenness of her delivery. "No one's coming after you. No one even cares that we've got you."

"Ah, Landis." Atwood squirmed in his saddle. "That brother of hers was there."

Bundy's eyes flew toward Ab. "Thought I told you to kill him."

"I did. I mean I thought I did. I'm sorry, Landis. Don't be mad with me."

Landis ignored his brother's sniveling and looked back toward Atwood. "Why in the hell didn't you take care of him?"

"The bitch here bit me and I dropped my gun. The boy was there diving for it and some dog was nipping at my horse. I figured it was time to git." Bundy straightened his shirt. "Besides the kid was hurt. Something wrong with his leg. He ain't nothing to worry about."

Moore leaned over his pommel. "Let's move. We'll be across the border by sundown. And then we'll have ourselves a little fun."

This time Bundy pulled Samantha up in front of him. She was spared the humiliation and discomfort of being tossed across the saddle. But she did have to contend with his ongoing description of what he had planned for her that night.

"And that's only me," he crowed into her ear. "All these other men is just as anxious for a piece of you before we're done."

His leg throbbed but he kept riding. Lovey, the mare, was breathing hard, her sides lathered, and Will considered slowing down. Then he thought about his sister and what she must be suffering and he urged the horse to move faster.

He had to get to town. He had to get to the army, and send them to help Sam and Jake.

He remembered what Landis Moore had done to his father. He'd only been a kid, but he remembered.

Will didn't see the snake slither out of the tall grass beside the road, but Lovey did. She whinnied

388

and bucked, catching Will off guard.

Riding was second nature to him. He'd been doing it for years. But never with a broken leg. Will tried to hold on. But when Lovey reared up a second time, he felt himself slipping from the saddle.

Searing pain shot through his leg as he landed in the dirt. And tears stung his eyes as he watched Lovey gallop away.

He'd trailed them all day, and with the coming of dusk, Jake knew he was close. He recognized the area. There were times during the endless hours that he wanted to stop hanging back and gallop up on them, his gun blazing. He hated what Samantha must be going through.

But he didn't. Jake figured his best chance of getting her away from Moore's men was after dark — after they reached Moore's uncle's farm.

Jake dismounted behind a stand of oak trees and worked his way up to the split log fence that surrounded the house. He watched in the dusky light as Landis Moore, Ab, and Atwood got off their horses in front of the weatherboard farmhouse.

Atwood yanked Samantha from the animal's back, again making Jake fight the urge to rush them. Instead he clenched his jaw and checked his gun, telling himself that any rash action would only get her killed.

He rubbed his itching palms down the fine wool of his pant leg, and waited. The rest of the men headed for the barn with the horses, then the front door opened, bathing the porch and Samantha in the soft glow of candlelight. Moore's uncle stepped out and greeted the three men.

"Well, what do we have here, Landis?" Jake heard the old man ask, then guffaw when Moore said it was a present for him.

"Now I don't know that I'm not too old for this kind of gift," he said before lifting a lock of Samantha's hair. She slapped at him and Jake's hand tightened around his gun.

Atwood raised his arm to backhand her and Jake took aim. But the uncle's laughter stopped both men's reaction. "No need for that, Bundy. She just needs to get used to us. Bring her on inside." The older man opened the door wider. "She can start by fixing us something to eat. I'm sure as hell tired of my own cooking."

No curtains blocked his view through the windows, and for that Jake was thankful. He could see Samantha and the men clearly once they reached the main room. Atwood shoved her toward the stove, and Samantha defiantly turned on him. But apparently she figured the same thing Jake was thinking. As long as she was cooking, they weren't going to do anything else to her.

"That's it, Samantha," Jake murmured. "Take down the mixing bowl and get busy." He watched as she hesitated, then did just that, almost as if she could hear him.

"Now fix them something filling and fix it slow." She moved across the room, coming within an arm's length of Atwood, who reached out and grabbed her. "Stay clear of him," Jake admonished as she jerked away and hurried back toward the stove. Atwood stayed in his chair and Jake let out his breath.

The men who'd gone to the barn emerged and made their way to the house. There were five of them. With Landis, Ab, Atwood, and the uncle, it made nine. Jake rubbed his chin. Not very impressive odds. But the army didn't seem in any hurry to show up, and Jake was going to have to do something soon.

The question was, what? Moore's gang was all in one place. He could see the newcomers dragging chairs toward the table. The problem was Samantha was in the same place.

Jake leaned against the fence and kept his eyes riveted to the window. The sky darkened, and crickets and bullfrogs vied to be the noisiest creature of the night. Samantha kept stirring, looking up nervously at the men seated at the table. They were obviously having a grand time. A jug was being passed around and every now and then the breeze caught a strain of their laughter and sent it Jake's way. They were getting drunk and rowdy.

Jake stood, deciding this was as good a time as any to move closer to the house when he heard a noise behind him. He crouched low and froze, intent on listening.

The sound came again, closer this time. It was someone . . . more than one someone by the amount of noise they were making . . . coming toward him from the road. They were talking—not loud—but loud enough to tell Jake it wasn't the army. Soldiers would know enough to be quiet.

Moving as quietly as he could, Jake followed the fence away from the lane then doubled back behind.

Damn. As if the odds weren't already one-sided enough, now more of Moore's cohorts had to show up.

Jake was behind them now. He could make out shadows in the twilight — four men — cautiously moving toward the house. One lagged behind and Jake crept closer, grabbing him about the neck. The man dropped his gun and gave a small yelp, which Jake smothered with his palm. His other hand held a revolver gauged into the man's ribs.

"The rest of you drop your guns or your friend is a dead man." Jake no sooner got the words out before three men turned, tossing their guns and throwing their hands up.

"You all right, Seth?" one of the men gasped, and Jake twisted his captive around so he could see his face.

"Nelson, is that you?" Jake squinted in the dim light. The head in his grasp nodded and Jake dropped his hands. "What in the hell are you doing here?"

Seth sucked in air and muffled a cough. "Will," he whispered as the others gathered around. "One of my sons found him in the road near my lane. A snake had spooked his horse and he'd fallen off. He was hobbling along at a frantic clip to get to my farm. Told me all about Samantha being taken and you following."

"What about the army?"

"I sent one of my boys to town to get them, but in the meantime some of the other farmers here were helping me out with my harvesting and we decided to come see what we could do."

392

"Yeah?" Jake couldn't help grinning as the men picked up their guns. He imagined what Samantha would think of her neighbors coming to help her. The thought made him glance back toward the house. "Damnit!" Jake moved forward, followed by the four farmers.

"What is it?" Seth crouched next to Jake behind the fence.

"Atwood has Samantha in another room," Jake whispered before bounding over the split logs. It had only taken one quick look at the house to see that two windows were now lit up and that Samantha was missing from the scene inside the main room. So was Atwood. And a quick scan of the other window showed Samantha enveloped by Atwood, her arms twisted high behind her back and her head thrown to the side. She screamed and the strident sound brought a round of riotous cheers and laughter from the other room.

"I'm going into the bedroom to get her." He threw the words hastily over his shoulder. "There are eight others — all in the house. When I give the signal — a shot — open fire on the rest of them." With those rather sparse orders, Jake raced toward the side of the house.

He reached the corner then rounded it, heading toward the side window when he heard breaking glass, followed by more loud laughter.

Inside, Bundy grabbed Samantha and shoved her onto a rumpled bedstead. He brushed shards of the broken pitcher she'd thrown at him from his shoulder and began unfastening his pants. "You'll pay for that, bitch!"

Glass shattered, splintering over the ground as Jake poked his gun barrel through the window. "Get down!" he yelled to Samantha, who'd already bounded from the mattress, ready to continue her fight with Atwood. She turned and froze, her eyes enormous as she recognized Jake.

"Get down," he screamed again, for she stood in the line of fire between Atwood and him. Between Atwood and hell.

In that instant Samantha seemed to recognize the problem, for she tried to throw herself to the side. But Atwood was quicker, grabbing her to him as his revolver cleared his holster. The gun barrel gouged into Samantha's ribs. "Throw the gun down and get in here, Morgan, or I kill her. I swear I will."

"He will anyway. Don't do it, Jake!" Samantha's outburst won her a vicious poke with the revolver and she cried out in pain.

"Stop it!" Jake shoved his hand through the broken pane to toss his gun just as the bedroom door slammed open.

"Hey, what's going on in here? You're taking too long. The stew's burning." Ab Moore came barreling through the opening, bumping into Bundy.

Samantha twisted away, Atwood aimed at Jake, and Jake fired, all in lightning-quick succession. Blood splattered on the grimy wall and across Ab's startled features. "Landis," he squealed as Bundy's body fell back against him.

But Landis and the others had their own problems.

The shot Jake used to kill Atwood served as the signal for Samantha's neighbors to open fire on the other room. And they'd done it with abandon, firing in rapid volley. This time Jake didn't have to warn Samantha to get down. She did so quickly as Jake kept his bead on the hapless Ab. He cocked his gun, remembering Will and the harm the slow-witted man had done, but before Jake could fire, Ab tossed Bundy aside and ran from the room.

Using the butt of his gun, Jake cleared away the remaining shards of glass and reached through the window. "Come here," he urged Samantha. "But keep your head down."

Gunshots were still ringing through the night air and the bedroom door was ajar. Jake kept his gun aimed at the opening as Samantha scurried toward him. She gave him a quick smile, which Jake returned, before he lifted her through the window opening.

"Oh, Jake." Her arms wound around his neck as he pushed her against the outside wall. "You came." He kissed her hard and quick then faced her toward the barn behind the house.

"You get in there and stay. And take this." He shoved his gun into her hand and gave her a small push toward the barn. One that didn't keep her going.

"But what about you? I can't take your gun. Where are you going?"

"Samantha."

"And who's doing all the shooting? And—"

"Go! Now!" His tone brooked no argument. But it didn't stop her from turning and grabbing his hand.

"Be careful," she whispered, then ran across the opening toward the barn. Jake watched her go by moonlight, then hoisted himself up through the window.

Atwood's pistol was on the floor. Jake scooped it up and checked the cylinder. Then moving quickly, he grabbed the lamp off the bureau, opened the bedroom door wider, and heaved it into the main room.

Several men stopped shooting out the front window and jerked around at the sound of the explosion of glass and burning oil. Jake dove behind the door as they fired off a barrage toward the bedroom. Then they were too worried about the flames erupting from the lamp, and running along the spilled oil, to care about Jake.

Jake fired several shots into the room then bolted toward the bedroom window as smoke began filling the house. Once outside he circled back to where the farmers had taken cover behind a wagon and motioned for two of them to follow him. "The rest of you keep firing and watch the front door. I have a feeling they'll be filing out of there soon."

"There are a couple of windows across the back we have to watch plus one off the side," Jake told the men that followed him.

Samantha leaned against the board siding and wished she could see what was happening. There were still shots being fired and she could smell smoke. Tentatively she pushed the barn door open a crack and peered out.

The farmhouse was on fire, with flames billowing up into the night sky. She laced her fingers around the gun and prayed that Jake hadn't gone back inside.

That was when she noticed the shadowy figure running toward her.

At first she thought her wish had been granted and it was Jake—he was the only one who knew where she was—but in the next instant she realized it was Landis Moore.

Panic seized her and she threw herself against the wall just moments before he burst into the barn. The inside was dark and musty and Moore obviously didn't see Samantha as he made his way toward the stall. He was breathing hard, loud enough for Samantha to keep track of his movements as he headed toward the horses.

A startled whinney told her he'd mounted and she could hear him coming toward her and the door.

He was going to get away. He'd killed her father and ordered the same for Will and he was going to get away. Before she could change her mind, Samantha stepped out, blocking his exit.

The horse pranced to the side and Landis peered down to see what the problem was. "Well, if it isn't little Miss Lowery, hiding in the barn." His voice had an inhuman quality that made Samantha's fingers icy cold.

They came out of the house hacking and coughing and trying to keep their hands in the air. Jake and the farmers gathered up their guns and set about tying up Moore's gang—all seven of them.

"Wait a minute." Jake tightened a knot behind Ab's back and jerked him around. "Where's Landis." When Ab didn't answer right away, Jake grabbed him by the shirtfront. "Where's your brother? Is he still inside?"

"You can't kill Landis," Ab said, smoke-induced tears streaming down his broad face. "He done left through the window."

"Hell!" He could have made it out the back before Jake put men there. And if he were loose, he'd probably be after a horse . . .

Jake drew his gun and took off toward the barn before he completed the thought. The doors were open and the light from the flaming house cast a macabre brightness to the scene inside.

Samantha stood, her right arm stiff, clutching Jake's revolver. It was pointed toward Moore, toward the gun Landis aimed at her. Jake didn't have time to think.

"Moore!" The word seemed to echo through the barn. Landis twisted in the saddle and his face was a mask of hate as he leveled his gun.

Jake fired.

For an instant, like a picture frozen in time, Moore stared at Jake. His expression, the straight-shouldered posture of his body, belied the blossom of crimson spreading across his shirtfront. Then he looked toward Samantha and slumped forward in the saddle. Before Jake could reach him, Moore slid to the ground and a riderless horse pranced into the night.

Jake glanced around and saw Samantha staring down at the rumpled heap on the barn floor.

"Samantha," he called softly. With a shudder, Samantha dropped the gun and walked into Jake's open arms.

"He laughed about hanging my father," she sobbed into Jake's shirt. "He laughed about Will and he said he'd kill me too."

"I know." Jake's arms tightened around her. "But it's over. It's all over now."

But it wasn't over and Jake knew it even before Seth reminded him that the army would be coming along soon. He'd worn a gun . . . killed two men with it. And Lieutenant Farrow had made it very clear what would happen if he caught him with a gun.

"I'll talk to him," Samantha pleaded when her neighbors were resting around a small campfire and she and Jake had walked out of earshot. "Maybe he'll listen to me."

"And do what?" Jake turned and cradled her shoulders. "Give me a reprimand and say it better not happen again." He shook his head. "Hell, Samantha, that's the best that can happen." He lowered his voice. "I can't live like that. I was leaving anyway. Now I know you really are safe." He let his hands drop.

Dawn was just breaking across the Missouri countryside and he expected to see a column of bluecoats coming up the road any minute.

"Where will you go?" She shouldn't question him, Samantha knew that. He was leaving and there was nothing she could do about it. But oh, it was hard.

"I don't know." Jake untied his horse.

"Jake." She rushed into his arms and returned the kiss he gave her with all the passion she could. With all the love and desire she felt for him. He held her close a moment longer, then moved away.

Without another word, he mounted and rode out of her life.

Chapter Twenty

Last night's frost clung to the browned blades of grass growing by the porch steps. Samantha wrapped her shawl more tightly about her shoulders and scattered the grain in a wide, graceful arc. The chickens flocked around their feed and Samantha stood watching them fluster and peck about, her mind far away.

But soon the creeping morning chill coupled with the warmth promised by the smoking stove pipe enticed her inside. She shivered, then moved toward the stove after hanging up her wrap. Holding out her hands, Samantha waited for the heat radiating from the iron surface to warm her.

But she didn't think it would do any good.

She was empty inside, and cold. And nothing, not the extra quilt at night, or the late autumn sunshine that seemed to warm everything around her, did any good.

Samantha sighed as she brewed herself some tea. Another futile attempt to escape the chill inside her. Today she'd do laundry and clean out the cabin.

Maybe if there was daylight left after that, she'd black the stove, and then maybe . . .

Samantha sipped her drink and paused. There was only so much a body could do in one day, even if they were trying to stay busy. And that was definitely what Samantha was doing. Trying to keep herself so busy that she had no time to think.

"Sam!"

Will's voice made her glance toward the door moments before her brother and Charity blustered in. The splints were off his leg, and each day he favored it less. Will set his pail of frothy milk on the dry sink and shrugged out of his jacket. "Looks good," he said before pulling out a chair and settling down at the table for breakfast.

He scooped a forkful of fried potatoes into his mouth. "Aren't you going to eat?"

Samantha sat across from him. "I had something earlier." Not a complete lie, Samantha assured herself. She'd munched on a slice of toasted bread.

Her appetite was gone too.

At first she thought her change in eating habits a result of being with child. It was possible, after all. More than possible, Samantha admitted. And she was pleased at the prospect of having Jake's child.

Not that it would have been easy . . . for any of them.

But as it turned out, there would be no child. It was not Jake's baby but the lack of Jake that took away her appetite and the warmth from her life.

"You sure you don't want to come along? Loni Nelson said she'd love to see you."

Samantha looked at Will through the steam rising

from her cup. "No, thanks anyway, Will, but I have some things to do."

"You can't just stay by yourself all the time, Sam. I miss him too, but —"

Samantha pushed out her chair. "If you're going to spend the day with the Nelsons, you should get started. I baked you a couple pies to take along." She settled the pastries into a basket and handed it to Will, adding with a smile on her face, "Have a good time."

"Sam." Will drew her name out. He looked at her, his freckle-faced expression one of pity. Pity Samantha couldn't stand.

She faced him, hands on hips. "What, Will? What would you have me do that I haven't? Take the corn to be milled?" She'd seen that done. "Fix your meals or mend your clothes?" He couldn't deny she did those things, or anything else that needed to be done. "Well, Will, what do you want from me?"

"Only to see you happy," came his quiet reply, and Samantha turned away before Will saw the tears well in her eyes.

Will must have sensed her distress. He picked up the basket and, after giving Samantha's shoulders an awkward squeeze, grabbed up his coat and reached for the latch. "You going to be all right here alone?"

Samantha blinked back her tears and turned toward her brother, a smile on her face. "Of course, I am." She settled a kiss on her brother's cheek. "You have a good time and be home before dark."

"Aw, Sam."

"Don't 'Aw, Sam' me, William Lowery." They were back on familiar ground again and Samantha was pleased that they could tease each other and laugh.

But when she stood on the porch watching him ride away on Pru, his jacket collar turned up under his ears and the basket propped precariously in his lap, she couldn't help the loneliness that swept over her.

She shook her head and went back in the house, deciding to finish her tea before hauling water up from the creek. But she wasn't going to sit around and sulk. What she'd said to Will was true. From the very first after Jake had left, she'd accomplished everything that needed to be done.

There were no self-indulgent pouts for her. Will was the one who had to be coaxed out of his surliness . . . reminded the corn harvest wasn't complete. He railed against Jake. Then he switched tactics and blamed Samantha for his friend's leaving. "If you'd asked him to stay . . ." Will had said. And Samantha had reminded her brother of Lieutenant Farrow's order about Jake leaving the area.

"Yes, but if you'd—"

"Stop it, Will," she finally said. "He's gone and there's nothing either of us can do about it."

Will had grumped around a few more days. Then because there was work to be done, and because for the first time since her father died, the neighbors had come to help, he snapped out of it.

Will seemed to be over the worst of his disappointment about Jake leaving. Oh, he still talked about his friend, wondering what Jake was doing now, where he was. And he practiced on the harmonica constantly.

Jake had given it to Samantha for Will before he

rode away. Something to remember him by.

But where Will had something tangible, Samantha had only memories and the awful suspicion that maybe she could have done something so that she'd still be with Jake.

Pushing away from the table, Samantha carried her cup to the dry sink. She was *not* going to succumb to melancholy. She hadn't asked him to stay. She hadn't begged Jake to take her along. And that was that.

If she knew where he was, maybe she'd do something about it. But she didn't. Texas was a big place. And life went on. Her shoulders squared, her chin raised, Samantha reached for the bucket.

The footsteps on the porch scared her all the more because she hadn't noticed anyone riding up. Instinct made her grab for the musket over the mantle. She aimed it toward the door just as someone lifted the latch. Samantha's heart thudded and her palms were damp.

The door swung open.

"Good Lord, Samantha! You're not going to shoot me again, are you?"

"Jake!" She lowered the gun and her hand fluttered to her throat.

"I didn't mean to scare you." Samantha looked as if she'd seen a ghost and he guessed he was about the last person she expected to see come through her door. Hell, this was the last place he expected to be again. That was till about a week ago.

At the time he was heading south, down through Texas, thinking he'd left Samantha Lowery in his past . . . where she belonged.

"May I come in?" Jake finally asked after he'd stood in her doorway for what seemed like forever. Not that he really minded because it was wonderful just seeing her again. Her golden hair was brushed back and caught in a blue ribbon that matched her eyes. Eyes he'd seen in every cerulean sky since he rode away.

But as much as he enjoyed studying her, her short, straight nose, the full bow of her bottom lip, the peach perfection of her silky skin, he hadn't backtracked all this way just to look.

"Oh." Samantha finally found her voice. "Oh yes, come in." She set the musket back over the mantle. "Have you eaten breakfast? Are you hungry?"

"No and no." Jake removed his hat, combing fingers back through his hair. When he noticed her lift her brow in question, he explained, "No, I haven't eaten. But I'm not hungry either."

This last statement caused her brow to arch higher. Jake chuckled. "I guess you have a hard time believing that, don't you?"

"That you're not hungry?" Samantha smiled. "It is a bit unusual."

Jake couldn't agree more. But when he'd risen at dawn to finish the last leg of his journey back, food had been the farthest thing from his mind. It still was.

"How about some coffee, then . . . or tea. I could just—"

"No, nothing." Jake measured his hands around the battered brim of his felt hat. Now that he was here, he was nervous. "Do you suppose we could talk some?" Talking wasn't really what he wanted to do either. But she wasn't exactly throwing herself into his arms like she did in all the dreams he'd had about this moment.

"Talk?" Samantha realized she sounded like she didn't understand the meaning of the word. She nodded, her hand indicating the table. "Of course," she answered calmly, though her mind was racing. Now was her chance to say all the things she hadn't said to him before. But first she'd find out what he was doing here.

"Didn't you like Texas?"

Jake sat down across the corner of the table from her. He was close enough to smell her fragrance, a scent that had haunted him for the long weeks he'd been gone. "It was all right. Big," he added. "But I didn't get down to the southeastern part."

"You didn't?" Samantha realized she was staring and tried to look away. But she couldn't. He was so handsome. His skin was tanned from the sun and that made his eyes look all the more clear, like the creek on a spring day.

"I ran into a wagon of settlers heading west. One of the boys had been accidentally shot while he and his brothers were hunting." Jake glanced down at his hands, then back up at Samantha. "I stayed with them awhile."

Samantha nodded, trying not to smile. "Is he all right?"

"The boy? Yeah, he's fine. . . . Anyway, when I left the Harrisons—that was their name—I started back to Kansas."

"Why?" Samantha's heart was pounding, and when her head felt light, she remembered to breathe.

Jake gathered Samantha's hands in his. They were cold and he smiled, thinking how he'd enjoy warming her up. "Samantha," he began. "I've made some mistakes in my life. And I've blamed myself for some that were beyond my control." He took a deep breath, not at all sure how she'd feel about what he had to say next. "But the biggest mistake I ever made was leaving here."

"We're doing all right, you know, Will and I." It suddenly occurred to her that he might feel responsible for their well-being. He had before. He'd stayed when he wanted to move on because he thought she and Will needed him. And he was a caring man. She knew that about him.

"I'm glad for you," Jake said, hoping it was the truth. He couldn't help feeling a little put out that she didn't seem to need him anymore.

"Yes. Seth Nelson organized some neighbors to assist with getting our corn to the mill." Her voice trailed off. "Everyone's been wonderful."

"Does that everyone include Lieutenant Farrow?" The question was out of his mouth before he could stop it. He sounded jealous—the last thing he wanted to do. And by the confused expression on her face, she noticed it.

Jake didn't know what he expected from his return—hell, yes he did. He expected . . . wanted her to fall in his arms and tell him how much she'd missed him. That she couldn't live without him. Because, damnit, that's how he felt about her.

But she just sat there, hands in lap, looking fit and content.

"Well, yes." Samantha carefully measured her

words, knowing Jake's dislike of Farrow. "He took charge of transporting Moore's men to Fort Scott for trial."

"Does his assistance include calling on you?" There he went again. He just couldn't seem to keep quiet. But while he was riding all over the damn country, Farrow had been here courting Samantha.

"He's called a few times, but— Where do you think you're going?" Samantha rose and flung herself at the door before Jake could get to it.

Jake took a step back, surprised at her quick movement and her question. Her eyes were large and very blue. And her chest beneath the plain calico gown heaved with each breath. Jake pulled his gaze away and rubbed his jaw. "I think I should get going."

"Back to Texas?" Samantha didn't budge an inch.

"I suppose." She seemed to be blocking the door. "You all seem to be getting on fine without me."

There was getting on and there was getting on. "Will misses you terrible. He hasn't let the harmonica out of his sight since you left."

"I miss him too. He's a fine boy." Moments stretched on as Samantha looked at Jake and Jake looked at her. He could feel the tension in the air, almost like the time he interrupted her bath. But, of course, this was different. They were both dressed, for one thing. And for another, he wasn't going to carry her off to bed no matter how much he craved her.

If Farrow was courting her, it should be Farrow taking her to bed . . . after he married her, of

409

course. Jake gritted his teeth and the crease between his brows deepened. Damnit, he couldn't stand the thought of Farrow—or anyone else—touching her.

"Samantha—"

"Jake—"

They spoke simultaneously, as if on cue, and politely stopped with as much precision.

"You go ahead," Jake offered gallantly.

"No you," Samantha countered.

Jake took a deep breath. Damn, he hated feeling nervous like this. Not knowing how Samantha would take what he was about to say.

It had been different with Lydia. They had known each other since childhood. There was never any doubt that they'd marry. But this. . . . If Samantha had fallen for the lieutenant—which she had every right to do, even though Farrow was an arrogant son of a bitch—then there was nothing Jake could do. And he'd have to go on without her.

When faced with that alternative, pride seemed foolish. He stared into her clear blue eyes. "I came back because of you."

"You did?" Samantha felt a smile form on her lips.

"Yes." Jake swiped his palm across his chin. "Damnit, Samantha, I love you. I know you might not feel the same, but—"

Samantha's mouth against his cut off the rest of what he planned to say. And the way she threw her body into his, he quickly forgot what it was.

Her arms were around his neck, his clasping her to him. Samantha breathed in his scent and showed him by her actions that she felt the same way about him. Their kiss was slow and deep and it was a long time before they separated. When they did, Jake's grin matched Samantha's.

"So what are you trying to say here?" Jake ran his hands along the length of her spine.

"I love you, too," Samantha whispered, tugging his head down for another kiss. "I thought you were gone forever and I missed you so much."

His lips brushed along her cheek and across her jaw. "I couldn't stay away." His breath fluttered the pale curls behind her ear. Then his mouth was again on hers, devouring her, melting her in his arms . . . flooding her with heat.

Desire raged through him. Jake cupped her breast, shaping the soft mound through her clothes. The nipple tightened and her soft moans scorched his blood.

"Oh, Jake. Jake." Her plea was a siren's song, one he wanted with all his heart to follow. But he'd ridden hundreds of miles to ask her a question. He pulled away, his breath catching as her lashes lifted and he saw her passion filled eyes.

"We need . . . to talk." He could barely get the words out and she writhed against his lower body. He didn't hesitate when she grabbed his hand and led him toward her bedroom.

"We can talk later," she said, then smiled broadly when he scooped her into his arms.

Undressing her was magic.

Each new expanse of flesh he revealed to the golden sunlight streaming through the window was beautiful, and begged to be kissed. His tongue wet the base of her neck as he stripped the dress from

411

her shoulders. When her breasts were free, he sat on the edge of the bedstead and pulled her into the V of his thighs.

She braided her fingers deep into the rough silk of his hair and he suckled her nipples. Samantha's back arched, offering herself more completely as his large hands rode the crest of her hips.

Her moans were as uncontrollable as the undulating waves of her body when he tugged free the bow of her pantaloons and skimmed them down her legs. His breath sighed across the tight curls at the apex of her thighs and Samantha's knees folded.

But before she could fall, Jake hauled her to him. His rough clothing rasped across her tender skin in a motion she found wildly erotic. Still she longed to feel the heat of his skin slide along hers.

As if he'd read her mind, Jake settled Samantha on the faded quilt and tore at his own clothes. When he stood before her bold and powerful, splendid in his readiness, Samantha opened her arms and he followed her down on the mattress.

He cupped her head between his hands and Samantha looked up into the impassioned intensity of his gaze. "I love you so much," he said, and plunged into her moist heat.

She wanted to return the words, but the next moment he thrust deeper and Samantha's legs wrapped about his hips. She couldn't speak, could barely think as his movements quickened.

But Jake needed no more affirmation of her feelings for him than the gentle touch of her hands on his shoulders. Or the open way she met and matched his rhythm as they moved toward the pinnacle of pleasure. Or her wild spasms and cry of joy when he sent her spiraling to the heavens. Her actions were the language of love eternal, her sigh of his name its benediction.

Jake shifted only far enough to take his weight from her then gathered her close. "It feels so good to hold you," he said as she snuggled against his hard chest.

They lay like that, content in each other's arms while their hearts quieted and their breathing returned to normal. The chilled temperature of the room finally registered on their love-slick bodies so Jake reached down to cover them with the quilt folded at the foot of the bed.

"Samantha?" Jake felt her cheek slip across his chest as she looked up at him.

"It's time to talk?" she questioned and his chuckle vibrated through her.

"Yes, I think it is." Jake hiked himself up against the headboard and settled Samantha with him. "I want to be with you," he began without preamble. "Always."

Samantha rested her elbows on his chest and smiled. "I want to be with you too."

"But I can't stay here," Jake hurried on. "The reasons for my leaving haven't changed. I know you don't want to give up your farm after you've worked so hard and it's a lot for me to ask. Especially knowing how you feel about Texas. But—"

"What do you mean, how I feel about Texas?" Samantha traced her finger along his jaw.

"Well, you told Will there was nothing there for him."

Samantha settled more comfortably along Jake's hard length. "Oh, that was Will. I just didn't want him getting any ideas about running off."

"But you would?" Jake's brow arched as she let her fingers drift down his muscled ribs.

"Run off to Texas?" Samantha pressed her lips to his collarbone, then glanced up through a veil of golden hair. "In a minute." She nibbled the underside of his chin. "Of course, I'd have to be asked to go first."

"Consider yourself asked."

"And I wouldn't go with just anyone." Samantha slid down his body, letting her mouth skim across his chest. "I'd want the man I ran off with to have a profession." She paused in her inspection of the arrow of hair that trailed down his chest. "I'd like him to do something where he helped people."

"Like, say, a doctor?"

Samantha giggled as Jake flipped her onto her back and settled on top of her. "Yes, a doctor would be just fine," she breathed.

"Good. Because I've decided that's what I'll always be." Jake fanned her glorious hair across the pillow. "You helped show me that. You gave me back my life." Jake's lips brushed hers. "Marry me," he whispered, then smiled when she did. "I want to take you to Texas, you and Will. We'll start a new life."

"Together," Samantha sighed.

"Mmmm." Her skin was soft and smooth as he trailed his mouth down her neck. "We'll find a town that needs a doctor and settle down—"

"And raise lots of babies," Samantha said, smiling

up at him.

"And raise lots of babies."

"And be happy."

"Oh, yes," Jake agreed, love for her filling all the empty spaces inside. "And be *very* happy."

HEART STOPPING ROMANCE BY ZEBRA BOOKS

MIDNIGHT BRIDE (3265, $4.50)
by Kathleen Drymon

With her youth, beauty, and sizable dowry, Kellie McBride had her share of ardent suitors, but the headstrong miss was bewitched by the mysterious man called The Falcon, a dashing highwayman who risked life and limb for the American Colonies. Twice the Falcon had saved her from the hands of the British, then set her blood afire with a moonlit kiss.

No one knew the dangerous life The Falcon led—or of his secret identity as a British lord with a vengeful score to settle with the Crown. There was no way Kellie would discover his deception, so he would woo her by day as the foppish Lord Blakely Savage . . . and ravish her by night as The Falcon! But each kiss made her want more, until he vowed to make her his *Midnight Bride*.

SOUTHERN SEDUCTION (3266, $4.50)
by Thea Devine

Cassandra knew her husband's will required her to hire a man to run her Georgia plantation, but the beautiful redhead was determined to handle her own affairs. To satisfy her lawyers, she invented Trane Taggart, her imaginary step-son. But her plans go awry when a handsome adventurer shows up and claims to *be* Trane Taggart!

After twenty years of roaming free, Trane was ready to come home and face the father who always treated him with such contempt. Instead he found a black wreath and a bewitching, sharp-tongued temptress trying to cheat him out of his inheritance. But he had no qualms about kissing that silken body into languid submission to get what he wanted. But he never dreamed that *he* would be the one to succumb to *her* charms.

SWEET OBSESSION (3233, $4.50)
by Kathy Jones

From the moment rancher Jack Corbett kept her from capturing the wild white stallion, Kayley Ryan detested the man. That animal had almost killed her father, and since the accident Kayley had been in charge of the ranch. But with the tall, lean Corbett, it seemed she was *never* the boss. He made her blood run cold with rage one minute, and hot with desire the next.

Jack Corbett had only one thing on his mind: revenge against the man who had stolen his freedom, his ranch, and almost his very life. And what better way to get revenge than to ruin his mortal enemy's fiery red-haired daughter. He never expected to be captured by her charms, to long for her silken caresses and to thirst for her never-ending kisses.

Available wherever paperbacks are sold, or order direct from the Publisher. Send cover price plus 50¢ per copy for mailing and handling to Zebra Books, Dept. 3691, 475 Park Avenue South, New York, N.Y. 10016. Residents of New York and Tennessee must include sales tax. DO NOT SEND CASH. For a free Zebra/ Pinnacle catalog please write to the above address.